The
Sacrifice

NOVELS BY JOYCE CAROL OATES

With Shuddering Fall (1964)

A Garden of Earthly Delights (1967)

Expensive People (1968)

them (1969)

Wonderland (1971)

Do with Me What You Will (1973)

The Assassins (1975)

Childwold (1976)

Son of the Morning (1978)

Unholy Loves (1979)

Bellefleur (1980)

Angel of Light (1981)

A Bloodsmoor Romance (1982)

Mysteries of Winterthurn (1984)

Solstice (1985)

Marya: A Life (1986)

You Must Remember This (1987)

American Appetites (1989)

Because It Is Bitter, and Because It Is My Heart (1990)

Black Water (1992)

Foxfire: Confessions of a Girl Gang (1993)

What I Lived For (1994)

Zombie (1995)

We Were the Mulvaneys (1996)

Man Crazy (1997)

ecco

An Imprint of HarperCollinsPublishers

The
Sacrifice

Joyce
Carol
Oates

THE SACRIFICE. Copyright © 2015 by The Ontario Review. All rights reserved. Printed in the United States of America. No part of this book may be used or reproduced in any manner whatsoever without written permission except in the case of brief quotations embodied in critical articles and reviews. For information address HarperCollins Publishers, 195 Broadway, New York, NY 10007.

HarperCollins books may be purchased for educational, business, or sales promotional use. For information please e-mail the Special Markets Department at SPsales@harpercollins.com.

FIRST EDITION

Designed by Suet Yee Chong
Title page photograph © artcphotos/Shutterstock, Inc.

Library of Congress Cataloging-in-Publication Data has been applied for.

ISBN 978-0-06-233297-4

15 16 17 18 19   OV/RRD   10 9 8 7 6 5 4 3 2 1

for Richard Levao
and for Charlie Gross

Acknowledgments

"Angel of Wrath" was first published in *Tweed's Magazine of Literature & Art*, Issue #1, in 2014.

The Mother

*S**een my girl? My baby?*

She came like a procession of voices though she was but a singular voice. She came along Camden Avenue in the Red Rock neighborhood of inner-city Pascayne, twelve tight-compressed blocks between the New Jersey Turnpike and the Passaic River. In the sinister shadow of the high-looming Pitcairn Memorial Bridge she came. Like an Old Testament mother she came seeking her lost child. On foot she came, a careening figure, clumsy with urgency, a crimson scarf tied about her head in evident haste and her clothing loose about her fleshy waistless body. On Depp, Washburn, Barnegat, and Crater streets she was variously sighted by people who recognized her face but could not have said her name as by people who knew her as Ednetta—Ednetta Frye—who was one of Anis Schutt's women, but most of them could not have said whether Anis Schutt was living with this middle-aged woman any longer, or if he'd ever been living with her. She was sighted by strangers who knew nothing of Ednetta

Frye or Anis Schutt but were brought to a dead stop by the yearning in the woman's face, the pleading in her eyes and her low throaty quavering voice—*Any of you seen my girl S'b'lla?*

It was midmorning of a white-glaring overcast day smelling of the Passaic River—a sweetly chemical odor with a harsh acidity of rot beneath. It was midmorning following a night of hammering rain, everywhere on broken pavement puddles lay glittering like foil.

My girl S'b'lla—anybody seen her?

The anxious mother had photographs to show the (startled, mostly sympathetic) individuals to whom she spoke by what appeared to be purest chance: pictures of a dark-skinned girl, bright-eyed, a slight cast to her left eye, with a childish gat-toothed smile. In some of the photos the girl might have been as young as eleven or twelve, in the more recent she appeared to be about fourteen. The girl's dark hair was thick and stiff and springy, lifting from her puckered forehead and tied with a bright-colored scarf. Her eyes were shiny-dark and thick-lashed, almond-shaped like her mother's.

S'b'lla young for her age, and trustin—she smile at just about anybody.

In Jubilee Hair Salon, in Ruby's Nails, in Jax Rib Joint, and the Korean grocery; in Liberty Bail & Bond, in Scully's Pawn Shop, in Pascayne Veterans Thrift Shop, in Passaic County Family Services and in the crowded cafeteria of the James J. Polk Memorial Medical Clinic as in windswept Hicks Square and several graffiti-defaced bus-stop shelters on Camden there came Ednetta Frye breathless and eager to ask if anyone had seen her daughter and to show the photographs spread in her shaky fingers like playing cards—*You seen S'b'lla? Yes maybe? No?*

She grasped at arms, to steady herself. She appeared dazed, disoriented. Her clothes were disheveled. The scarf tying back her stiff-oiled hair was askew. On her feet, waterstained sneakers beginning to fray at each outermost small toe with a quaint symmetry.

Since Thu'sday she been missin. Day and a night and a nother day and a night and most this time I was thinkin she be with her cousin Martine on Ninth Street comin there after school like she do sometimes and she forgot to call me, so I—I was just thinkin—that's where she was. But now they sayin she ain't there and at her school they sayin she never showed up Thu'sday and there be other times she'd cut since September when the school started that wasn't known to me and now don't nobody seem to know where my baby is. Anybody see S'b'lla, please call me—Ednetta Frye. My telephone is . . .

Her beautiful eyes mute with suffering and veined with broken capillaries. Her skin the dark-warm-burnished hue of mahogany. There was an oily sheen to her face, that glared in the whitely overcast air. From a short distance Ednetta appeared heavyset with large drooping breasts like water-sacks, wide hips and thighs, yet she wasn't fat but rather stout and rubbery-solid, strong, resistant and even defiant; of an indeterminate age beyond forty with a girl's plaintive face inside the puffy face of the aggrieved middle-aged woman.

Please—you sayin you seen her? Ohhh but—when? Since Thu'sday? That's two days ago and two nights she been missin . . .

Along wide windy Trenton Avenue there came Ednetta Frye lurching into the Diamond Café, and into the Wig-a-Do Shop, and into AMC Loans & Bail-Bond, and into storefront Goodwill where the manager offered to call 911 for her to report her daughter missing and Ednetta said with a little scream drawing back with a look of anguish *No! No po-lice! How'd I know the Pascayne police ain't the ones taken my girl!*

Exiting Goodwill stumbling in the doorway murmuring to herself *O God O God don't let my baby be hurt O God have mercy.*

Sighted then making her way past shuttered storefront businesses on Trenton Avenue and then to Penescott to Freund which were blocks of brownstone row houses converted into apartments and so to Port and Sansom which were blocks of small single-story stucco and wood frame bungalows built close to cracked and weed-pierced sidewalks. An observer would think that the distraught woman's route was haphazard and whimsical following an incalculable logic. Sometimes she crossed the street several times within a single block. There were far fewer people on these residential streets so Ednetta knocked on doors, called into dim-lighted interiors, several times boldly peered into windows and rapped on glass—*'Scuse me? Hello? C'n I ask you one thing? This my daughter S'b'lla Frye she missin since Thu'sday—you seen anybody looks like her?*

Crossing vacant lots heaped with debris and along muddy alleys whimpering to herself. She'd begun to walk with a limp. She was panting, distracted. She seemed to have taken a wrong turn, but did not want to retrace her steps. Somewhere close by, a dog was barking furiously. Overhead, a plane was descending to Newark International Airport with a deafening roar—Ednetta craned her neck to stare into the sky as at a sign of God, unfathomable and terrible. Here below were abandoned and derelict houses, a decaying sandstone tenement building on Sansom long known as a hangout for drug addicts, teenagers, homeless and the mentally ill which Ednetta Frye approached heedlessly. *H'lo? Anybody in here? H'lo! H'lo!*

And daring to step into the street to stop vehicles to announce to the startled occupants *'Scuse me! I am Ednetta Frye, this is my daughter S'b'lla Frye, she fourteen years old. Last I seen of S'b'lla she be leavin for school and now they sayin she never got there. This was Thu'sday.*

She passed the pictures of Sybilla to these strangers who regarded them somberly, handed them back to Ednetta and assured her no, they hadn't seen the girl but yes, they would be on the look-out for her.

At Sansom and Fifth there came sharp gusts of wind from the river, fresh-wet air and a sickly-sweet odor of leaves and strewn garbage in the alleys. And there stood Ednetta Frye on the curb pausing to rest like a laborer who is exhausted after an effort that has come to nothing. No one so alone as the bereft mother seeking her lost child in vain. The heel of her hand pressed against her chest as if she were stricken with heart-pain and she was staring into the distance, at the Pitcairn Bridge lifted and spread like a great prehistoric predator-bird and beyond at the slow bleed of the sky and on her face tears shone unabashed, so little awareness had Ednetta of these tears she hadn't lifted a hand to wipe them away.

■

THAT POOR WOMAN SHE SCARED OUT OF HER WITS LIKE SHE AIN'T EVEN aware who she talkin to!

Primarily it was women. During Ednetta Frye's several hours of search and inquiry in the Camden Avenue–Twelfth Street neighborhood of inner-city Pascayne on the morning of October 6, 1987.

Some sixty individuals would recall Ednetta, afterward.

Of these a number were women who knew Ednetta Frye from the neighborhood and who'd seen her frequently with children presumed to be hers including the daughter Sybilla—but they hadn't seen Sybilla within the past forty-eight hours, they were sure.

Of these were women who'd known Ednetta Frye for years—as long as thirty, thirty-five years—when they'd been girls together in the old Roosevelt projects, long since condemned and razed and replaced by a never-completed riverfront "esplanade" that was a quarter-mile sprawl of concrete and mud, rusted chain-link fences, frayed flapping plastic signs DANGER DO NOT ENTER CONSTRUCTION. They'd gone to East Edson Elementary in the 1950s and on to East Edson Middle School and to Pascayne South High. Some of them had known Ednetta when she'd been a young mother—(she'd had her first baby at sixteen, forced to quit school and never returned)— and during those years when she'd worked part-time as a nurse's aide at the Polk clinic taking the Clinton Street bus along Camden Avenue, a husky straight-backed good-looking woman with a gat-toothed smile, warm-rippling laughter that made you want to laugh with her.

And there were those who'd known Ednetta in the past decade or so since she'd been living with Anis Schutt in one of the row house brownstones on Third Street. Some of these women who'd known Anis Schutt when he'd been incarcerated at Rahway maximum-security and before that at the time of Anis's first wife's death— "manslaughter" was the charge Anis had pleaded to—had (maybe) wondered at Ednetta who was younger than Anis by at least ten years falling in love with such a man, taking such a risk, and her with three young children.

Ednetta had always belonged to the AME Zion Church on First Street.

She'd sung in the choir there. Rich deep contralto voice like Marian Anderson, she'd been told.

Good-looking as Kathleen Battle, she'd been told.

Never missed church. Sunday mornings with her mother and her grandmother (her old ailing grandmother she'd helped nurse) and her aunts and her girls Sybilla and Evanda, Ednetta's happiest times you could see in her face.

Anis Schutt never came to the AME Zion Church. No man leastway resembling Anis Schutt was likely to come to the AME

Zion Church where the shock-white-haired minister Reverend Clarence Denis frequently preached himself into a frenzy of passion and indignation on the subject of "taking back" Red Rock from the "thugs and gangsters" who'd stolen it from the good black Christian people.

A few years ago there'd been a rumor of Ednetta Frye fired from the Polk clinic for (maybe) stealing drugs. Ednetta Frye charged with "bad checks" when it was claimed by her that she'd been the victim. Ednetta working at Walmart—or Home Depot—one of those big-box stores at the Pascayne East Mall where you were lucky to get minimum wage and next-to-no health benefits but you could buy damaged and outdated merchandise cheap which all the employees did especially at back-to-school and Christmas time.

Over the years there'd been rumors of ill health: diabetes? arthritis? (Seeing how Ednetta had put on weight, fifty pounds at least.) Taking the children to relatives' homes to hide from Anis Schutt in one of his bad drunk moods but Ednetta had not ever called 911 and had not ever fled to St. Theresa's Women's Shelter on Twelfth Street as other women (including her younger sister Cheryl) had done at one time or another nor had she gone to Passaic County Family Court to ask for an injunction to keep Anis Schutt at a distance from her and the children.

Ednetta Frye, who loved her children. Who did most of the work raising Anis Schutt's several children (from his only marriage, with the wife Tana who'd died) along with her own—five or six of them in the cramped household though Anis's boys being older hadn't remained long.

One of the sons at age nineteen shot dead on a Newark street in a drive-by fusillade of bullets.

Another son at age twenty-three incarcerated at Rahway on charges of drug-dealing and aggravated assault, twelve to twenty years.

They were an endangered species—black boys. Ages twelve to twenty-five, you had to fear for their lives in inner-city Pascayne, New Jersey.

Ednetta had a son, too—ten years old. And another, younger daughter, Sybilla's half-sister.

Of the women to whom Ednetta Frye showed Sybilla's picture this morning several knew Anis Schutt "well" and at least two of them—(Lucille Hersh, Marlena Swann)—had had what you'd call "relations" with the man, years before.

Lucille's twenty-year-old son Rodrick was Anis's son, no doubt about that. Marlena's eight-year-old daughter Angelina was Anis's daughter, he'd never contested it. Exactly how many other children Anis had fathered wasn't clear. He'd started young, as Anis said, laughing—hadn't had time for counting.

It was painful to Ednetta of course—running into these women. Seeing these women cut their eyes at *her*.

Worse, seeing these women with children the rumor was, Anis was the father. *That* was nasty.

You could see that poor woman scared out of her wits like she ain't even aware who she talking to. I saw it myself, Ednetta come up to me an my friend Jewel in the grocery like she never knew who we were—Ednetta Frye be Jewel's enemy on account of Anis who ain't done shit to help Jewel out, all the time he promise he would. And Ednetta looks at us with like these blind eyes sayin 'Scuse me! Hopin you can help me! My daughter S'b'lla—you seen her?

That big girl gone only a day or two and Ednetta was actin like the girl be dead, we thought it was kind of exaggerated but when you're a mother, you do worry. And when a girl is that age like S'b'lla, you can't trust her.

You wouldn't ask Ednetta if she'd called the police, knowin how Anis feel about police and how police feel about Anis.

So we said to her, we will look for S'b'lla for sure! We will ask about her, everyone we know, and if we see her, or learn of her, we will inform Ednetta right away.

And she was cryin then, she like to hugged us hard and she say, Thank you! And God bless you, I am praying He will bless me and my baby and spare her from harm.

And we stand there watchin that poor woman walk away like she be drunk or somethin, like she be walkin in her sleep, and we're sayin to each other what you say at such a time when nobody else can hear—Poor Ednetta Frye, sure am happy I ain't her!

The Discovery

OCTOBER 7, 1987

EAST VENTOR AT DEPP

PASCAYNE, NEW JERSEY

You hear that? That like cryin sound?"

In the night she'd heard it, whatever it was—had to hope it wasn't what it might be.

Might be a trapped bird, or animal—not a baby . . . She didn't want to think it might be a baby.

A soft-wailing whimpering sound. It rose, and it fell—confused with her sleep which was a thin jittery sleep to be pierced by a sliver of light, or a sliver of sound. Those swift dreams that pass before your eyes like colored shadows on a wall. And mixed with night-noises—sirens, car motors, barking dogs, shouts. The worst was hearing gunshots, and screams. And waiting to hear what came next.

She'd lived in this neighborhood of Red Rock all of her life which was thirty-one years. Bounded by the elevated roadway of the New Jersey Turnpike some twelve blocks from the river, and four blocks wide: Camden Avenue, Crater, East Ventor, Barnegat. Following the "riot" of August 1967—(*riot* was a white word, a police word, a word of reproach and judgment you saw in headlines)—Red Rock had become a kind of inner-city island, long stretches of burnt-out houses, boarded-up and abandoned buildings, potholed streets and decaying sidewalks and virtually every face you saw was dark-skinned where you might recall—(Ada recalled, as a child)—you'd once seen a mix of skin tones as you'd once seen stores and businesses on Camden Avenue.

She'd gone to Edson Elementary just up the block. She'd taken a bus to the high school at Packett and Twelfth where she'd graduated with a business degree and where for a while she'd had a job in the school office—typist, file clerk. There were (white) teachers who'd encouraged her to get another degree and so she'd gone to Passaic County Community College to get a degree in English education which qualified her for teaching in New Jersey public schools where sometimes she did teach, though only as a sub. There was prejudice against community-college teacher-degrees, she'd learned. A prejudice in favor of hiring teachers with degrees from the superior Rutgers education school which meant, much of the time, though not all of the time, white or distinctly light-skinned teachers. Ada didn't want to think it was a particular prejudice against *her*.

She'd lain awake in the night hearing the faint cries thinking it was probably just a bird trapped in an air shaft. This old tenement building, five floors, no telling what was contained within the red-brick walls or in the cellar that flooded in heavy rainfall when the Passaic overflowed its banks and sewage rushed through the gutters. A pigeon with a broken wing, that had flung itself against a window-pane. A stray dog that had wandered into the building smelling food or the possibility of food and had gotten trapped somewhere when a door blew shut.

"Nah I don't hear nothin'. Aint hearin anything."

"Right now. Hear? It's somebody hurt, maybe . . ."

"Some junkie or junkie-ho'. No fuckin way we gonna get involved, Ada. You get back here."

Ada laughed sharply. Ada detached her mother's fingers from her wrist. She was a take-charge kind of person. Her teachers had always praised her and now she was a teacher herself, she would take charge. She wasn't the kind of person to ignore somebody crying for help practically beneath her window.

Down the steep creaking steps with the swaying banister she was having second thoughts. In this neighborhood even on Sunday morning you could poke your nose into something you'd regret. Ma was probably right: drug dealers, drug users, kids high on crack, hookers and homeless people, somebody with a mental illness . . .

She couldn't hear the cries now. Only in her bedroom had she really heard, distinctly.

Years ago the factory next-door had been a canning factory—Jersey Foods. Truckloads of fish gutted and cooked and processed into a kind of mash, heavily salted, packed into cans. And the cans swept along the assembly line, and loaded into the backs of trucks. Tons of fish, a pervading stink of fish, almost unbearable in the heat of New Jersey summers.

Jersey Foods had been shut down in 1979 by the State Board of Health. The derelict old building was partially collapsed, following a fire of "suspicious origin"; its several acres of property, including an asphalt parking lot with cracks wide as crevices, as well as the rust-colored building, lay behind a six-foot chain-link fence that was itself badly rusted and partially collapsed. Signs warning NO TRESPASSING had not deterred neighborhood children from crawling through the fence and playing in the factory despite adults' warnings of danger.

In the other direction, on the far side of the dead end of Depp Street, was another shuttered factory. Even more than Jersey Foods,

United Plastics was off-limits to trespassers for the poisons steeped in its soil.

You'd think no one would be living in this dead-end part of Pascayne—but rents were cheap here. And no part of inner-city Pascayne was what you'd call *safe*.

It was Ada's hope to be offered a full-time teacher's job in an outlying school district in the city, or in one of the suburbs. (All of the suburbs were predominantly white but "integrated" for those who could afford to live there.) Then, she'd move her family out of squalid East Ventor.

Six years she'd been hoping and she hadn't given up yet.

"God! Don't let it be no *baby*."

(Well—it wouldn't be the first time a baby had been abandoned in this run-down neighborhood by the river. Dead-end streets, shut-up warehouses and factories, trash spilling out of Dumpsters. Some weeks there wasn't any garbage pickup. A heavy rain, there came flooding from the river, filthy smelly water in cellars, rushing along the gutters and in the streets. Walking to the Camden Street bus Ada would see rats boldly rooting in trash just a few feet away from her ankles. [She had a particular fear of rats biting her ankles and she'd get rabies.] Nasty things fearless of Ada as they were indifferent to human beings generally except for boys who pelted them with rocks, chased and killed them if they could. And what the rats might be dragging around, squeaking and eating and their hairless prehensile tails uplifted in some perky way like a dog, you didn't want to know. For sure, Ada didn't want to know. Terrible story she'd heard as a girl, rats devouring some poor little baby left in some alley to die. And nobody would reveal whose baby it was though some folks must've known. Or who left the baby in such a place. And the white cops for sure didn't give a damn or even Family Services and for years Ada had liked to make herself sick and scared in weak moods thinking of rats devouring a baby and so, whenever she saw rats quickly she turned her eyes away.)

Ada was uneasy remembering Ednetta Frye from the previous morning. She'd seen the distraught woman first crossing Camden Avenue scarcely aware of traffic, then in the Korean grocery, then approaching people in Hicks Square who stared at her as you'd stare at a crazy person. Ednetta had seemed so distracted and disoriented and frightened, nothing like her usual self you could talk and laugh with—it was Ednetta who did most of the talking and the laughing at such times. There'd been occasions when Ednetta had a bruised face and a swollen lip but she'd laugh saying she'd walked into some damn door. You guessed it had to be Anis Schutt shoving the woman around but it wasn't anything extreme, the way Ednetta laughed about it.

Ada was at least ten years younger than Ednetta Frye. She'd substitute-taught at the middle school when Ednetta's daughter Sybilla had been a student there, a year or two ago; she knew the Fryes from the neighborhood, though not well.

They were neighbors, you could say. East Ventor crossed Crater and if you took the alley back of Crater to Third Street, somewhere right around there Ednetta was living in one of the row houses with that man and her children—how many children, Ada had no idea.

With her education degree and New Jersey teacher's certificate Ada Furst liked to think that there was something like a pane of glass between herself and people like the Fryes—it might be transparent, but it was substantial.

But the day before, Ednetta hadn't been in a laughing or careless mood. She'd been anxious and frightened. She'd showed Ada photos of Sybilla as if Ada didn't know what Sybilla looked like—Ada had had to protest, "Ednetta, I know what Sybilla looks like! Why're you showing me these?"

Ednetta hadn't known how to answer this. Stared at Ada with blank slow-blinking eyes as if she hadn't recognized Ada Furst the schoolteacher.

"She's probably with some friends, Ednetta. You know how girls are at that age, they just don't *think*."

Ednetta said, "S'b'lla know better. She been brought up better. If Anis get disgusted with her, he goin to discipline her—serious. S'b'lla know that."

Ada said another time that Sybilla was probably with some friends. Ednetta shouldn't be worried, just yet.

"I don't know how long you'd be wantin me to wait, to be 'worried,'" Ednetta said sharply. "I told you, Anis don't allow disrespectful behavior in our house. S'b'lla got to know that."

Clutching her photographs Ednetta moved on. Ada watched the woman pityingly as she approached people on the street, imploring them, practically begging them, showing the pictures of Sybilla. Most people acted polite, and some were genuinely sympathetic. There was something not right about what Ednetta was doing, Ada thought. But she had no idea what it was.

Ada was ashamed now, she'd spoken so inanely to Ednetta Frye. But what did you *say*? Girls like Sybilla were always "running away"— Ada knew from being a schoolteacher—meaning they were staying with some man likely to be a dozen years older than they were, and giving them drugs. What she could remember of Sybilla Frye from the middle school, the girl was sassy and impudent, restless, couldn't sit still to concentrate, had a dirty mouth to her, and hung out with the wrong kind of girls. Her grades were poor, she'd be caught with her friends smoking out the back door of the school—in seventh grade. None of that could Ada tell poor Ednetta!

Ada knocked at the second-floor door of a woman named Klariss— just a thought, she'd ask Klariss to come with her. But Klariss was as vehement as Ada's mother. "You keep outa that, Ada. You know it's some drug dealer somebody put a bullet in, or some druggie OD'ing. You get mixed up in it, the cops is gonna mix you up with them and take you all in."

Weakly Ada tried to cajole Klariss into at least coming outside with her, in back of the building—"You don't have to come any farther, K'riss. Just, like—see if anything happens . . ."

But Klariss was shutting her door.

In the front vestibule were several tall teenaged boys on their way outside—ebony-black skin, mirthful glances exchanged that signaled their awareness of / disdain for stiff-backed Ada Furst they knew to be some kind of schoolteacher—(these were boys born in Red Rock of parents from the Dominican Republic who lived upstairs from Ada)—and for a weak moment Ada considered asking them to accompany her . . . But no, these rude boys would only laugh at her. Or something worse.

Outside, Ada walked to the rear of the building. No one ever went here, or rarely: behind the tenement was a no-man's-land of rubble-littered weeds and stunted trees, sloping to a ten-foot wire fence at the riverbank, against which years of litter had been blown and flattened so that it resembled now some sort of plaster art installation. In this lot tenants had dumped trash that included refrigerators, mattresses, chairs and sofas and even badly broken and discolored toilets. (Ada recognized a broken lamp that had once belonged to Kahola, her sister must've tossed out here. For shame!)

Ma and Karliss were right: Ada shouldn't be here. Hadn't there been a murder in this block, only a week ago, one in a series of young black boys shot multiple times in the back of the head, dragged into an abandoned house to bleed out and die . . .

But this person, if it was a person, was alive. Needing help.

Noise from jetliners in their maddening ascent from Newark Air-

port a few miles away, that began in the early morning and continued for hours even on weekends. Ada couldn't hear the crying sound,
with those damn jets!

Ada checked to see: was anyone following her? (The tall black-
skinned Dominican boys, who hadn't said a word to her though
she'd smiled at them?) She made her way through the debris-strewn
lot to the fence, that overlooked the river. Here she felt overwhelmed
by the white, vertically falling autumn sunshine, that blinded her
eyes. And the wide Passaic River with its lead-colored swift-running
current that looked to her like strange sinewy transparent flesh, a
living creature with a hide that rippled and shivered in the sunshine.
Oil slicks, shimmering rainbows. The Passaic had once been a beautiful river—Ada knew, from schoolbooks—but since the mid-1800s
it had been defiled by factories and mills dumping waste, all sorts
of debris, tannery by-products, oil, dioxin, PCBs, mercury, DDT,
pesticides, heavy metals. Upriver at Passaic was Occidental Chemical, manufacturers of the most virulent man-made poison with the
quaint name—Agent Orange. Supposedly now in the late 1980s in
these more enlightened times manufacturers had been made to comply with federal and state environmental laws; cleanups of the river
had begun but slowly, at massive cost.

When she did move away from East Ventor, Ada thought, she
would miss the river! That was all that she would miss, even if it was
a poisoned river.

It had long been forbidden to swim in the Passaic—(still, boys
did, including Ada's twelve-year-old nephew Brandon: you saw them
on humid summer days swimming off rotting docks)—and most of
the fish were dead (if any survived you'd be crazy to eat them but every day, every morning at this time in fact, there were people fishing
in the Passaic, mostly older black men with a few women scattered
among them).

Ada's grandfather Franklin had been one of the fishermen down by the docks, in the last years of his life. He'd been happy then, Ada had wanted to think. Bringing back shiny little black bass for her grandmother to clean, gut, sprinkle with bread crumbs and fry in lard. How much poison they'd all eaten, those years, not knowing any better or indifferent to knowing, Ada didn't want to speculate.

This morning the river was bright and choppy. There were a few boats, at a distance. On the farther shore were shut-down factories and mills that hadn't been operating since she'd been in high school. Vaguely she could remember her father and grandfather working at Pascayne Welding & Machine when she'd been a little girl in the 1960s, then later her father worked at Rand Alkali Pesticides until his health deteriorated and he'd been laid off. (The pesticide factory sprawling among seven acres of "hazardous" land within the Pascayne city limits had been shut down by the New Jersey Board of Health in 1977 for its toxic fumes and carcinogenic materials. There'd been a settlement between Rand Alkali and the State of New Jersey but whatever fines had been paid had made little difference to the sick employees like Ada's father whose disability pension was less than his Social Security, and the two checks together came to less than he required to live with any dignity in even the shabby tenement at 1192 East Ventor.)

Ada listened: there came the crying again. Now, it sounded like a plaintive mewing, that had all but given up hope.

Definitely, the sound was coming from the old Jersey Foods factory next-door.

The fish-canning factory was a ruin that would one day slide into the river, next time it flooded. Last time, the spring of 1985, filthy river-water had risen into the factories on the riverbanks as into the dank dirty cellars of residences like Ada's. A powerful stink had prevailed for weeks. The state had declared a disaster area for some and a makeshift shelter had been established in the high school gymnasium and the Pascayne Armory. Fortunately, Ada and her family hadn't had to be evacuated. Kahola had been living with them then.

Approaching the factory with its broken, boarded-over windows Ada tried not to think *This is a mistake. I am making a mistake.*

There was no man in her life, as there'd been in her sister's life. Not a single man in Kahola's life but numerous men. Ada was too free to make decisions of her own, too reckless. It was the price of her female independence and a certain stiffness, resentment even, about inhabiting a fleshy female body. Oh, she was frightened now. But damn if she'd turn back. She cupped her hands to her mouth and called: "Hello? Is anybody there?"

The cries seemed to be coming from the factory cellar. Bad enough to be inside the nasty fish-factory, but—in the *cellar*! There were steps leading down, a door that had been forced open years ago. Everywhere was filth, storm debris and mud. Ada drew a deep breath and held it.

She thought—*It's only a cat. A trapped starving cat.*

A wounded cat.

Planning how she would trap the cat—in a box?—somehow—and take it to an animal shelter.

(But how practical was that? The shelter would euthanize the cat. Better to keep the cat.)

(But she couldn't keep the cat! No room for a scrawny diseased alley cat in their place already too small and cramped for the people who lived there.)

It was 8:20 A.M. It was a bright cool Sunday morning in October. Ada Furst would recall how she made her way into the cellar down a flight of steps littered with broken glass and pieces of concrete as she continued to call in a quavering voice—"Hello? *Hello?*" A pale, porous light penetrated the gloom, barely.

The cry came louder. Desperate.

Ada blinked into the shadows. Ada took cautious steps. She could hear someone whispering *Help me help me help me.*

Then she saw: the girl.

The girl was lying on the filthy floor in the cellar not far from the entrance, on her side facing Ada, on a strip of tarpaulin, as if she'd been dragged partway beneath a machine. She appeared to be tied, wrists and ankles, behind her back. It looked as if there'd been a wadded rag in her mouth, she'd managed to spit out. And around the girl's head was a cloth or a rag she'd worked partway off. Her hair was matted with mud and something very smelly—feces? Ada began to gag. Ada began to scream.

"Oh God. Oh God! My God."

A girl of thirteen, or fourteen. On the filthy floor, she looked like a child.

Ada was stricken with horror believing that the girl was dying: she would be a witness to the girl's death. She'd wasted so much time—she'd come too late—the girl was shivering uncontrollably, as if convulsing. Ada crouched over her, hardly daring to touch her. Where were her injuries? Was she having a seizure? Ada had a confused sense of blood—a good deal of blood—on the tarpaulin, and on the floor. It seemed to her that the girl had been mutilated somehow. The girl's bones had been broken, her spine deformed. Ada would swear to this. She would swear she'd seen this. Certainly the girl's face was swollen, her eyes blackened and bruised. Dark blood had coagulated at her nose, that looked as if it had been broken. How young the girl seemed, hardly more than a child! Her clothing was torn and bloody. Her small breasts were bared, covered in a sort of filthy scribbling. Cruelly her legs were drawn up behind her back, hog-tied.

Ada was telling the girl she was here, now. She would take care of her, now. The girl would be all right.

"Is it—Sybilla? Sybilla Frye?"

Feebly the girl tried to free herself, moaning. Ada pulled at the ropes binding her wrists and her ankles, which were thin ropes, like clothesline—tugged at them until a knot came loose and she could lift the girl in her arms, into a partially sitting position on the filthy tarpaulin. The stench of dog shit was overwhelming. The girl was shivering in terror. Saying what sounded like *They say they gon come back an kill me—don let em kill me!* When Ada tried to lift her farther, out of the filth on the tarpulin, the girl began to squirm and fight her, panting. She seemed not to know who Ada was. Her eyes rolled back in her head. She fell back heavily, as if lifeless. Ada would not wonder at how readily the knotted rope had come loose, at this time. Ada was begging the girl: "Don't die! Oh—don't die!"

Yes I saw she was Sybilla Frye. I saw that right away.

Ada Furst ran stumbling and screaming for help.

A first-floor resident in her building called 911.

An ambulance from St. Anne's Hospital, two miles away on the other side of the river, arrived in sixteen minutes.

The first query on the street would be—*She goin to live?*

Then—*Who done this to that girl?*

"White Cop"

J esus help me

Say they gon kill me, I tell anybody Dear Jesus help me, they hurt me so bad and they will do worse they say next time my mama they gon hurt bad an my lit sister an any nigra they find where I live, they told me they will murder us all

They was hopin I would die, they leave me in this place to die sayin you be eaten by beetles nasty black cunt you deserve to die you are SO UGLY

Thought I heard say there was other dead nigras in this place they was laughin about where they drag me thinkin I would not live this like cellar-place they say, you will die here an beetles eat you only just bones left nobody gon recognize by the time those beetles finish with you

They had white faces an one of them a badge like a cop would wear or a state trooper an they had guns an one of them, he put that gun barrel up inside me and it hurt so bad I was crying so bad they said Nigra cunt you stop that bawlin, we gon pull this trigger an all yo' insides gon come splashin out your ugly nappy head

And they laugh, laugh some more

All the time they be laughin like they are high on somethin smokin crack, I could smell

The Pis'cyne cops they con-fis-cu-ate the crack an smoke it for themselves, why they are crazy to kill black people they white bosses tell them, you give us our percent of the money we be OK how you behave

Grabbed me from behind where I was walkin from school in the alley behind the car wash on Camden some kind of canvas they pulled down over my head like a hood and I was screamin but couldn't get free to breathe Thought I would die an was cryin Mama! Mama! till they stuffed a rag in my mouth near to choking me O Jesus

It was in the back of a van it was a police van, I think there was a siren they were laughin to use a cop can use a siren any time he wishes they drove to underneath the bridge I could hear the echo up under the bridge I could recognize that sound like when we were little and played there, and put our hands to our mouths and called up under the bridge and it was like pigeons cooing and the echo coming back and the water lapping except now, I could not hear any echo the white men were laughin at me took turns kicking and beating and strangling me raped me like with they guns and fingers sayin they would not put their pricks in a dirty nasty disease nigra cunt they jerked themselves off onto my face that's what they done they said, swallow that, you ignorant nigra bitch how many times how many of them they was who hurt me, I could not see I thought five, maybe five—their faces were white faces—there was a badge this one was wearin, shiny spit-in-your-face badge like a cop wear or a state trooper an they laughin at me sayin nobody will believe a dirty nigra cunt taking her word against the word of decent white men

The van, they drove somewhere else then here was maybe other men came into it it was a night and a day and a night I was hurt so bad, my eyes was puffed shut I was fainted from the bad hurt and bleedin up inside me it was all sore and bleedin and my mouth, and my throat they'd stuck the gun barrel down into my throat too there was more than one of them did it they said, this is what you like black nigra cunt aint it

Tied me so tight like you'd tie a hog no water and no food, they was hopin I would weaken and die some of them went away, an other ones came in their place Nigra hoar of babyland they was laughin

I could not see their faces mostly I heard their voices

There was one of them, a young one he was sayin why dint they let him blow out the nigra cunt's brains he would do it, he said

In my hair and on my body they smeared dog shit to shame me when they was don with me two of them dragged me from the van to that place in the cellar they put they foot on the back of my head to press into the earth they would leave me there, they said beetles would eat me and nobody give a damn about some ugly nappy lit nigra girl if she live or die and nobody believe her, that a joke to think!

O Jesus help me I am afraid to die, Jesus help me I have been a bad girl is this how I am punished, Jesus an Jesus say, the last shall be first an the first shall be last an a litl child shall lead them AMEN

St. Anne's Emergency

OCTOBER 7, 1987

She'd been left to die.

She'd been beaten, and raped, and left to die.

She'd been hog-tied, beaten and raped and left to die.

Just a girl, a young black girl. Dragged into the cellar of the old fish-factory and if she hadn't worked the gag out of her mouth, to call for help, she'd have died there in all that filth.

It was that 911 call. That call you'd been waiting for.

You'd expect it to be late Saturday night. Or Friday night. Could be Thursday night. You would not expect the call to be Sunday morning.

And that neighborhood by the river, East Ventor and Depp. Those blocks east of Camden Avenue. *High-crime area* the newspapers call it. After the fires and looting of August 1967 spilling over from the massive riot in Newark, the neighborhood hadn't ever recovered, Camden Avenue west for five or six miles looking like a war zone twenty years later, shuttered storefronts, dilapidated and abandoned houses, burnt-out shells of houses, littered vacant lots and crudely hand-lettered signs FOR RENT FOR SALE that looked as if they'd been there for years.

Many times, the calls come too late. The gunfire-victim is dead, bled out in the street. The baby has suffocated, or has been burnt to death in a spillage of boiling water off a stove. Or the baby's brains have been shaken past repair. Or there's been a "gas accident." Or a child has discovered a (loaded) firearm wanting to play with his younger sister. Or a man has returned to his home at the wrong time. Or a drug deal has gone wrong. (This is frequent.) Or a drug dose has gone wrong. (This is frequent.) Or a space heater has caught fire. Or a carelessly flung burning cigarette has caught fire. Or a woman has swallowed Drano and has lain down to die. Or a gang of boys has exchanged multiple shots with another gang of boys. Or a pit bull maddened by hunger has attacked, sunk its fangs into an ankle and will not release the crushed bones until shots from a police service revolver are fired into its brain.

Calls of desperation, dread. But exhilaration in being so summoned, in a speeding ambulance, siren piercing the air like a glittering scimitar.

You are propelled by this speed. You are addicted to the thrill of danger, this not-knowing into which you plunge like a swimmer diving into a swirling river to "rescue" whoever he can.

But now there is *this call*—to change your life in a way you will regret.

Damn it wasn't true the ambulance had *taken its time* getting there! Sixteen minutes but we'd been slowed down on the bridge and the 911 dispatcher had given us an incomplete address.

It being a *black neighborhood*, it would be claimed. The EMTs from St. Anne's had *taken their time*.

We'd responded to the dispatcher as we always did.

We said, there was no difference between this emergency summons and any other—except what would be made of it, later.

When we arrived at the corner of East Ventor and Depp we hadn't known immediately where to go. The dispatcher hadn't been told clearly where the injured girl was.

Something about a factory. Factory cellar.

So we'd wasted minutes determining what this meant. We'd been told "cellar"—so we had flashlights in case flashlights were needed. Searching for a way through the chain-link fence until a woman appeared and screamed at us about a "dying girl"—a girl "bleeding to death"— and directed us where she was.

First thing we observed was that the girl (later identified as "Sybilla Frye") lying on her side on the cellar floor on a strip of tarpaulin seemed to be *conscious* but would not respond to us, as if she was *unconscious*.

When we came running down into the cellar with flashlights we saw that the girl's eyes were open but immediately then she shut them when the light came onto her face. We saw her lift her hands to hide her face from the bright light.

It was our concern that the girl was in severe physical distress, in shock, or bleeding internally, we had to determine immediately, or try to determine, before lifting her onto a stretcher.

Her face was bloodied and battered. There was a towel or a rag partly tied around her head and her hair was matted with filth.

There were no evident deep lacerations of the kind made with a sharp weapon or gunshot. Wounds were superficial, though bloody. There did not appear to be a severe or life-threatening loss of blood.

There was a strong smell of excrement—possibly human, or animal.

It looked like the girl had been tied with a clothesline but when we arrived, the clothesline had been untied. The woman who'd met us outside said she'd found the girl tied and had untied the girl. Her wrists and ankles had been tied behind her—"hog-tied."

Well, we thought there was something strange—the injured girl had been communicating with the woman who'd found her, the woman told us—but then, she wouldn't communicate with *us*.

She was limp and her arms were, like, falling loose—like a person would be if she was unconscious. But when we touched her she stiffened up. She'd shut her eyes tight and kept them shut.

That girl was in a state of shock! She didn't know who we were.

We identified ourselves. She had to know we were a rescue team.

But she was scared! She was terrified. She was just a girl and somebody had almost killed her. She might've thought we were her assailants coming back. She was shivering—her skin felt clammy when I touched her.

She never did talk to us. Not a word.

It was possible, I thought, she was—you know—mentally disabled like retarded, or autistic. She communicated with *me* . . .

She did not communicate with you. She was not observed communicating with you.

She didn't *talk* to me exactly but, but she—*communicated* . . .

Look—this was not a "cooperative" individual. First thing when we came down into the cellar with flashlights we saw the girl's eyes were open and she's staring at us—then, she shut her eyes. We saw her lifting her hands to hide her face from the bright light—which you wouldn't do if you were *unconscious*.

The lights blinded her and scared her . . .

Had a damn hard time taking her blood pressure and pulse and trying to check for injuries, she kept bending her legs and wouldn't lay them flat so we could strap her down.

Sometimes it happens, an injured person is panicked and doesn't want to be taken to the ER.

But this girl refused to talk to us. She wasn't screaming or saying she didn't want medical treatment. She wasn't hysterical or crazy. She was trying to simulate being unconscious but she was awake and alert. You could see her eyeballs kind of jerking around behind her eyelids. You could see she'd been assaulted, a strong possibility she'd been raped, her clothes were torn partly off except she was still wearing jeans—bloodied jeans.

The visible injuries were lacerations and bruises on her face, her chest, her belly—where her clothes had been ripped, you could see.

The woman had been screaming the girl was "bleeding to death" but that was not the case.

Most of the blood appeared to be dried, coagulated. Whenever she'd been beaten, it hadn't been recently.

She'd been beaten and left to die! Tied and a gag in her mouth and left to die in that nasty place! When we found her, she was in a state of shock.

Actually she was not in a "state of shock"—her blood pressure wasn't low, we discovered when we were finally able to take it, and her pulse was fast.

She was in, like, emotional shock . . .

The woman was explaining she'd been wakened by "some kind of crying" in the night then in the morning she'd searched outside and found the girl tied and bleeding and left to die and she was worried since she'd moved the girl a little, started to lift her off the tarpaulin, maybe the girl had a skull fracture or broken spine or internal injuries she might've made worse, she wanted to tell us that.

The woman was kind of hysterical herself. She looked like her heart was jumping all over inside her chest. Said she was a schoolteacher and the girl had been one of her pupils . . .

Kept saying she'd thought the girl had been thrown down from some height, and her back was broken. She'd thought the girl was bleeding to death, that's what she'd told us when we first arrived. And the girl had been raped, she was sure of *that* . . .

She'd wanted to come in the ambulance with us but we had to tell her *no*. We told her to notify the girl's mother.

That poor girl was in a state like panic. Maybe it wasn't "shock" but she was panting—hyperventilating. Her skin was clammy like death.

Well—anybody would be scared and upset, in her circumstances. With just the flashlights we could see it had been a vicious attack. And you'd think for sure, rape. The disgusting thing was what was smeared in her hair and on the parts of her body that had been naked—mud and dog shit. And in the ambulance we saw something spelled out on her body.

These nasty words! Smeared in dog shit on that poor girl.

It wasn't *dog shit* the words were written in, it was some kind of smeared ink like a marker pen.

It was dog shit, too. I saw it.

The scrawled words were in black marker pen. It was hard to make out what they were because the ink was smeared, and the girl's skin was kind of dark . . .

The thing is, if you are unconscious, your limbs are not stiff and you don't resist medical intervention. If you are conscious, you might resist—if you are terrified and panicked. But we got a blood pressure reading finally and she wasn't in shock—or anywhere near—her pressure was 130 over 115. Her pulse was fast but not racing.

You could see that somebody had hurt her bad! There'd been

more than one of them, they'd kicked her and cut her and left her to die in that nasty place.

In the ER in the bright lights you could see these words scrawled on her chest and belly you couldn't read too well because the letters were smeared and distorted NIGRA BITCH KU KUX KLANN.

(Right away I had to wonder—why'd anybody write words on somebody's body *upside-down*?)

NIGRA BITCH—this was just below the girl's breasts, on her midriff.

KU KUX KLANN—this was on the girl's belly just above her navel.

Photos were taken of these racist words as photos were taken of the girl's injuries. This is ER procedure in such cases. When the flashes went off Sybilla Frye tried to hide her face making a wailing sound like *Noooo*.

It was our assumption she'd been raped—very possibly, gang-raped. Her clothes were ripped and bloody and her lower belly and thighs were bruised, we saw when we got the jeans pulled down. (She fought us pretty desperately about that—pulling down her jeans.) Her face had sustained the worst injuries. Both her eyes were blackened and her upper lip was swollen to twice its size, like a goiter.

A brutal gang-rape is not a common incident even in inner-city Pascayne. Yet, a brutal gang-rape is not an uncommon incident in inner-city Pascayne.

When she was first brought in Sybilla Frye hadn't been ID'd yet. We didn't know her name or address or who to contact. The EMTs couldn't help us much. We were asking her questions but she kept pretending to be unconscious and unable to hear us when it was obvious that she was conscious and she was hearing us.

I was the ER physician on duty, Sunday morning October 7.

Right away I said to her, "Miss? Open your eyes, please." Because

I had to examine her eyes. I had to determine if possibly she'd had a concussion or a skull fracture. I'd be ordering X-rays including X-rays of her skull. But still she wouldn't open her eyes. She was so tense, you could feel her body quivering. Yet she refused to cooperate. She pretended to be unconscious the way a small child might pretend to be "asleep." It isn't easy to pretend you're unconscious when you're conscious. You might think it is, but it isn't. I lifted one of her arms over her head and released it and immediately she deflected her arm to avoid striking her face—it's a reflex you can't help. Clearly, this girl who'd be identified as "Sybilla Frye" was conscious in the ER and in control of her reactions. I could see she'd been injured—that was legitimate—I felt sorry for her but this kind of uncooperative behavior would impede us in our treatment so I said, "Miss, you can hear me. So open your eyes"—and finally she did.

Looked at Dr. D___, like she was terrified of *him*.

Dr. D___ is Asian, light-skin. Later it came out she was afraid of him, he'd looked "white" to her.

Of the EMTs, just one of us was "white"—"white Hispanic." The others were dark-Hispanic, African-American. Yet, she'd acted scared of *us*.

She was terrified! Just so scared . . .

She wasn't hysterical but she was—she wasn't—you had to concur she wasn't in her right mind and under these circumstances you couldn't blame her for not cooperating. She didn't seem to understand where she was, or what was happening . . .

She understood exactly where she was, and exactly what was happening. She didn't wish to cooperate, that's all.

I did wonder why she wasn't crying—most girls would've been crying by now. Most women.

We treated her for face wounds. Lacerations, black eyes, mashed nose, bloody lip. A couple of loosened teeth where he'd punched her.

(You could almost see the imprint of a man's fist in her jaw. But he hadn't strangled her, there were no red marks around her throat.) The blood wasn't fresh but had coagulated in her nostrils, in her hair, etc. By their discolorations you could see that the bruises were at least twenty-four hours old. Also the blackened eyes. We gave her stitches for the deepest cuts in her eyebrow and on her upper lip. She reacted to the stitches and disinfectant so we had to hold her down but she still didn't say any actual words only just *Noooo*. We wondered if she was, like, a Dominican who didn't know English, or—there's Nigerians in Pascayne—maybe she was Nigerian . . .

There were Hispanic nurses we called in, to try to talk to her in Spanish—she ignored them completely.

Where (presumably) the rope had been tied around her wrists and ankles there were only faint red abrasions on the skin. No deep abrasions, welts, or cuts.

We couldn't get a blood sample. *That* wasn't going to happen just yet.

Pascayne police officers were just arriving at the factory when the EMTs bore the girl away in the ambulance. The bloodied tarpaulin and other items were left there for the police to examine and take away as evidence.

Soon then, police officers began to arrive at St. Anne's ER.

The hard part was—the pelvic exam . . .

We had to determine if she'd been raped. Had to take semen samples if we could. Any kind of evidence like pubic hairs, we had to gather for a rape kit, but the girl was becoming hysterical, not pretending but genuinely hysterical kicking and screaming *No no don't hurt me NO!* Dr. D___ was angry that the girl seemed determined to prevent a thorough examination though such an examination was in her own best interests of course. We were able to examine her and treat her superficially and it took quite a while to accomplish that with her kicking, screaming, and hyperventilating and the orderlies having to hold her down . . .

(Now we knew, at least—she could speak English.)

She continued to refuse to allow Dr. D___ to examine her just clamped her legs together tight and screaming so Dr. D___—(flush-faced, upset)—asked one of the female interns to examine her; this young woman, Dr. T___, was a light-skinned Indian-American who was able to calm the girl to a degree and examined her pelvic area by placing a paper cover over the girl's lower body but when Dr. T___ tried to insert a speculum into the girl's vagina the girl went crazy again kicking and screaming like she was being murdered.

Like she was being raped . . .

It was a terrible thing to witness. Those of us who were there, some of us were very upset with Dr. D___'s handling of the situation.

By this time, the mother had arrived. The mother had been notified and someone had driven her to the hospital and before security could stop her she'd run into the ER hearing her daughter's screams and began screaming herself and behind her, several other female relatives, or neighbors—all these women screaming and our security officers overwhelmed trying to control the scene . . .

Pascayne police arrived at the ER. Trying to ask questions and the girl refused to acknowledge anyone shutting her eyes tight and screaming she wanted to go home and the mother was saying *My baby! My baby! What did they do to my baby!*

You couldn't get near the girl without her screaming, kicking and clawing. We'd have sedated her but the mother was threatening to sue us if we didn't release her daughter.

(It is strange that a mother would want her daughter released into her custody out of the ER, before she knew the extent of her daughter's injuries. It is strange that the mother, like the daughter, refused X-rays, a blood test, but it is not so very uncommon under these circumstances. We are accustomed to delusional behavior and violence in the ER. We are accustomed to patients dying in the ER and their relatives going berserk. Yet, this seemed like a special case.)

We were trying to explain: the girl had to have X-rays before being discharged.

It was crucial, the girl had to have X-rays.

If she'd suffered a concussion, or had a hairline fracture in her skull, or had broken or sprained bones—it was crucial to determine this before she left the hospital.

If there was bleeding in her brain, for instance.

And we needed to do blood work. We needed to draw blood.

Mrs. Frye didn't give a damn for any of this. In a furious voice saying how her daughter had been missing three days and three nights and wherever she'd been there were people who knew more than they were revealing and she'd come to take her daughter home, now.

They took my baby from me, now I'm bringin my baby home can't none of you stop me.

The Pascayne police officers set her off worse. When an officer from Child Protective Services tried to speak with Mrs. Frye she backed off stretching her arms out as if to keep the man from assaulting her. She was saying *You aint gon arrest me, you aint gon put cuffs on me, you leave me alone seein what you done to my baby aint that enough for you.*

Mrs. Frye's fear of the police officers appeared to be genuine.

By this time Sybilla Frye was sitting up on the gurney with her knees raised against her chest trying to hide herself with the crinkly white paper and making a noise like *Nnn-nnn-nnn*—like she was so frightened, she was shivering convulsively. You could hear her teeth chatter. And now she was crying, like a child *Mama don let them take me, Mama take me home* . . .

The mud and dog-feces had been removed from the girl's hair.

We'd had to cut and clip some of her hair in order to get this matter out. It would be charged afterward that we had *defiled and disfigured* Sybilla Frye—we had deliberately cut her hair in a careless and jagged fashion.

Her body covered in filth had been washed but the racist slurs in black Magic Marker ink remained on her torso and abdomen, more or less indecipherable.

(It would be recorded in the ER photos that these words had been written upside-down on Sybilla Frye's body.)

(Well, you'd think—as if Sybilla Frye had written the words herself, right? But a clever assailant might've written the words on her body standing behind her so that she could read the words. Or—he'd written the words upside-down purposefully so the victim would be accused of lying. *That* was possible.)

(Seeing the racist words on the girl's body we'd had to notify the FBI right then. This is protocol if there is a probable "hate crime" as there certainly was in this case.)

In an emergency unit in a city like Pascayne, New Jersey, you are half the time reporting crimes and taking such photos for forensic use. If your patient dies, you may be the only witnesses.

The FBI had to be notified immediately which the ER administrator did without either the injured girl or her mother knowing at the time.

Mrs. Frye was demanding to speak with her daughter "in private" if we wouldn't release the girl so she could take her home. Dr. D___ allowed this.

Mrs. Frye jerked the curtain shut around the cubicle.

For some minutes, Mrs. Frye and Sybilla whispered together.

Police officers were asking the ER staff and the EMTs what had happened and we told them what we knew: Mrs. Frye had ID'd her daughter who was "Sybilla Frye"—"fourteen years old"—(in fact, it would be revealed later that Sybilla Frye was actually fifteen: she'd been born in September 1972); the girl had been assaulted and had sustained a number of injuries; she'd been struck by fists and kicked, but she didn't seem to have been attacked with any weapons; cuts in her face had been made with a fist or fists, not a sharp instrument; there were no gunshot wounds; her face, torso, belly, legs and thighs were bruised, and there appeared to be evidence of bruising in the vaginal area, but without a pelvic exam it wasn't possible to determine if there had been sexual penetration or any deposit of semen.

Skin samples taken from the girl's body would be tested for DNA and these might contain semen. Other tests would be run, to determine if a sexual offense had been committed.

Mrs. Frye had claimed that her daughter had been "kidnapped" and "locked up" somewhere for three days and three nights. During this time, Mrs. Frye had been looking for the girl "everywhere she knew" but no one had seen her. Then, that morning, Sybilla Frye had been discovered by a woman who lived near the Jersey Foods factory, who'd heard the girl "crying and moaning" in the night.

So far, Sybilla Frye had not identified nor even described her assailant or assailants. She had not communicated with the ER staff at all.

She had not allowed a pelvic exam, nor had she consented to a blood test.

Despite the mother's claim that she'd been kept captive somewhere for three days, Sybilla Frye did not appear malnourished or dehydrated.

This is some of what we told Pascayne police.

After approximately ten minutes of whispered consultation, Mrs. Frye drew back the curtain. She was deeply moved; her face was bright with tears. She'd been wiping her daughter's face with tissues and now she was demanding that she be allowed to take her daughter home, it was a "free country" and unless they was arrested she was taking S'billa home.

(Ednetta Frye would afterward claim that she'd had to clean her daughter of mud and dog shit herself, the ER staff had not "touched a cloth" to Sybilla. She would claim that she'd carried her baby in her arms out of the ER, filth still in the girl's hair and on her body, and her body naked, covered in only a "nasty" blanket as the ER staff had cut off her clothes for "evidence.")

An officer from Juvenile Aid had arrived. But Mrs. Frye refused to allow Sybilla to speak to this woman, as she'd refused to allow Sybilla to speak to the officer from Child Protective Services.

It was explained to Mrs. Frye that since a crime or crimes had been committed, Sybilla would have to be interviewed by police officers— she would have to give a "statement"—when she was well enough . . . Mrs. Frye said indignantly *That girl aint gon be "well enough" for a long time so you just let her alone right now. I'm warnin you—let my baby an me alone, we gon home right now or I'm gon sue this hospital an every one of you for kidnap and false imprisonment.*

But finally Mrs. Frye relented, saying she would allow Sybilla to talk to a cop—*One of her own kind, and a woman—if you have one in that Pas'cyne PD.*

The Interview

It was not an ideal interview. It did not last beyond twenty stammered minutes.

It would be the most frustrating interview of her career as a police officer.

She'd been bluntly told that a black girl beaten and (possibly) gang-raped had requested a black woman police officer to interview her at the St. Anne's ER.

Getting the summons at her desk in the precinct station late Sunday morning she'd said, D'you think I'm black enough, sir?—in such a droll-rueful way her commanding officer couldn't take offense.

She couldn't take offense, she understood the circumstances.

She was not minority hiring. She didn't think so.

She'd been on the Pascayne police force for eleven years. She had a degree from Passaic State College and extra credits in criminology and statistics as well as her police training at the New Jersey Academy.

She was thirty-six years old, recently promoted to detective in the Pascayne PD.

As a newly promoted detective she worked with an older detective on most cases. This would be an exception.

Iglesias did not check *black* when filling out appropriate official forms. Iglesias did not think of herself as a *person of color* though she acknowledged, seeing herself in reflective surfaces beside those colleagues of hers who were *white,* that she might've been, to the superficial eye, a *light-skinned Hispanic.*

Her (Puerto Rican–American) mother wasn't her biological mother. Her (African-American) father wasn't her biological father. Where they'd adopted her, a Catholic agency in Newark, there was a preponderance of African-American babies, many "crack" and "HIV" babies, and Iglesias did not associate herself with these, either. Her (adoptive) grandparents were a mix of skin-colors, a mix of racial identities—Puerto Rican, Creole, Hispanic, Asian, African-American and "Caucasian." There was invariably a claim of Native-American blood—a distant strain of Lenape Indians, on Iglesias's father's side. The Iglesias family owned property in the northeast sector of Pascayne adjacent to the old, predominantly white sector called Forest Park; they owned rental properties and several small stores as well as their own homes. It was not uncommon for a young person in Iglesias's family to go to college—Rutgers-Newark, Rutgers–New Brunswick, Bloomfield College, Passaic State. The most talented so far had had a full-tuition scholarship from Princeton. They did not think of themselves and were not generally thought of as *black.*

Iglesias did not take offense, being so summoned to St. Anne's ER. Something in her blood was stirred, like flapping flags in some high-pitched place, by the possibility of being in a position unique to her.

For racism is an evil except when it benefits *us.*

She liked to think of being a police officer as an opportunity for service. If not doing actual good, preventing worse from happening. If being a *light-skinned female Hispanic* helped in that effort, Ines Iglesias could not take offense and would not take offense except at the very periphery of her swiftly-calculating brain where dwelt the darting and swooping bats of old hurts, old resentments, old violations and old insults inflicted upon her haphazardly and for the most part unconsciously by white men, black men, brown-skinned men—*men*.

With excitement and apprehension Sergeant Iglesias drove to St. Anne's Hospital. The emergency entrance was at the side of the five-story building.

This was not a setting unfamiliar to Ines Iglesias. She had witnessed deaths in this place and not always the deaths of strangers.

Just inside the ER, a patrol officer led her into the interior of the unit where the (black) girl believed to have been gang-raped was waiting, inside a curtained cubicle.

In the ER she noted eyes moving upon her—fellow cops, medics—in wonderment that this was the officer sent to the scene as *black*.

Cautiously Iglesias drew back the curtain surrounding the gurney where the stricken girl awaited. And there, in addition to the girl, was the girl's mother Ednetta Frye.

Sybilla Frye was a minor. Her mother Ednetta Frye had the right to be present and to participate in any interview with Sybilla conducted by any Pascayne police officer or social worker.

Too bad! Iglesias knew this would be difficult.

Iglesias introduced herself to Sybilla Frye who'd neither glanced at her nor given any sign of her presence. She introduced herself to Ednetta Frye who stared at her for a long moment as if Mrs. Frye could not determine whether to be further insulted or placated.

Iglesias addressed Mrs. Frye saying she'd like to speak to Sybilla for just a few minutes. "She's had a bad shock and she's in pain so I won't keep her long. But this is crucial."

Iglesias had a way with recalcitrant individuals. She'd been brought up needing to charm certain strong-willed members of her own family—female, male—and knew that a level look, an air of sisterly complicity, shared indignation and vehemence were required here. She would want Mrs. Frye to think of her as a mother like herself, and not as a police officer.

Extending her hand to shake Ednetta Frye's hand she felt the suspicious woman grip her fingers like a lifeline.

"You ask her anythin, ma'am, she gon tell you the truth. I spoke with her and she ready to speak to you."

Mrs. Frye spoke eagerly. Her breath was quickened and hoarse.

Not a healthy woman, Iglesias guessed. She knew many women like Ednetta Frye—overweight, probably diabetic. Varicose veins in her legs and a once-beautiful body gone flaccid like something melting.

Yet, you could see that Mrs. Frye had been an attractive woman not long ago. Her deep-set and heavy-lidded eyes would have been startlingly beautiful if not bloodshot. Her manner was distraught as if like her daughter she'd been held captive in some terrible place and had only just been released.

But when Iglesias tried to speak to Sybilla Frye, Mrs. Frye could not resist urging, "You tell her what you told me, S'b'lla! Just speak the words right out."

The battered girl sat slumped on the gurney wrapped in a blanket, shivering. Iglesias found another blanket, folded on a shelf, and brought it to her, and drew it around her thin shoulders. Close up, the girl smelled of disinfectant but also of something foul and nauseating—excrement. Her hair was oily and matted and had been cut in a jagged fashion as if blindly.

With both adult women focused upon her, Sybilla seemed to be shrinking. Her shut-in expression was a curious mixture of fear, unease, apprehension, and defiance. She seemed more acutely aware of her mother than of the plainclothes police officer who was a stranger to her.

Between the daughter and the mother was a force field of tension like the atmosphere before an electric storm which Iglesias knew she must not enter.

Iglesias asked the girl if she was comfortable?—if she felt strong enough to answer a few questions?—then, maybe, if the ER physician OK'd it, she could go home.

A trauma victim resembles a wounded animal. Trying to help, you can exacerbate the hurt. You can be attacked.

"Sybilla? Do you hear me? My name is Ines—Ines Iglesias. I'm here to speak with you."

Gently Iglesias touched Sybilla's hand, and it was as if a snake had touched the girl—Sybilla jerked back her hand with an intake of breath—*Ohhh!*

There was something childish and annoying in this behavior, Iglesias thought. But Iglesias wanted to think *The girl has been badly hurt.*

Mrs. Frye said sharply to her daughter, "I'm tellin you, girl. You just answer this p'lice off'cer's questions, then we goin home."

Sybilla continued to hunch shivering inside the blanket. She had shut her eyes tight as a stubborn child might do. Her upper lip, swollen like a grotesque discolored fruit, was trembling.

Iglesias had been told that the girl's assailants had rubbed mud and dog excrement into her hair and onto her body and that they'd written racist words in black ink on her body.

When she asked if she might see these words, Sybilla stiffened and did not reply.

"If you could just open the blanket, for a minute. The curtain is closed here. No one will see. I know this is very unpleasant, but . . ."

Sybilla began shaking her head vehemently *no*.

In a plaintive voice Mrs. Frye said, "She don't need to do that no more, Officer. S'b'lla a shy girl. She don't show her body like some girls. They took pictures of the writing, they can show you. That's enough."

"I would so appreciate it, if I could see this 'writing' myself."

"Ma'am, that nasty writin is all but gone, now. I think they washed it off. But they took pictures. You go look at them pictures."

"If I could just—"

"I'm tellin you *no*, ma'am. It's enough of this for right now, S'billa comin home with me."

Iglesias had been briefed about the "racist slurs"—scribbled onto the girl's body "upside-down." Clearly it was already an issue to arouse skepticism—*upside-down?* She would study the photos and see what sense this might make.

Iglesias had placed a recording device on the examination table. Mrs. Frye objected: "You recordin this, ma'am? I hope you aint recordin this, I can't allow that."

The small spinning wheels were a provocation. Iglesias had known that Mrs. Frye would object.

Carefully she explained that it was police department policy that such an interview would be recorded. "A recorded interview is for the good of everyone involved."

"No it ain't, ma'am! Like with pictures you can mess up what people say to twist it how you want. Like on TV. You can leave out some words an add some others the way police do, to make people 'confess' to somethin they ain't done. *You* got to know that, you a cop you'self."

Mrs. Frye spoke sneeringly. The sudden hostility was a surprise.

Iglesias had wanted to think that she'd been persuading Mrs. Frye, making an ally of her, and not an adversary. It was a painful truth, what the woman was saying, yet, as a police officer, she had to pretend that it wasn't so.

"Not in this case, Mrs. Frye. Not *me*."

Mrs. Frye folded her arms over her heavy breasts. She was wearing what appeared to be several layers of clothing—pullover shirt, long-sleeved shirt, sweater, and slacks. On her small wide feet, frayed sneakers. Iglesias saw that Ednetta Frye's nails had been done recently, each nail painted a different color, zebra-stripes on both thumbnails, but the polish was chipped and the nails uneven. The girl's nails were badly broken and chipped but had been polished as well, though not recently. The daughter wore no jewelry except small gold studs in her ears. The mother wore gold hoop earrings, a wristwatch with a rhinestone-studded crimson plastic band, rings on several fingers including a wedding band that looked too small for her fleshy finger.

"See, ma'am, I can't allow my daughter to be any more mishandled than she's been. No recordin here, or we goin home right now."

The woman didn't remember Iglesias's name or rank. You had to suppose. She didn't intend a sly insult, calling Iglesias *ma'am*.

Iglesias could only repeat that recording their conversation was for the good of everyone concerned but Mrs. Frye interrupted—"Nah it ain't! You must think we are stupid people! Have to be pretty damn stupid not to know that white cops turn your word around on you, or say you goin for a 'weapon' when you're reachin for your driver's license so they can shoot you down dead."

Iglesias spoke carefully to the excited woman saying she understood her concern, but this was an entirely different situation. In the heat of confrontations, terrible mistakes sometimes happened. But allowing Iglesias to record a conversation with her daughter, in the safety of the ER, was not the same thing at all.

Mrs. Frye said, snorting with indignation, that that was just some white folks' bullshit.

Iglesias said, pained, that "white folks" had nothing to do with this—with *them*. They could both speak frankly to her, that was why she'd come to speak with them.

Mrs. Frye was unimpressed. She said to Sybilla she was going to get her some decent clothes to put on, and they were getting out of this place. Unless they were arrested, nobody could keep them.

"Mrs. Frye, please—let me speak to Sybilla without recording our conversation. For just a few minutes."

Iglesias had no choice but to relent, the woman was about to take away the girl. Arranging for another interview would be very difficult.

"Nah I'm thinking we better be goin. Talkin with you aint worked out like I hoped, see, ma'am, you one of *them*."

Mrs. Frye spoke contemptuously. Iglesias felt dismay.

I am one of you, not one of them. Believe me!

"Please, Mrs. Frye. Just a few minutes. No recording."

All this while Sybilla had been sitting mute and shivering. Only vaguely had she seemed to be listening to the adult women, with an air of disdain.

Iglesias saw herself in the girl, she believed to be fourteen. She saw herself at that age, sulky, sullen, defiant and scared.

She'd been sexually molested, too. More than once. And many times sexually harassed and threatened. But never raped, never brutally beaten. Not Ines Iglesias.

The Fryes lived on Third Street, in that run-down neighborhood by the river. Abandoned factories, shuttered and part-burned houses, streets clogged with abandoned and rusting vehicles. Pascayne South High, lowest-ranked in the city. The Fifth Precinct, with the highest crime rate. You had to grow up swiftly there.

In the Iglesias neighborhood, adjacent to Forest Park, there were blocks of single-family homes, neatly tended lawns and attached garages. There were streets not clogged with parked, abandoned vehicles. There was Forest Park High from which an impressive number of students went on to college and where there were no fights, knifings, rapes on or near the premises.

But I am one of you! Please trust me.

Though she hadn't grown up in the inner city, Iglesias had had good reason to fear and distrust the Pascayne police. Family members, relatives, friends, neighbors had had encounters with (white) police of which you had to say the good thing was, none of these encounters had been fatal.

Though she knew of encounters that had been fatal.

Though she knew police officers who were racists, even now—in 1987. After the Pascayne PD had been "integrated" for twenty years.

It was a mark of their contempt for her, she supposed—making racist remarks when she could overhear.

Yet, racist remarks that weren't directed toward her or her kind—*light-skinned Hispanic.*

It was African-Americans they held in particular contempt—*niggers.*

Though maybe behind her back, in their careless, jocular way, that exaggerated the bigotry they naturally felt in the service of humor, they referred to her as *nigger,* too.

Iglesias not bad-lookin for a nigger, is she?

Man, not bad!

Got her an ass on her.

I seen better.

In a quiet urging voice Iglesias was telling Sybilla Frye how she wanted to help her. How she wanted to know who'd hurt her so badly, who the assailant or assailants were so that they could be arrested, gotten off the street.

With a little shiver of dread Sybilla drew the blanket closer around her. She seemed to be rousing herself out of a dream.

Shaking her head looking now scared and miserable. Iglesias was wondering how a rape victim returned to her life—to school, to her friends. Already news of the missing Frye girl found hog-tied in the canning factory was on the street.

Sybilla leaned to her mother and murmured in her ear. Her swollen lips moved but Iglesias couldn't make out what she was whispering.

"Oh honey, I know," Mrs. Frye said to the girl; then, to Iglesias, with grim satisfaction, "S'b'lla sayin they gon kill her, ma'am. Told her they gon kill her whole family, she tells you."

It was strange how Mrs. Frye addressed her daughter gently and lovingly, or harshly and reproachfully. If you were the daughter you would have no way of guessing which Mama would emerge.

Though generally, it was safe to surmise that when Sybilla did not oppose her mother in any way, in even the expression on her face, the tilt of her head or the set of her back, the gentle-loving Mama emerged.

"But we can protect you, Sybilla. We can put you in protective custody until your assailants are arrested."

Iglesias was a police officer, she said such improbable things.

How many times uttered by police officers in such situations in Pascayne, to whatever futile end.

"Off'cer, that is such bullshit. Half the people we know believe that shit you tell them, they shot down dead in the street. Whoever do it don bother waitin for dark, he just shoot. You aint bein honest with my daughter an me, an you know it. Why I asked for an African-American woman, and you aint her."

"I *am her*. I'm here to help you."

"You a woman, you got to know what they gon do to my daughter if she say who hurt her. All she told me, it was five of them— men. Men not boys. Nobody she knew, from the neighborhood or her school. That's all she told me, she's too scared." Mrs. Frye smiled a sharp mirthless smile revealing a gap between her two front teeth like an exclamation mark.

Iglesias tried again with Sybilla. "So—you say—it was five men? No one you recognized? Could you begin at the beginning, please? Your mother says you went missing on Thursday . . ."

Slowly then, as if each word were a painful pebble in her mouth, Sybilla began to speak in a hoarse whisper. She was squirming inside the blanket, looking not at the police officer who'd fixed her face into an expression of extreme solicitude and interest but staring at the floor. There appeared to be a slight cast in her left eye. Perhaps this was why she didn't look up. Iglesias could not determine if the girl was genuinely frightened or if there was something childishly resistant and even defiant about her—an attitude that had to do less with Iglesias than with the mother who remained at all times close beside her, half-sitting on the examination table, a physical presence that must have been virtually overwhelming to the girl yet from which she had no recourse.

Iglesias could see that, though Sybilla's eyes were swollen and discolored, these were Ednetta Frye's eyes: thick-lashed, so dark as to appear black, large and deep-set. During her hurried briefing Iglesias had been told that the victim was possibly mentally defective, maybe retarded, which was why it was so difficult to communicate with her, but Iglesias didn't think this was true.

Iglesias asked Sybilla to repeat what she'd said, a little louder. She was leaning close, to listen.

In the hoarse slow whisper Sybilla recounted how she'd been

coming home from school Thursday afternoon when somebody, some men, came up behind her with a canvas they lowered over her head and grabbed her and dragged her away in a van and kept her there for three days—she thought it was three days, she wasn't sure because she was not conscious all the time—and punched and kicked her and did things to her and laughed at her when she was crying and later put mud and dog shit onto her and wrote on her "nasty words" and tied her up and left her in the factory cellar saying there were "other nigras" in that place who had died there.

Starting to cry now, and Mrs. Frye squeezed her hand, and for a moment it didn't seem that Sybilla would continue.

Iglesias asked if she'd been able to see faces? Could she describe the men—their age, race? Were they known to her?

Sybilla shook her head, they weren't known to her. She seemed about to say more, then stopped.

"You're sure that these men are not known to you, Sybilla? Could you describe any of them?"

Sybilla stared at the floor. Tears welled in her eyes and spilled over her bruised cheeks.

"Did they hurt you sexually?"

Sybilla sat very still staring at the floor. Her face was shiny now with tears.

Mrs. Frye said, gently urging, "S'b'lla, honey, you got to tell this lady, see? You got to tell her what you can. You aint told me all of it, has you?—you know you aint. Now, you tell *her*."

"Did they rape you, Sybilla?"

Sybilla shook her head just slightly, yes.

"More than one man, you've said?"

Sybilla shook her head yes.

"You told your mother—five men?"

Sybilla shook her head yes.

"Not boys but men."

Sybilla shook her head yes.

"And not men you know?"

Sybilla shook her head no.

"Can you describe them? Just—anything."

Sybilla stared at the floor. Mrs. Frye was crowded close beside her now, an arm around the girl's shoulders.

"The color of their skin? You said they used the word *nigra*—"

Mrs. Frye urged her to speak. "Come on, girl! Was they black men, or—some other? Who'd be sayin 'nigra' except some other?"

Sybilla stared at the floor. She didn't seem resistant or defiant now, but exhausted. Iglesias worried that the girl was about to faint or lapse into some sort of mental state like catatonia.

Once, interviewing a stricken and near-mute girl of twelve, Iglesias had given the girl Post-its upon which to write, and the girl had done so. Iglesias gave Sybilla a (bright yellow, cheering) Post-it pad and a pencil to write on and, after some hesitation, Sybilla printed:

WHITE COP

" 'White cop'—"

Iglesias tried not to show the surprise she felt.

Mrs. Frye took the Post-it from Iglesias's hand, read it and began to wail as if *white cop* was a death sentence.

Iglesias asked if the "white cop" had hurt Sybilla?

Sybilla shook her head yes.

"Was just one of the men 'white'—or a 'cop'?"

Sybilla shook her head to indicate she didn't know.

"How did you know the man was a 'cop,' Sybilla?"

Sybilla wrote on the Post-it:

WEAR A BAGDE

"He was 'wearing a badge'? When he raped you, he was 'wearing a badge'?"

Sybilla shook her head, she didn't know. Thought so, yes.

Her eyelids were drooping, her mouth was slack with exhaustion.

"Were any of the others 'wearing a badge'?"

Sybilla shook her head, she didn't know.

"Could you describe him? The 'white cop'?"

Sybilla printed on a Post-it:

YELOW HAIR

"Could you say what his approximate age was?"

Sybilla shook her head, uncertain.

"Thirty? Thirty-five?"

Sybilla shook her head.

"My age is thirty-six. Was he older or younger than me, do you think?"

Sybilla squinted at Iglesias. Her left eye seemed to be losing focus but her right eye was fixed on Iglesias. On a Post-it she wrote:

AGE 30

"Were the other men 'white' also? Could you see?"

Sybilla printed on the Post-it:

THEY WHITE

Sybilla took back the Post-it and printed:

THEY ALL WHITE

"These men abducted you, kept you captive in a van, beat and raped you, intermittently for three days and three nights? Where was the van parked, do you have any idea?"

Sybilla shook her head, she didn't know.

"Could you describe the van? Inside, outside?"

Sybilla shook her head slowly, she wasn't sure.

Sybilla smiled, a nervous twitch of a smile. How like a child she looked, a badly beaten child, with a gat-toothed smile, looking almost shyly now at the police officer.

Iglesias wanted to take the girl's hand, to comfort and encourage her. But she dared not touch her, after Sybilla had shrunk from her.

"If you saw a van, you could maybe compare it to the van they'd taken you in? You could try to describe it?"

Sybilla shook her head yes. She could try.

"When they left you in the factory cellar, they told you they would kill you, if you told anyone? Who said these words?"

Sybilla shook her head, she didn't know.

"Did one of the men say this, or others? Did they all say this?"

Sybilla hid her face in her hands. Mrs. Frye whispered to her, and drew her hands away.

The interview had exhausted the girl. Iglesias was exhausted.

Thinking *White cop! White cop.*

Thinking *None of this story is true. This is all a lie. The mother has coached her. The mother has beat her. The mother's boyfriend—her own boyfriend—someone she knows . . .*

Mrs. Frye was embracing her daughter. The two of them were weeping, wet-eyed.

"Ma'am, this interview over now. My girl got to get home where she safe, and her mama can take care of her."

And there was no recording of this interview! Iglesias had known that was a mistake.

Only her notes, and the bright yellow Post-its.

Only her word.

"Mrs. Frye, if we could just—a few more minutes, and . . ."

"I said no! My daughter's health come first, before anythin else. You got this girl to tell you somethin could get her killed, and you better not misuse it, or S'b'lla, I'm warnin you—Off'cer."

Off'cer was spoken in indignation as Mrs. Frye heaved herself up from the gurney and gathered Sybilla into her arms. The girl was unresisting now, and hid her face in the older woman's bosom.

Iglesias backed away sick and stunned.

"'White cop.'"

Her very mouth seemed to have gone numb.

And how many times in the weeks and months to come would the thought come to her, remorse like a stab in the gut—*But what if it is true? What if white men did debase her? And we didn't believe her? God help me to know what is truth and what is false.*

Red Rock

*H*og-tied and left to die.

The Frye girl, fourteen. Beaten and raped and shit-on and left to die in some factory cellar.

She sayin it was white cops. In a cop-van drivin around with a black girl they arrest like pretendin she a hooker so they use her like some sex-slave, then they rub shit on her, and write nasty words on her, and dump her and left her to die.

Except she ain't die, she been rescued. By her own lady schoolteacher!

Aint died and tellin what the white cops done now see what the fuckers gon do, to punish themselves.

In Red Rock it began to be told. In the small storefront businesses, in the taverns, rib joints and diners of Camden Avenue, Penescott, Ventor, Twelfth. In the brownstone row houses of Third, Fourth, Fifth and Sixth streets and in the tenements of East Ventor, Crater, and Depp. In the several towers of the Earl Warren high-rise project on the river at Twelfth Street, its gritty-floored foyers, erratically operating elevators, shadowy staircases and corridors and vast open courtyards ravaged as earth over which a Biblical pestilence has raged. In the hair salons, nail salons, wig shops, beer wine and liquor stores, groceries and pawnshops and bail-bond shops and Red Rock's single drugstore—(a bleak Walgreens of narrow corridors and a low stamped-tin ceiling doomed for closure within the year)—at the windswept intersection of Camden and Freund. In Passaic County Family Services, Polk Memorial Medical Center, Planned Parenthood and Veterans' Furniture Outlet and Goodwill as in the defaced bus shelters of Camden, Trenton, Crater, Jersey and West River Street. In the vicinity of the Pascayne Police Department Fifth Precinct on First Street with its commandeered side streets of white-and-green cruisers and vans parked as in a stalled but belligerent military formation. In the shadow of the Pitcairn Bridge rising hunched above the river and running parallel with the New Jersey Transit railroad bridge that in turn ran parallel with the elevated Turnpike bridge blotting out much of the eastern sky above Red Rock. In the sandstone tenement buildings like corroded pueblo dwellings of an ancient time jutting up against the elevated spiraling lanes of the Turnpike. In Hicks Square, in Polk Plaza, in the weedy no-man's-land littered with bottles, cans, styrofoam containers, junkies' needles and used condoms like shrunken sea slugs abutting the Passaic River at Washburn where the city had intended a park. In the drab factory-like Pascayne South High School where Sybilla Frye was a tenth-grade student and in Edson Middle School and in even Edson Elementary where she'd been a student when younger it began to be told, and retold.

That Frye girl gone missin you hear she been found? In that fish-factory cellar she left for dead all tied-up and bleedin these white cops grabbed her comin out of school Thu'sday sayin they got warrants to arrest her she be missin school an take her away in the police van. We saw it—right outside the school.

Left her for dead, they'd been beating and raping and starving her. She'd lost more'n half her blood. Branded KKK in her skin with hot irons. Carved nasty words on her back. They'd picked her up outside the high school there was witnesses saw the white cops takin her away in a cop van tryin to say she a nigger hooker her pimp give to them for payment. Kept the girl tied up for three days while her mother lookin for her on every street, we seen that poor woman showin pictures of the girl to anybody who would look. They raped her, beat and kicked her an rolled her in dog shit an told her they would cut her throat an her family's if she told and they told her nobody would ever believe her, take the word of a nigger slut against the word of white cops and they left her to die in that nasty place where in '67 they dumped people they'd shot in the street and nobody found the bodies for a long time. But this girl didn't die.

"S'quest'd"

here my baby? She s'quest'd. She aint here. She sick, and she gon get well. You leave my baby alone!

In the brownstone row house at 939 Third Street the agitated mother scarcely opened the front door but shouted through a narrow crack for would-be visitors to go away. Initially, Mrs. Frye had tried to determine who it was ringing the bell or rapping loudly at the door when the buzzer-bell failed to sound, a familiar face, relatives, girlfriends of Sybilla's, incensed and sympathetic neighbors or strangers—so many strangers!—then in a frenzy of fear and dismay she turned them all away slamming the door in their faces.

Through the windows Ednetta Frye could be seen, a shifting shadow-shape, peeking out at the edges of the drawn blinds. Her figure was both hulking and tremulous. Muttering to herself *God help us. God help us through this mis'ry.*

—

It was known, Sybilla Frye was being kept home from school. Days in succession following the news of her discovery in the Jersey Foods factory she was absent from Pascayne High South where she was a sophomore with what school authorities were acknowledging was a *spotty record*—a history of sporadic and unexplained absences already since the start of the fall term after Labor Day and the previous year in ninth grade as well.

Questioned by authorities about the assaulted girl, the principal of the high school had no recollection of her nor did her teachers speak of "Sybilla Frye" with much certainty—classes at Pascayne South were overcrowded, students sat in seats not always assigned to them, Sybilla's homeroom teacher had taken sick days in September during which time substitutes had monitored the thirty or more students in the homeroom and none of these had any clear recollection of "Sybilla Frye" still less any information about her.

Nor did Sybilla's classmates wish to speak of her except in the most vague terms—*S'b'lla be out of school, somethin happen to her.*

When someone from the high school called, Ednetta Frye interrupted without listening to whatever question, request, message this stranger had for her—*My daughter not livin in this house right now! She s'quest'd somewhere safe.* Repeated calls, Ednetta picked up the receiver and slammed it down without listening.

Juvenile Aid of New Jersey, Child Protective Services, Passaic County Family Services—calls from these agencies, Ednetta Frye dealt with in a similar fashion. Individuals from these agencies, even those dark-skinned and female like herself, Ednetta Frye turned away brusquely from her door.

She s'quest'd where you can't get her! Just go away an leave us like you ever give a damn for us!

The Hispanic female police detective who'd pretended to be Ednetta's friend in the hospital ER returned, with a (male,

Italian-looking) detective-companion who stared at Ednetta with an expression of barely concealed contempt. Ednetta had seen the white-and-green Pascayne PD cruiser park at the curb only a few yards away from the window at which she crouched pressing the palm of her hand into her chest as she panted in pain and apprehension—*Jesus help me. Jesus send these people away*—and she guessed she had no choice but to open the door to them, at least a crack, for possibly they had a search warrant? a warrant for arrest?— though which of them it might be, Sybilla, or herself, who'd be arrested, Ednetta had no idea. She was near-fainting with anxiety. High-blood-pressure pounded in her ears. As the female detective knocked Ednetta snatched open the door saying in a hoarse pleading voice what sounded to the detectives like—*My baby s'quest'd! She ain't here! Can't talk to you now gon shut this door.*

The female detective—(Ednetta hadn't caught the name, much of what other people said in recent days flew past Ednetta's consciousness like panicked birds whose beating wings you ducked to avoid)—tried to prevent her from shutting the door. Saying it was crucial that she speak with Sybilla, and with her. The female detective's companion was standing beside her grim-faced staring at Ednetta through the two-inch crack between the door and the doorframe and Ednetta saw in the man's ice pick eyes the look that signaled *We know you are lying you God damn fuckin nigger bitch you will regret this.*

The female detective—"Iglesias"—was trying to speak calmly to Ednetta. Seeing that Ednetta was in an excitable mood. (Both cops alert to whether the distraught and panting heavyset black woman might've been hiding a butcher knife behind her broad hips, or a hand gun.) Telling her that she, Iglesias, was her friend; and she'd brought with her Detective ___ —whose name Ednetta could not have heard even if she'd wanted to hear it, blood pumping in her ears; and they hoped for just a few minutes of her time, and if they could please speak with Sybilla . . . And Ednetta said sharply *Ma'am I told you you can't! My baby aint in this house she s'quest'd somewhere safe.*

Iglesias seemed not to hear. Not to understand.

S'quest'd? "Sequestered"?

Quickly Ednetta shut the door. Her heart was pounding so hard in her billowy chest, she'd have thought it was an angry fist demanding release.

From inside Ednetta could see Iglesias and the other detective outside on the step conferring what to do. Shrewdly she reasoned that the detectives didn't have a warrant to enter the house—if they had, they'd have entered the house; nor did they have a warrant to arrest her or Sybilla. (Could you arrest someone for being a *victim*? Could you arrest someone for being a *victim's mother*?) Still, Ednetta was remembering the martial law days and nights of August 1967 when SWAT teams stormed Red Rock houses in a hail of bullets or threw tear gas containers or firebombs into dwellings like this in a pretext of "neutralizing" sniper fire. She hadn't known Anis Schutt then but knew of how Anis's (unarmed) sixteen-year-old brother Lyander had been murdered by city police for stepping outside his mother's house on Freund Street five minutes after the 9:00 P.M. curfew. A sixty-year-old great-aunt of Ednetta's living in a first-floor apartment in the Roosevelt project had been shot dead through a window unwisely passing in front of a blind with a harsh light behind it—another "sniper" casualty.

Iglesias was calling through cupped hands not in a threatening-cop voice but a friendly-female voice—*Mrs. Frye? Please? We can just speak with you. This is crucial for our investigation.*

Ednetta retreated to the rear of the house. Ednetta climbed panting and sweating to the second floor of the house. Ednetta hid away in her and Anis's bedroom whimpering like a wounded creature sprawled on the bed covering her head with a blanket. *Jesus help me. Jesus forgive me. None of this my fault Jesus!*

When she revived, the house was quiet. She listened hard to hear if the detectives were knocking on the door, calling for her, but they were not.

She'd heard a vehicle in the street, pulling away. She hoped this was the police cruiser.

Damn phone began to ring, she'd thought she'd taken the receiver off the hook. She took that precaution now.

It was true: Sybilla Frye wasn't in the brownstone at 939 Third Street. Soon after they'd returned from St. Anne's Hospital and before Anis had returned to the house Ednetta had taken the girl away to stay with Ednetta's seventy-nine-year-old grandmother who lived in a ground-floor apartment in the dead end of Eleventh Street at the river.

High above Ednetta's grandmother's windows was I-95 north-bound, the elevated Turnpike. There was a near-continuous shudder and vibration of traffic in the apartment like the breathing of a great beast. The air was a pale-cinnamon haze.

Sybilla's great-grandmother Pearline Tice had not been informed of the nature of the terrible hurt done to the battered girl but only *S'b'lla needin to spend some time with you, Grandma. Somebody act bad with her now she gon conv'lesce. She give you trouble, call me quick!*

Ednetta's other children still living at home—the younger son and daughter—were in school when the detectives came to the door. Anis had been out and Ednetta didn't know for sure—often, she didn't know, and could not ask—if Anis intended to be back that night for supper.

(Anis had other places he stayed, some nights. Anis had sporadic if precisely unidentified "work" that seemed to pay fairly well—judging by cash he set out on the kitchen table for Ednetta when he was in a generous mood. It was enough for Ednetta that Anis Schutt kept his clothes and things with *her*—meaning he'd always be coming back to *her*. Other places, other women were temporary.)

Now that Sybilla was out of the house, that was a calming influence on Anis.

Ednetta hadn't told him about Sybilla hog-tied in the fish-food factory, and taken to the ER. She hadn't told him that Sybilla had been questioned by a Pascayne PD detective. Not yet.

Anis knew some of what had happened. But not all.

It was like Lyander shot down dead over on Freund Street and his body not found until morning when the curfew lifted. You know that something has happened, it will hit you hard and irrevocably but you don't know (yet) what it is and you are in no hurry to know.

That morning Anis had awakened late. You tiptoed around Anis sprawled naked and snoring in bed one of his muscled arms flung out like a gnarly tree limb. And his face that was an ugly-scarred not-young face twitching and grimacing in sleep. Standing above the man seeing his eyeballs shifting inside the tight-shut lids which meant he was dreaming Ednetta lapsed into a dream of her own recalling her friend from girlhood Natalia who'd murdered her common-law husband (as the newspapers would identify him) while he'd slept in just this way, gripping in both hands a revolver belonging to the man, pointing the barrel at the man's forehead from a distance of no more than three inches then pulling the trigger. *It was him or me, he'd have killed me* Natalia said and though this was true, they'd convicted Natalia of "cold-blooded" second-degree murder and sent her to the women's prison at Trenton twenty-five years to life.

Ednetta loved Anis too much for anything like *that*.

Even if it became necessary Ednetta wasn't the one for anything like *that*.

So, you moved quiet and took care not to close any door with a click, not to waken the man. Stumbling out of the room to dress in the bathroom and not to use the faucet that squeaked, and not to flush the toilet that made too much damn noise. And if you turned on TV to see local morning news you kept the volume down almost to mute.

(Nothing on the TV about "Sybilla Frye"—yet. There'd been no official charges made, no news released to the media. Ednetta reasoned that so long as she kept away from all cops, and kept Sybilla away, there would never be this news and maybe it would all just fade away like things do.)

The younger children had learned also to hush, to be very quiet not to awaken their stepdaddy. They were gone to school by the time Anis staggered out for breakfast and by this time Sybilla would have been gone also if she'd been in the house. No reason for Anis to ask about her and he hadn't asked. Hadn't said a word. Silent in the kitchen devouring the breakfast Ednetta had prepared for him which was a hot breakfast—sausages fried in grease, corn bread— and strong-smelling coffee whitened with milk the way Anis liked it and he hadn't looked at her in fury or in shame though he'd grunted in farewell rising from the table, grabbing his jacket and his cap and departing with footsteps quick for a man so heavy, like mallet-thuds on the floor.

All he'd been hearing on the street that week, had to be hearing and he hadn't said a word to Ednetta.

Between the girl and the stepfather was a treacherous wild place Ednetta tried to avoid.

They were two of a kind, Ednetta thought: the girl, the stepfather.

She was the responsible one. *She* was the mother.

First thing he'd said moving into this house he'd said if these kids are under my roof with me, they are going to be disciplined by me. In Anis's own way of speaking (which did not involve the employment of actual words you might recount, contemplate) he'd allowed her to know this. And he had his own boys he'd brought with him—big, brooding boys, not home half the time, or more than half the time, never mind them.

And Sybilla was just a young girl then, sixth grade, eleven years old, grateful to be taken up by the Tyne girls across the street, and the gorgeous Jamaican Gloria Estes who was their stepmother and braided the girls' hair including Sybilla's hair and it was like Sybilla *adored them all* and had no judgment. And the girls were running crazy-wild colliding with people on the sidewalk, elderly ladies, crippled men, that poor no-leg boy in his wheelchair in Hicks Square, giggling and screaming and in the Korean grocery two of them attracted the attention of the cashier (who was also the store owner) and another two wandered the aisles with schoolgirl inno-cence while slipping things into their pockets, licorice twists, salted peanuts, gummy worms, mints, no surprise the girls were caught—(disgusted Mr. Park could see the ghost-white-girls cavorting on a TV surveillance screen)—and when Anis found out that his eleven-year-old stepdaughter had been "arrested" for shoplifting with three other, older girls he'd disciplined her grimly in a way he said had to be done, it was the way his own father had done with all his chil-dren, beating the girl with his belt, a half-dozen harsh strokes, a dozen harsher strokes, and now the girl was screaming in pain and terror for her mama had never hurt her like this, even in a blind rage Ednetta had never hurt her children in such a way, but Anis who was the new stepdaddy believed in a different sort of discipline and finally Ednetta had dared to rush at the man to stop his hands terri-fied he'd injure her little girl seriously with the flying buckle that had inflicted hurt on her bare back, buttocks, legs, blood-oozing welts. And Anis had flung Ednetta from him to stumble stunned against a wall. And Anis had said afterward it was a good thing she'd stopped him for once he began in the way of disciplining which was his own daddy's way it was hard to stop.

Soberly and seriously he'd told Ednetta this. He had not exaggerated. Uneasily Ednetta recalled the rumor—(not a rumor but "fact" but Ednetta didn't want to think in such specific terms)—that Anis Schutt had beaten to death his first wife a beautiful Haitian named Tana and been convicted of second-degree manslaughter and incarcerated at Rahway for how many years exactly, Ednetta didn't know.

So it was a warning, Ednetta thought. A warning for the heedless stepdaughter and a warning for the mother.

Don't provoke Anis, girl. You know the man have this temper, he can't help.

Yet it was a desperate thing, how she loved Anis Schutt. A melting sensation in the region of her heart, Jesus! First time she'd seen him, and she had not been a naïve young girl then. And thinking he was an ugly man, large blunt face like something carved in weatherworn rock and an oily black skin ten times blacker than Ednetta Frye who wasn't what you'd call *light-skin*. And his eyes distinct and shiny as marbles in his head and restless, and his way of carrying himself like he was too restless to be confined in any space. And you would not ever want to cross Anis Schutt or draw his angry attention. And yet she'd stared at him, and stared. And he'd seen her, and smiled at her. And suddenly his face was changed, even boyish. Even kind-seeming.

You lookin at me, honey? You got somethin for me?

He'd been crazy for Ednetta Frye's gat-toothed smile. Big enough space he could stick the tip of his tongue into it, almost.

He'd been what you would call an older man—not even thirty!

She'd been just seventeen.

Ednetta smiled, recalling. O Jesus.

In a woman's life there is only one man like Anis Schutt. She'd had him, even if she lost him in some time to come she'd had him, that could not be taken from her.

What a woman would do for a man like Anis, Ednetta would do, and had done. And would keep doing, as long as she could.

What the first wife Tana might've done was *betray*. In no way did you *betray* Anis Schutt and not be hurt bad for doing it.

Ednetta wasn't always sure she loved the girl. So much of herself she saw in Sybilla, the almond-shaped eyes, the gat-toothed smile—it was like herself and how could you "love" yourself?

My baby, she myself. Why I feel so bad for her, and blame her.

Soon the sons-of-bitches intruding upon Ednetta's life returned to the brownstone at 939 Third. Ednetta saw the God-damn vehicles pulling up to the curb like her place was some kind of drive-in bank teller or fast-food restaurant. Now these were senior staff workers from Juvenile Aid, Child Protective Services, Pascayne County Family Services, and Save-Our-Children which was a white-folks' church volunteer organization with a storefront office in Red Rock. And Sergeant Iglesias. All looking for *your daughter Sybilla Frye,* and with warrants. And Ednetta said, pressing the heel of her hand against her bosom, eyes brimming with hurt and indignation *Ain't I told you! My baby s'quest'd where you can't find her.*

Because they had warrants, Ednetta couldn't keep them out. Let the sons-of-bitches search the house upstairs and down, the kids' bedroom, her and Anis's bedroom, Sybilla's closet-sized bedroom with picture-posters on the wall—Michael Jackson, Tina Turner, Whitney Houston, Prince, LL Cool J, Public Enemy. The fact was, Sybilla wasn't there.

Girl-Cousins

"Where's S'b'lla?"

"They sayin S'b'lla in some hospital."

"They sayin S'b'lla in 'custody.'"

"S'b'lla in Juvie."

"Nah S'b'lla ain't in Juvie—*she* the one got hurt."

Sybilla's girl-cousin Martine and several of her friends from the neighborhood went to her house looking for her and each time Mrs. Frye sent them away—*S'b'lla ain't here. Y'all get on home.*

Martine was Sybilla's age and in Sybilla's class at Pascayne South. Some of the rumors she'd been hearing about her cousin were so nasty, she'd had to press the palms of her hands over her ears and run away.

Through back-alleys she came to the rear of the brownstone row house in which her aunt Ednetta Frye lived with that man Anis Schutt. Thinking she would peek in the windows and see if she could see Sybilla inside, but Ednetta had drawn all the blinds down to the sills.

Martine thought, if her cousin Sybilla was dead, she would know it. That shuddery sensation like when someone walks over your grave-to-be.

All of Sybilla's girlfriends were talking about her, wondering where she was. Sybilla was starting to hang out with older guys but it had to be in secret—Ednetta couldn't know. (For sure, the stepfather Anis couldn't know. That man would whip her hard with his belt and give Ednetta a few swipes, too.) Her friends wondered if this disappearance, all these rumors, had to do with *that*.

Or maybe there was no connection. Sybilla was just grabbed in some alley, dragged into a car or a van and driven away, kept for three days and three nights and God knows what done to her.

"They sayin she in the hospital now, in some 'special care' ward. She on 'life support.'"

"Nah. They sayin she run away with that Jaycee."

It wasn't uncommon for a girl like Sybilla who didn't get along well with her mother to be *sent away*—somewhere. Martine wondered if this was the explanation.

Where's S'b'lla?—Martine nagged her mother who'd told her a dozen times she didn't know. There was something evasive in her mother's voice that suggested to Martine that she did know. (Martine's mother Cheryl was Ednetta's younger sister. Bullshit Ednetta hadn't confided in her.)

The last time Martine went to Third Street to knock on her aunt's door Ednetta cursed her with a choking sob *God damn girl ain't I told you! S'b'lla not here! Just go.*

For sure something had happened to Sybilla, you could tell by Ednetta's behavior. That guilty-ravaged look in Ednetta's face. How quick Ednetta flared up in a nasty temper.

Whatever it was, Ednetta knew. She just wasn't telling.

Martine hated it when people's mothers changed from who they were to somebody else, the look in their faces and in their eyes like they were strangers and didn't care for you like they'd always done. A man was different, it was never surprising a man might change, and a man might change back to who he'd been, or a man might just depart and you'd never see him again. But a woman like Ednetta who was Martine's aunt, her mother's older sister, who'd taken care of Martine a thousand times, and had always babied and kissed her like Martine was her own daughter, and (maybe) nicer than Sybilla in fact—if a mother like Ednetta could change, that made Martine want to cry.

■

"S'B'LLA?"—SOFTLY MARTINE CALLED CUPPING HER HANDS TO her mouth.

Standing on tiptoe in the alley outside her great-grandmother's ground-floor apartment on Eleventh Street. It was a wild chance Martine was taking but you had to figure if Sybilla had been *sent away*, likely it was here. Martine had been *sent away* to Grandma Tice's place herself more than once, when her mother didn't have time for her or was in the women's shelter and Martine didn't want to live there with her and the other pitiful beat-up women and kids.

"S'b'lla? Hey? It's me."

From where she stood in the alley, she couldn't see into the room behind the window. But this would be Sybilla's window if Sybilla was staying here.

Somewhere close by a dog was barking furiously, God damn thing she'd have liked to murder. If Grandma Tice came to the window instead of Sybilla and saw her, she'd send Martine away with a scolding.

Like a cooing pigeon Martine called gently, stubbornly—"S'b'lla! It's Martine."

Suddenly the window was tugged up. And there was Sybilla leaning out to Martine looking surprised and happy—like a little girl surprised and happy.

"M'tine! Jesus! Hi."

"S'b'lla! Jesus."

This was a shock: her girl-cousin *beat-up*.

Almost, Martine might not have recognized Sybilla.

Both Sybilla's eyes were puffy and discolored, her upper lip was puffy and scabby, one of her eyebrows was shaved and stitched like a weird horror doll, and her hair was cut jagged like a weird horror wig. It was like Sybilla had been dragged from the rear of a vehicle like they told of black people being dragged in the terrible old days in the South or some nasty place like Texas.

Sybilla tugged the window a few inches higher so that she could lean out, to pull Martine up and inside. Gave a little gasp of pain, blood rushing into her face must've been hot and heavy, and just leaning down the way she was seemed to be hurting her back. Martine grabbed hold of the window ledge and swung her legs up like a monkey, crawled through the window and fell into the room giggling into Sybilla's arms.

"Oh M'tine! It's *you*."

"Yah I been missin you, S'b'lla. Why're you here?"

"Mama made me come here."

The girl-cousins were the same age. Same height and same size except Martine registered shock, hugging Sybilla tight and feeling that Sybilla was *skinny*.

"Fuck baby, who hurt you so bad?"

"Jesus, M'tine! Shh."

Sybilla wriggled out of Martine's arms. Had to pull down the damn window quietly so Grandma wouldn't hear and bust in on them.

Pearline Tice was some ancient age but sharp-eared and sharp-eyed. People said admiringly of Pearline *you can't put anything over on that lady*. She'd had seven children, twenty-one grandchildren, more great-grandchildren than anyone could count scattered through the State of New Jersey and beyond.

"You OK, S'b'lla?"

"Yah. Aint gonna die, I guess."

Sybilla climbed up onto the big bed which took up most of the room. Only a few inches so the door could be opened, and a few feet for a battered old chest of drawers and an ugly old radiator. Martine climbed up beside her breathless and dazed.

"Worst thing is, I been lonely."

Sybilla wiped at her eyes. It looked as if she'd been in the sway-back bed sleeping or trying to sleep: she was wearing a flannel night-gown faded with many washings and over this a coarse-knit sweater of Ednetta's, and on her feet woolen socks. Hadn't gotten dressed for days she told Martine. (Smelling of her underarms without knowing it, Martine thought.) Taking "painkiller pills" her Mama had left with her grandmother to give to her, no more than three a day.

It made Martine feel sad, to think of her girl-cousin in *pain*.

Martine winced seeing the swollen bruised eyes, bruised cheeks and disfigured-looking mouth close up. Her cousin's familiar face made unfamiliar like her own face in a mirror, she couldn't recognize.

"Who hurt you, S'b'lla?"

"Ednetta said, I aint supposed to say."

"Why not?"

"They say they gon murder us all, that's why."

"S'b'lla you can tell *me*."

"Then they gon murder you, M'tine."

The girls shuddered together. Martine drew a forefinger gently over Sybilla's bruised face. She touched the swollen lip that felt burning-hot.

"There's stitchin in my lip, and my eyebrow, that comes out by itself the doctor said. You don't have to go back to the damn hospital." Sybilla spoke with a faint surge of pride.

"Jesus, S'b'lla! Why'd anybody hurt you so bad?"

Sybilla shuddered again, and laughed.

"Why'd anybody hurt *anybody*? Ask 'em."

"Some people sayin you're in the hospital, or worse. Sayin all kinds of things."

"Yah? What they sayin?"

So many terrible things Martine had heard, maybe she shouldn't tell Sybilla. It was the worst part of something happening to you, that everybody knew about it. And if it hadn't happened to you, or not in exactly that way, and people were saying it had, that was worse. You would just want to die if—certain things were said for instance at school.

Any kind of *sex-thing. Sex-hurt, humiliation.*

Girls felt pity for you but something else—a feeling you deserved whatever it was.

Guys would not want to touch you. Or, they'd want to touch you real bad.

"M'tine? What the fuck they sayin?"

Martine noticed that her cousin's breathing was thick and audible as if her head was stuffed with mucus. Her skin was fever-hot and she seemed short of breath as if she'd been running and not lying sprawled on this bed cooped up in an airless box of a room.

"Well—an ambulance took you to St. Anne's. Somebody found

you on Sunday morning where you were 'bleedin to death'—you been stabbed and left to die in the fish-food factory in the cellar. But I guess that didn't happen?"

"Nah I aint been stabbed. At least not *that.*"

Sybilla laughed, and winced. Her fingers sprang to her jaw, that seemed to hurt her when she laughed. Martine wondered if Sybilla's jaw was dislocated, her face was so swollen. Martine's jaw had been dislocated when she'd been a little girl, in some shoving accident on the stairs where they'd lived at the time.

"People sayin you were in the ER at St. Anne's."

Sybilla shrugged yes, she guessed that was so.

"They brought you there in one of them ambulances with a siren?"

Sybilla shrugged yes. Guess so.

"That must've been scary."

Sybilla giggled. Nah! It wasn't.

"Wasn't?"

Sybilla shrugged like she wasn't remembering too clearly. Like whatever it was had happened in a kind of cloud, a haze-cloud that made you cough and choke at the time but then just drifted away and you forgot about it.

"See, you tryin to stay *alive,* like. When you hurt bad you concentratin on getting the breath in, an the breath out, an back in again—just that, an that's enough. You thinkin *Jesus get me through this!* No time for 'scary' or shit like that."

Sybilla snuggled close to Martine, and Martine hugged her like a little baby might be hugged. Sybilla wasn't smelling too fresh—not just underarms but (maybe) stale-dried blood as well. Probably Martine wasn't smelling too fresh either.

Sybilla asked what people were saying about her at school and Martine hesitated before saying just that people were wondering where she was, and feeling bad for her.

"What the teachers sayin?"

"They askin *us*. We just sayin we ain't seen you and don't know nothing."

"Any cops come around?"

Martine thought so, yes. But Martine didn't want to tell Sybilla, for fear of worrying her worse.

"There's people over at your house, knocking on the door. Ednetta don't let them in."

"What kind of people?"

"I don't know. White people . . . Not all white people but like that, like from the county or the city, 'family services' shit. You know."

"'Social worker' shit?"

"Yah like that."

"Some female cop, 'detective'—she been there?"

Martine didn't know. She hadn't seen any uniform-cops at the house but then, she hadn't been at Sybilla's house every minute.

Sybilla was breathing in that harsh labored way. Every so often she made a snuffling-choking noise like trying to clear her sinuses.

"Jesus! Your nose ain't broke, S'b'lla, is it?"

"Nah. My nose OK."

"You sure?"

"Ain't fuckin sure of anything." Sybilla laughed, and winced. "Guess whose ol' nightie this is!"

"Grandma's."

"Yah! Her socks, too."

"Why'd Ednetta bring you here?"

"Ask her."

"Can't ask Ednetta anything, she in a rotten mood. Like she fuckin scared of somethin."

"Yah my mama scared. *She* got reason for it."

Abruptly Sybilla sat up, opened her sweater, tugged the nightgown off her shoulder to show her cousin the bruises and welts on her chest. It was a shock for Martine to see Sybilla part-naked like this— and to see how bruised and battered she was. Her small soft breasts looked like they would register hurt if you touched them.

"Ohh S'b'lla! What the hell . . ."

Sybilla squirmed to lift the nightgown, pulling it up over her hips. The way she was lying, her little taffy-brown belly button was so pinched it was nearly invisible. She was wearing white cotton panties she pried down with awkward fingers to show Martine more bruises and welts on her belly, abdomen, the soft flesh of her inner thighs.

"Oh hon. He hurt you—*there?*"

"Yah pretty bad. Not his nasty old thing, he didn't stick that in, but something else, like his fingers I guess—like grabbin up inside me, and his damn fingernails was sharp, I just screamed and screamed so loud, he punched me on the jaw and knocked me out. I guess."

"Who?"

A sullen pouty look came into Sybilla's battered face.

"Told you, M'tine—I can't tell."

"You can tell me."

"Nah that's stupid. I aint gon 'danger you. Anyway there was more'n one of them—there was five of them."

"Five!"

"Five I counted but maybe more. Comin and goin, there was three days an three nights they had me in the van. Fuck anybody could keep track how many fuckers there were."

Sybilla spoke in a strange mocking voice. Martine could not recognize that voice.

"Some guys in the neighborhood? Some gang?"

"Nah! Nobody in the neighborhood."

"Herc'les an them?"

(Hercules Johnston was a boy with whom they'd gone to school who was several years older than the girl-cousins but kept back often so he'd spent most of his time in the class just ahead of theirs. Hercules had dropped out of school at sixteen and now he and his friends were errand-boys for the drug-dealer bosses in Red Rock.)

"I said *no*. Not Herc'les or anybody you know."

"Who, then?"

"I told you, M'tine—I can't tell you. They threatened me they would murder me if I did. And my mother, and anybody in my house or my family and that includes you." Sybilla spoke with a kind of exasperation, as if there was something here, plain-faced and obvious, that Martine wasn't getting.

Martine tried to think. What Sybilla was saying wasn't irrational but made total sense to her. You *did not tell*—if *telling* meant naming an individual or individuals who could punish you worse than you'd been punished. Even if it was an open secret who'd done what to who—which usually in Red Rock it was—you *did not tell*.

" 'Nother thing they sayin, there was 'writin' on you. Like 'nigger'— 'slut'—'Ku Kux Klann.' Like, in dog shit."

Martine giggled, this was so weird and so awful! But Sybilla only just made the snuffling-snorting sound like this was some old boring news.

"They sayin you talked to cops. You told cops—somethin."

"I *did not talk to fuckin cops*. There was that female 'detective'—I told you—Puerto Rican tryin to jive my mama an me, she was a 'sister'—fuckin bullshit!— came to see me in the ER when I wasn't halfway conscious, an Mama was there, an she got me to say some things. Mama said we had to do that—but no more than that. Nobody 'filed charges'—that's what they want me to do, Mama says. You have to go to the police station and report that a crime was perp'trated on you and make that charge. And they write it down, and you can't erase it. They ask you a thousand stupid questions and take 'evidence' like from the hospital—take pictures of you and you look at pictures in the police station—they *never let up,* once it starts. So they aint gonna get me. And I aint goin back to any white doctor, either. They could give me some kind of 'truth serum' without Mama or me knowing, Mama says." Sybilla spoke hotly, squirming in distress.

Ednetta had taken her to a doctor on Trenton Avenue before bringing her to Eleventh Street, Sybilla said. Ednetta didn't trust "white" doctors. (To Ednetta, any Asian-looking professional person was "white"—or worse than "white." Looking at you with that pissy-polite face so you know they're thinking how pitiful you are.) This "Dr. Cleveland" had a diploma on the wall certifying him as a *chiropractor* but he had painkiller pills he could dispense in his office, chalky-white pills so large you had to cut them in two with a knife-edge.

"This 'Dr. Cleveland'—Mama said he could 'xamine me, like, my 'gina, where I been hurt so bad, an there was more bleedin so I had to wear a damn Kotex—but I wouldn't let him. God damn I told Mama, I had enough pokin up there, let them poke *her big fat 'gina* see how she like it."

"S'b'lla! You didn't say that to your mother!"

Sybilla giggled. Her heavy-lidded eyes were blinking sleepily.

"You didn't say *big fat 'gina* to Aunt Ednetta—I bet."

Sybilla giggled, yes she had.

"'Nother thing they been sayin, it was 'white cops' hurt you."

Martine spoke hesitantly. Sybilla stiffened and did not reply.

"'White cops' picked you up on the street and kept you handcuffed for three days an three nights in some police van, an raped you an beat you all that time then left you in the fish-factory cellar to die. *That* the worst thing people sayin."

Martine was hoping that Sybilla would deny this. So nasty!

But Sybilla only just shrugged. "Yah. Some shit like that. 'White cops.'" Again Sybilla spoke in that curious mocking voice, a mock-child-voice, as if she were reciting words prepared for her which she resented.

"You sayin—'Five white cops.'"

"Five—or six. Or seven. White-cop fuckers."

Sybilla laughed, and winced. Her jaw was hurting her.

Martine said, carefully, "The 'white cops' got you—like, last Thu'sday? That's what Ednetta says."

"Yah I guess—'Thu'sday.' Some day like that."

Yet more carefully Martine said, "How'd you get out, then, to visit Jaycee at M't'nview? His sister Shirley been sayin you were there on Friday? Visitin hours Friday mornin?"

Sybilla lay very still, snuffling deep inside her head.

"Shirley sayin you cut school and you an her went together on the bus and she got you in sayin you was Jaycee's little sister Colette?"

Sybilla lay still making no reply. Martine wondered if her cousin had fallen asleep.

Martine continued, cautiously.

"Anyway, that's what Shirley goin around sayin. Of course, if you visited Jaycee at M't'nview, an it wasn't your name on the books, nobody gon prove you were there an not Colette. Nobody gon prove you were *anywhere* at that time."

Martine had been hearing about Sybilla and Jaycee Handler—not from Sybilla but from others. Jaycee was nineteen, a big hulking boy with a scarred, shaved head, tight-muscled arms and legs, a way of making you laugh with him even if you were damned scared of him. Jaycee had met Sybilla Frye at somebody's place at the Justice Warren project when she'd been in just eighth grade and crazy for hip-hop music. Martine had never heard that Sybilla and Jaycee were a *couple* exactly—one of them built like a pro wrestler six foot three weighing beyond two hundred pounds and the other just five foot one inch tall weighing less than one hundred pounds. (That'd be scary for Sybilla especially if Ednetta or the stepfather Anis Schutt found out.) Back last spring Jaycee had been incarcerated at Mountainview Youth Facility, an hour bus-ride from Pascayne, on charges of drug possession and aggravated assault. Martine hadn't heard that Sybilla had visited Jaycee in the past but maybe Martine just hadn't heard.

Martine wasn't jealous of her cousin! Not over Jaycee Handler who used up silly little girls like toilet paper. (And they sayin something wrong with Jaycee, he prefer these young girls still in school.)

Lots of guys Martine knew including relatives were at Mountainview but Martine had never gone to visit. Wouldn't have gone except her mother took her. There was nobody there wanted to see *her*. At Mountainview you were released at age twenty-one no matter your crime which seemed strange to Martine, but a damn good deal. If you went in at fourteen, on a serious charge, like aggravated assault, or even manslaughter, you'd stay in until twenty-one; but if you went in at eighteen, as Jaycee had done, you'd only stay in until twenty-one. It was the same for girls of course, at the girls' correctional facility at Barrow. What sense that made, you'd have to ask the assholes who make up the laws.

Martine nudged Sybilla to answer her but Sybilla only said, snuffling, it was like she'd been telling people—"Thu'sday comin home from school in the alley behind the car wash, where I was walkin alone, somebody come up behind me with a—one of them—like a 'tarpaulin'—an drop it over my head, an drop me down like—some kind of animal bein hunted. And taken me in a van. And there was a white cop—I saw his badge. And—five white cops. Or six. Like that."

Sybilla's voice trailed off into silence. Martine didn't feel that she could challenge her cousin, who spoke flatly and defiantly.

"Ohh hey. Just remembered."

In her school bag Martine had brought things for Sybilla: chocolate chip cookies, tortilla chips, a twelve-ounce plastic bottle of Coke the girls could share, purple-sparkle nail polish, hairbrush and combs. Ravenously Sybilla began to devour the cookies though her jaw made her wince. She complained to Martine that their grandma was feeding her food to make her gag like collard greens, hominy, fatty ribs and that nasty slimy white stuff—"okra." The girls made gagging sounds together.

Soon then Sybilla began to cry. Martine began to cry, too.

This windy afternoon of October 14, 1987, in their great-grandmother Pearline Tice's apartment on Eleventh Street, the girl-cousins fell asleep exhausted in each other's arms.

The Investigator

Overheard as she'd passed them in the precinct corridor. *That the one? Hot spic chick is she?*

She'd made her initial report. She'd reported to the Lieutenant. She'd told him all that she'd learned. Not a taped interview with Sybilla Frye and her mother but "notes." She'd smoothed out the yellow Post-its on the Lieutenant's desk so that he could see them, each singly.

WHITE COP

YELOW HAIR

AGE 30

THEY WHITE

THEY ALL WHITE

The Lieutenant stared at the Post-its with their painstakingly printed words. The Lieutenant laughed harshly.

"This is what she's saying? That black girl? Bull*shit*."

With the back of his hand the Lieutenant pushed the Post-its off his desk. A beat, and Detective Iglesias decided to interpret this as a joke, just playful, fucking with her but not seriously, or anyway not seriously enough to register as shock and not rather amusement, so she laughed to show she's a good sport, one of the guys, stooped and picked up the precious Post-its with care and returned them to her file marked SYBILLA FRYE.

How alone this was going to be.

How she'd been shunted into it as a farm-creature—cow, calf, hog—is shunted along a chute into the slaughter-house.

Because the mother Ednetta Frye had requested a black police officer. A black woman police officer.

Black had always seemed harsh to her. *African-American* was a preferable term. And there was *Negro,* no longer fashionable.

If she was anything, she was *Hispanic.* In crude mouths, *spic.*

Yet among Hispanic Americans she was "too white"—not just her appearance but also her way of speaking, her manner.

Her life had been, since adolescence, an effort to overcome the crude perimeters of identity. Her skin-color, ethnic background, gender. *I am so much more than the person you see. Give me a chance!*

Must've been, in her early twenties Ines Iglesias had some confused idea—idealism—about *serving the community, serving the country.*

Several of her (male) cousins had enlisted in the U.S. Army. Scattered among the Iglesias relatives were women who'd made decisions similar to Ines's—inner-city teacher, social worker, psychiatric nurse, Red Cross nurse, youth facility psychologist.

An older relative, an uncle of her (adoptive) father's father, had been a New Jersey State trooper. Another relative, also in her father's family, was a Pascayne police captain in the Forest Park precinct—the first Hispanic officer to rise to that rank.

When she'd graduated from the police academy and began to wear the patrol officer's uniform she'd felt suffused with pride. She'd thought *Now I am one of—something. Now there are many like me.*

Apart from the Forest Park captain Ramon Iglesias there were few Puerto Rican–American police officers in the Pascayne PD. Very few African-Americans. And very few women.

Not quite out of earshot her fellow officers had begun saying of her *If Iglesias believes that rape bullshit she's crazy. She's finished.*

Driving the streets of Red Rock.

Not wanting to think she was becoming obsessed with Sybilla Frye.

The girl, and the mother.

White cop. White cops.

Talkin with you ain't worked out like I hoped, you one of them.

She'd never lived in Red Rock. She'd grown up across the river scarcely a mile away. A thousand miles away.

She'd been sixteen in August 1967, when the inner city of Pascayne had erupted into several days and nights of sporadic gunfire, burning and looting, martial law, the deployment of the New Jersey National Guard to control violence. Twenty-seven people had died in what was called a "race riot" and of these twenty-four were black.

Of the twenty-seven deaths, at least twenty were individuals un-involved in the violence, unarmed, incidental bystanders who'd been in the wrong place at the wrong time or who'd come unwisely to stand at a window in an area in which "sniper gunfire" was suspected by police officers. Three were children younger than twelve and two were elderly women shot inside their homes by National Guardsmen firing into windows.

Two had been police officers, determined to have been shot by "friendly fire"—"in the line of duty."

Pascayne PD officers had been outfitted in riot gear, carried tear gas canisters, automatic weapons, shotguns. They'd shot freely at individuals with dark faces who'd been perceived as behaving "suspiciously"—"threateningly." They'd shot at passing vehicles and into the windows of houses and apartment buildings. Many had re-moved their badges and covered the license plates of their vehicles with tape. Of investigations into wrongful deaths in the months fol-lowing the riot not one condemned the use of extreme force by any officer.

In the wake of August 1967, much of Red Rock was burnt-out and would not be rebuilt. But in the wake of August 1967, a new city administration and a new police chief initiated an era of reform in the Pascayne PD. There were campaigns to integrate the police force, programs to train minorities and women. A new era, an era of social justice, and Ines Iglesias had wanted to be part of it.

Now it was twenty years later. The inner city had lost population, like most of Pascayne. Red Rock still resembled a battle zone.

In her (unmarked) police vehicle driving the devastated streets of Red Rock. Neighborhoods of single-story woodframe houses and two-story brownstone row houses. Churches, soup kitchens. Pub-lic housing projects by the river. Human habitations in clusters surrounded by empty lots, acres of abandoned and derelict buildings. Along the riverfront, miles of desolate old factories, mills. And one of these Jersey Foods where the girl had been found.

Iglesias had studied photographs of the scene: the cellar, the stairs leading down to the cellar, the exterior of the building covered in graffiti to a height of about ten feet. As in much of Red Rock there was an exhilaration of violence enacted against what you could see: walls of buildings, broken windows, fences.

It seemed fitting, the badly beaten, sexually abused black girl had been found in the cellar of one of these condemned buildings. *Left to die* was the refrain heard on the street.

White cops, kept her tied up, raped, left to die. This was the refrain of the street.

It hadn't been clear, from Sybilla Frye's fragmented statement, how long she'd been "hog-tied" in the cellar. There was evidence that the girl had wet herself but minimally on the tarpaulin which suggested that she hadn't been in the cellar more than a few hours. Countless footprints in the cellar's soft sinking floor both human and animal, and much evidence of human activity over a period of time, but nothing that suggested recent activity except in the specific area where the girl had been found lying on the tarpaulin. Here there were seemingly fresh footprints belonging to just two individuals and these were not likely prints made by adult men. Scattered throughout the cellar were the desiccated remains of small animals. Bones to which mummified tufts of fur accrued. Despite rumors on the street there'd been no human bones discovered in any area of the factory.

The filthy tarpaulin upon which the girl had lain, clothesline allegedly used to bind the girl's wrists and ankles, dish towels allegedly wrapped around the girl's head and shoved into her mouth to gag her—these had been examined by Pascayne PD forensics team, and had yielded "inconclusive" evidence. On the tarpaulin were badly smudged fingerprints and encrustations of mud and dog excrement. Iglesias had requested that the department forensics team examine virtually everything in the cellar, but this wasn't possible—there was just too much, and resources were limited.

Of the debris accumulated in the cellar over a period of years it was possible that there was an item—for instance a soft-drink bottle or can tossed into a corner— bearing the prints of Sybilla Frye, that would suggest the girl having come or having been brought to the cellar voluntarily, to stage the scene.

Her story is a lie. Yet, no story is entirely a lie.

She is telling us—she was badly hurt, and her life was threatened. That's real—isn't it?

Yes. That is real.

"Off'cer, I'm telling you Sybilla *not here*. She stayin in some safe place to convalesce. The doctor say she had a 'severe trauma'—she 'anemic' from all that blood she lose."

Iglesias had come with a warrant to search the premises for Sybilla Frye. With two patrol officers she gained access to the household at 939 Third Street in which Sybilla Frye lived with her mother, a younger sister and brother, and the mother's common-law husband Anis Schutt. But as Mrs. Frye had angrily insisted, the girl wasn't there.

"Go ahead, Off'cer, look! Nothin to see!"

Iglesias stood in the doorway of the girl's closet-sized room. A narrow bed over which a soiled comforter had been drawn. Bare floorboards, chenille throw-rugs. A chest of drawers. A single window with a cracked blind. Stuffed animals, a limp Raggedy Ann doll with a sallow face. Photos of smiling black faces, predominantly young, Scotch-taped to a dingy wall—Sybilla's relatives and friends.

The rest of the wall space was covered with glossy posters of rock musicians. Iglesias recognized most of the figures—Tina Turner, Whitney Houston were her own favorites.

"Mrs. Frye, please tell me where Sybilla is. She may need further medical care. You should want to cooperate in this investigation."

Ednetta had come up behind Iglesias incensed and panting. Just barely audible Ednetta murmured what sounded like *God damn bitch.*

Iglesias felt her face flush with heat. But she spoke calmly and without rancor.

Telling Ednetta Frye that her daughter had made "serious charges" and that it would be determined eventually what had happened to her—"It will be better for you, and for Sybilla, if you cooperate now. We only have your daughter's welfare in mind."

Ednetta snorted in derision. She was badly out of breath from the stairs. "Off'cer, you best go away now. You see Sybilla ain't here like I told you."

"Where is she? With relatives?"

Ednetta frowned. The way in which she stared at Iglesias suggested that yes of course, Sybilla was staying with relatives. And probably not far away.

"She stayin where she safe. Ain't gon do any good if you hound her, ma'am."

Iglesias was pained that Ednetta Frye so disliked and distrusted her. There seemed nothing she could say to persuade the woman otherwise.

The animosity of men, she could comprehend. Sex-hatred of the female was common in the culture. But the animosity of a woman so like herself—so essentially *herself*—was something very different.

"We both want what is best for Sybilla, Mrs. Frye. I wish you would cooperate with the investigation and with me. I wish you would help *me*."

"No cop is gonna help us. No 'white cop' is gonna arrest any 'white cop.'"

Thinking *But I am not a "white cop."*

Iglesias was satisfied that Sybilla Frye wasn't at her mother's house but still the brownstone had to be thoroughly searched, upstairs and down. And the dank smelly cellar into which, as she descended the wobbly stairs, flashlight in hand, Iglesias felt a thrill of sheer visceral revulsion for people who lived in such quarters—who could not help themselves to live in any other way.

Within a day Iglesias had traced the girl to Mrs. Frye's grandmother's home in an apartment building on Eleventh Avenue.

Here, the elderly white-haired Pearline Tice told Iglesias that her great-granddaughter was "resting" and couldn't "speak with a stranger." But Iglesias managed to talk the elderly woman into opening the door to the room in which Sybilla lay in bed with a cover pulled to her chin, staring stonily in Iglesias's direction. When Iglesias greeted the girl, Sybilla gave no sign of hearing her.

The girl's eyes were still bruised but not so badly swollen as they'd been when Iglesias had last seen her. Her face was near-normal except for stitches in her lip and above her eyebrow.

Her hair had been washed and brushed. Wild frizzed and nappy dark hair tied up in a scarf.

"See, Off'cer, S'b'lla all right—she ain't *sick*—just needin to conval'sce. Her mother don't want her to start back at school till she is feelin strong again."

Politely Iglesias requested if she might ask Sybilla just a question or two?—and Pearline Tice said sharply that Iglesias should ask *her,* and she would ask the girl.

In this way Iglesias conducted a kind of interview with the girl— hardly an "interview" of any substance.

Asking if Sybilla could provide any further descriptions of the *white cops,* or of the van in which she'd been kept; and if she would allow a doctor to come to her, to examine her, since the examination at St. Anne's ER had not been completed.

Pearline Tice shut the bedroom door while she conferred with Sybilla. Whatever the elderly woman and her great-granddaughter said together, in lowered voices, Iglesias couldn't hear. She thought *But I have found her, at least. She is still alive.*

Iglesias had learned about Pearline Tice by questioning some of Ednetta Frye's neighbors. When she'd arrived at the weatherworn old sandstone apartment building on Eleventh Street, that looked at a little distance as if it were uninhabited, she'd had the impression that Sybilla Frye had been out of bed, and watching TV in the front room; when Pearline Tice admitted Iglesias into the apartment, the TV had been switched off and Sybilla had hurriedly retreated to a back bedroom.

"Off'cer, S'b'lla not feelin strong enough to talk right now. Ednetta has got to be here, if S'b'lla be 'questioned.' So, I'm askin you to leave."

Already! Asked to leave.

Iglesias was accustomed to interviewing individuals who lied to her, who claimed forgetfulness, and sometimes ill health. A police officer expects dishonesty. A police officer is not naïve. Yet, in the matter of Sybilla Frye, Iglesias was baffled. She didn't believe the girl's story—yet, there was a story, which she was determined to expose. She protested to Pearline Tice that at least Sybilla Frye should be examined by a doctor, more thoroughly than she'd been examined in the ER. There'd been no rape kit, and now it was too late. There was the risk of infection, sexually transmitted diseases, complications following the girl's injuries . . .

"S'b'lla been examined by a doctor, her mother take her to. *She* all right and just restin now, I'm tryin to explain."

"A doctor? A private doctor? Who? I need his name, please . . ."

"You need to ask Ednetta about that."

Mrs. Tice spoke stubbornly. Iglesias made a note—*Doctor?*

The mother had taken Sybilla to a black doctor in the neighborhood, very likely. Iglesias hoped this doctor was competent. She had a dread of Sybilla Frye infected with HIV and not knowing until it was too late.

Over Pearline Tice's shoulder, not more than five feet away, the girl in the bed gazed at Iglesias with heavy-lidded slow-blinking eyes; not overtly defiant or impudent, yet with a subtle twist of her puffy upper lip, that suggested a sneering little smile. *Can't make me talk to you! Can't make me do any fucking thing I don't want to do.*

A single window in the room and no furnishings except a bureau. The air was overheated, and smelled of the girl's hot body and bedclothes that needed changing.

Iglesias tried to address the girl over the great-grandmother's shoulder, but Pearline Tice blocked her and shut the door, firmly.

"Off'cer, this girl not a 'criminal'—this girl was *hurt*. You and anybody else got no right to harass her. Please leave my home, now."

"Mrs. Tice, may I speak with *you*? Your great-granddaughter was found badly beaten, she has accused 'white cops' of having repeatedly raped her, beaten her, left her to die . . . You must understand that she needs further medical treatment, and she should have psychological counseling; whoever hurt her has committed a serious felony, and must be apprehended. We can't just—pretend that nothing has happened . . ."

Pearline Tice escorted Iglesias to the door. The elderly woman was scarcely five feet tall, frail-bodied, yet suffused with the strength of indignation.

"Mrs. Tice, how much do you know of what happened to Sybilla? What did they tell *you*?"

Pearline Tice had opened the door to the hall and was waiting for Iglesias to depart. Her face was a mass of fine wrinkles, like a soft glove that has been crumpled. Her hair was silvery white, thin, plaited shoulder-length. Her eyes were intelligent, alert, wary. Iglesias understood that the elderly Mrs. Tice was by nature a polite, gracious woman—it was painful to her to be rude to a visitor.

White cop. White cops. The enemy.

In a lowered voice, as if reading Iglesias's thoughts, and touching Iglesias's elbow in a grandmotherly gesture, Pearline Tice said, "How you come to be one of *them,* Off'cer? You have got to know the Pascayne PD, they racist and vicious to black folks however they can get away with it. They still killin us, treat us like animals like in the 'riot' in '67—not so many of us being killed like in the past, so they call that 'progress.' If S'b'lla tells what they did to her, she would not ever be safe in Red Rock. And her mother, and anybody in her family. Our minister say, if she 'bear witness' it will be on TV and in the papers. But if she 'bear witness' she will be in danger. It will be hard for her to return to school where everybody talking about her. Say there are police officers—like you—wantin to help her. But they would never find the ones who hurt her, we know that. No white cops is ever gon be 'arrested' for hurtin a black girl. By this time they probly been transferred to some other police department downstate in some southern county of New Jersey where the Klan still rides."

Mrs. Tice laughed. Still she was gripping Iglesias's elbow in an oddly intimate gesture.

"Mrs. Tice, if nothing is done, whoever hurt Sybilla will get away with it. If she's been sexually assaulted—he will do it again. Or—they will do it again."

Now gravely Mrs. Tice said, "Yes ma'am. They will do it again. Nobody gonna stop that."

Angel of Wrath

Ednetta sayin to me, Anis my daughter is hurt bad.

It was white men hurt Sybilla, she sayin white cops—five, six of them that kidnapped her and hid her away, raped and beat her, and hog-tied her in the cellar of the fish-food factory leavin her to die.

And she looking at me. Scared, and her eyes wet with tears, and her face kind of melted-looking, and her mouth like something bruised.

Anis? You hear me?—it was white men done it.

And I'm—I am—in the kitchen of the house. Dragged a chair around, and leaning on the back of the chair heavy enough to break it. Damn leg hurting so, the pain come so fast.

Anis? That's where she was. S'b'lla missin, the white cops arrested her on the street she say. S'b'lla comin home from school Thursday, an they arrested her. And all that while when she was gone, the white cops had her.

Anis, it was when I was lookin for her. All that time, lookin for S'b'lla on the street and beggin people help me find her an she be captive to these men.

And Ednetta looking at me, that way of hers. Her face smudged like somebody rubbed his thumb over it.

Ednetta breathing quick, and her hand against her heart like it be jumping in her chest.

Sayin, Anis the terrible things they wrote on her—in dog shit on her body! Such hate for us, we are animals to them. NIGRA BITCH. KU KUX KLANN. Like they done to black people in the South— hangin from trees, cut with knives and burnt alive.

S'b'lla life be saved, she be found in the fish-factory by some neighbor. She be taken by ambulance to the hospital—St. Anne's. She gon have face-scars all her life. They will never arrest the white cops. Some kind of nasty joke, they pretendin to "investigate." Anis I am *so afraid*.

Coming against me the woman cryin with her eyes shut and pushin into my arms that feel like lead, so heavy. And I'm tryin to think what is the meaning of the woman's words. What does the woman know, why the woman sayin these words? *White men done it. White cops.*

Ednetta hidin her face against me. Hidin her eyes. Falling against me like she be drunk, or takin those damn pills of hers. A woman's tears wettin my shirt, and my arms not wantin to touch her to push the woman away. That smell of her, and her stiff-greasy hair in my face. Wantin to take hold of her, the woman, sink my fingers into her fat arms, shake and shake shake *shake* like you'd shake a wailing baby to shut it up forever.

Forty years tormented by the fuckin black-feather thing like a vulture—Angel of Wrath.

Sayin *Kill you one of them white cops. You know you ain't goin to re-spect yourself nor anybody else respect Anis Schutt if you ain't accomplished this at least. Should have done when you was a boy, and they shot Lyander down in the street. And things they done to you, and you as a witness. And you ain't no boy now, nigger.*

Fifty-two years old, Christ that *old.*

Never thought Anis Schutt would live so *old.*

Where the cops beat me, my throat, there's something broke so people can't hear me when I try to talk it's like wind rustling in tall grasses. The doctor said *trach-y-a.*

First thing I knew this foot, this foot in a heavy boot kicking me. Can't remember how I got there—down on the pavement. Cops must've grabbed me from behind and the other boys ran. Threw me down and one of them was kicking me and pressed his boot against my neck pressing pressing like he wanted to break every bone of my neck and the other cops was yellin so maybe he stop. Left me there, and somebody came along to help me up saying the cops was lookin for some other black boy you damn lucky Anis Schutt it wasn't you.

Of my brothers an cousins Anis about the only one still alive. One son dead and the other in Rahway ain't gon think of *that.* My girls all grown and moved away and they livin they lives without they daddy fuck them that's all right, Anis ain't beggin after anybody. Sisters and female cousins OK—a woman will find a way to live even if she crawl like a dog. But a man different.

How many of people I knew they'd killed or beat or incarcerated including my boys, the white cops.

Any color skin of a cop, he's a *white cop.*

Has to be. If he isn't, he ain't a cop.

This black-feather thing sayin *Your time runnin out Anis. You gettin old an your sorry ass slow.*

Takin them painkiller pills Ednetta gets for arthritis, fuckin bad arthritis in my hands, legs, hips. Wet weather ridin the garbage truck, Pascayne city sanitation, last time I quit walkin off the job they say *Anis you quit again you ain't ever comin back* and I'm telling them *That's right motherfuckers. Ain't never comin back.*

Ednetta say, This female cop come to the house lookin for S'b'lla an wantin to talk to you Anis.

All I been telling her Anis, you ain't here a lot of the time. And that is true.

An I been telling her, you a good father to my children. And that is true.

What Ednetta wants me to say to her, I ain't goin to say it. Fuck the woman tryin to manipulate *me*.

Like she is *savin me*. Like she is *put herself between the cops and Anis Schutt*.

Ednetta a good woman if you could mash a pillow over her face when she talk too much an get excited an her eyes jumpin in her face and sweat on her face. I know, Ednetta a good woman an a Christian woman an Ednetta *love me*.

All these years I been with Ednetta she never once ask about my wife Tana or any other women.

Tana my wife I was crazy for, beat with my fists till she wasn't screamin or movin any longer an her face broke, that had been a beautiful face. And Tana's eyes that were beautiful eyes, that turned against me.

A flame came over my brain like the flame of the gas stove flarin up higher than you expect. Never knew what I had done except to see the results of it, and had to know it was me and nobody else.

Anis what did you do? Anis—what did you do to your wife?

Tana my only true wife. That was long-ago. Of the women since Tana too many to count or recall. She the only one meant anything to me, my first woman I feel that way about. Crazy for that woman and when I killed her, I killed that feelin too.

Ednetta say, A woman loves a man more than her own babies if she is a real woman. Anis, that how I love *you.*

On her knees on the kitchen floor, an sobbin. Grabbin me around the legs like it's all I can do to keep from kickin the woman away.

That girl too young to be whorin like she is, and the mother not fit to discipline her. None of this I'm gon say to the woman, she know already who to blame and that is *herself.*

This was late that Friday night. Middle-of-the-night. I'd been out, and come back now. Been drinkin and that heaviness in my head, arms and legs. And the woman cryin, and wettin my shirt and my knees and beggin, Anis do you love me, please Anis you love me, an I'm not answering anything and she says again begging, Anis you love me don't you, so I say *Shit. Yes.*

After a heavy rain, and the damn river floodin. And the streets like little rivers. And our school was shut, there was oily water in the first-floor classrooms, and the lights gone out. A gang of us runnin wild on Trenton Avenue where the stores were closed early and some of the iron gratings not all the way down so you could break the glass an reach up inside like at the liquor store where people be helpin themselves but by the time we get there, everythin gone. And there's a squad car pulls up and the cops get out yelling at us and their guns is in their hands. There's water in the street, rising onto the sidewalk, and river water mixed with rain rushing so your feet are almost pulled out from under you. And it's *dark*—no light except the squad car and cops' flashlights. And there's a telephone pole tilted like it's about to fall and a cable is hanging from it in the water. And the cops say to Oscar, he's the oldest of us, and the biggest, though he ain't more than fourteen, get over there, boy, and pick up that cable. And Oscar is tryin to laugh like he believe the cops is joking— (we don't believe they is joking nor does Oscar)—and the cops say it again, You boy, you stupid nigger, get your ass over there an pick up that cable. And Oscar is scared, we all scared but afraid to turn our back on the white cops pointin they guns at us, to provoke them to shoot us in the back—(this had happened to people we knew, sometimes the cops tell you to run before they shoot)—but finly Oscar wades into the water, he don't even touch the cable with his hand but only step on it beneath the water and in that instant Oscar go up in flames, it is a "live wire" he has stepped on and in an instant electrocuted and hardly time for Oscar to scream, he has fallen down burning alive into the nasty water.

And the cops yellin at us, climb back inside the squad car and drive along Trenton and are gone.

That was 1947. I was twelve years old.

You'd find the bodies in the street or in an alley where they ran and fell. The white cops had told them to run, and shot them in the back. In August 1967 they said it was the "spill-over" from Newark—"race riot." They was waitin for Pascayne to go up in flames, the cops was practicing tear gas in a place in Red Rock behind the precinct where the tear-gas smell would make you sick, coming out of the building and everybody in the neighborhood could smell it, the cops was hoping for a "race riot" and the mayor say on TV the police force was given instructions "shoot to kill" if there was burnin and lootin like in Newark and Detroit. And the state troopers, and the National Guard where some of the white farm-boys who'd never seen Negro faces close up were shooting their rifles into windows at those faces. After the first few hours of burning and shooting there was "martial law" in Pascayne meaning the cops could shoot anybody they wanted—any age from babies to elderly if their faces were black. There was shots fired back at them—plenty of shots. There was fires set, Molotov cocktails tossed at cop cars. There was firemen carryin guns on the firetrucks, then the trucks stopped coming into Red Rock. And fires burnin out of control. And our mothers screaming *No no no!—you are burning where we live.* And if you stepped outside into the street, if you were a black boy, no matter your age, they had the right to shoot you down dead like my brother Lyander. And if you stood by a window, and there was snipers on the roof of your house, you would be shot dead. Forty, fifty shots fired into a bedroom, and a baby and his grandmother killed. Any shots fired by the cops and soldiers including machine-gun fire, into people's darkened windows, or lighted windows, or vehicles in the street, or at somebody in a doorway trapped there when the shooting started, or two people walking fast together to get home by curfew—"snipers" was the reason.

Came the Angel of Wrath with black-feather wings sayin in a loud voice every hour of every day since that time *You got to kill you one of them white cops Anis. You ain't gon die a righteous death if you fail in this.*

The Good Neighbor

All these days, then a week, two weeks—she'd waited.

Waited for a proper time. Not wanting to be intrusive or pushy. She *was not* intrusive or pushy. That was not Ada Furst's personality.

Waited for the mother Ednetta Frye to call her, or send some word to her—at least. Some word thanking Ada Furst for saving Sybilla Frye's life, and inviting Ada to visit the girl and her.

That poor girl Sybilla Frye?—I was the one who found her.

Hog-tied in that factory cellar. Left to die by white cops who'd beat her and raped her.

Heard her calling for help—nobody else heard.

Never shut her eyes to sleep now without hearing the girl's plaintive cry like a trapped creature. Never shut her eyes without seeing the girl hog-tied in the cellar lying on her side, on that filthy tarpaulin.

And the girl's (blackened, swollen) eyes shifting to her, in such hope, eagerness.

Hadn't been for me, Sybilla Frye would be dead now.

She'd run for help. Run screaming, so a woman in the next-door apartment building called 911.

Then, she'd returned to the girl. She'd waited for the medics. She'd called to them, to direct them to the girl.

Heard her crying in the night. I knew—knew it was something terrible . . .

Red Rock was talking of nothing else except *that girl, white cops, rape, beatin and left to die* but then, after a while, people weren't talking about Sybilla Frye so much.

Each day Ada looked eagerly through the Pascayne newspaper searching for a headline about Sybilla Frye, a photograph—her own name in print, possibly, as the person who'd rescued Sybilla—(Ada had been interviewed by police officers at the scene)—but there was nothing. Several times a day she listened to radio news, turned on TV news, but—nothing.

No arrests! They pretending nothing happened!

In virtually every issue of the *Pascayne Journal* there were news articles about assaults, rapes, murders. When a seventeen-year-old (white) girl "disappeared" from her suburban home in Summit, there had been front-page articles for days in succession. An accident on the Turnpike in which the driver of a trailer truck lost control and veered into a car containing a (white) family killing or badly injuring several children . . . Yet, so far as Ada knew, there had yet to be a single article about Sybilla Frye.

She wondered: should she contact the newspaper herself? Should she write a letter—signing her name, or anonymously?

There was the local TV station WNJN. On the six o'clock news, a glamorous African-American "anchor" rumored to have lived in Red Rock at one time. Ada wondered if she could interest this young woman in the Sybilla Frye story . . .

An outrageous assault upon a young black girl by "white cops" and not a single article in the newspaper and no arrests—of course.

Who am I?—a neighbor. Hadn't been for me the girl would not be alive now.

Ada stood at her bedroom window. At a little distance the Passaic River moved slow as molten lead and of that hue and when she shut her eyes just slightly and stood very still she could hear beyond the beat of her heart the faint plaintive yearning cry *Help me . . . Help me.*

"Ada? C'n you come help me please? Where you *at?*"

Ma calling to her, panting and breathless. She'd have to help Ma to her feet, so that Ma could use her walker to get to the bathroom. A dozen times a day, or more. She'd tried not to count.

As, subbing in a school where "Miz Furst" was known but not well-known, and some of the students recognized her, she tried not to count, during a class, those students who were paying attention to her, some of them avidly, in that shy-black-girl way that reminded her of herself, and those students who were obviously, rudely not paying attention.

Ma leaning on Ada's arm, heavier each day.

"That Ednetta Frye—she ain't exactly friendly to you, is she? Should've called you, by now."

Words like nettles stinging Ada's sensitive skin. Ma wheezing and mean-smiling knowing how Ada must feel about the Fryes ignoring her.

"Like you hadn't anything to do with them—like they's forgotten you. I'd be feelin real funny about that, Ad', if I was you."

Stiff-smiling Ada said, "Well, Ma. I'm not *you.*"

Two or three times a week Ada Furst was called by the Pascayne public school district to substitute-teach. In most cases the calls were last-minute for the teachers she was replacing "called in sick" just an hour or two before they were due to arrive at their schools.

Hello? Ada? Can you come to Edson Elementary by 8:30 A.M., sixth-grade class? The teacher is . . .

Yes of course! Yes thank you. I'll be there.

Occasionally Ada was summoned to teach elsewhere in the city, from time to time even in one of the predominantly white suburbs, but never so frequently as in Red Rock. Only logical, Ada thought. Red Rock was where she lived.

The Red Rock schools were the poorest in the city. No surprise there, either.

Most teachers in Red Rock public schools were black. A few Hispanics, a scattering of whites. It did not go unremarked that most of the principals were white.

Ada didn't want to speculate whether the checks she received for her substitute-teaching were lower than the checks other substitute-teachers received for the same essential work, for instance white teachers. Ada didn't want to speculate how much lower her checks were than the checks full-time teachers received.

She had a reputation as a good, reliable teacher. Even if "Miz Furst" couldn't always maintain control in her classrooms, if older students sometimes disobeyed and disrespected her, she could be relied upon to teach those students who wanted to be taught, and to protect them against their aggressive classmates; she could be relied upon to show up on time, to keep careful attendance records, to fill out required forms.

She was well-groomed. She dressed attractively. She was courteous, she was intelligent and she was *nice*.

Since Sybilla Frye, however, Ada Furst was drawn to speak of the abused girl to whoever would listen to her—teachers, administrators—in the schools in which she was subbing. Where previously Ada had been a quiet person, friendly but unassuming, now she was vehement. *That poor girl! Kidnapped, beaten and raped and left to die. And there has been nothing in the newspaper—at all. And no arrests.* Ada spoke with the aggrieved air of one who believes herself among sympathetic listeners and was stunned and baffled when she was met with a very different sort of response.

She was cautioned not to speak of "Sybilla Frye" within earshot of any students. Above all, not to alarm and upset any of her young girl students.

At Edson Elementary a friend who taught eighth grade science took Ada aside to warn her that the Sybilla Frye "situation" was maybe not a good subject for Ada to be discussing, so much; and when Ada asked why, her friend's reply was evasive.

"There might be something wrong about it, Ada. No one is sure."

" 'Wrong about it'?—what do you mean?"

"Something about the girl's story. And the mother's story. What we've been hearing . . . Things that can't be corroborated."

"Of course they can't be 'corroborated'—the girl is too terrified to give police a statement, when her rapists are *white cops*."

It was unlike Ada Furst to speak so passionately on any subject. It was unlike Ada Furst to feel that, so frustrated, so confused, she might burst into tears at any moment.

"Well. You don't want people here to think you might be talking to your students about Sybilla Frye, Ada. You need to maintain an air of professionalism . . ."

"I am! I do! 'Professionalism'—I *do*."

Ada went away hurt, resentful. She hated it that her black teacher-colleagues were so *timid*.

Ada had always thought that *integration* was the highest social goal for black Americans. Her heroes had been Reverend Martin Luther King

Jr., Rosa Parks, Booker T. Washington, Medgar Evers, the three civil rights activists who'd been murdered in Mississippi in 1964, President John F. Kennedy and Attorney General Robert Kennedy, President Lyndon Johnson . . .

The most eventful incident of Ada's life had been the passage of the Civil Rights Act when she'd been eighteen, in the summer of 1964— the struggle of President Johnson to get the legislation passed over the opposition of Southern racist senators. At Pascayne High South in those years there had been a black social studies teacher who'd made the civil rights campaign her subject and had been enormously influential, at least with serious students like Ada Furst.

Ada recalled the great excitement in Red Rock when the bill had finally been passed. Lyndon Johnson had been everyone's hero at the time. Memories were strong of John F. Kennedy who'd been assassinated for championing black people. Then, Reverend King Jr.—of course. Robert Kennedy, Malcolm X—assassinated for their beliefs in social justice. Medgar Evers who'd been among the earliest to die.

Her social studies teacher had said that if you knew your history, you would be empowered by this knowledge. And if you failed to know your history, you would be deprived of power.

As a girl Ada had been told by her grandmother of how the factories on the Passaic River had been mostly textile mills at one time. How in the 1930s hundreds of strikers at the Pascayne mills had marched over the Pitcairn bridge and helmeted police were waiting for them with clubs, firing at the unarmed workers. It had been like war—the workers were led by Communist union-organizers who wanted to unionize the mills—the police were on the side of the factory owners. A strike meant martial law, police shot to kill.

Like the 1967 "race riot" in Pascayne except those were white cops beating, shooting, and killing white men—immigrant Poles, Hungarians, Ukrainians. Negroes hardly figured in the strike except as strike-breakers hired by the cynical factory management which was not only a dangerous sort of employment but temporary—when the strike was settled, no strike-breaker would be allowed to join a union, and no non-union worker could get a job.

Ada's grandmother had known black men who'd been killed, maimed or paralyzed in the striking wars of the 1930s. Ada had thought it was lucky her grandfather hadn't been one of them.

Ada's grandparents had come north to New Jersey from rural Georgia, where they'd been dirt-poor and in fear of their lives. (They'd come from Dundee County which had the highest frequency of lynchings in Georgia.) They'd lived in Newark, Passaic, and finally Pascayne. Ada had loved them and missed them, still. Her grandmother had been nicer to her than her mother had ever been. Her grandfather had been one of those fishermen down by the docks, in his old age—except, when Ada's grandfather had fished in the Passaic River, the river hadn't been so polluted as it was now.

Younger people didn't care so much about their family histories any longer. "Colored" history was a bore to them, or an embarrassment. It had become a school thing—like special holidays nobody gave a damn about except they meant no school. Hearing of people who'd migrated north from a backwoods place like Georgia, looking for work in a place like Pascayne, New Jersey—boring. Most of the grandparents of schoolchildren Ada taught had migrated north to New Jersey in the 1940s to work in defense plants, and when defense-manufacturing ceased at the end of the war, there'd been little factory work for black workers since (white) veterans were given back their old jobs. Same with women who'd worked in these factories. Being a woman, and being *black*—that was the most disadvantaged you could be.

Now, younger generations scarcely knew the names of Booker T. Washington, King, Kennedy, Malcolm X. They had little interest in civil rights activists whether white or black. They knew and revered the names of athletes and rock musicians, movie actors—these were the black Americans who dominated the culture, not politicians or civil rights activists who'd been martyred for the cause.

The rude kinds of boys and girls Ada sometimes had to teach, or had to try to teach, in schools like Pascayne South High didn't give a damn as they'd tell you almost to your face. She'd had disastrous classes at the high school ending with her screaming at students to sit down, take their proper desks, be quiet—totally out of control until another teacher or the principal's assistant came to her rescue.

It made Ada uneasy to recall that Sybilla Frye had been in one of those classes that had raged out of control. She couldn't remember clearly but—yes, she thought so.

If you didn't stop them from rebelling immediately, Ada had been warned, you would lose the class. Oh but she'd tried!—she had tried.

Jeering mouths, narrowed eyes, shrill laughter—like wild creatures the adolescents were, united in opposition to "Miz Furst." She'd pleaded for them to settle down, almost she'd begged them—*Don't do this to me! Please don't! I want so badly to love you.*

She'd waited. And finally, she couldn't wait any longer.

On a weekday morning when by 11:00 A.M. the phone hadn't rung to summon her to work and she was feeling anxious, lonely, and— didn't know what else! *Boiling mad.*

Told Ma she was "going out." Kahola's children had been given breakfast and sent off to school. *She* had only housework including laundry (which she hated: so much of it, and the kids' clothes so dirty, and Ma's so smelly) with which to occupy herself. A young woman of her intelligence, talents, idealism, motivation—whom teachers had praised.

God damned unfair.

It was nearing Hallowe'en. Lurid orange plastic pumpkins in

Walgreens window, ugly black silhouette-witches. In long-ago times "witches" were unmarried females of a certain age. *God damned unjust.*

Ada walked to 393 Third Street. A mile or less, and some of the walk along the riverfront. She tried not to think *If they wanted to see you they'd have called you.* She preferred to think that Sybilla had never told Ednetta about her, Ada Furst. The more she thought about it, the more convinced Ada was that Sybilla hadn't known her name, and in the confusion and fear of that time she'd forgotten Ada entirely.

If there'd been newspaper articles. Possibly, a photo of Ada Furst would have been published.

She was bringing the abused girl a little gift. Not one she'd bought but something she'd owned herself, and had prized for years.

As Ada approached the row house in which Ednetta lived with her family, which was two houses down from the intersection with Union Street, she saw a man leaving the house—had to be Anis Schutt.

Ada knew of Anis Schutt, a little. *His wife he'd killed with his fists and the (white) prosecutor had allowed him to plead guilty to manslaughter.*

Black-on-black crime. Hard for white folks to take seriously in the courts.

Anis Schutt had been incarcerated in Rahway. At the most, he'd been away seven to ten years.

Though Ada was hanging back the bull-necked black man sighted her. Stopped in his tracks and stared at her without smiling.

"You comin here? You a friend of 'Netta?"

Ada stammered no, not a friend exactly—a neighbor . . .

"You from the city, eh? Pass'c County?"

Ada shook her head no, she was just a—a neighbor . . .

No matter how casually she dressed, Ada looked like a school-teacher. Canny Anis Schutt had no difficulty identifying her as some-one allied with *them.*

Anis Schutt in a frayed leather jacket, open to show his high, hard-looking stomach. He was bare-headed, with dense nappy stone-

colored hair trimmed close to his skull. Ada felt slightly faint seeing
the big mangled-looking fingers.

As a girl she'd seen Anis Schutt in the street. Younger then, seeming taller, with a dark pitted yet handsome face like that famous
(white) actor—Richard Burton. And the man's eyes alert, bemused.

"You comin to see the girl?"—Anis Schutt spoke sneeringly.

Ada tried to behave as if she hadn't heard this question, or hadn't
quite understood it. She was thinking it wasn't too late to cross the
street and walk away briskly—not too fast—as if she had other business on Third Street. (But she'd admitted to coming to see Ednetta,
hadn't she? The raw blunt way Anis Schutt stared at her was driving
all her thoughts out of her mind.)

"I ast—you comin to see my stepdaughter?"

Ada stammered yes, she hoped so. If Sybilla was home . . .

"You sure you ain't no police officer? Social worker? Psychol'gist?"

"Just a neighbor, Mr. Schutt."

Mr. Schutt. The words seemed to placate the black man as one
might placate a dangerous animal in the most obvious of ways.

Anis Schutt climbed into a vehicle parked at the curb. Its chassis
was riddled with rust like bullets and its back rear fender was hanging
low. Yet, the vehicle exuded an air of crude street-glamour. Ada felt a
sexual shudder at the thought of Anis Schutt pulling her into that car
with him, laughing as he settled her into the passenger's seat, shut the
door and drove away.

She'd heard that Anis Schutt worked for the county. Sanitation
services, roadwork. But maybe that hadn't been for a while.

On the front door at 393 Third Street was a tinsel Christmas
wreath from a previous year. On the stoop, rotted newspapers and
flyers. She had an impression of someone just inside the door staring
at her and so she maintained her stiff-friendly smile.

She rang the doorbell. A buzzer sounded inside. *This is a mistake! These are not my kind of people.*

Third Street had not recovered from the fires and break-ins of 1967. Ada had had a school friend who'd lived on this street when the houses hadn't been so run-down and shabby.

Small ravaged lawns, cracked sidewalks. It was a surprise to see that several houses in the block appeared to be vacant.

Entire blocks in Red Rock could be ravaged in this way. Houses without tenants were always burning. They became crack-houses, squatters moved in. Graffiti covered the facades like crazed screams. Bodies began to be found on the premises. Ada felt a revulsion for this place in which she'd lived her life until now—she could only bear it if she believed it would be temporary.

The door was finally opened, as if in exasperation. There stood Ednetta Frye in a soiled chenille robe staring at her. Ednetta's hair was tied up in a scarf so tight it had caused her forehead to pucker.

"Yah? What d'you want?"

Awkwardly Ada introduced herself: "Maybe you remember me? Ada Furst? I—I live over on Ventor, by the fish-food factory . . ."

Ednetta blinked at her slowly. Her eyes were heavy-lidded, reddened.

"I'm not with the city or the county, I'm just—one of your neighbors. You know my sister Kahola, I think? I'm—Ada."

Ednetta's expression showed no recognition. Maybe there were ill feelings between Ednetta and Kahola—maybe Ednetta resented being reminded of Ada's sister.

Damn she wished she hadn't dressed so attractively for this visit! That was poor judgment. Shouldn't have brushed her hair and fastened it with a barrette like a schoolgirl.

With an eager smile she stammered: "I was the one—Ada Furst—

who found your daughter in the factory cellar. I heard her calling for help and I—I found her . . . I ran to get help."

"'Ada Furst.'" Ednetta pronounced the name doubtfully. "Was you the one called the ambulance?"

"Yes."

"Was you at the hospital with all them?"

"No—I wasn't allowed to come to the hospital with Sybilla. I found her, and I untied her, and I ran for help . . ."

"Jesus! You the one saved my girl's life, I guess."

Ednetta was smiling now, though her eyes remained heavy-lidded, and wary. Ada saw with disappointment that Ednetta had no intention of inviting her inside: she stood blocking the door, sway-backed, contemplative, stroking her left arm.

"Well, Anna. S'b'lla real grateful to you, an I am also. S'b'lla whole family grateful. This nasty thing happen to my girl, everybody sorry for us an talk about us but treat us like we was lepers. Everybody know the white cops aint gon do a God-damn thing, they just waitin for this to fade away. Fuckers!"

Ada murmured sympathetically. She wasn't sure how to respond. She hesitated to introduce herself as a schoolteacher, who had contact with the white world; this might backfire, and Ednetta would lose trust in her.

Ednetta was saying, "Somebody say, one of them social workers comin around here, there is a 'fund' for lawsuits, you can sue the police force, like there is 'wrongful arrest'—but . . . You need God-damn witnesses, an who gon test'fy against *white cops*? Every time I ask them, they say some bullshit takin you back to where you begun. They say, 'You need S'b'lla to *test'fy*. When you gon bring her into the courthouse to *test'fy*." Ednetta broke off in disgust.

"Yes. I think that Sybilla would have to give a formal statement. We can accompany her to the police station—people from the neighborhood. There's a protocol for reporting a crime—if the victim is able to participate in the investigation . . ."

Ednetta stiffened, as if Ada had said the wrong thing.

"Ma'am, I got to go now. Somebody callin."

"Oh but wait, Mrs. Frye—how is Sybilla? Is she home? I hoped I could see her."

"We real grateful to you, Anna—that your name?—*Ada*. We real grateful but see, S'b'lla not here right now."

"Where is she?"

"*Where* is she?" Ednetta frowned. "She where she bein taken care of, that's where."

"I'd like so much to see her. Just to say hello."

Ada spoke naïvely, wistfully. She believed that, if she and Sybilla could meet, if Ada took Sybilla's hand in hers, the girl would remember her, and smile at her.

Sybilla Frye and Ada Furst in a photograph in the newspaper. "Ada Furst Saved My Life."

Her school colleagues would see that photograph. The staff at the school district headquarters, that was responsible for hiring her.

But Ednetta was saying, "Nah, S'b'lla aint here. She stayin somewhere safe till she 'convalesce.' She real grateful to you, though—she say 'Thank you!'" Ednetta bared her teeth in a forced smile. She would have shut the door in Ada's face but Ada protested:

"Mrs. Frye, wait! Please! I brought a—a little present for Sybilla. If she's 'convalescing'—this is just ideal."

Ednetta stared at the paperback book Ada gave her: Maya Angelou's *I Know Why the Caged Bird Sings*.

"It meant so much to me, when I was Sybilla's age. And I have other books she might like, if . . ."

Ednetta glanced at the book, frowning and exasperated. She muttered "Thanks" and shut the door.

Ada walked back home feeling very tired. But smiling to herself.

"'Your neighbor! Your friend.'"

Klariss on the stairs asking her about the Sybilla Frye thing.

"You know that mother? Ednetta Frye? Couple weeks ago I seen her and the girl out back by the factory, tryin to get through the fence like they didn't know where the fence is broke, you can push through. This was just gettin-dark. They carryin something like a canvas an the girl have somethin wrapped on her head like a scarf. And I was watchin thinkin what the hell they doin here? Why'd they be out back of this place? An next I know, next morning you're sayin there's somebody over there needin help—and it's the daughter be found in the factory cellar all tied up and 'white cops' put her there an beat her and raped her. Jesus!" Klariss laughed, shaking her head. "That's some shit Ednetta is saying, ain't it?"

Ada hadn't listened to most of this. Ada was eager to avoid Klariss if she could. The woman consorted with low-level drug dealers, you had to assume she took drugs herself. Not long ago Klariss had been a good-looking woman of about Ada's age, now she looked ravaged. Dyed-beet-color hair looking like a cheap wig, shirt half-unbuttoned so you could see more than you wanted of the woman's fleshy breasts, and that smell coming off her—you didn't want to think what it was. Stiffly she said:

"You don't know Ednetta Frye, Klariss, and you don't know Sybilla. I'd be careful what kind of stories you spread about them, that could get back to them."

The Lucky Man

On Camden Avenue in the shadow of Pitcairn Memorial Bridge he was stopped by police.

Coming up swiftly behind his car the Pascayne PD squad car siren deafening.

He knew to pull his car over without hesitation. Seeing how traffic moved past, drivers' eyes easing onto him in curiosity and pity and a measure of brotherly sympathy, and away.

His heart was a fist pounding inside his rib cage. Myriad bone-aches and muscle-aches in his limbs faded to invisibility in the face of such danger.

Two patrol officers approached his car. One advanced to his window and the other held back.

Both officers' hands lightly resting on their holstered weapons.

He was asked for his driver's license, vehicle registration. He hesitated only because he wasn't sure—though it was not yet 9:00 P.M., and Camden Avenue was far from deserted—that, when he reached for his wallet, or leaned over to open the glove compartment, the police officers might not shoot him dead.

Going for a weapon. We told him stop but he did not stop.

There were two choices: silent, or deferential.

Silent might be mistaken by the cops for sullen, dangerous. Deferential might be mistaken for mockery.

So far as they knew he was a black man and armed. Might be armed. And good reason to be armed. On the floor of the car, or in the backseat, a weapon. Firearm, tire iron. Judging by his face not only the darkness of his skin but its rough and irregular texture this man was a killer.

He'd killed, and he would kill again. He'd (maybe) killed a white person. White people. He'd liked the taste of (white) blood and could be trusted to kill again.

His (shiny dark) eyes gleamed (wetly, whitely) in his rough black face like something hacked out of stone. The flash of his (not white, but white-seeming) teeth inside his (fleshy, blood-tinctured) lips.

He considered asking what he'd done wrong, had he been speeding, had he crossed over the yellow line, or was he driving without headlights, or a taillight burned out. Such questions were but the reasonable questions of an innocent man stopped by police for no (evident) reason. A (white) man might ask such questions of (white) cops. Though it was clear to him that he hadn't been speeding, at less than thirty miles an hour on Camden Avenue as dusk came on accelerated by the massive bridge blotting out half the sky.

Yet, he didn't trust himself to speak. Even in the way of (carefully cadenced, black) deference. His (ruined, rasping) voice might sound to the white cops like a voice of threat.

He was cursing us, sounded like. Couldn't make out what the fuck he was saying like maybe he was—Haitian? Domin'c'n?

High on some drug seemed like.

He decided to say nothing. Not even muttering *Yes Officer* as every adult woman had taught him when he'd been a boy.

The Pascayne PD officers said nothing frowning at his driver's license and vehicle registration with a flashlight. Quietly he sat unmoving as a statue arms lightly resting on the steering wheel. He owned a weapon, a Smith & Wesson .45-caliber revolver, but he was not transporting this weapon in his car at this time. He was in possession of "stolen goods"—(electrical supplies)—but he was not transporting these goods in his car at this time. The elder of the cops had taken his driver's license back to the squad car to run through the PD computer while the other cop waited outside the car brandishing the flashlight. He was very quiet waiting for them to order him out of the car, to lie down on the oil-splotched pavement, at least to kneel on the pavement with his hands on his head. Waiting to be so ordered, humbled and humiliated as traffic passed slowly on Camden Avenue, approaching the intersection with Eighth Street.

His arms remained on the steering wheel of his vehicle. He would not make any sudden moves. His heart was still beating rapidly and hard inside his chest. He would not allow himself to cough, or to sneeze. Such sudden movements might cause the police officers to defend themselves by shooting him to death.

It was police protocol, the cops shot twice. Two cops, four shots.

A minimum of four shots. There was no maximum.

A few weeks ago a young black Hispanic had been shot to death by Pascayne PD officers on a ramp of the Turnpike less than a mile from Camden and Eighth. He'd been speeding—(this was the officers' claim)—and when they'd flagged him over he had *gone for his weapon, looked like*—though occupants in the young man's car insisted that he'd had both hands on the steering wheel of his car and had not moved at all even to remove his wallet when they shot him to death.

A fusillade of bullets, the media had reported. Not less than thirty shots fired of which at least half had entered the young man's body and two had ricocheted, injuring passengers.

An investigation was pending. Police officers involved in the shooting temporarily suspended.

He had to think, that was how Lyander died. On a Pascayne street. The claim was his brother had fired shots at a passing police cruiser but Lyander hadn't had any gun.

Witnesses said there'd been no weapon in Lyander's hand. Face so messed up, nobody could mostly recognize him except for his new jacket and shoes.

"'Anis Schutt.' You the father of a high school girl named 'Sybilla Frye'?"

Shook his head *no*. Didn't trust his raspy, ruined voice to communicate with the police officers staring at him from a distance of less than three feet.

"You livin with her, though? At '939 Third'—right?"

Shook his head *yes*.

"You livin with the mother, is that it?"

Shook his head *yes*.

In his raspy ruined voice saying he lived with the mother Ednetta, that was right.

"The girl is, like, your 'stepdaughter'—right?"

In his raspy ruined voice saying *yes*.

Near-inaudibly so the police officers asked him to repeat what he'd said.

He repeated what he'd said. Dry-mouthed having to swallow as with deadpan expressions the police officers regarded him. He understood how they were wanting badly to shout at him *Get out and run! Run for your life motherfucker!*

Many times in his life he'd run. Many times in his sleep he'd run. In his dreams he'd run. The shotgun blast had blown his back open. The hail of bullets had torn his chest open, ripped at his face. There were special kinds of bullets, dumdums, that tore your organs out as they traveled through your body. A shot at the back of the neck exiting at the groin and every organ in the torso and gut carried out with it. He felt his lungs torn out, astonished as the hot-rushing bullets ricocheted through his body soft as a mollusk and out.

They'd ordered him to step into the rushing sewer water. Ordered him to pick up the fallen wire with his hands. Cursed him and laughed at him as he'd burst into blue flame.

It was the white cops' happiest times, the times for which they lived when they shouted such orders. No time so thrilling, you understood seeing their snake-flat foreheads and pinprick eyes.

Run! Run and we'll let you go black motherfucker.

Steeling himself for the bullets—but the bullets had not come.

With disdain and contempt as you'd contemplate a cockroach goading it with your foot the police officers requested of the black man that he open the trunk of his car. As with care, caution, the stoop of an elderly man he popped the trunk, he cooperated.

They ordered him out of his vehicle then in the stinging rain. Like acid rain it felt against his warm face and hands.

They asked if he was carrying a concealed weapon or anything that was "sharp" and when he said no, one of the officers briskly patted him down. The (gloved) hands were swift, rough, practiced in all parts of his tense quivering body for there was no part of the black man that was *private, untouchable.*

Pascayne PD officers wore gloves, that they would not leave incriminating fingerprints on any surface. Present-day officers were not so crude as their predecessors.

The black-feather thing, the Angel of Wrath brushed near. With his teeth he could rip out the throat of the steely-faced officer close beside him except the other cop would shoot him dead even as the jugular vein spouted blood.

He had not ever ripped out the throat of any human being with his teeth. But he'd seen throats slashed with knives. Once, with a machete.

His shoes had been splattered with blood. More than once, in his lifetime.

But always black blood. Not yet the blood of the enemy.

The police officers continued to examine the vehicle, front and back, glove compartment, beneath the seats, every square inch of the trunk. He was kneeling now on the dirty pavement, hands on his head. It was a matter of shame to him, his knees were excruciating in pain. His ruined knees, his arthritic knees, shooting pains that left him dazed and breathless running from the base of his spine into his legs and through the length of his (kneeling, bent) legs into his very feet. He bit his lower lip to keep from sobbing aloud. He had never felt such pain, he could not bear it. Leaping from the sanitation truck, he'd been a young man when the pains had first started years ago. Drinking helped. Heavy drinking helped most. Painkiller pills. His right knee, and his right thigh, and later both his knees and both his thighs. And his fingers were becoming gnarled like claws. And the nails were splitting, so dry. The woman kissed his hands. The woman's warm breath on his hands. She was forgiving him, he knew. But she had no right to forgive him. The woman had no right to forgive *him*.

The examination of his vehicle had netted them nothing. The elder of the officers handed back his driver's license with a look of contempt.

"Lucky this time, Schutt."

———

The black-feather Angel of Wrath whispered to him gloating *Lucky this time, Schutt. Ain't you shamed.*

On ruined legs he struggled to rise but could not. At last crawling to his car to hoist himself erect he hoped the cops hadn't observed as they'd driven away.

The Stepdaughter

The intrusions at 939 Third Street were fewer now. Telephone calls from city-county agencies. Unannounced visits.

Search warrant from Passaic County Family Services.

Social worker visit. *Ednetta Frye? I need to see your daughter Sybilla immediately.*

Questioned by agency officers the girl replied in a voice so hushed, you could barely hear her words.

Weeks after the (alleged) assault her face was still slightly bruised and her upper lip appeared swollen. There was a sickle-shaped scab in her left eyebrow. In her left eye, a just-perceptible cast that gave her a sly drifting impudent look.

A girl of fifteen, lanky-limbed, attractive but wary-looking, unsmiling. Her fingernails had been polished sparkly-purple and there were gold studs in her ears. She sighed often, shifted in her seat.

She'd been "returned home"—as Mrs. Frye explained—after having stayed with her great-grandmother Pearline Tice who lived over on Eleventh Street for several weeks—"S'b'lla been convales'in, an she feelin good now."

The mother was eager and attentive to the officers' questions even as the girl appeared sulky and withdrawn.

When the girl failed to reply to a question the mother murmured *S'b'lla!* and the girl roused herself to answer in monosyllables.

Agency officers visiting the Frye household at 939 Third Street were disappointed, baffled—for it seemed, Sybilla Frye was refusing now to speak of *what had happened* to her the previous month.

Stiffly Mrs. Frye said, "We aint gon talk about *that*. No more."

And, "We got 'freedom of speech'—we exercisin that."

Some questions the girl didn't seem to hear. These questions were repeated carefully and the girl mumbled vague replies or shrugged her shoulders with downcast eyes. You would think—almost—that Sybilla Frye was *mentally impaired* but medical records and school records did not indicate this.

It was surmised that the girl had been *traumatized*. Psychological therapy, counseling were strongly advised for both the girl and her mother but had been refused, adamantly by the mother who'd drawn in the minister of her church and a Red Rock physician, in fact a chiropractor with strong opinions about "psycho"-therapy.

In her chair the girl shifted restlessly as if to avoid the stinging of small ants. She sighed, swiped at her nose with the edge of her hand, didn't trouble to conceal a yawn. From time to time she cast a narrow sidelong glance at her mother, unreadable to outsiders.

The pouty mouth twitched in amusement, or in anger?—this wasn't clear.

Asked if she was *being coerced* in any way the girl shook her head vigorously *No.*

Asked if she knew what *coerced* meant the girl shook her head vigorously *Yes*.

"Seem like what you doin with me now, ma'am. 'C'erced.'"

That drifting left gaze, detached and mocking even as the girl spoke in a way to placate the anxious mother.

"Yes ma'am. I am feelin OK. Yes I am goin back to school soon. You c'n write all that shit down."

It was the first week of November, Ednetta brought Sybilla back home. Soon then, Sybilla returned to Pascayne South High.

But late morning of Sybilla's first school day since her long absence Ednetta heard a thudding noise in the front hall—and a door slammed hard—and there came Sybilla into the kitchen to toss her backpack onto a counter, scowling. "Don't you scold me, Mama. I am *home*. I am not takin any more shit."

Ednetta had been afraid of this. Ednetta knew her daughter's headstrong ways and her unpredictable behavior since—what the mother called *that nastiness happened to you*. But Ednetta professed surprise and disappointment asking what had happened at school and Sybilla said there was God damn boys pressin against her in the hall and knockin into her on the stairs, God damn assholes lookin at her like she was some kind of slut. And her asshole teachers not much better lookin at her too.

"I told them go fuck themselves. Just walked out."

"Well girl, you can't 'just walk out.' You aren't old enough to quit school."

"I'm gon get a job an make some money. Grandma said she could find work for me. There's a lady in her building has two little children an the person who was takin care of them got sick. I can do that."

"S'b'lla, you *too young.*"

"Fuck 'young'! There's girls my age had babies by now, an you know it. Fuck you lookin at me like I am crazy, Mama—*you* the crazy one, got us into this shit."

Sybilla spoke with a peculiar sort of elation. She'd picked up her backpack and let it fall again now, onto the floor. She kicked the backpack shouting with laughter and stamped her feet until Ednetta hugged her tight, to calm her.

Very still mother and daughter stood panting and hot-faced. It made Ednetta uneasy that Sybilla was her height now—Ednetta stood somewhat stooped as if her body was settling in upon itself while Sybilla stood wiry and straight.

Sybilla giggled and said, quietly, "Where's *he?*"

"I told you. He ain't here."

"Where, then?"

Ednetta shrugged. "He ain't say."

"He comin back here tonight?"

"No."

"He been callin you?"

"No."

Sybilla pushed out of Ednetta's arms. "Bullshit, Mama. You must be simple, thinkin I would believe *you.*"

Carelessly Sybilla rummaged in the refrigerator. Lifted a quart container of milk and drank from it before Ednetta could stop her. Took up a jar of grape jam, slices of bread, and a bread knife, and ran back into her bedroom and slammed the door shut.

Ednetta stood in the hall calling after her. Inside the room, Sybilla screamed what sounded like *Fuck fuck fuck you big fat Mama ass* then lapsed into a fit of laughter, or coughing.

———

"If you go to the police and make a formal charge, as I think you should, Ednetta—they will have to investigate. They will at least have to pretend to investigate. It may get in the media then—it may receive some attention. But if you don't, then the police will never act—they will claim they don't have enough evidence, and they don't have a cooperating witness. They might even know who hurt your daughter in this outrageous way, but they won't investigate. We can't tolerate such injustice in our community—this is 1987, not 1967."

The woman from Crisis Ministry, speaking to Ednetta in a fast-clip way like she was scolding Ednetta. A light-skin black woman with fussy speech sounding like a radio or TV voice.

Or, no—maybe this was the woman from NAACP. Maybe a lawyer? Same way of scolding like Ednetta Frye was some rural-South fool had to be set right.

"Mrs. Frye? If you're reluctant or afraid to go alone with your daughter, I will accompany you. I'll bring two or three of my colleagues, in fact. We will *march into* the police station here in Red Rock—I've done it in the past, and you do get attention."

Ednetta said evasively, stroking her arm, "Well. That might maybe happen . . . Trouble is, S'b'lla not feelin like she want to 'cooperate.' That girl, it's hard for me to get to her sometimes, she fifteen years old . . ."

"I need to talk to Sybilla, Mrs. Frye. I'd thought she would be home this morning—I thought you'd said so. But I can come back. We have to move ahead with this, and quickly. The longer a crime goes uninvestigated, the less likely the perpetrator or perpetrators will be found."

God damn, Ednetta hated this female! "Herring-bone" pantsuit and lace-up grannie shoes, eyeglasses, not a touch of makeup on her face that had to be young like early thirties, and a sneering look to her mouth. *A lawyer is the worst kind of son-bitch* she'd heard Anis remark,

he get paid for just talkin an you can't shut his mouth. Had to be, the females were no different than the males.

Ednetta had been crinkling her face to show that she was listening. Saying in a dull-whining voice, "Ma'am, nobody expect justice
from the racist cops an pros'cutors anyway. The thing that would
happen is, S'b'lla get in more trouble, all kinds of nasty attention
and threats. Her whole family get in trouble. Already at the school
her teachers look at her funny—she refusin to go back, and I'm gon
get in trouble for *that*. These 'white cops'—God knows how many
of them they are, and how high-ranking. They could drive by in the
street here an shoot in our windows, like they did in '67. They could
harass S'b'lla so she runs away from home—she that desp'rate!
They could harass *me*. And Anis, the police always stopping him
and friskin him, askin where he live, where he goin, pretendin they
don't know who in hell he *is*. One of these days, Anis say he gon take
his gun and blow some white cop's head off. Get him a shotgun, and
go to war."

The female lawyer stared at Ednetta and didn't speak for a moment.

"Mrs. Frye, I don't think that's a good idea. To think that way, or
to talk that way. Is Mr. Schutt your husband?"

"Yes, he is my husband."

"You don't want him to provoke the police, do you? There's strain
enough in Red Rock without provoking more. My suggestion is that
you allow the NAACP to take up your case, and I will drive you to
police headquarters—not the precinct here, but headquarters, at Flint
Square across the river. I think that's a much better idea than the Red
Rock precinct. There, your daughter will file formal charges of abduction, aggravated assault, rape, with evidence from the hospital. You
may be correct—the local police won't conduct a serious investigation. But there are other police forces in New Jersey, for instance the

state police. If this is a 'hate crime'—as it obviously is, with obscene racist epithets written on your daughter's body—the FBI should already be involved."

Ednetta was staring at the floor. Caressing her arm slowly, to ease the arthritic pain in her joints. The woman's sharp voice had rattled by like a freight train.

Thinking how Anis had said of lawyers *They will sell you out to the pros'cutors. Telling you one thing an they make a deal with the other law'ers behind your back.*

"Ma'am, it's one thing for you to say all this, but somethin else for S'b'lla and me. You ain't got to live with it. You gettin some salary at the NA'CP, but we ain't gettin any salary to be spendin all that time at the police station where S'b'lla be treated like some freak an insulted. Who is goin to protect my daughter, when all this start? *You?*"

"We can certainly try to protect your daughter, and you. We could arrange for a place for her to live . . ."

" 'Place for her to live'—where? S'b'lla got to live *here*. Her family here, and her school an friends. Bad enough people talkin about her now, without anything in the paper or on TV. There's people lookin at me like I was some leper already."

The female lawyer stared at Ednetta. She removed her wire-rimmed eyeglasses to stare at Ednetta more closely.

"But—you want justice for your daughter, don't you, Mrs. Frye? You don't want these rapists to remain free, do you?"

"Ain't what I want, ma'am. It's what the mother of a black girl in Pascayne got to expect."

"But, Mrs. Frye, I don't understand. Just a few minutes ago . . ."

Ednetta was on her feet. Ednetta would usher the astonished female out of her house with flurried gestures of her hands as you'd drive away annoying chickens.

"Mrs. Frye, please—"

"Excuse me, ma'am! The migr'n headache come over me! Good-bye."

Shut the door behind the stunned-looking woman almost catching her heels. Stood at the front window peering around the edge of the blind to make sure the woman got into her car and drove away. Ednetta was quivering with laughter.

Ednetta was thinking how, before this *nasty thing* happened, just back in September she'd been a young woman yet. Skin around her eyes not so saggy, and her breath not so short, and in the street she'd looked good in men's eyes, and laughed back at them they whistled in her direction, or made some wise remark leaving her feeling damn good.

But now—things had got strange. Unpredictable day to day.

The car was gone from the curb. Ednetta had to think for a moment who it had been, in her living room. Mashed her knuckles against her mouth, laughing aloud.

So funny!

You thinkin you can manuplate Ednetta Frye! Fuck all of you.

Hauled herself up the stairs that seemed to be getting steeper every damn day. And there was Sybilla in her cubbyhole room languidly brushing her snarled hair. That big girl sprawled on her bed amid a scattering of stuffed baby-animals not troubling to glance up when her out-of-breath Mama appeared in the doorway.

"That law'er gone now, girl. You don't need to hide up here."

Ednetta was thinking, she'd take Sybilla to the Jubilee Salon and have her hair done right. Hot comb, and (maybe) cornrows. On his way out that day Anis had handed her a wad of bills including two crumpled fifties.

"I ain't hidin up here, Mama. Jesus!"

"Well, that NA'CP law'er gone. Who she's been talkin to, I don't know. Neighbors, maybe. God damn I hate to think what people be sayin—*we* the last to know."

Sybilla winced, as if the pit of her belly hurt her. A chill thought came to Ednetta—*Is that girl pregnant?*

She knew, this could not be. From what Sybilla had told her, in bitter little fragments like a shattered mirror you'd have to sweep up from the floor with care, there was no likelihood of *pregnancy.*

"Is Martine comin over? Want for her to stay for supper?"

That sly mocking look in Sybilla's drifting left eye.

"Martine comes, an you be bitchin we don't do the dishes right. Or the dish towels too *wet.* What we want to see on TV ain't what you want."

Ednetta was hurt, was this how Sybilla thought of her? And Martine, her favorite little niece—did Martine think Ednetta was a bitch, too?

Ednetta came to Sybilla, and lay the back of her hand against the girl's forehead. In the instant before Sybilla pushed her hand away, Ednetta registered the girl was *warm.*

"Everybody want to 'represent' us, like we was the Supremes. Must be thinking they can make money out of us." Ednetta laughed hoping Sybilla would laugh with her.

Coldly Sybilla said, without a blink of an eye, "Make money out of *me.* Fuck 'us.' They all comin about *me,* Mama."

The Mission

Black girl kidnapped beaten & raped by white cops & left to die in abandoned factory in Pascayne, NJ. No arrests, news blackout & censorship by white media, power structure & politicians.

No more than this, and this was enough.
Left a message for his brother Byron.

En route to Pascayne NJ
Prepare for emergency

Reverend Marus Cornelius Mudrick, Attorney-at-Law Byron Randolph Mudrick.

Fraternal twins born 1943 in Penn's Mill, Virginia. Moved to Camden, New Jersey, with parents in 1952 where, after the departure of their father from the household, they lived with their mother and several siblings in a public housing project. By the age of five Marus's gift for preaching had been cultivated by a minister in the African Methodist Episcopal Church in Penn's Mill, Virginia; by the age of eight Marus was a regular guest-preacher in the St. Matthew AME Church in Camden, and, in time, a guest-preacher in other AME churches in New Jersey and New York City; by the age of twelve, Marus was enrolled as a "special-studies" part-time student at the Camden Bible College and Seminary, and by the age of fifteen he'd been ordained as a minister in the AME Church—the youngest in the history of the Camden Seminary. At the same time, Marus often sang solo hymns at church services; as a child, he had a beautiful boy's voice, and in late adolescence he had a strong baritone voice. At the age of eleven Marus was a contestant on the popular TV quiz show *Twenty One:* the first child, and the first African-American, to appear on the show, though Marus only appeared for three weeks before losing to the young white "genius" Herbert Stempel. Years later, as a controversial public figure in the New York City area, Marus Mudrick appeared on the quiz show *Let's Make a Deal* where he won several thousand dollars which he announced would be donated to the National Black Youth Fund, a nonprofit organization devoted to helping impoverished young black people.

Both brothers graduated from Booker T. Washington High School in Camden, in 1962; Byron with honors, as class salutatorian, and Marus, by this time an ordained minister, voted "most likely to succeed." Marus enrolled at the Newark campus of Rutgers University with the intention of studying political science but soon dropped out to work for two years in the Harlem office of Congressman Adam Clayton Powell, while Byron remained at the university, graduated in 1966 (*summa cum laude*) and earned a degree from Rutgers-Newark Law School in 1971. Byron qualified for the New Jersey bar in 1972 and began work as a Legal Aid attorney in the state capitol at Tren-

ton, while Marus, associated with no single black church, continued
to give guest sermons while working for a succession of civil rights
organizations—NAACP, CORE (Congress of Racial Equality), the
Summer Freedom School Project, and the National Black Youth Fund
for which he became New Jersey coordinator in 1979. (In 1983, Marus
was investigated on suspicion of "misuse of funds" by the national
NBYF; though never formally charged with any crime, Marus paid
back approximately $12,000 to the organization and resigned his
position. Byron was involved in Marus's defense and, following the
lengthy investigation, the Mudrick brothers were estranged for several years.) While Byron kept a low profile in civil rights litigation,
Marus acquired a reputation as a flamboyant black agitator more in
the tradition of Congressman Powell than of the Reverend Martin
Luther King Jr.; from Powell, Marus learned to organize black communities in rent strikes, the boycotting of selected (Jewish, Chinese,
Korean) stores and services, civil rights demonstrations and picketing;
he led marches through "lily-white" suburban communities in New
Jersey and in the New York City area; he challenged the legitimacy
of police shootings of black "suspects" and agitated for the hiring of
black law enforcement officers, firemen, and bus drivers in Newark.
Marus's most publicized activist projects were the 1981 march of
more than a thousand individuals to the New Jersey State Legislature
in Trenton protesting the death-sentence conviction of a black man
who'd been convicted on rape and murder charges primarily on the
basis of a (white) jailhouse informer, and the even larger protest rally
in Newark, in 1984, following the shooting-death of an (unarmed)
black former Marine hero by New Jersey state police who'd stopped
him on the Turnpike with a claim that he'd been speeding.

Marus had himself been arrested by law enforcement officers numerous times, charged with "inciting riot," "disturbing the peace,"
organizing and marching without a permit, disobeying police orders

and resisting arrest. It was Marus's custom to drive new-model vehicles, favoring Cadillacs and Lincolns, with the consequence that
he was many times stopped on charges of DWB—"Driving While
Black." (Often these stops escalated into arrests and bookings when
Marus displayed an "uppity" tendency to confront police officers.)
He'd been beaten and jailed in Albany, Georgia, in the summer of
1964, for his participation in the Freedom School, and again in the
late 1960s and 1970s for his political activism in New Jersey–New York
City. (In Rikers Island for several days in 1977, Marus Mudrick deliv-
ered impassioned sermons of black liberation to his fellow prisoners,
until prison authorities intervened.) In 1985, Marus established the Urban Care Ministry of Central New Jersey, with the financial support
of the Lewentine Foundation and other well-to-do (white) donors;
the Ministry targeted underprivileged youths, helped find training
programs and jobs for them, as well as temporary housing for their
families. At the same time, less publicly, and less controversially, Byron Mudrick continued in civil rights/social activism law as well as
adjunct teaching at Rutgers-Newark Law School; much of his work
was *pro bono,* in alliance with the Innocence Project. (Byron Mudrick
was one of several lawyers arguing on behalf of the boxer Hurricane
Rubin Carter, for instance, wrongly convicted of murder in the late
1960s, and released from prison in 1985.) It was said of the Mudrick
brothers *Marus proposes, Byron deposes.*

From his early, charismatic mentor Adam Clayton Powell, whose
1967 conviction on charges of embezzlement, bribe-taking, and an
assortment of similar petty crimes Marus Mudrick had protested as
an "egregious example of race-discrimination"—(it was an open secret that Democratic Congressman Powell was but one of countless
politicians of the era, predominantly white, who were understood to
be involved in what the press called *corruption;* Powell was singled
out because he was black, not because he was *corrupt*)—Marus Mud-

rick had learned the importance of looking his best at all times, but particularly when photographers or TV crews were at hand. Like Powell, Marus dressed carefully—in three-piece, custom-made suits, often worn with striking silk ties, silk shirts and monogrammed cuff links; his footwear was elegant, and never less than highly polished. Like Powell, Marus cultivated a thin mustache; his dense, oily-dark hair was carefully barbered and pomaded; his fingernails were manicured, and he wore gold jewelry—rings, watch band, bracelet. Marus would no more wear clothing that had even the slightest appearance of being rumpled, soiled, or out-of-date, than he'd have stepped into a vehicle that wasn't gleaming with newness. *Black is beautiful* came naturally to Marus, who hadn't doubted, since he'd been a child-preacher of five, that he was beautiful—not because he was black but because he was Marus, who happened to be black.

In the mid-1970s posters began to appear in black neighborhoods of the sleekly handsome Marus Mudrick in his signature three-piece suit with a flowing necktie, sternly smiling, vibrant and alert, exuding strength, masculinity, Christian resolution—*"Black is Beautiful"*— *Rev. Marus Mudrick, Care Ministry of Central New Jersey.* And, at times, provocatively—*"I bring not peace but a sword" says Jesus—Rev. Marus Mudrick, Care Ministry of Central New Jersey.* Though Marus was in his thirties at the time of these controversial posters he appeared a decade older, with fattish jowls, a puffy face, the portly, dignified air of a chief justice. His smile was enigmatic, a faintly sneering smile with a curled upper lip—*My people I will do battle for you against our enemies. Believe in me—I am the man.* Marus had been married, divorced and remarried, and often seemed to be living apart from his family; in his early thirties Byron had married a woman he'd known since high school in Camden, and lived with her and their children in an integrated inner-city neighborhood in Newark where his wife was a public schools administrator.

Born within minutes of each other, the twins did not—at first glance—closely resemble each other. Six minutes older than Byron, Marus behaved as if these six minutes had given him a mandate of authority in their twinness which Byron, quieter by nature, self-effacing and given to irony, didn't contest. There was no competing with Marus Mudrick—you were a follower, a disciple, or an enemy; in Byron's case, you were a *younger brother.*

Both brothers had suffered from birth injuries that caused their upper spines to be slightly twisted and stunted their growth: Marus never grew beyond five feet five, Byron was at least an inch shorter. Marus compensated for this "short" stature by wearing shoes with substantial heels, standing very straight and holding his head high, speaking clearly and decisively, often in a loud, assured, preacherly voice; his staffers and associates were chosen partly for their height, and it was rare, except in celebrity-photographs, that Marus allowed himself to be photographed with individuals who were taller than he.

Byron, who professed himself bemused by his brother's vanity, yet not wholly unsympathetic with it, compensated for his stature by immersing himself in his work, in which he exerted, at times, an extraordinary *will*—he liked to think of himself as a pit bull that never barks but sinks his teeth in his opponent's ankle and will not be pried loose. Where Marus thrived upon attention, thrilled to be heard, to be seen, to be photographed and on TV, even to be reviled and attacked so long as he was able to exert influence in the cause of advancing his race, Byron was content to win court cases and to negotiate settlements behind the scenes, out of the glare of publicity.

Because of their spinal condition and short stature the Mudrick twins were classified 4F for the U.S. draft, and were not called up for service in the Vietnam War. Marus was (publicly) sympathetic with black draft resisters (like Cassius Clay) but overall not so sympathetic with the white-radical-led anti-war movement of the late 1960s which he believed might be "Communist"-inspired as well as a movement generated by "hippies" who didn't give Marus Mudrick the respect and recognition to which he was accustomed in the black community. Byron, a believer in black patriotism, in the wake of the Paul Robeson scandal careful to identify himself as an "enemy of communism," had nonetheless defended a number of young black conscientious objectors in the 1960s, without much success in keeping them out of federal prisons. Of black activist attorneys, Byron Mudrick was hated less than most, for his cordial, professional, and non-declamatory manner; even politicians, public officials, and judges who sided against him, whose (covert) racism made of Byron Mudrick an ideological enemy, were courteous to the man, and admiring of his courtroom skills. He liked to joke that he should have cards printed—THE MUD-RICK BROTHER PEOPLE COME TO FOR HELP WITH MARUS.

■

FIVE WEEKS AFTER SYBILLA HAD BEEN FOUND IN THE FISH-food factory, Ednetta Frye was introduced to Reverend Marus Mudrick.

It was the pastor of Ednetta's church, Reverend Denis, who brought the two together. He'd told Ednetta that "someone very special, one of our great black Americans" wanted to meet her.

Why'd this person want to meet *her?* Ednetta asked, frightened.

Ednetta knew of Marus Mudrick of course. Not only had she heard Reverend Mudrick preach in Reverend Denis's church on several occasions, but she'd been seeing his photograph in newspapers for more than twenty years; she'd read admiring articles on the dynamic civil-rights-activist-minister and interviews with him in such publications as *Ebony, Essence,* and *Black Digest.* The Pascayne newspaper had reported on Marus Mudrick's "illegal" protest marches and "inflammatory" public addresses in the state capitol, and in Newark; in any white publication, Reverend Marus Mudrick was likely to be denounced as "race-baiting." Since girlhood Ednetta had revered Adam Clayton Powell, like everyone she knew; she knew that Marus Mudrick had been a young protégé of Powell.

Ednetta felt that she might faint when Reverend Mudrick took her hand in his and gazed into her eyes with an expression of tender interest and concern. Her nostrils took in his fragrant hair pomade, and his cologne. She had never seen, at close quarters, so suavely handsome a man, so elegantly *masculine* a man; she was conscious of his dazzling-white smile, his burnished, caramel-colored skin, the fine-trimmed mustache on his upper lip. Reverend Mudrick wore a three-piece suit of a dark, soft wool, with a waistcoat in a lighter fabric, a white silk shirt and a rich, resplendent salmon-colored silk tie. On his right hand he wore a gold signet ring and on his left wrist, a gold stretch-band watch. His gold cuff links engraved MCM glittered. His voice was low, sibilant. *Mrs. Frye, Ednetta, your daughter Sybilla*— Ednetta's breath grew short, and her eyes brimmed with moisture so sharp it hurt.

In the front room of Reverend Denis's house adjacent to the AME church on Seventh Street, Marus Mudrick spoke with Ednetta Frye for more than an hour, explaining his "mission" in seeking her out; his outrage over the "race-rape" of her daughter by white police officers; and his conviction that he was the one to secure "justice for her daughter, and for her."

Though scarcely taller than Ednetta, and much shorter than Anis Schutt, Marus Mudrick exuded an air of remarkable authority. He spoke intensely and with passion. His gestures were grandiloquent. His very soul seemed to quiver with heat. Several times Ednetta tried to draw breath to speak but stammered and fell silent, overcome by the man's personality.

He'd been sent to her by a "direct action of God," he said. To her, and to her daughter Sybilla.

As soon as he'd learned of the outrage that had befallen them, and of how Pascayne police were ignoring the case. And of the *white news boycott* of the case.

A fourteen-year-old black girl. Kidnapped, beaten and raped and left to die in that terrible place by white cops; and their superiors protecting the rapists; and the white-establishment media choking off all news pertaining to the rape.

Such was—almost—worse than murder. Nothing like this would be countenanced in any civilized society, in any true democracy but only in a *Nazi-racist state.*

Marus Mudrick was breathing quickly. His air of excited good news confused Ednetta for she felt responsible for it, and uneasy—why hadn't Reverend Denis warned her that she would be meeting Marus Mudrick! (She'd supposed it would be another of the dreary social-worker types with nappy hair, flat-heeled shoes, short-filed fingernails who'd been coming around for the past month.)

She'd dressed hurriedly to come to Reverend Denis's. At least, her clothes were decent—recent purchases, and not wrinkled: suede trousers tight at the waist, "fox"-fur jacket, V-neck tinsel sweater and around her neck the plain gold chain and cross she'd been wearing since age ten when her grandma Pearline had given it to her. And she'd had Chloe at the Jubilee Salon do her hair, that had been looking like a rat's nest for the past month. And on her feet, high-heeled shoes not those damn sneakers she'd been wearing because of her bunions. And makeup—*After Dark* lip-gloss.

The look that passed between them, Reverend Mudrick, and Ednetta Frye—like a match-flame, so quick.

The Reverend clearly thinking *Here is a beautiful woman where I was expecting a fat middle-age Mama.*

Ednetta was too distracted to ask Marus Mudrick how he'd heard about her daughter and her but Marus Mudrick explained that "evil news" travels fast and that he had his finger on the pulse of injustice suffered by blacks especially in the State of New Jersey where his Care Ministry was located. Soon as he'd heard of the outrage perpetrated upon Sybilla Frye, he'd contacted Reverend Denis who was one of his oldest and most trusted friends in the cause of black justice.

Now, Ednetta was truly feeling faint. Reverend Mudrick helped her to a chair, and pulled up a chair so close before her, their knees touched.

Marus Mudrick paused in his excited speech to tell Ednetta that he'd heard—from Reverend Denis—that Ednetta had a beautiful contralto singing voice—like Marian Anderson. He'd heard that Ednetta didn't sing with the church choir any longer—and that everyone missed her. *He* had a love for music, too—he'd begun singing solos in church as a little boy, in Virginia—the old gospels, hymns—he'd taken up the saxophone in high school—his great hero was Charlie Parker—but he hadn't much spirit for music any longer, in these turbulent times.

In the 1960s, the enemy assassinated black leaders. In the 1980s, the enemy was more insidious—"Like they sittin on our chests, cutting off our oxygen. One day you wake up and you ain't alive—you a zombie—but don't know it."

Seeing that Ednetta Frye was looking dazed—(this was an effect he often had upon women of a certain age)—Marus Mudrick said in a lowered voice, "You might not know, Mrs. Frye, but the original zombies were blacks—slave-blacks—in the Caribbean. They were poor innocents drugged, and buried alive, and made to believe they had died, then dug up by their cruel masters, and made to 'live'—that's to say, to work for the slave-master. So long as they thought they were dead—they *were dead*. But they worked—they had no other life except to work. In the old days, a zombie had no one to free him—but now, in 1987, a zombie has no excuse to remain enslaved."

Ednetta had never heard anyone speak more persuasively. She recalled Reverend Mudrick's impassioned sermons from the pulpit in the AME church—you went away convinced that Reverend Mudrick was right, though it was sometimes difficult to explain exactly what he'd said.

Now, Marus outlined his proposed "crusade" for Ednetta and her daughter as their "spiritual advisor." He would be working closely with his younger brother Byron, a noted civil rights attorney qualified to practice law in New Jersey, he said; he and Byron Mudrick had worked on many cases together. "We will begin by calling a press conference in Newark, as soon as possible, but no later than next Monday, and demanding an investigation into the Pascayne police department that has been 'derelict' and 'obfuscatory' in pursuing justice for your daughter. We may then move to the state capitol at Trenton where I have contacts in the legislature, and where I might petition to see the governor. As soon as you designate Byron as your 'legal counsel,' he will demand to see all pertinent records—Pascayne PD, the local ER. If the FBI has been on the case, seeing that this is a 'hate crime,' we will acquire their records, too. We will begin with an assault on the white enemy, and we will never let up."

Ednetta's heart was beating so quickly, she could barely draw breath. She could barely comprehend what the man was saying, only that he was speaking in an urgent, intimate manner to *her*.

This renowned black minister—this black *celebrity*—was addressing Ednetta Frye in a way no one had ever addressed Ednetta Frye in her entire life; even in her silly girlhood fantasies in which such celebrity-figures as Aretha Franklin, James Brown, Wilson Pickett, Diana Ross had addressed her. (Singing in her room, swaying in front of a mirror, and there came Diana Ross to invite Ednetta to join the

Supremes, to take the place of poor Florence Ballard—*It would mean giving up your Pascayne life, and touring with us. But you got the voice for it, Ednetta! And the looks.*)

"I want to meet your daughter, Mrs. Frye. Will you take me to her, now?"

"N-now?"

"Yes. I've come to Pascayne today, having canceled several important engagements, to speak to you, and to your daughter Sybilla. Will you take me to her, Sister Ednetta?"

Sister Ednetta! Ednetta felt a melting sensation in the region of her heart.

"Reverend Denis says you live close by, sister. I have a car—we can drive."

"But—they will kill us, Rev'nd Mudrick. The white cops—they threatened S'b'lla, and all her fam'ly—"

"But now, Marus Mudrick will protect you. No more 'they' to terrify black women—there is *Marus Mudrick.* Soon as they learn that I have taken up your cause, they will back off."

"Rev'end, I—I don't know where S'b'lla is . . ."

"You have heard of Joan of Arc? The French peasant girl who became a martyr, and a saint?"

Ednetta nodded, uncertain.

"'Joan of Arc'—just a young girl when the visions came to her, sent by God. Your daughter is—how old, Ednetta? Fourteen?"

"S'b'lla fifteen . . ."

"We will raise the consciousness of white America, through the exposure of what was done to Sybilla Frye—your daughter is a martyr now, but she will be a saint one day."

Ednetta nodded slowly. She felt the dazed lethargy of a creature mesmerized by a cobra—the handsome sleekly glistening head, the "piercing" eyes.

"But—S'b'lla say she don't want to talk about it, any more—S'b'lla a young girl, you know how they are . . ." Ednetta's voice trailed off weakly.

"Not only will you be protected from the white swine, and elevated above them in the consciousness of America, but you will be handsomely rewarded, Sister Ednetta. Sybilla's story—Sybilla's 'exclusive interviews'—lawsuits filed against the Pascayne Police Department, Passaic County, the district attorney's office—for failure to prosecute a crime and to protect a minor . . . Do you recall the march my associates and I led, in 1984, in Newark, protesting the police-murder of the black former Marine hero Tyrell Rourke on the Turnpike? We were 2,300 strong marching past phalanxes of the Gestapo, jeered-at, threatened by white racists, but we had our signs, and we had our protest songs, and we had God on our side—the black side of history. That march was on the front page of the *New York Times* and on every news channel in the region. And what do you think the Rourke family was offered in settlement from the State of New Jersey, Sister Ednetta?"

Marus Mudrick spoke so triumphantly, Ednetta feared that he would discover how little she knew of black history even during her own lifetime.

"The sum was two point five million dollars, Sister Ednetta. That was the overall settlement, to be divided among a number of individuals. But—two point five million. Think of it! Prior to this, most protest marches were 'disbanded' by the police—possibly, there were bottles and rocks thrown, and a few gunshots fired, and the police rushed in to 'quell the riot.' The State of New Jersey had to consider that the white racists were getting off easy, this time. And the gang rape of a fourteen-year-old black girl on her way home from school by 'white cops' in Passaic County in 1987, will be worth more, I predict."

Ednetta was feeling so dazed now, she had to clutch at Marus Mudrick's arm.

"But, Rev'end—S'b'lla say she never saw any *faces*. Or maybe just one—a 'yellow-hair' man—S'b'lla say he had a 'badge'—but she never saw it close up, you know? It was all like—S'b'lla say—some kind of nasty dream, you can't explain to another person."

"Which is why I need to speak with Sybilla, Sister Ednetta. This very day."

"But—I'm tryin to say—S'b'lla ain't . . ." Ednetta's voice trailed off weakly.

"We will broker Sybilla's interviews, and yours, Sister Ednetta, in this tri-state area: Newark, New York City, Philadelphia. Pascayne will be the hub. I promise, Sister Ednetta—your life will be trans-formed, in a way you could never have imagined."

In his sonorous, sibilant voice Reverend Mudrick spoke. It seemed to Ednetta that he hadn't heard a single word she'd said.

In desperation she looked to white-haired Reverend Denis, sitting close by, his hands clasped over his belly, eyelids shut as if he were lightly dozing. Ednetta wondered if her pastor, too, had fallen under the spell of Marus Mudrick's mesmerizing speech.

"'Scuse me Rev'end Denis, what you thinkin? You think S'b'lla is up to this—talkin to people? Being 'interviewed' . . ."

Slowly, gravely Reverend Denis shook his head. It wasn't clear if he meant *no,* or if he was admitting to having no idea.

"My baby S'b'lla—she ain't—ain't always—ain't what you'd call a girl who obeys her mother, see, Rev'end Mudrick? She, like, 'headstrong'—how she got herself in this nasty situation, prob'ly . . ."

"I will talk with Sybilla, and we will move forward. Next Monday at the latest, we will call a press conference at my headquarters in Newark. I insist that—"

But abruptly Ednetta was on her feet. Damn weak-ankled in these high-heeled shoes with a tiny strap, the very shoes of vanity her heart accused her, *faux crocodile skin*. Sybilla had tried them on jamming her big feet in the high heels as she's jeering *Shit Mama, these shoes too sexy for some old lady like you.*

Ednetta stammered: "I'm just rememberin—my grandma, she needs me to drop by the house. She feelin poorly an she needs me *now*. Some other time, Rev'end Mudrick, we c'n talk—maybe . . . Right now, 'scuse me, Rev'end Denis, Rev'end Mudrick, I'm havin to leave."

Before Marus Mudrick could protest, and snatch up her icy-stricken hands in his, Ednetta stumbled out of the room.

"Sister Ednetta! My dear, *wait*."

But she fled! Fled Reverend Mudrick!

Astonished, the minister in the three-piece dark-wool suit stood in the doorway of Reverend Denis's house, calling after Ednetta. She could imagine his bright eyes snapping in alarm, and in rage. She could imagine his fingers twitching with an urge to catch hold of her, and haul her back inside the house. For Ednetta knew men well: you did not ever cross even the weakest of them, and Marus Mudrick was of the strongest.

But it was the only way, the way of desperation, and fear and shame—to walk out of the room breaking the spell of the man's eyes not daring a backward glance.

The Temptation

L ike to escaped with my life. Jesus!"
        She was laughing telling whoever she met. Whoever
came by the house. Even Anis Schutt, she'd debated telling.
*You know Rev'end Marus Mudrick? He come to Pasc'n to meet with me spe-
cially today.*

But no, Ednetta knew better than to tell Anis Schutt.

Anything of her private life, her private-womanly-life, she'd never
have told Anis Schutt or any damn man.

Martyr. Saint. Joan of Arc.

   Sister Ednetta. Will protect you.

Could not sleep for hearing the man's velvety words! With Anis
snoring and snuffling beside her yet she heard the other's voice like
the very voice of Jesus.

In her veins flowed something molten-hot, behind her eyelids her seared and blinded eyes filled with tears of such emotion, Ednetta could not have said if it was excitement, or fear, or simple gratitude she was feeling like when Jesus touches you to raise you from the dead, returns the breath to you like Jairus's daughter you would not doubt Jesus but fall to your knees weeping *Jesus thank you for my life O Jesus thank you for my life restored to me.*

Never had Ednetta met anyone like Marus Mudrick. Her soul felt ravaged, slaked. Like Anis Schutt that first time when Anis had been young, and Ednetta had been young, delicate and succulent as a newly ripened peach, which had not been, Ednetta thought, for a long time now.

Black justice. Two point five million.

The Seduction

Doorbell, and Ednetta in her chenille robe peering to see who the hell it was.

"Ma'am? Is this 'Sister Ednetta Frye'?"

Sister! Blindly Ednetta took the pen from the delivery man's fingers, and signed the receipt.

Blindly signed, and blindly stumbled into the kitchen with a bouquet of one dozen long-stemmed bloodred roses in her arms *from your friend & protector Reverend Marus C. Mudrick.*

"Jesus, Mama! They be bringing that shit to the wrong house, an you gon have to pay for it!"—Sybilla laughed.

Ednetta was feeling too faint to argue with the girl. Just too—too faint—and her heart pounding so hard—it was easier to set the delicate flowers in the sink and search for a vase while Sybilla jeered and mocked as if the sight of the roses was frightening to her, too.

"Got to be the first time anybody sent flowers *here*."

Seeing her mother's stricken smile, and the way Ednetta slumped into a chair as if her legs had given way beneath her, Sybilla quieted and searched for the card, that had fallen into the sink.

"Mama, who the fuck's this—'Reverend Marus C. Mudrick.' Ain't that some famous name like 'Martin Luther King'?"

Ednetta shook her head *yes*.

"What's some famous rev'end want with you, Mama?"

"Not me, S'b'lla. *You.*"

She was determined to say *no*. Yet somehow, she said *yes*.

Sybilla had said *no! Fucking no, Mama*. Yet somehow, Sybilla too said *yes*.

Arrangements were made for Ednetta Frye and her daughter Sybilla to be brought by limousine to the headquarters of the Care Ministry of Central New Jersey, on Fort Street, Newark. A Lincoln Town Car, shiny-black as a hearse, driven by a uniformed driver, bore the apprehensive mother and daughter dressed as for Sunday church services to what had been a private home, a red-brick Federalist town house, in a once-exclusive neighborhood of Newark now mostly small businesses, medical offices, and churches in need of renovation.

In the Care Ministry, Ednetta and Sybilla were seated in Reverend Mudrick's outer office which was staffed by young light-skinned black women so attractive, so stylishly dressed, personable as TV anchors, both mother and daughter stared in abashed silence. The outer office appeared to have been a dining room at one time: the white ceiling was high, and ornately molded; there was a single crystal chandelier, and an elegant marble floor, just slightly begrimed but impressive. A curved staircase led to the second floor—very likely, the Reverend's private quarters. Prominent on the walls were dozens of framed photographs at which Ednetta and Sybilla stared in amazement: there, at various stages of his life, and always smiling broadly, was Reverend Marus Mudrick with Charlie Parker ("Harlem, 1954"), Mahalia Jackson ("Harlem, 1957"), Jackie Robinson ("NYC, 1963"), Reverend Martin Luther King Jr. ("Alabama State Capitol 1964"), U.S. Congressman Adam Clayton Powell ("Washington, D.C., 1965"), Reverend Jesse Jackson ("Newark, 1969"), Aretha Franklin ("Harlem, 1974"), Muhammad Ali ("NYC, 1977"), New Jersey governor Brendan Byrne ("Trenton, 1980"), Sammy Davis Jr. ("Las Vegas, 1982"), James Brown ("Newark, 1983"), Diana Ross ("NYC, 1984"), former president Jimmy Carter ("NYC, 1985"), Bill Cosby ("NYC, 1985"), Tina Turner ("NYC, 1986"), Michael Jackson ("Newark, 1986"), Whitney Houston ("LA, 1987") . . . Sybilla had gone to stand before the more recent of these, whispering to Ednetta: "Ohh Mama, look here—Whitn'y Houst'n? Michael *Jack*son? Jesus."

Also prominent in the Reverend's outer office were plaques and medallions commemorating "New Jersey Citizen of the Year Reverend Marus Mudrick"—"New Jersey Black Outreach Honor Roll Reverend Marus Mudrick"—"New Jersey Hall of Fame Reverend Marus Mudrick"—as well as a number of framed honorary doctorate diplomas from Rutgers-Newark, Rutgers-Camden, Trenton State, Stockton State, Bloomfield College, and Howard University.

"Mama, I'm scared. What's this Rev'end want with *us*?"

Ednetta took Sybilla's hand which was icy-cold and seemed small to her, a child's hand.

"Honey, I got some idea. We gon be all right."

After forty suspenseful minutes, one of the smiling young women escorted Ednetta and Sybilla into Reverend Mudrick's office. At once the Reverend came to them to take their hands, each in turn. For a portly man he was light on his feet, nimble as a boxer. His smile was quick and dazzling-white with the most subtle hint of a gold filling in an upper incisor. A pungent scent wafted from his oiled hair. "Sister Ednetta! So good to see you again." And there was Sybilla looking very young and dazed. "And this is—Sybilla? 'The little lady who will start a great war'—we hope!"

Side by side mother and daughter were seated facing Reverend Mudrick across the expanse of his gleaming mahogany desk. Abashed and mostly silent for the better part of the next hour they listened to the Reverend speak. He began—quietly—by explaining that black women were "race victims"—"potential prey" for white men—"all black women, at all times." During slave-times, black females were the actual possessions of white masters, and their "white-bastard spawn" were possessions; these white "masters" still existed in America. Where there were whites, there were masters.

"You, Sybilla, are a race victim, a martyr, and a sacrifice. But you will be our saint—our Joan of Arc."

Sybilla licked her lips, uncertain how to reply. Martyr? Sacrifice? Saint? She had heard of Joan of Arc, but vaguely.

"What was done to you, Sister Sybilla, was an unspeakable crime. And that is the issue—it is *unspeakable* by the white press, the white cops, the white politicians, the *whited sepulcher*. But that which is *unspeakable* by the white enemy is *speakable* by us. That is my mission, Sister Sybilla—Sister Ednetta. That is why I have brought you to the Care Ministry today."

Enthralled and intimidated by these words which were both matter-of-fact and beautifully modulated, like speech you might hear from the pulpit, or on TV, mother and daughter sat scarcely breathing.

Marus Mudrick's desk was the largest desk either Ednetta or Sybilla had ever seen, and made of the most elegant wood; it was piled with important-looking letters, papers, documents. Even the phone was unusual—a black phone, but trimmed in gold. In a corner of the room was an American flag on an eight-foot pole, hanging at half-mast; on the walls more photographs and diplomas.

"You are wondering why the flag is at half-mast, Sister Ednetta and Sister Sybilla? It is at half-mast *in perpetuity*—to commemorate the thousands of lynched black men and women in the history of the United States—the *unspoken history*. What was done to you, Sister Sybilla, is a kind of *lynching*—except you have lived to name your accusers, and to see justice done." Marus Mudrick paused, seeing that his listeners were rapt with—was it awe of him? shyness of him, who represented to them a way of being, even of speaking, utterly foreign to them?—or was it female unease, anxiety, in the presence of a dominant male?

"When you are unjustly and cruelly treated, your instinct is to retreat—to 'turn the other cheek'; but such an instinct is contrary to God's plan for the black people. Jesus said, 'I bring not peace but a sword'—this is the Jesus to which the black people must cling. Our martyred brother Reverend King knew, as Gandhi knew, that you cannot meet force with force when the oppressor will slay you—your strategy must be a different way, that of passivity, strategic 'nonviolence.' This was not an ideal situation for many civil rights activists who were murdered or beaten in the South in the early days of the crusade—but there was the 'Dream'—and it came to be, in time. 'We shall overcome'—and we did, to a degree. But you cannot confront an enemy like Hitler with 'passivity'—'non-violence'—such a man will destroy you. Strategies must be modulated, to meet changing situations. The 1960s were a time of struggle that is—in some quarters—past; in 1987, in confronting the enemy, we will use a different strategy. Yes—one day soon we may march—we may 'demonstrate' in the streets—but initially, we will use white weapons against the white enemy—the *media*."

A poisonous merriment shone in Marus Mudrick's eyes. Ednetta could not have named it but was thrilled to see it. She clutched at

Sybilla's icy-cold hand to comfort the girl. How touchingly small the hand felt to her. *Her child!*

As the Reverend continued to speak, his voice grew louder by degrees, and more declamatory; you could hear the preacherly cadences, with a faint trace of a Virginia accent, beneath the percussive rapid-fire New Jersey accent.

"Sister Ednetta, and Sister Sybilla—know this: whites were livin in caves, when the black race built empires. The ancient world was ours. Out of the bowels of Africa—our empires. Philosophy, math, astrology—before Socrates and the Greek queers, we had taught these. We had discovered and refined these. All of the arts—painting and sculpture, speech, music—music be our special gift, all the world know that!—the black race originated, and the paler races replicated. This is plain-fact history—you aint gon find in any white-folks history book!"

Ednetta said hesitantly, "*I* heard this. Yessir."

"In this campaign for justice, Reverend Marus Mudrick vows that he will extract victory from the jaws of humiliation and defeat, and he will protect both the mother and the daughter from further harm by the white rapists. He will raise you to a level far beyond anything you know—you will no longer be martyrs but *saints*. Tell me, Sister Sybilla, what was done to you, exactly as you recall."

Ednetta, holding Sybilla's hand, felt her daughter flinch as if she'd been slapped.

Sybilla turned to Ednetta like a little girl, hiding her face in Mama's neck. Whispering *Mama no, I can't.*

Though Reverend Mudrick urged Sybilla to speak, gently, without a hint of impatience, Sybilla cringed against her mother, and would not even look at him.

Reverend Mudrick exchanged a glance with Ednetta. Curtly the

Reverend nodded, and frowned. "Sister Ednetta, tell your daughter please speak."

But Sybilla refused. Now turned awkwardly in her seat, hiding against her mother who was trying both to comfort her, and to urge her to answer Marus Mudrick. But Sybilla only just wept *Mama no! Don't make me, Mama.*

Ednetta said, apologetically, "Rev'end, I tried to tell you—my girl been hurt bad, an in her mind she have bad dreams and memories—we was hopin they would heal, an go away. Tried to explain—"

"Yes, but you are here now in the office of the Care Ministry of Central New Jersey, as others have failed you and will fail you. And we are deliberating strategy, Sister Ednetta. There is no doubt in my mind—in my soul—that we are going forward with this campaign. We are not going backward, we are not admitting defeat. You will cooperate with us—for the sake of black liberation. Each black individual has a 'small' destiny, and a 'large' destiny. The one is just the personal life but the other is the life of the race—where you matter to your race. In some of us, the small, personal life is sacrificed to the larger life—Jackie Robinson, for instance, 'integrating' Major League Baseball—the courage of that great man!—enduring years of abuse from the most ignorant vicious brayin racists who'd have lynched him if they could've got to him. *There* was a great man, and a great black man—for Robinson, the sacrifice was not in vain but an alteration of history. For your daughter, the sacrifice will not be in vain—I am certain. The fact is, Sybilla Frye was kidnapped, raped, beaten and left to die by white police officers in early October of this year, when she was fourteen years old and returning home from school—that is the essence of the terrible crime, Sister Ednetta—yes?"

Ednetta, hugging Sybilla, pressing her face against the girl's hair, shuddered. It wasn't clear that she'd heard Reverend Mudrick's question. Mother and daughter huddled together as if very cold.

"Sister Ednetta? The accusation is a true one, is it not?"

Ednetta, not meeting Reverend Mudrick's eye, nodded *yes*.

Adding then, still not meeting the man's eye, that Sybilla was fifteen, not fourteen.

"In the simplest terms: the black girl was attacked by white cops. Yes?"

Hesitantly, Ednetta nodded *yes*.

"There have been no arrests, and hardly any investigation by the Pascayne police, or by any law enforcement officers?"

Ednetta nodded *yes*.

"No coverage of the case in the local media. In any media."

Ednetta nodded *yes*.

"But there are medical records? At the Pascayne ER?"

Ednetta nodded *yes*.

Reverend Mudrick contemplated the mother and daughter before him for several seconds, brooding and silent. Ednetta was uneasily aware of the man's attention, and did not dare to lift her eyes to his.

He don't believe us! He will let us go.

But then, Reverend Mudrick drew in a deep breath. Ednetta dared to glance up at him, and saw that he was smiling.

How handsome Marus Mudrick was! Especially when he smiled, and you felt his approval, his manly affection, sweeping over *you*.

A warm melting submissive sensation. Like kneeling to take Jesus into your heart—you didn't know you would do it, you didn't want to do it, the risk of ruining stockings if you knelt on the church floor, but then suddenly a sensation like weeping rose in your chest, into your throat, you began to bawl, you were on your knees bawling to Jesus to come into your heart.

In a kindly voice Reverend Mudrick was saying, as if something had been decided: "Dear Sister Ednetta! And dear Sister Sybilla! My brother Byron—the revered civil rights attorney-at-law Byron

Mudrick—will work with me on this crusade for justice. Next time we meet, Byron will have some questions for you. If Sybilla doesn't care to discuss this traumatic incident, she will not be obliged to. We are here to protect, not intimidate. All questions I need answered I can ask *you,* Sister Ednetta. That will be sufficient. I promise to shield you and your daughter from harm—we will control all access to Sybilla—as she is a minor, as well as a rape victim, it is not up to her to be interrogated; she will not be required to answer police questions, to 'testify,' or 'swear on a Bible'—that white-folks shit they use to intimidate us. It will be the *court of public opinion* we gon apply to, not the Nazi-racist-swine court that ain't gon give a black man justice unless it is dragged out of his white-honky ass." With the timing of a TV comedian the Reverend slurred these last words, in comic-black-menace dialect. Ednetta was too startled to respond but Sybilla, huddling in her arms, laughed.

"There will be media 'interest'—requests for interviews—many people wanting to purchase your story—both your stories. The mother's story in such a case is almost as interesting as the victim's story—you will see. We will be discreet about this. We will look before we leap. We will *not leap.* The kind of white folks we gon appeal to is likin to punish white folks—not themselves—but other white folks. The feeling is, white folks want to think they are 'friends of the Negro'—while they neighbors are racist cracker-swine. Jews the most like this, they anxious they ain't 'hundred-percent *white.*'" Reverend Mudrick laughed heartily now, seeing the look of bafflement in Ednetta Frye's face.

It seemed that the Reverend had a document for them to sign— "Not a contract per se but a 'letter of agreement' drawn up by my brother Byron. Before you leave, Sister Ednetta, and Sister Sybilla, I will ask you to sign this—here is a pen . . . I'll call in my assistant to witness our signatures."

Ednetta took the contract from the Reverend's fingers and looked at it warily.

"As your daughter is a minor, Sister Ednetta, you will sign beside her name as her guardian, as well as by your own name. D'you see?"

"Yes . . ."

"The 'letter of agreement' is a formality only. It addresses the issue of 'exclusivity'—that, so long as Reverend Marus Mudrick and Attorney-at-Law Byron Mudrick are your representatives, you will not engage with any other 'representatives'; and you will follow our strategy at all times."

Sybilla burrowed deeper into Ednetta's embrace. "Mama! What'm I spost to do?"

"You will do only as you are told," Marus Mudrick said in his kindly voice, as if he were speaking to a small child and not a big girl of fifteen as tall as her mother. "You will not need to make decisions, ever: I will make them. My brother Byron will be your 'legal counsel.' If it's required for anyone to talk to the police, or prosecutors, or the media—Byron and I will talk to them. Your mother will give your statement to me, and we will work on it. We will perfect it. The 'kidnapping'—'inside the police van'—the 'white cops'—what they did to you, and how many times; how long you were kept captive, and where you were found; the injuries you sustained, which are in the medical files at the hospital ER. We will practice your statement until you have memorized it and you will not ever have to re-think it, or re-word it, Sister Sybilla. That is my promise."

Sybilla fretted licking her lips. She had the look of one who is gazing into a blinding light, trying bravely not to flinch.

"If you'd rather not speak directly of the rape even to your mother, that will be honored. You are a young, shy girl—you are a virginal girl—except for this rape. In your soul, you are *virginal*. You can write down what happened to you—as you did with the Pascayne police.

The fewer words, the better. The simpler our message, the more effective. It is not expected that the surviving child-victim of a violent sexual assault will remember ev'y least little detail of that assault. We will swear by your words. We will not ever let you be 'questioned' or 'interrogated' by any police officer or prosecutor except we are right beside you, and you are not obliged to reply in any case. You are a minor, and you are exempt from many laws that pertain to adults. You are your mother's child, and Ednetta Frye is your guardian. And Reverend Marus Mudrick is your spiritual counsel, and Byron Mudrick is your legal counsel."

Ednetta was glancing distractedly through the document, which was a single page of several paragraphs. A surprise to see her name at the bottom—*Ednetta Frye*. Beside this, Ednetta signed her name.

Sybilla fumbled the pen signing beside her name, dropped the pen and had to snatch it up, with a wild little laugh.

"Like signin for a record, Mama! Like this my first 'hit-single.'"

As he was about to escort Ednetta and Sybilla from his office, Reverend Mudrick said, "This is for you, Sister Ednetta, and for your daughter Sybilla. It is a gesture of my faith in our cause and a prophecy of what lies ahead for you."

Counting out ten one-hundred-dollar bills into Ednetta Frye's quivering hand.

The Crusade

*B*lack girl, white cops, kidnap, rape, assault & left to die.

Quickly then it became a poem. An incantation. These few words uttered again, again and again.

"There's this 'Occam Razor'—he say how the simplest you can make things, the more effective they be. More urgent the sound, the more it will be heard. And the angrier the voice, the more emotion it will arouse."

In the final, tense two weeks of a trial of eight-months' duration—a class action suit brought against the Passaic County Board of Education on behalf of a number of African-American custodial employees claiming to have been wrongfully dismissed from their jobs in the years 1978 to 1985—he hadn't had time for more than cursory research into the Sybilla Frye case. He'd made a few telephone calls to contacts in Pascayne, he'd questioned a few potential witnesses, but he hadn't yet spoken with Ednetta Frye face-to-face, nor had he spoken with Sybilla Frye even on the phone; he was working approximately ninety hours a week, and he was exhausted, but hopeful, for the lawsuit would be adjudicated soon, and the long effort would be over. *And the plaintiffs would win. And the settlement, though not large, would constitute a great moral victory.* Byron Mudrick would burst into tears in the courtroom, and his clients would embrace him.

Hope is a stimulant. His heart raced with hope. But hope can cloud judgment, as he should have known by now. He was forty-three, not a young man.

He'd taken a deep breath. He'd gripped his brother Marus's arm at the elbow as if to steady Marus, or himself. For Marus had been speaking passionately about the Frye girl—what had been done to her, how she and her mother had been traumatized by the assault, how dazed and helpless they were, like victims of war. Byron had often seen his brother in elated, excitable moods, but he'd rarely seen him so moved—genuinely moved, Byron thought.

He'd brought his face close to his brother's face, regarding him searchingly. The eyes of twin brothers, each peering into the soul of the other.

Byron was thinking *But he has deceived you in the past. He has begged forgiveness, but he has deceived you. Why would you believe him now?*

(It was true: Byron had been shocked to learn, belatedly, that his preacher-brother Marus Mudrick had been an FBI informant in the late 1960s and early 1970s. Marus had been an *anti-Communist informant* relaying confidential information about the Nation of Islam, the Black Panthers, Malcolm X, Stokely Carmichael, Howard University anti–Vietnam War protesters, and others, to the FBI; he'd told Byron defensively that he was an American citizen as well as a black man, and he wasn't ashamed of it. And Byron had said, incredulously *But you informed on our brothers, our black brothers* and Marus said *We are all brothers in Jesus. We are Christians before we are black but the Nation of Islam is not Christian. We hate and abhor godless communism.* It had not seemed to Byron that his brother was speaking coherently or honestly but in the end, he'd forgiven Marus. But he had not forgotten.)

Yet now, Byron was weakening. Marus had shown him a photograph of Sybilla Frye, who looked younger than fifteen, with swollen and discolored eyes and mouth, creased forehead. This was a child who'd been kidnapped by "white cops" and held captive for several days, raped repeatedly, and beaten. Dog feces had been rubbed into her hair and onto her body and racist epithets had been scrawled on her body. She'd been hog-tied and left in the filthy cellar of a boarded-up factory on the Pascayne waterfront and only through the accidental discovery by a neighbor had her life been saved. In a voice that trembled with indignation Marus said *This is a lynching in which the victim has been let live, that her humiliation and shame will endure through her life.*

Byron felt a sensation of vertigo as if he were crossing a narrow board above an abyss. For he had daughters, of whom the oldest was sixteen and the youngest eleven. He adored and feared for his daughters in this world that, for all the gains of the past two decades, was yet a vicious, racist world. He'd spent much of his legal career dealing with the consequences of racism—direct racism, indirect racism (where the victims of racism harm one another as tortured or starving animals might harm one another, being unable to reach the source of their misery). He'd represented countless individuals who'd been mistreated by white cops—the least of their problems had been false arrest. He knew how cops—some, not all—but a sizable some—treated poor women of color who were helpless against them. The thought of his daughters being subjected to such horror made him feel—literally—sick.

He asked Marus simply: did Marus believe the girl?

Marus said *Yes. Yes* he did believe.

Still Byron gripped his brother by the elbow. Here was the "elder"—larger—Mudrick brother Marus with his smooth handsome face, the fattish dignity of a Buddha. Byron leaned close to Marus in a way that only an intimate might do, peering into his brother's eyes.

You are sure, Marus?

Yes. She is telling the truth, and I am sure.

Byron regarded his brother for a long moment, then decided to believe him.

"We movin forward now. We ain't never movin *back*."

The Mudrick brothers were not strangers to righteous crusades. But rarely had they joined forces as they would in the crusade for justice for Sybilla Frye.

"My brother Byron with us now, an his staff workin with mine, we will have an *army*."

The sexually abused Sybilla Frye had been so traumatized, she was near-mute in public. Only her mother could communicate with her. Though sometimes, at his specially convened news conferences, Reverend Mudrick would approach the girl and address her in a kindly, lowered voice, and elicit from her timid responses that signaled *Yes* or *No*.

The first news conference of the Crusade for Justice for Sybilla Frye was held at Care Ministry of Central New Jersey headquarters on Fort Street, Newark, on November 11, 1987. Rows of chairs had been set up to accommodate 150 individuals who'd been invited by the Reverend's staff, of whom forty-two came: journalists who worked for newspapers and news services, and journalists who called themselves "freelance"; writers of whom some were published, and some were not; academics associated with Afro-American Studies departments in the Newark area; civil rights activists and associates of varying ages; a scattering of social workers, welfare workers, lawyers and paralegals, law students from Byron Mudrick's classes at Rutgers-Newark Law School. Gazing out over the small but rapt audience, which was almost exclusively black and about equally divided between male and female, Reverend Mudrick cried: "Welcome, sisters! Welcome, brothers! You are blessed by the Lord: you will find yourselves at the fulcrum of history, by answering my heartfelt appeal on behalf of a martyred Christian black girl."

As the harrowing story of Sybilla Frye was revealed to the public for the first time, Ednetta Frye and her daughter Sybilla appeared stiff with fear, or anxiety; at Reverend Mudrick's insistence they were seated just behind and to the left of the podium at which Reverend Mudrick stood to speak. Mrs. Frye was perceived to be an attractive black woman in her early forties, who looked as if she'd been through an emotional ordeal; her gaze was downcast and she was dressed in the dark, somber clothing of a mourner, with a skirt that fell nearly to her ankles, and black leather pumps with a low heel. Around her neck was a small gold cross on a chain. Close beside her, so that the two could grip hands, sat Sybilla Frye, who wore schoolgirl clothes—dark pleated skirt, white cotton long-sleeved blouse, white socks, prim little patent leather shoes. Sybilla's hair had been fashioned into pigtails: she looked much younger than fifteen. Her face no longer bore obvious marks of the beating she'd received several weeks before but when she was observed walking she carried herself like one who anticipates pain in her back, hips, and legs.

Sybilla, too, wore a little gold cross on a chain around her neck.

To the right, rear of the podium sat Byron Mudrick, known also to most of the individuals in the room. To some, Dr. Mudrick was their mentor, their professor. Small of stature, yet stern-faced, he resembled the more flamboyant Marus Mudrick like a younger, less consequential but staunchly loyal brother.

Reverend Mudrick wore one of his custom-made dark three-piece suits, with an elegant silver silk necktie and a gold watch chain across his vest. His oily, dense hair had been freshly barbered. His gold-rimmed eyeglasses shone. Those who were familiar with Marus Mudrick's sermons and public addresses were not surprised that the Reverend began speaking so very softly, individuals at the back of the room could barely hear him; by degrees, his beautifully modulated voice that was a subtle blend of New Jersey and Virginia would rise, gain strength, fill every corner of the room. Outrage was Reverend Mudrick's highly combustible fuel—stoking the outrage of his listeners. In a voice quavering with emotion he described the "Nazi-racist white atrocity" that had been perpetrated upon the "black child Sybilla, on her way home from school" in Pascayne, New Jersey, just the previous month, that had never been reported in any newspaper or on any news program: "A shameless 'whitewash'—'white boycott.' A 'gag-rule' from on high, some are sayin the governor of New Jersey conspirin with the Pascayne police chief an head of the state police."

In Pentecostal tones, fierce, then subdued, then again fierce, and again subdued, with grandiloquent gestures of his beringed hands, and tears brimming conspicuously in his large, alert eyes, Reverend Marus Mudrick continued to shock and outrage his audience, as Sybilla Frye hid her face in her hands, weeping, and Mrs. Frye comforted her, as one might comfort a young child. All eyes in the room were riveted on the Fryes—the loving and protective mother, the stricken and abused daughter.

In the audience were several photographers who'd been encouraged to take photographs when they wished. If it seemed surprising to some observers that a child-rape victim was to be so publicly identified, and openly photographed, no one remarked upon it, or protested.

"That which has been *concealed,* will now be *revealed.*"

Often it happened at Reverend Mudrick's news conferences that Ednetta Frye would have to comfort her weeping daughter, as Marus Mudrick spoke in his ever-escalating, stormy and impassioned voice; sometimes, both mother and daughter broke down, and had to be escorted from the room as audiences stared in rapt silence.

"My sisters and brothers, you seein brave people here—Sybilla Frye an her mother Ednetta Frye darin to come forward to charge their accusers an not hidin away like the 'white cops' been expectin these black sisters to do—under threat of death not just to them but their family. Jesus watchin over them—but they need our prayers! They needin all the help we can give them."

Within hours of the first press conference, word began to spread of the abused black girl in Pascayne: the Care Ministry was flooded with calls, answered by Reverend Mudrick's staff who directed callers to the Pascayne Police Department and the *Pascayne Journal,* as well as soliciting donations to the Crusade for Justice for Sybilla Frye; in time, callers were also directed to the mayor of Pascayne, local New Jersey state congressmen and U.S. congressmen, U.S. senators, the govenor of New Jersey. Angry and incredulous callers were urged to walk into Pascayne police headquarters and demand justice for Sybilla Frye, and to "ply" the media with appeals for justice.

Soon then, brief articles on *Sybilla Frye* began to appear in the press and on TV. In a few, photographs of Reverend Marus Mudrick and the Fryes began to appear.

The first news item in a major, white publication was in the Newark *Star-Ledger* on November 15, 1987; though on page six of the Metropolitan section the article was beneath a striking headline—

ABDUCTION, RAPE CHARGES MADE AGAINST
UNIDENTIFIED PASCAYNE POLICE OFFICERS

The Newark *Star-Ledger* was the preeminent daily newspaper in New Jersey, one of a chain of papers that included the Trenton *Times,* in which a similar article appeared on November 16, on page three of the first section.

On November 18, Reverend Mudrick scheduled a second news conference, this time in an auditorium at Rutgers-Newark Law School, which had been secured by Byron Mudrick. To this conference came an unexpected number of persons, estimated to be as many as three hundred; predominantly black, yet including a number of white-skinned individuals as well, many from out of town. Black publications like the *Chicago Messenger, Black Digest,* and *Essence* were represented by more than one reporter each. As many as a dozen photographers arrived, as well as TV news reporters and camera crews from local New Jersey stations, to whom Reverend Marus Mudrick willingly gave interviews.

At last the *Pascayne Journal* published its first story on the subject beneath a headline on page three of the first section: "Pascayne PD Denies 'Groundless' Charges in Alleged Rape." The Newark *Star-Ledger* and the Trenton *Times,* as well as other Jersey papers, featured articles titled "The Crusade for Justice for Sybilla Frye"—"Cover-up Charged by Reverend Marus Mudrick in Alleged Rape Case"—"The Mysterious Case of 'Sybilla Frye,' Pascayne, NJ."

In all of these articles, Reverend Marus Mudrick, identified as an African-American Episcopal minister and a civil rights activist, a "former aide" of Reverend Martin Luther King Jr., was quoted, at length. In some articles, "Civil Rights Activist-Attorney" Byron Mudrick was also quoted.

Neither Ednetta Frye nor Sybilla Frye was quoted in the press, for both were inaccessible to journalists.

The Pascayne Police Department was flooded with calls. Reporters arrived at police headquarters and at the Red Rock precinct. There were roaming photographers. TV news reporters appeared with camera crews, stationed on the street and causing traffic jams. Initially these were local New Jersey stations, then they were network affiliates of NBC, CBS, ABC. Pascayne patrol officers were approached on the street by reporters before they'd been informed who "Sybilla Frye" and "Marus Mudrick" were. Reporters and photographers for the Associated Press, the United Press, *USA Today* arrived. There was a frantic search for Sybilla Frye and her mother Ednetta, but canny Marus Mudrick had made arrangements for them to stay with friends of Reverend Denis in another area of the city; eventually, Ednetta and Sybilla would be moved several times, as Marus Mudrick said for their "protection."

Photographs were taken of the Frye residence in the weatherworn brownstone at 939 Third Street. Photographs were taken of the derelict Jersey Foods factory from the outside, and inside the dim-lit cellar. If there'd been a "crime scene," this scene was thoroughly trampled.

Then, a great leap to the front page of the tabloid *New York Post:* "Black Minister Charges Cover-up in Pascayne, NJ, Race-Rape Case."

After a cautious interlude, quick in the aftermath of the *Post* the *New York Times* began to report, initially on an inside page in the city news section, then on the lower-left front page.

"Man, this crossin the Rub'icon! Crossin the Hudson! We in the *New York Times* now! An this just the beginning."

To his staff, Marus Mudrick appeared jubilant. And on the phone speaking with "Sister Ednetta" (who never saw a newspaper but watched TV news and listened to the radio through the day) he was triumphant. To his brother Byron, Marus appeared slightly dazed, like a man who has had too much to drink, too quickly.

"They believin the girl—lib'ral white folks? Jews the kind sure don't want to be *racists* like the redneck crackers." Marus's jowls shook with laughter.

They were in Marus's inner office at the Care Ministry. Telephones had been ringing through the day. Reporters were even now waiting out on Fort Street. Reverend Marus Mudrick was to be interviewed in the morning on NJN-TV—New Jersey Network—and later in the day, by a reporter for the Trenton *Times*. Byron said: "They should believe her. It's got nothing to do with 'Jews.' The girl is telling the stark, terrible truth." He'd studied the articles in the *New York Times* with a stab of something like shock, dismay. It was astonishing to him—the "Crusade for Justice for Sybilla Frye" had made the priceless front page of the great newspaper that, for the many years Byron Mudrick had labored in civil rights litigation, for the many brilliant but hard-won cases he'd fought for his clients, for all the doubts, despair, misery and self-disgust he'd had to endure, had steadfastly ignored him.

"Until now, man. Now, them New York Jews gon chase after *New Jersey niggers*."

"Nazi-Racist Swine"

Black girl, white cops, kidnap, rape, assault & left to die.
White cover-up, Pascayne police, Nazi-racist swine.

Calls had come for her at the precinct. Calls were routed to her. A trickle at first, and then a flood. Reporters, TV people wanting quotes, interviews with Detective Ines Iglesias who'd been identified as the only Pascayne police officer who'd spoken with Sybilla Frye and her mother Ednetta.

And was this because, Detective Iglesias, you are a woman, and you are of an "ethnic minority"?

And what can you tell us of the progress of the investigation? Have you identified the "white cops" in your department who are accused of having kidnapped, raped, nearly beaten to death the fifteen-year-old African-American victim?

———

"Yes, I am Detective Ines Iglesias. I am the Pascayne PD officer assigned to the 'Sybilla Frye' case."

She'd been the investigating officer, she would bear the brunt of the blame.

She knew, her fellow officers spoke meanly of her. Maybe not the women—the few women . . . But the men, yes.

Iglesias was the sacrifice, was she? The detective burdened with an impossible case and (unspoken) task of exonerating the Pascayne PD.

It was no secret, the Lieutenant disliked her. When he happened to see her, in the precinct house. Passing on the stairs, in the parking lot. The man's flushed skin, bulldog mouth, furious eyes. *Blame the female. Ethnic minority hire.*

She wanted to protest—the investigation is continuing.

She wanted to protest—but you assigned me!

When she'd been a new hire on the force, this Lieutenant had seemed to like her. A lot.

She'd been smiling and friendly but not *in that way.* The Lieutenant was a veteran of the Pascayne PD, with a not-smooth history of dealing with "ethnic minorities" and he'd tried to make an impression on Ines Inglesias and when fairly quickly he'd understood that she wasn't interested in him *in that way* his manner toward her changed—not mean, not nasty, but matter-of-fact, impersonal-professional. He'd been genial enough, even courteous to Iglesias, at least to her face; obviously, he had not sabotaged her promotion to detective.

But all that was changed, now. Since Sybilla Frye.

That first call. A rock thrown through a window of her life.

It had come to Iglesias, at home. In that dead time-lull after she'd returned from the precinct and changed into a sweatshirt, jeans, sneakers but before she'd prepared a meal and had her first glass of wine of the day while watching TV; as, later, she would lie in bed and read until she couldn't keep her eyes open any longer, a book from the local library, often a novel by a woman writer frequently but not exclusively Hispanic-American. And so utterly unprepared she'd answered the phone with what would seem to her in retrospect a naïve hopefulness, a wish to speak with someone, a friend, a relative, anyone who knew her as *Ines* and not *Iglesias*. And it had been a fellow detective, in fact a former partner, who'd told her sneeringly to turn on her TV to channel four, the 6:00 P.M. Newark news.

Iglesias's first glimpse of fiery crusader Reverend Marus Mudrick.

She'd known the name, and something of the reputation, but she hadn't realized immediately that the ranting black man on the TV screen, on a sort of stage, was in fact Marus Mudrick; she had no idea what he was talking about in such fierce, declamatory tones, like a Pentecostal preacher, until she heard a name—Sybilla Frye?

Iglesias groped for a chair, to sit. All strength had drained from her legs.

Sybilla Frye! Iglesias's first thought was that the girl had been murdered.

Sybilla Frye's mother had insisted that Sybilla's life was in danger. The lives of the Frye family were all in danger. Iglesias had supposed there might be truth to this charge, if not the truth the Fryes were insisting upon.

Since early October Iglesias had made little headway in the Sybilla Frye case. She'd been thwarted at every step. Yet, Iglesias hadn't given up.

Now on TV Reverend Mudrick was no longer ranting before an audience but being interviewed by a lithe blond reporter. It was the conclusion of a "news conference" he'd convened in Newark to "expose" the Sybilla Frye case to the world.

White cops. Rape. Cover-up. Death threats.

Permanently traumatized fifteen-year-old black girl.
Pascayne cops. Nazi-racist-swine.

The news clip had been brief, scarcely three minutes. Iglesias would catch it again on the 11:00 P.M. Newark news and hear the righteous accusatory black voice reverberate as in a vast echo chamber inside her skull through the long, insomniac night. At 4:00 A.M. staring at her sick, sallow face in a bathroom mirror eyes pleading *This can't be happening. It will be the end of my career, that has scarcely begun. How can this be happening!*

"They refuse to meet with me. They refuse to meet with anyone associated with law enforcement. The mother refuses to bring the daughter to headquarters, or to come to headquarters herself. They've said they are 'fearful of their lives'—'white cops' will kill them. Now that Marus Mudrick is their 'spokesman,' and his brother Byron is their 'legal counsel,' they are not accessible to any law enforcement officers. We have no power to bring them into custody. We can't arrest them. They haven't formally reported a crime. They haven't pressed charges. At the news conferences Reverend Mudrick accuses 'white cops'—he accuses the 'white power structure' of a cover-up—but Reverend Mudrick never names names. He is very careful never to make specific charges against specific individuals. The 'interview' I had with Sybilla Frye in St. Anne's Hospital wasn't recorded—the mother refused to allow me to record it. The mother and the girl were cooperative initially—for a few minutes—then abruptly ceased to be cooperative. At the Frye residence, on Third Street, I spoke briefly with Mrs. Frye—she ordered me from the premises. At the great-grandmother's apartment on Eleventh Street where Sybilla was staying, I was allowed to have a glimpse of Sybilla, who was in a back bedroom, 'convalescing'—not in any evident physical distress, that I could see. Sybilla did not speak to me and I was not allowed to speak to Sybilla. And then, I was ordered from the premises.

"Ednetta Frye has said she will not bring her daughter back to St. Anne's for further medical examinations. When the girl was brought in, the mother refused to allow a 'pelvic exam.' There is no 'rape kit'—no evidence of 'sexual assault.' Yet, rape is claimed. Multiple rapes are claimed. The mother has taken the girl to a doctor in Red Rock. And this doctor—who refuses to be 'interrogated'—confirms only that Sybilla Frye is his patient. His patients' records are private, he says. He will acknowledge that the girl is 'under his care,' and 'doing well.'

"We have interviewed many people. Social workers, welfare workers, the girl's teachers, family and relatives. Neighbors of the Fryes, residents of Red Rock. We know that the mother Ednetta went 'searching' for the girl on the day before she was found. We know the circumstances in which she was 'found.' But we can't get to the girl. We can't interview her. We can't stop Reverend Mudrick from making charges against the department. He speaks of 'justice' for Sybilla Frye but he refuses to cooperate with the Pascayne PD or the district attorney's office."

Her voice was calm, reasonable.

Her voice was raw, rattling like a runaway freight train.

Always she was hearing her voice. Words that were truthful and yet deceitful-sounding, desperate.

A coldly sober voice. A drunken bawling voice.

In her sleep, and in that twilit interlude between sleep and waking, and waking and sleep. Alone, in her car, driving to the precinct in the devastated interior of Red Rock; alone, as she felt herself increasingly isolated and ostracized within the Pascayne PD, at her

desk scarcely less than three feet from neighboring desks, yet remote
from her neighbors; in the women's restroom, where frequently she
fled to hide in a toilet stall, to soak paper towels to dampen and cool
her face hot as fever. As in a nightmare of disintegration and despair
even as the earth sinks away beneath your feet you will hear your
voice in a semblance of manic calm *O God You would not let this happen. I have been a good person, I have tried so hard to be a good person
believing that I can make a difference and this is true, I know this is true,
I could make a difference in that girl's life, even in Ednetta Frye's life if she
would allow me. How has this gone wrong, why do they hate me who wants
only to be their friend?*

These words she could not speak to the Lieutenant. She would
find other words with which to speak to the Lieutenant. For she could
not believe truly that the man despised her.

As it's said we can't believe that we are mortal and must die, so we
can't believe that, unfairly, unreasonably, someone despises us.

■

SEVERAL TIMES, IGLESIAS AND HER PARTNER HAD SOUGHT OUT
Anis Schutt, the common-law stepfather of Sybilla Frye.

Anis Schutt, who'd spent seven years in Rahway for having beaten
his first wife to death.

Anis Schutt, who had a criminal record dating back to 1950. A
man of whom it was said *Anis he have some temper!*

Ednetta had been reluctant to speak of Anis Schutt to the detectives. Saying it was hurtful to her, it was shameful to her, Anis was
away from the house so much not telling her where in hell he was,
with whom he was staying or what he was doing, if she asked he'd get
furious with her sayin *That aint your fuckin bus'ness, woman.*

The way he said *woman,* Ednetta felt the disgust.

Ednetta had sworn, Anis had nothing to do with Sybilla, or any of the children—*Like, he don't take no mind of them, Officers. He didn't take much mind of his own chil'ren. All they need remember is stay out of Anis's way when he be home, and things be OK. Like, Anis is not a stingy man, he got money he will be generous. Nobody here ever went hungry or at Christmastime didn't have presents.*

In person Anis Schutt was not forthcoming. One of those many citizens of Red Rock who hated, feared, distrusted cops.

The man frowned, grimaced, sucked at his mouth, stared at the floor. It wasn't clear if he understood what was being asked of him.

He was a thick-bodied man in his early fifties, looking older. Broken capillaries in close-set eyes. A flat broad broken nose. Very dark skin in which light seemed to disappear. Mangled-looking fingers. Labored breathing. His employment was sporadic—most recently, Passaic County sanitation.

Mr. Schutt where were you when. What is your relationship with. When was the last time you saw Sybilla Frye before she went missing on October 4 for two days.

Anis Schutt had known that the girl had been "missing" but he hadn't seemed to know where she'd been "found" nor did he seem to know beyond a vague idea of "assault" what had happened to her, and what the charges of "white cops" meant. He'd kept asking the detectives *What? What you sayin?* His breathing grew alarmingly labored. His forehead oozed sweat. In the man's face, in the small damp bloodshot eyes, an expression of consternation and something like horror.

They smearin—what on her? Dog shit you sayin?

Who's this—"white cops"? Who the fuck done this?

It soon seemed evident to Iglesias and her partner that Ednetta hadn't told Anis Schutt about what had happened to Sybilla, or at least she hadn't told him crucial details. Astonishing that the man didn't seem to know what most of Red Rock had known within a few days. Or maybe—Iglesias thought this must be the case—no one had wanted to bring up the subject to Anis Schutt out of fear of the man's reaction.

They'd tried to explain to Anis Schutt what had happened, or was believed to have happened, to Sybilla; they'd told him about the factory cellar, the ambulance, St. Anne's ER. Anis Schutt cupped his hand to his ear as if hard of hearing. *What—what you sayin? Ednetta's big girl? Who done this to her?*

Anis Schutt had been a heavy drinker for much of his life. Possibly now, he'd become mentally impaired.

Iglesias wondered how Ednetta dared live with such a man. You could see that Anis Schutt had been handsome at one time—a swaggering masculine presence—a man for whom a woman might feel many kinds of desire; but now he was a wreck of a man. When he heaved himself up on his feet, in a sudden need to end the interview, his right knee nearly buckled.

Afterward Ednetta complained bitterly they hadn't needed to upset her husband like that. Anis didn't know anything much about Sybilla or the other children—for the man the crucial thing was, they weren't *his*—and now lately this past year or two he had symptoms that worried her but trying to get him to a doctor or a clinic was hopeless, God knows she tried. *But Anis sayin he all right. Or, Anis sayin he don't give a shit he live or die, already been livin long enough. Like to break my heart hearin that!*

■

HER (NEW, RELUCTANT) PARTNER HARVEY CURZDOI SAID *It was a gang thing. Raping the girl, the dog shit, hog-tied and they knew she wouldn't die because someone would find her. Or, they told someone to find her. No one will ever name names, we're totally fucked with this.*

And Iglesias had said *Or maybe the stepfather? And no one will ever name him.*

■

PLAINCLOTHED AND OFF-DUTY AND ALONE INES IGLESIAS MADE a decision to attend the third "news conference" convened by Reverend Marus Mudrick, this time in Pascayne.

Overnight, posters festooned the city, most concentrated in the Red Rock neighborhood—CRUSADE FOR JUSTICE FOR SYBILLA FRYE—DEC. 3, 4:00 P.M. AME ZION CHURCH CAMDEN AVE. PASCAYNE NJ.

The previous two news conferences had been held in Newark where Reverend Mudrick had his headquarters. Moving to Pascayne which the Reverend called the "scene of the heinous race-crime" was a provocative act. The mayor's office was on high alert. The Pascayne PD was on high alert. Six hours before the event was scheduled uniformed officers began to assemble on the streets surrounding the church. Police on foot, police in several types of vehicles including those vans used to transport the arrested and imprisoned. There was a clattering static of police radios like a ubiquitous buzzing of angry hornets.

Uniformed men—(Iglesias could see only men, and virtually all of them white-skinned)—like soldiers waiting to defend an embattled city, hoping for an attack so that they could use their weaponry.

The stucco church on Camden Avenue was one of the few buildings in the area that hadn't been burnt down in the "riot" of 1967. Iglesias recalled tales of how terrified black people had fled into the church to escape police gunfire; how in several instances police officers had stormed the church, shooting. How many had been shot in the church, taken prisoner or left to die . . . But the mustard-colored church with its brave weatherworn cross had survived in the desolate neighborhood, and adjoining empty lots had been cultivated as AME community gardens, dormant now in early winter.

Intimidation was police strategy, Iglesias knew. You tried to discourage crowds from gathering, with a visible display of police force.

The high saturation of cops on Camden Avenue seemed to be having the effect of discouraging some people, older women, and women with children, from approaching the church—you could see them at a little distance, hesitating, and turning away. But most others pressed forward, unintimidated. Iglesias thought—*Good for them!*

Already by 3:30 P.M. a crowd had gathered in the street, to file into the church; the church was too small for the numbers of people who wanted to come inside. And there were several rows of pews at the front of the church reserved for "press." Since the assembly was in the church and on private property, police couldn't charge the organizers with having failed to get a permit for the event; but there were sure to be many people left outside on the sidewalk, and in the street. It had been a shrewd decision of Mudrick's, Iglesias thought—a way of provoking tension between the black crowd and the Pascayne PD.

Marus Mudrick had a reputation for "innocently"—that is, deliberately—sowing confusion among even his followers; he'd led protest marches in Newark and elsewhere that had ended in racial violence, police retaliation and arrests. Iglesias dreaded the hour when Mudrick would be injured or killed by a white racist. Or shot by a white cop. Leading his marches, Mudrick liked to boast that he wasn't wearing a bulletproof vest and he wasn't carrying a weapon.

In front of the church were photographers, reporters, TV camera crews and bright lights, unnatural at this hour of the day. Here were "media people"—sought by Reverend Mudrick to promulgate his crusade.

Not all of the media people were white. But even the dark-skinned among them looked and dressed conspicuously different from most Red Rock residents.

Amid the yet-peaceful crowd filing into the church Ines Iglesias passed unnoticed. Not one police officer had so much as glanced at her, still less recognized her. No one among those entering the church knew her. Hispanic female in a long black leather coat, leather boots to the knee. Her fedora was pulled low over her forehead and her hair was pulled back into a neat Spanish knot. She wore tinted glasses of the hue of smoke. Her mouth was pale, with her sharp sculpted features Iglesias wore no makeup. Inside her clothes she carried her 9 mm police service revolver.

Iglesias made her way to the front of the church and sat in the fifth row which was filling up quickly. The first several rows of pews had been reserved for "press."

It was stirring, to see so many concerned residents of Red Rock.

Primarily these were adults, but there were also high-school-aged girls, and slightly older boys. Word had spread quickly of "Sybilla Frye" who was one of their own.

Iglesias had been thinking, since her conversation with Harvey Curzdoi: it wasn't likely that any black man would smear dog-shit and scrawl racist words on a black girl, still less the daughter of his common-law wife. A black man might murder such a girl, for the reasons that men murder females, but he wouldn't defile her in such a way.

But maybe gang members. Some sort of nasty initiation. And Curzdoi was right—it would be virtually impossible to get anyone in Red Rock to snitch on a black youth gang.

The "news conference" began shortly after 4:00 P.M. when Reverend Marus Mudrick appeared at the pulpit with his arms lifted in welcome. In a grave sonorous voice amplified by a microphone he introduced himself as "Reverend Marus C. Mudrick, director of the

Care Ministry of Central New Jersey, headquarters in Newark, New Jersey." There was a scattering of excited applause. Reverend Mudrick then welcomed "Sister Ednetta Frye" and "Sister Sybilla Frye" and "my brother, renowned civil rights attorney Byron R. Mudrick" who joined him at the front of the church, to more applause.

The audience was riveted observing Ednetta Frye and her daughter Sybilla taking seats behind and to the right of Reverend Mudrick. Many knew Ednetta and Sybilla—and so it was intriguing to see them in this new way, dressed in prim church-clothes, strangely modest and downlooking. Ednetta was self-conscious and somber, her face puffier than Iglesias recalled; she wore tasteful dark clothing, and no evident makeup. Sybilla appeared stricken with shyness, her hair plaited into pigtails; she wore a very pretty white silk long-sleeved blouse with a bow and a dark, pleated skirt, white woolen socks and black patent leather shoes. At the hollow of her throat a small gold cross gleamed. Her facial injuries had faded, or were not visible at a little distance. The sly drift of her left eye was not visible. Iglesias wondered if Sybilla's friends and relatives recognized her—the lanky-limbed, sassy teenager reinvented as a demure doll of another era.

As Reverend Mudrick spoke, voice swelling with righteous indignation at the "outrage" perpetrated upon "a daughter of Red Rock," the pigtailed girl sat with her knees tightly pressed together and her eyes lowered, but well aware, Iglesias thought, of the audience staring at her and her mother.

At one point, flinching at a statement of Reverend Mudrick's, Sybilla groped for her mother's hand. A shiver of sympathy rippled through the audience.

Those TV crews allowed inside the church were using bright blinding lights. Instead of staying in the area set aside for them, photographers began to wander about taking flash pictures, several crouched directly beneath the pulpit. Reverend Mudrick's eyes glared red in the flashes. He seemed consumed by an inner, thrumming energy.

Mudrick was wearing one of his signature three-piece suits, custom-made, Iglesias had read, to fit his deformed upper spine. His head appeared large for his body, even as his legs appeared foreshortened. His torso seemed to fall outward, softly, restrained by his clothes. Yet Mudrick was an attractive man, thrilling in the Pentecostal mode with a deep rich voice that soared and swooped like a bird of prey. He spoke in a way to incorporate Biblical imagery, the wisdom of Jesus Christ, quotations from Abraham Lincoln, W. E. B. DuBois, Booker T. Washington, Martin Luther King Jr. There were no preachers like the Pentecostals in the Roman Catholic church in which Ines Iglesias had been confirmed as a young girl; sitting through the Catholic mass each Sunday with her family, Ines had tried to keep her mind from leaping and darting restlessly about, but without success; she'd known herself a *bad girl,* for the mass was deeply boring to her. She had tried to see that familiarity might be a spiritual comfort and not deadening. The truth was, she had not ever *felt anything* for her religion. Communion was awkward and embarrassing to her, a ritual for children. The entire mass was a ritual for children, or child-sized minds. *This is my body, and this is my blood. Take ye and eat.* She'd been too skeptical to believe such brazen nonsense! Yet, she'd never argued with her parents. She'd never so much as hinted at her disbelief. She'd been brought up to respect her elders and would not have wished to challenge them, or hurt them. And she loved them.

As she had minimal interest in visiting Puerto Rico, her grandparents' birthplace, so she had minimal interest in replicating their lives in any way. This included marriage, having babies. As a girl she'd preferred playing with her brothers' toy guns to dolls.

As a police officer, Iglesias had not yet fired her weapon. She'd drawn it as a patrol officer more than once but had not fired it and did not like to think of the prospect of having to fire it—self-defense . . .

Bold and brash of Reverend Marus Mudrick to boast that he didn't wear a bulletproof vest. There had been no security check at the front entrance of the church.

Yet she was fascinated by the man. You had to admit, Mudrick was *charismatic*. Everyone jammed into the pews was swept along by his words including those reporters and TV people who should've evinced more skepticism. Mudrick was a master of preacherly rhetoric seasoned with brilliantly timed lapses into black dialect—you listened to him as you would listen to the improvisations of a jazz musician. His sarcasm made you laugh, even when it was tinged with black racism: words like *honky, cracker* like whip-lashes, stinging without exactly drawing blood.

Iglesias was uneasy, amid the crowd. Thinking *He is a black racist but who can blame him. None of us can blame him.*

Any of these people—who can blame them!

She felt the seething excitement, the thrill of a common enemy. In the church there were no "whites" except in the pews reserved for the media.

Iglesias had investigated: The CRUSADE FOR JUSTICE FOR SY-BILLA FRYE had been established as a non-profit charitable organization with headquarters in Newark, and Marus Mudrick its CEO. The Passaic County district attorney's office intended to look into its finances; the New Jersey attorney general had been alerted. "Misuse of charitable donations" seemed a likely charge, to Marus Mudrick's (white) enemies.

Mudrick had campaigned for office, but had failed to get the Democratic nomination from his Newark district. Riding the waves of the

Sybilla Frye publicity, he would very likely try again for a U.S. congressional seat.

After forty minutes of stirring rhetoric, Mudrick introduced his brother Byron—"the internationally renowned civil rights attorney"—who spoke much more calmly, rationally, and flatly. Within a few minutes the audience grew restive.

"Law is civilization, and there is no civilization without law. Yet, there are times when . . ."

Byron Mudrick was a diminutive man with a wise, creased face and hair much thinner and grayer than his brother's; his clothes were not distinctive, and his voice neither swooped nor soared as he reiterated Marus Mudrick's main points and added, with painstaking thoroughness, points of his own. The kind of attorney you would want for legal advice, but not the kind of fiery attorney you would want to defend you in court. By the time Byron finished his prepared talk, he seemed as relieved as the audience.

Another time now, but with renewed zest and revulsion, Mudrick recounted the "unspeakable outrage" perpetrated upon Sybilla Frye. "When white men assault a black girl, it is 'blackness' they are assaulting—that is, all of us."

With salacious indignation Mudrick described the kidnapping—the repeated rapes and beatings—the terrified girl kept captive in a van for two nights—smeared with dog feces and "Nazi-racist-swine words written on her body"—hog-tied in the cellar of an abandoned factory and left to die. "Only through the intervention of Jesus Christ was Sybilla Frye discovered by a good Samaritan, who heard her cries. Her rapists are white men dwelling and working right here in Pascayne; they are law enforcement officers of some kind, believed to be in the Pascayne PD, who remain unidentified, unapprehended, and free to this day. Sybilla could no more than glimpse them in her terror, as her eyes were blindfolded. It is believed that there are four or five of them, though they might have been joined, in the course of several days of captivity, by others. Only one of the men was seen by Sybilla Frye more clearly than the others, who had 'yellow hair'—one of the younger men. And she saw a badge—or badges."

At this recollection Sybilla Frye seemed about to faint, and Ednetta Frye caught the girl in her arms. A seismic shudder ran through the church.

Iglesias was thinking *Blindfold? Sybilla was blindfolded?*

This was the first she'd heard of a *blindfold.* There was nothing in her original notes about a *blindfold.*

Possibly, Mudrick had made this up, on the spot. The Reverend seemed to be improvising with much zest, as waves of emotion from the audience encouraged him. Or, Sybilla Frye had told him— *Blindfold.* If she'd been abducted, it was plausible to think that she'd also been blindfolded; but maybe not for such a duration of time as she was claiming. Or: if you were composing a plausible statement of having been abducted, you might decide to add *blindfold.*

"Jesus here with us now. You feelin Him?—is you?—I'm feelin Him! Jesus gon protect us in this place of holiness and the 'white cops' will not harm us though they be out on the street a thousand-fold, the Nazi-racist-swine hopin there will be a 'riot' an they can shoot us down dead like they done in 1967 here in Pascayne as in Newark, Detroit, Los Angeles. If there is blood to be spilt in this crusade for justice for Sybilla Frye, I pray Jesus it be *my blood,* and all innocent sisters an brothers spared. The white man will never confront the evil in hisself, but when he see you, he see the burning finger of Truth. The blaze that will never be extinguished. Amen!"

Amen! the audience responded.

Everyone around her appeared to be deeply moved. Iglesias saw individuals wiping their eyes, and these were not solely women.

Breathing hard, mopping his forehead with a white handkerchief, Mudrick paused to take questions from the media people, who'd become increasingly restless. Several reporters called out the same question—why hadn't Sybilla Frye and her mother cooperated with the police if she was a "legitimate rape victim," why was Marus Mudrick intervening in this public way?—and Mudrick said, indignantly, "Cooperate with the po-lice? In this Nazi-racist city? When the Pascayne po-lice is *the problem?*"

There were shouts of agreement—*You tell it, Brother!*—*You tellin them!* Mockingly Mudrick spoke over the reporters' raised voices: "Tellin that poor ravaged girl to go to the po-lice is like tellin Jews to appeal to the Nazi Führer. Only a white-skinned person with no notion of life in a Nazi-racist state would ask that foolish question. Some white lib-rals might be fools but we sure ain't! We ain't goin to no local po-lice, nor even New Jersey State Police, they all brothers together under the skin, that 'blue line' nobody gon cross."

In this vein Mudrick continued, in a voice of ballooning wrath. Iglesias could feel the temperature in the pews rise as she could feel her heartbeat accelerate. There came many more shouts and cries of agreement.

Iglesias wondered if the media people, sequestered in the first few rows of the church, felt trapped and vulnerable. Their responses to Mudrick's assertations were surprisingly tame. Since the *New York Times* had started covering the case, with extensive, damning quotes from Mudrick, Iglesias had been reading the paper with increasing bewilderment and chagrin—the *New York Times,* giving columns of its front page to the race-baiter's unsubstantiated charges. Slandering the Pascayne PD, in virtually every issue of the paper, with very little space given, at the end of the articles, to statements from the Pascayne PD chief of police.

White liberal credulousness, Iglesias thought. Liberals eager to ally themselves with black accusers. Ready to believe the worst of their fellow whites and the worst of cops.

In this crowd, *she* was "white"—unless you knew Ines Iglesias.

Most of the media coverage she'd seen had stressed the girl's accusations and Reverend Mudrick's charges but failed to make it clear that, as soon as Marus Mudrick had become the official "spiritual advisor" for Ednetta and Sybilla Frye, and Byron Mudrick had become their "legal counsel," they'd been invited to meet with high-ranking police officers and attorneys from the Passaic County district attorney's office, and repeatedly they'd refused. Byron Mudrick, previously an attorney who'd cooperated, to a degree, with legal adversaries, seemed to be concurring with his radical brother. Their first obligation was to their clients, the brothers claimed. These clients had been threatened by police officers in the Pascayne PD. The Fryes' lives were at risk, as were their relatives' lives. They were living in fear and terror "as of the Nazi Gestapo." Both Sister Ednetta and Sister Sybilla had been threatened by police officers, and by the "hierarchy of law enforcement" in New Jersey. They could no longer dwell in their home on Third Street, but had to take refuge in a safe house.

The other night, someone had thrown a rock through the Fryes' window on Third Street. There'd been shots fired. Cries of *nigger slut*. More than one witness had claimed to see what appeared to be "unmarked police vehicles" cruising Third Street at all hours of the day and night.

It was no secret in Red Rock that law enforcement claimed fraudulently all the time that they would protect police informers and witnesses against criminals, then left them to die in the street. *That* was how cops treated their own "nigger-snitches."

The Reverend spoke in a voice heavy with sarcasm. There was startled, harsh laughter in the church.

A journalist in the front row stood to ask that if Reverend Mudrick had no intention of meeting with the police, not even the chief of police, or with the district attorney of Passaic County, what was the purpose of his news conferences?

" 'What is the *purpose?*'—you aint been listenin, has you. Our purpose is to bring this tragic story of Nazi-racist-swine rape of black women to the attention of the world. To the 'court of public opinion.' We are exposin the rotten core of the police state. White privilege. White 'masters.' The rich white capitalists settin they foot on the back of our necks, an they act surprised when we throw it off. They act surprised when we defend our women. This badly wronged girl Sybilla Frye is our Joan of Arc here in New Jersey—but the girl is no martyr. She has been hurt deep in her soul, you can see, but she be strong in her soul, and she will survive. And we will find justice for her, long prison terms for the white rapists and monetary reparation from the Pascayne police department, many millions of dollars for all who have suffered the white boot on the nape of the neck. All the white cap'lists give a damn for is the mighty buck which is where we will kick them—hard. This, we swear."

Amid cries of approval one of the reporters managed to ask if Reverend Mudrick would be appealing to the New Jersey attorney general and Mudrick said he hadn't yet decided. He was demanding a "statewide" and "federal commission" to investigate the case but it would have to include black investigators—black lawyers—from both New Jersey and out of state; and it would have to involve an investigation of the entire Pascayne PD as well as the Pascayne mayor's office and the district attorney's office. "The whole hive of them is sick, rotten with corruption, and Nazi-racist. You from out-of-town—from New York City—are thinkin it would be a good strategy for us here in Jersey to try to cooperate with the officials that are not so sick and corrupt, and clear out the rogue cops and corrupt politicians. But consider—this is the hallowed state of New Jersey which is number two in corruption in U.S. history, behind only the state of Louisiana which takes that dubious trophy." These remarks were greeted with raucous laughter. Reverend Mudrick frowned as if such mirth was inappropriate, and gravely continued: "Now, I am a Christian minister, and I am a reasonable man—I understand, there are 'good cops' in this city—maybe even a majority of 'good cops.' There are 'persons of color' on the force—a few. Putting pressure on the entrenched white bosses to hire black and Hispanic, like they putting pressure on the firemen in the big cities to cast aside their race-bigotry. But these are not the law enforcement officers with authority or seniority, and they are vulnerable to their superior officers. They *take orders,* or they out on the street. These brothers and sisters are not the ones who are the problem. Outside this house of worship at this very hour—you saw them, intimidatin you as you entered this church of Christ—as you exercise your God-given and Constitutional right to 'freedom of assembly' without harassment and fear of police violence. And the 'superior officers' who ain't present givin them orders—that is the problem, that is the challenge before the *Crusade for Justice for Sybilla Frye.*"

As the press conference was ending, Mudrick turned to Ednetta Frye to take her hand, and to Sybilla Frye to take her hand. As the audience stared rapt with attention Mudrick brought both Ednetta and Sybilla to the pulpit.

"We are not askin these victims of race violence to speak this afternoon, as they are not accustomed to public speaking, and it has been my promise to them, they need not be subjected to any public scrutiny at this time. But, Sister Ednetta, will you say just a few words to this gathering?"

Meekly Ednetta Frye stood at the pulpit, rapidly blinking and smiling awkwardly; her gaze darted about the audience before her, she licked her lips and said, in a barely audible voice, "I—I am Ednetta Frye—I thank you all for comin here today—in support of my daughter Sybilla and her 'crusade for justice.'"

Mudrick turned to Sybilla, saying, "Sister Sybilla, will you say just a few words to this gathering, that is filled with love and support for you in your suffering?"

Meekly Sybilla Frye stood at the pulpit, rapidly blinking and smiling awkwardly; if she'd been coached to speak as her mother had spoken, she seemed to have forgotten what to say, overcome by the rows of raptly staring people before her, and the distractions of flash and TV cameras.

"Just tell these good people your name, dear. They have come to help you."

Sybilla was trembling. She spoke in a whisper, inaudibly.

"Just a little louder, dear."

"Sy-Sy-b'lla F-Frye . . ."

The audience murmured sympathetically. Cries of *S'b'lla! S'b'lla!*

Iglesias had a sudden impulse to stride to the pulpit, push the hulking Reverend aside and seize the girl's hands in hers—explain to her, and to her naïve mother, that Marus Mudrick had a reputation for exploiting "black victims" in the past: collecting money on their behalf, brokering interviews and media features, using them to promote himself and dropping them when the public lost interest.

He is not your friend. You are making a mistake to trust him.

If you could trust me . . .

Yet when a collection basket was passed, Iglesias slipped a five-dollar bill into it. She'd been deeply moved.

In farewell Reverend Mudrick blessed the audience and urged them to take the crusade to the enemy—to repeat after him "JUS-TICE FOR SYBILLA FRYE—JUSTICE FOR SYBILLA FRYE" as they left the church. "March then along Camden Boulevard—to Pitcairn Bridge—in a *peaceful and orderly manner*—and across the bridge, and to City Hall where the mayor and his white minions are hiding. Chanting loud so all can hear 'JUSTICE FOR SYBILLA FRYE'—'JUSTICE FOR SYBILLA FRYE—JUSTICE FOR SYBILLA FRYE.'"

The chant was taken up at once. A frenzied excitement rippled through the crowd. Pressing her fingers over her ears Iglesias managed to exit the church, just barely. She hadn't noticed so many black youths in the church, unless they'd been waiting outside in the street—now shoving, jostling, chanting "JUSTICE FOR S'B'LLA FRYE—JUSTICE FOR S'B'LLA FRYE."

Police were waiting for them. Flanked like soldiers.

Iglesias thought panicked *If there is gunfire!*

On all sides were cries of elation, and warning. Cries of fear.

Move along! Move along! Police officers were shouting.

Portions of the unruly crowd were dispersing. Allowed by police officers to cross wide, windy Camden Avenue, which had been blocked off for traffic, and make their way along side streets. But others were trapped on this side of the avenue, and others were resisting the officers' orders. Iglesias wasn't sure how to proceed. She would have liked to help disperse the crowd—but had no idea how. As she hesitated, she was being shoved, struck. The chant of "JUSTICE FOR S'B'LLA FRYE" continued ragged and halting and yet ferocious on all sides. Iglesias's training was to control such a situation—physically—but she could not; she wasn't with fellow officers, she wasn't in uniform, she had not the authority of a police officer. She found herself on the street, pushed into the gutter. A line of patrolmen surged forward with batons drawn. What remained of the crowd was being forced back. There were cries, screams of fear, fury, pain. Individuals slipped or were pushed, and fell. A heavyset woman with a ravaged dark skin yanked at the sleeve of Iglesias's leather coat. Her stylish black fedora was knocked from her head. The back of her neck felt exposed, vulnerable. She managed to slip free of the clutching woman, trying to make her way to the line of uniformed officers.

She cried out to them, her fellow officers—"I'm a cop! Hey! Here!" Her badge was in her hand, but suddenly her hand was struck, and the badge was lost.

The heavyset woman was pursuing her: "You a cop? You sayin you a cop, bitch?" Another, younger woman tore at her hair. She was called bitch, spic, cunt, slut. She was being punched, kicked. She lost her balance in the tight-fitting boots and was grabbing at arms, panting, falling.

Her hair was in a tangle on her shoulders. A coin-sized swath of hair had been torn from her scalp. She was bleeding but not seriously. She was bleeding from a scalp wound which can mimic serious bleeding but is not. Her stylish clothes, stained with blood. She was frightened, but she would not panic. In the New Jersey Police Academy she'd been trained not to panic. Dared not draw her weapon here. Seen with a weapon, she'd be shot by police. A few yards away, a black man in his twenties was being subdued and arrested by six police officers, bleeding from a cut in his scalp. Other black men, a black woman. Subdued, arrested. One of the men was shirtless, and his muscled dark chest glistening with blood. Police were shouting, beating back the crowd. On Camden Avenue were police vehicles advancing like tanks. Amid the screaming young people were older men and women unable to escape. Appalling to see children here—some of them clutched in adults' arms, crying in terror. Sirens, deafening. A furious-looking black woman clawed at Iglesias's face. The smoke-tinted glasses were knocked off. There was an explosion—gunfire, and a smell of gun-smoke—so close to Iglesias's head, she was blinded, stunned. She fell to the pavement amid screams and desperation as people tried to get away, her left hand was trampled, and her left arm, she could not get to her feet to protect herself, something was wrong with her legs, and with her vision—so suddenly gone . . .

"Reassigned"

First you think *I am alive.*

Astonishment washes over you, bright and vivid and narcotic—*I am alive, still.*

Not until later the pain.

Humiliation, and shame.

Still, I am alive. I made it.

She would recall the gunshot—close beside her head. She'd thought—she'd assumed—she'd been shot.

Lifted onto a stretcher. Dazed and bleeding from head and facial wounds, and her clothes torn. Oxygen fitted to her nose and mouth, she could not breathe deeply enough.

But vaguely she was aware of voices urging her—*Breathe!*

Vaguely aware of ambulance doors being slammed shut, and the vehicle propelled into motion.

Her brain was faltering, dying. She'd been struck a savage blow to her right temple. She'd been kicked, trampled, terrible pain in her ribs, her lower back, left arm and left leg. Something wet and sticky in her hair. The leather coat had been torn, she would never wear her fancy leather coat again. She could feel her face swelling. A loose tooth. Her badge was gone, they'd taken it from her. She would not discover until later that her 9 mm police service revolver was gone.

In the brightly lit ER, trying to explain—something . . .

Trying to explain who she was, why she had to be allowed to leave, why she didn't want anyone in her family called . . .

I am a police officer. Detective Ines Iglesias. Pascayne PD. My ID is in my . . . My badge . . .

And when she returned to the precinct after several days' "sick leave" at once she was summoned to the Lieutenant's office.

Disgusted with her. Could barely bring himself to look at her.

"Clear your desk, Iglesias. You're out of here."

So abruptly, Iglesias had barely stepped inside the Lieutenant's office. The door had not been shut—he hadn't asked her to shut it.

She was stunned and disbelieving. She wasn't sure what she had heard.

"You're off the Frye case. You're being reassigned. But you're out of this precinct, so clear your desk and get out."

She was stammering—her words were indistinct—*I don't understand . . .*

It must have been, Iglesias had been expecting a very different greeting from the Lieutenant. She'd cut short her sick leave eager and anxious to return to the precinct. She'd been prepared to tell the man

Thank you Lieutenant I'm fine. I was never in serious danger.

The Lieutenant had not the slightest interest in Ines Iglesias's

medical condition. Her still-swollen mouth, bruised eyes hidden behind dark glasses, the wincing limp with which she walked—(and
this limp much less in public than in private)—these aroused in the
man a roiling contempt he would only allow her to infer from the
way in which he could not bring himself even to look at her, fully in
the face.

"No need to close the door when you leave, Iglesias. But leave."

The Good Son

*Zahn, Jerold ("Jere"). Born March 22, 1960. Died De-
cember 11, 1987. Patrol officer, Pascayne Police Department
and lifetime resident, Pascayne, New Jersey.*

Nine-twenty A.M. that day which was approximately eighteen hours
after he'd got the terrible news he was at his parents' house repairing
the roof. Squat-climbing the peak of the roof in cold stark overbright
December sunshine. Dark glasses protecting his red-veined eyes.
He'd always been a good handyman, carpenter. Throwing himself
into tasks at his former house. He was *the good son* though it embarrassed him to be so named, through childhood and now into adult-
hood approaching the (hard-to-believe) age of thirty.

Maybe he'd anticipated the news. Had to be an open secret at the
precinct by this time nearly two weeks after the Camden Avenue disturbances.

Or maybe, just maybe there was no actual connection. Between anticipating the news, and receiving the news. And driving across town to his parents' house to repair a section of (rotting, leaking) roof-shingles. And once he'd done with hammering on the roof—(which was how his mother Mimi Zahn knew Jere had come over: heard him before she saw him, hurried to a window to see, yes Jere's car was in the driveway which was like her youngest son to just show up unannounced at the house, immediately throw himself into the carpentry and handyman tasks his older brothers with their busy lives and families wouldn't have thought of doing for their parents)—he carried the ladder around to the garage to replace burnt-out floodlights on the garage roof and while he was up there, to secure a loose drainpipe.

Taking care then to place the heavy long ladder back in the garage exactly where he'd found it which was where, in fact, he'd put the ladder a few months ago which was the last time the ladder had been used by anyone in the Zahn family.

Too wired to stop work. Anxious to clear away debris from last week's storm scattered through the backyard in time for trash pickup later that week. *Jere is such a good person. Even as a boy he was always the first to volunteer help. His dad and I just wish he did more for himself not always other people . . .* Which meant a mother's concern that her youngest son was living alone at the age of twenty-seven, no (apparent, desirable) prospects for marriage, obsessed with his job (which by calling a mere "job" Mimi hoped to minimize) as a new recruit in the Pascayne Police Department.

Rookie cop Jerold Zahn. Rank Police Officer I.

The Zahns were proud of him. Anxious for him.

He hadn't had an easy time at the New Jersey State Police Academy in Sea Girt. Never certain why, when he'd been so excited about being accepted. Graduating in the lowest third of his class of cadets.

In the Pascayne PD, in the Red Rock precinct which was the worst precinct in the city, highest crime rate, blocks of burnt-out buildings, Zahn was the rookie feeling the most stress.

(Not that Jere complained to anyone. He'd never been the kind to complain.)

(On the Pascayne North High varsity team Jere Zahn was known for having finished a championship game limping on a sprained ankle. Another time, concussed for as long as a minute flat on his back on the ground but insisted on going right back into the game.)

In a haze of grief the Zahns would claim *We had no idea. No warning* but in fact Mimi had been concerned, something in the boy wasn't quite right. The intensity with which he threw himself into handyman tasks. Anything you'd ask him to do and some things he volunteered, you hadn't even thought to ask like thinning the old straggly shrubbery around the house, replacing cracked bricks in the patio. And his old room, he'd cleared out and painted a pale yellow for his mom's sewing room, his own idea entirely.

So that day December 11, 1987, when Jere turned up at the house before 9:00 A.M. (after his dad left for work at 7:30 A.M.) without having called first, hauled the long ladder out of the garage and leaned it against the side of the house with a thud and climbed the steps rapid and unerring and then heavy-footed on the roof hammering in a fury of concentration for the remainder of the morning—she'd sensed that something was possibly wrong but was determined to make a joke of it, a jest, that was the Zahns' way, four boys and a younger sister and their dad a great kidder so Mimi had learned to laugh as the first line of defense. Tugging open a second-floor window to call out to her son overhead (and out of sight) who failed to hear her and so she'd gone outside into the backyard to call plaintively up to him—*Jere? Hi! Did you tell your dad you were coming over, honey?*—shivering hugging herself in just a cardigan sweater, and her son on the roof a startling sight in bright cold sunshine in his old hunter-green high school hoodie, knitted wool cap pulled down over his creased forehead, boyish face grim and unsmiling. He seemed embarrassed, possibly annoyed, his mom outside in the cold calling up to him through cupped hands, he was hoping neighbors wouldn't hear. Jere's way to shrug and say *No big deal* when people made too much of the least little thing he did for them. Mimi chided him come inside and get warm, she'd make him something hot to eat reasoning he'd had just cold cereal and coffee for breakfast as usual if he'd bothered to eat at all. With a grimace he waved at her *I'm OK Mom, I'm almost done with this, go back inside Mom OK?* Definitely he was embarrassed by her solicitude but she could see he was losing weight, since summer he must have lost at least ten pounds. Actually becoming lean-faced which wasn't like any of his brothers. And his eyes ringed with a kind of adult fatigue she'd never seen in Jere before.

Henry had said to the older sons *Spend some time with Jere can you? Invite him over for supper? He needs something I'm not sure that your mother and I can supply.*

After he'd cleared away a sizable portion of the fallen tree limbs in the backyard and raked brush into a pile Jere came into the kitchen to get warm, removed his hoodie and wool cap and Mimi couldn't resist brushing hair out of his face as she'd done without thinking for most of his life. Jere's hair was white-blond, pale-silvery-blond like her own, though her own was mostly gray now, and Jere's eyebrows and lashes pale like hers, almost invisible so growing up he'd hated the color of his hair which was freaky he'd complained, like a girl's hair. Mimi had felt a mother's (small, finite, contained) heartbreak assuring him *Don't be silly, honey! You are a very good-looking boy. Girls would kill for hair natural-blond like yours.*

And Jere's eyes, ghost-eyes, pale eyes, pale blue or gray, like Mimi's eyes also, that looked raw, vulnerable.

She'd insisted, he had to sit down for a few minutes at least, have something to eat so he said with a smile *OK, Mom, you're the boss* and she felt a little thrill of triumph—thinking she would keep her son with her for a while longer, and the big house not so empty, and when Henry came home she would tell him with a quiet kind of pride *Jere came over this morning and surprised me, repaired the roof and changed the outside garage lights and we had a nice talk like we haven't had in a while. He told me . . .*

Instead after he'd eaten only about half the food on his plate— (scrambled eggs, bacon and toast which was a special breakfast in the Zahn household)—he'd seemed to lose appetite suddenly, and ceased eating; and Mimi asked him if something was wrong, and evasively he'd said *Nothing is wrong, Mom. I'm OK.* She knew that he'd been seeing a young woman named "Kim"—"Kimba"—who wasn't ideal, from Mimi's perspective, being a single mother, and not younger than her son, and this person Mimi had not ever met, and hoped she would not. And yet—*I want Jere to be happy. I want him to get married, someday. He can't live alone, he needs someone to take care of him.*

She knew that since the "disturbances" on Camden Avenue following a meeting in a black church, when so many police officers were involved in quelling a near-riot, things had been tense in the Pascayne Police Department, particularly in Jere's precinct in Red Rock. (It was their son's bad luck, to be assigned *there*. But Jere never complained even to his brothers or his sister with whom he'd always been close, so far as Mimi knew.) Jere said of the incident that it could've been a hell of a lot worse, and the fact was nobody got killed, nobody got seriously injured, no police cars were overturned and burned, and there was "zero" looting.

His father had said *When a class of individuals can't support themselves, have to live on food stamps and welfare, and no jobs, it's a powder keg. Thank God worse didn't happen.*

They'd heard of a black teenager in Red Rock charging white police officers with kidnapping and rape, and how preposterous these charges were—totally unsubstantiated. Jere's father had asked him about it and Jere had said with a shrug he didn't know anything about it except people said it was a "race-thing."

Jere had had enough of his mother's breakfast, and was eager now to get back outside and finish clearing the yard. Through a window she observed him for a while, working fast, pushing himself as if punishing himself; she could see no logic to it, no reason, but their youngest son had often behaved this way. As young as twelve, in seventh grade, when Jere had begun to play on sports teams, and to be a player whom coaches singled out for particular attention.

She thought of putting on a fleece-lined jacket and joining her son outside. Vigorous exercise in fresh air would be good for her—cheer her. Helping Jere rake debris into those big black plastic trash bags which was a task requiring two people. But she knew—oh, she knew—Jere wouldn't have liked that. He was a sweet boy but sad-hearted and right now he wanted to be alone with his thoughts.

Well—Mimi assumed Jere would come back inside to say good-bye but around 2:00 P.M. she noticed his car was gone from the driveway.

He was going to tell me, I think. I see that now.

I didn't, then. I guess I . . . missed it.

First thing was thinking of Mimi. Thinking of Mom.

In fact he'd come over to tell her. That was why he'd come.

Then, lost courage. Sick-hearted.

Intending to tell her when no one else was around. Just Mom, and she could tell Dad later, in her own words, and he wouldn't be there, and that would be a way of doing it. And his parents would tell his brothers and his sister, in a way they could. But he needed to tell her in some way that wasn't direct.

How disappointed she'd be. But sympathetic, wanting to hug him. (Could he bear being *hugged*? Jesus! He was twenty-seven years old.)

And his dad stunned with disappointment. And his brothers pitying him so for once they wouldn't tease or torment him. (But—what would they say to him, when they saw him? Something inside him shriveled and died, trying to think what he'd say to *them*.)

Kind of shitty news. Can't talk about it right now OK?

On patrol with his training officer he'd made some mistakes. It was his "probationary period"—they'd kept reminding him—which made him more anxious and more likely to fuck up like freezing when advancing on an altercation in the street, black youths with guns, drug dealers, knowing what he was supposed to do but totally unable to do it, unable to draw his weapon as commanded, hyperventilating so he'd nearly fainted. And on Camden Avenue assigned to crowd control at the black church he'd had something of the same thing happen, a swirling in his vision, pounding heart, breathing quick and shallow and he'd heard gunshots and his instinct was to duck, actually wasn't able to hear—*to hear and process*—what his training officer was shouting at him. He'd been utterly, hopelessly—could not even think of the word to describe his state—terrified? panicked? paralyzed? Like at the gun range in the academy when he was being examined he'd misfire while before that, at practice, he'd done fairly well—it was the pressure on him that was suffocating him, felt like a vise tightening around his chest.

A cop obeys orders. A rookie cop doesn't fucking think!

He'd tried to explain, he loved being a cop. He'd always hoped to be in law enforcement. City cop, state trooper, highway police. He'd had his heart set on it. He wanted to "enforce" law—"protect" people. He liked the uniform—he loved the uniform. Carrying a firearm was a symbol, like a badge. The uniform, the badge, the holster and revolver but something in him was uncomfortable with the gun, not the object but the firing of the gun in the presence of others, the loud *crack!*—the sense that, having pulled the trigger, you could not nullify what you'd done. Pull the trigger, it was *done*.

Ironically for a law enforcement officer he hadn't been a kid who'd played much with guns. He'd taken little pleasure in "killing" his friends and he'd been dismayed when they'd shot at *him*.

And he wasn't "political." Rarely read a newspaper or watched TV news except local news. Like everyone he knew he'd voted for Ronald Reagan. Reasons behind things didn't engage him as things-in-themselves engaged him. You're a cop, you follow orders.

You're a rookie cop, all you do is follow orders.

He'd been praised for his skills with low-stress rookie-cop duties like traffic control, taking notes at an accident scene and comforting people, typing and filing reports, accompanying older officers on school visits. "Neighborhood Rapport"—a new feature in the Pascayne PD in the aftermath of the State of New Jersey Law Enforcement Reform Project.

There were COs—"corrections officers"—in the Zahn family, though not in Jere's immediate family. A parole officer, in Rutherford. But no cops in Jere's immediate family.

His brothers had been surprised, and impressed. Kid brother Jere admitted to the police academy in Sea Girt.

The nicest of the Zahn brothers. Sweet kid, you could see he wasn't cut out to be a cop.

Why'd they let him? We all knew it was a bad idea.

Jesus! Just 'cause he was big and strong-seeming, doesn't mean he'd make a good cop.

And not in Red Rock.

His training officer told him the news. Brusque in his speech so

Zahn wouldn't see how sorry he felt for the poor kid, the look in the kid's face, like he'd been kicked in the gut and out of nowhere, total surprise.

How could it be a total surprise, hadn't Zahn known? Hadn't he *sensed*?

That was one of Zahn's problems, like something was missing in his brain like, what's it called, "synapse"—"synapses"—something not quite connected. So he'd seem to understand what you were telling him, nodding and saying *Sir, yeh* but it wasn't being absorbed so a few days later he'd screw up and each time was like the first time. You had to like the kid, but you'd never trust him out on the street. The kind of guy who if he fired his weapon might shoot his own foot or worse yet, your foot.

There were two more weeks of the rookie probationary period but they called Zahn in early, to inform him. Better sooner, than later. Better now, than nearer Christmas.

Give the kid time to start looking for another job or return to school for more credits.

Don't understand sir, you're telling me—what?

You aren't being promoted, Jere. You aren't moving up to grade two.

He'd sat there, facing the officer whose responsibility he'd been since early summer. Like an older brother McGreavy had been and between them there'd been—(so Jere had believed, naïvely)—a special understanding of the kind between older and younger brothers *If you fuck up expect your ass to be kicked but basically it's OK. You can keep trying.*

Except somehow this was wrong: Zahn wasn't being told that he could *keep trying*.

That was the meaning of "probation"—you were being judged, assessed, and if you were found lacking, you were not promoted but asked to resign from the force.

He seemed to understand this, yet sat unmoving. His eyes blinked slowly and his mouth had stiffened into a kind of half-smile, his lips parchment-dry.

There were pathetic older patrolmen in the Red Rock precinct. Middle-aged, fat-bellied. Never promoted past Officer III and so just waiting out their time to be retired with pensions. A sound of gunfire on a Red Rock street, these police officers were likely to drive their cruisers in the opposite direction. Their radios often broke down, their reports were confused and incomplete. Like zombies they seemed to the rookie-cops. Going through the motions of the job. You'd never turn into one of *them.*

Like you'd never turn into most of the older men, the veterans, officers with ranks of sergeant and above, all looking older than their ages. Some of them frankly fat, puffy-red-faced and only in their early forties—Christ! Jere was thinking he was better off without the uniform. Better off in some other line of work, maybe public school teaching since he liked kids and kids liked him and it had to be low-stress compared to being a beat-cop.

His father, his brothers would be ashamed of him. They would pity him, as the loser they'd always (secretly) known he was, which fact his loving mother had never known, and would never accept. His sister adored him, he'd been her protector against their brothers. His sister would never doubt *him*—but she'd be disappointed too, and maybe she'd cry. (If she cried, and Mom, he couldn't bear it, Jesus!—run out of the house and slam the door.) His brothers wouldn't tease and torment him as they had when they were living in the same house together because this was serious. *Did'ya hear, Jere got canned from the force? Sons of bitches aren't keeping him on, those fuckers who the fuck do they think they are? It's this "firmative-action"—they got to hire blacks and spics—son-of-a-bitch! I'm telling Jere he should sue.*

There was Kimba Jacyznek, with whom he hadn't spoken since

October 14. Kimba would learn the news, and feel sorry for him; and maybe, he hated to think this, Kimba would think *That loser! I knew.*

He'd been so happy with Kimba, those nights—and she'd seemed so happy with him. Just not possible he'd imagined it all—was it? He could not believe this.

Though maybe it hadn't been altogether real, Kimba's little girl staying with Kimba's mother on those nights. So Kimba missed the little girl and missed being Mommy, at the same time resolved to relate to Jere Zahn as a woman to a man: the sex-relationship but also, and primarily, an emotional relationship. The sex she could do, the emotion she had difficulty with.

He'd guessed she was playing an old, outgrown role—the girl she'd been before she had married and had a baby at the age of twenty-two nearly a decade ago. Yet, he hadn't the experience with women to free her from this role. He had not adequate words.

Yet, overall, she'd seemed pretty happy with him. In a good mood, with him. Laughing, and eyes shining, and seeming to listen intently to him as somewhat falteringly he spoke.

Just three times they'd been intimate, in her apartment. Making love in her bed in pale-peach sheets, and a bedside lamp with a rose-colored shade like the lamp in Jere's sister Elise's bedroom. Each of these nights the little girl was away with the grandmother, but there were traces of the child everywhere so Jere felt he should ask about her, but asking about her involved a sort of play-acting since the prospect of being a kind of father to a stranger's child was disconcerting to him. And he felt that this stranger's child would be judging *him*—comparing him to the child's father (who barely paid child support, lived out of state and rarely troubled to visit or even to call). Kimba had seemed to like Jere's lovemaking—that was the impression he'd had. Kimba hadn't said much. She was quiet, secretive. Jere was a quiet person who talked nervously when women didn't talk as normally they did, to fill the silence; feeling at such times like a bat that needs to send out jittery little waves of air-vibrations to situate himself with other bats and with objects. Some people, it's how you define yourself—talking and being heard. And so, he'd talked but wasn't sure he was being heard though the woman leaned forward listening to him with that air of female intensity that could be turned on and off like a light switch.

He'd thought impulsively *I love you!*

The last time, she'd asked him to leave by 2:00 A.M. and not stay through the night, she'd had a reasonable excuse but he'd been hurt and anxious. Next day he'd called and she didn't call back. And next day he'd followed her, not really following her since he'd been driving in that direction anyway, south on Amsterdam Street, and there was Kimba in her car, driving just ahead of him. And a few days later at the mall he'd seen her and considered calling to her but decided against it.

And he'd called her, and left another message. And she had not called back.

Then, astonishing to Jere Zahn, Kimba Jacyznek lodged a complaint against him at the Red Rock precinct!

Sometime that week she'd called, and one morning his sergeant asked him if this female was someone he knew?—she'd claimed he was "stalking" her.

Jere had been shocked. He hadn't ever stalked anyone in his life! Possibly two or three times he'd driven past the duplex on Irving Street where Kimba and her daughter lived, out of curiosity to see if Kimba's car was in the driveway, or whether other cars were parked there, that might belong to friends of Kimba's, or the ex-husband. Off-duty, driving home to his single-bedroom apartment two miles away he'd fallen into the habit of driving past Kimba's house and slowing his speed as he approached; gazing at windows lighted from within, and shades drawn. He'd had a premonition that Kimba might be in trouble and needing him and she'd call his cell phone and he'd be at her door within minutes, having been, by chance, in the neighborhood.

One of those things they'd look back upon. *That night, when I called you. And you came.*

The sergeant was saying all right, he believed him, or at any rate he wasn't taking the female's complaint seriously. She'd sounded hysterical on the phone, some kind of ethnic accent, half of what she'd said the sergeant couldn't make out. Jere insisted he hadn't ever even considered stalking this woman, or any other.

At the precinct, maybe they'd put it into Jerold Zahn's file. The sergeant had indicated the complaint had been dropped but, who knew?—Jere was sick at heart thinking he couldn't trust anyone.

He'd loved Kimba Jacyznek. Badly, he'd wanted to love her.

Made it a point never to drive past her house on Amsterdam, since that day. Though he'd called her and left a friendly message which wasn't an unnatural or an illegal thing to do, with the pretense that she hadn't complained to the sergeant, or that he knew nothing about it. But this message, or messages, were not returned. He had to wonder why, at the start of their relationship several months before, when he'd left messages for Kimba at home or at her work she'd called him back within hours, even minutes—what had gone wrong? What had been the disappointment she'd felt for him? Was it his intelligence? His personality? His *body*? The way he'd made love to her, that was wrong somehow? That was in error, somehow? Not a normal way of lovemaking, or inadequate in some way, but what way? Was his breath repulsive, was his body repulsive? (Examined himself in the bathroom mirror with its pitiless overhead light. He hated the white blond hair, eyebrows and lashes, some kind of albino freak, but apart from that he looked OK, he thought. Not so different from any other guy, he thought.) Then in the Mill River Mall he'd seen Kimba pushing a cart, and the little girl Edie with her, quickly he'd turned and exited the mall before Kimba could see him and register surprise, dismay, fear—before she had grounds to report him another time.

Yet, his heart was broken. They would say, his sister Elise would say, it wasn't just the Pascayne police letting my brother down it was that woman.

In the Zahn household, *that woman* would not have a name. "Kimba Jacyznek" would not be named.

He was religious about cleaning his revolver. He'd never failed to clean his revolver each week. He took pride in the revolver that had been issued to him: Police Officer Jerold Zahn, Pascayne Police Department. He was supposed to turn in the revolver, with his badge. His uniform, he could not wear. They were taking all these things from him. He had not ever used his revolver, except at the firing range. He was not a good "shot." He'd been shaky, he'd had to take longer than others. But his instructors at the academy had liked him. His schoolteachers had liked him. Guys had liked him, especially guys on the team. Girls liked him, though a girl had not ever "loved" him.

His mother said *When you smile, Jere honey—you light up the room! Wish you smiled more, honey.*

"This, too, shall pass."

("This, too, shall pass"—a familiar saying of his grandfather, his mother's father who'd died when Jere was ten years old. Jere hadn't known what the words meant but guessed they were intended to be a consolation, yet not a happy consolation. Like saying that, if you're in a wheelchair, it's raining out anyway, you can't go out to play.)

But they didn't want him now. Kimba, or the others. Any of the others including those girls he'd never called, knowing beforehand how they wouldn't want him. And guys he'd been friendly with from school, but wasn't seeing much any longer like they'd lost interest in Jere Zahn or had forgotten him. And the Pascayne PD. *Probation means you're promoted or out on your ass. No second chances for losers.*

His size was misleading. In high school he'd lifted weights, he'd been diligent and possibly a little obsessed, and it had paid off. And his smile—Jere Zahn's "nice" smile. (You smiled to show you were cool, you weren't anxious or fretting. You smiled to show you had some good reason to smile.) The Zahn kid was never sarcastic like most teenagers. Always sincere. But they didn't want him now, anyway. None of them wanted him: the Pascayne PD, and the woman. They just didn't want him. He felt sick, having to know this. It was a fact simple as a nail driven through a hand. Later that day after stopping by his parents' house he'd driven to a liquor store and bought a bottle of gin with a nasty boar's head on it, he'd never had a swallow of gin before in his life and now drinking gin in mouthfuls trying not to vomit, like kerosene it tasted, what you'd imagined kerosene would taste like. His badge he'd been so proud of, he'd leave on the kitchen table in his little apartment. No note, he wasn't the kind to express himself clearly in words. Any words he'd ever used seriously he had fucked up. He couldn't trust just *words.* He was getting sicker, drinking, not a good idea to drink but there was some reason he'd begun. Cleaning the revolver for the final time, smelling the oil, the nickel-finish, shutting his eyes in wonderment and a loss beyond all thoughts as beyond all words hearing a voice bemused and chiding *Oh shit Zahn just do it. C'mon just do it. The bullets are in, it's in working condition, you ain't gonna miss from close range. Now's your opportunity to do something right for one fucking time in your sorry-ass life.*

The Twins

G od *damn*."

He'd tripped on a step. Hurrying, breathless, and he hadn't glanced down, or having glanced down hadn't seen the step, for his vision was occluded and the beat of his blood strong and distracting in his ears and there were strangers watching, whose faces he couldn't see—a TV audience? And these blinding lights?

"Jesus help me . . ."

Waking then, abruptly. Sweating. And for a moment not recalling where he was except *not home*.

Not in his own bed, in his home. But in a spare bedroom, in a lumpy bed, at his brother's place in Newark.

For he and Klarinda had had a rare quarrel and the consequence was that in the heated aftermath he'd said God damn it all right, he would move out, and Klarinda said she thought that might be a good idea, for now.

How furious he'd been! How quick to be wounded, how sensitive to Klarinda's every word, every glance these past several weeks—his wife whom he'd loved for too long perhaps, he'd become overly dependent upon the woman, and so weakened in himself, as a man.

Unlike his brother Marus: dependent upon no female, on principle.

Hot-faced, shaking, relenting just slightly, for his pride had been grievously wounded by the woman's accusations, if she so distrusted him, if she had no faith in him—if she wanted him to move out *he would*.

And gazing at her husband with frank pitying eyes Klarinda had said: "Yes. I think so, Byron. As long as you're aligned with *him*. That might be a good idea, for now."

Excited by the prospect of combat, he could not easily sleep.

In dread of public failure, exposure and humiliation, he could not allow himself to sleep.

Recalling how in the hot damp darkness of their mother's womb he'd fought for nourishment, most desperately he'd fought against *being consumed* by his larger twin. For sometimes it happens, more often than a surviving twin would wish to think, that the larger fetus drains life from the smaller, and sucks the smaller being into itself to lodge like a secret tumor in some region of the chest, the gut, the skull.

Some measure of prenatal memory lay deep within him, the instinct of an animal that has never seen the prairie, for instance, but knows how to raise itself cautiously on its rear haunches, and then its front legs, and its head lifted warily, for the flat landscape is a place of predators.

There are animals for whom all landscapes contain predators, as there are animals for whom all landscapes contain prey.

"Time to escalate, Brother."

"Why do you say that? 'Escalate'—how?"

Dreading what plan Marus had next.

Aligned with his brother Marus, Byron Mudrick had at last received the public attention long withheld from him: TV and radio interviews, a joint-profile titled "The Crusading Mudrick Brothers of New Jersey" in *Essence,* the most astonishing respectful coverage in the *New York Times,* the *Washington Post,* the Newark *Star-Ledger,* the Trenton *Times,* the *Nation* and *Mother Jones* as well as black publications.

Yet, despite this early, vertiginous success it had begun to be evident that interest in the Crusade for Justice for Sybilla Frye was waning by the second week of December. A spike of publicity in the New Jersey–New York City area would bring with it almost immediately thousands of dollars in donations to the Care Ministry of Central New Jersey, and pledges for more, but these quickly leveled off as a fickle public became distracted by other racial issues, and outrages, publicized by the media.

After the near-disaster of the "march" along Camden Avenue to the Pitcairn Bridge and across the river to City Hall . . . Narrowly, chaos had been averted; the deployment of hundreds of law enforcement officers had saved them, ironically. If there'd been fewer cops, the crowd would have swarmed out of the church and along the avenue, like a great beast without a brain; older and slower individuals would have been trampled; stores would have been looted, vehicles and buildings set afire, and the Crusade for Justice for Sybilla Frye would have ended, as such poorly organized gatherings often did, in the destruction of the marchers' own neighborhood. Reverend Mudrick had protested to TV cameras the "Nazi-Racist Police State" that curtailed the march before it had begun, but Byron Mudrick had been greatly relieved; only a half-dozen individuals had been injured in the melee, that had been contained within a single city block; police had arrested few marchers, hadn't used excessive force so far as Byron knew, and, thank God!—had shot down no one.

Inside the church, Byron had heard gunshots on the street. Like the white-skinned journalists and media people trapped in the first several rows of the church he'd been terrified by the sudden explosion of energy his brother Marus had unleashed, with the reckless aplomb of a boy tossing a match into dried tinder.

Having exhorted the crowd to march out of the church and across the river to City Hall, Marus had held back, himself. He'd escorted Ednetta Frye and the girl out of the church, at the rear, to take refuge in Reverend Denis's house next-door.

Byron hadn't had any warning that Marus was going to make the announcement he'd made from the pulpit of the church, charging his followers to march across the river seeking "justice." He'd been stunned, appalled. He'd been terrified. His brother had always behaved unpredictably, following his instinct for attracting attention and provoking controversy; but Byron could not forgive him for not having confided in *him*.

Jesus! My brother is insane.

Reckless, vicious . . .

But I'm the one who will be disbarred.

Afterward, Marus said with a shrug that he hadn't consulted with Byron because he'd known that Byron would have counseled him against the impromptu march. And Byron said, incensed, "You are right, Marus! You are absolutely right."

"You're a conservative by nature, Brother. I'm a radical."

"You're a *Christian*. You can't betray the basic tenets of our religion."

"Brother, there are 'conservative' and 'radical' Christians. Jesus

Christ was hardly 'conservative'—He died for his radical beliefs, and we must emulate him."

"You don't want to die for your beliefs, Marus—don't be ridiculous. Like King? Like Malcolm X? Not you."

Wanting to add, with a younger brother's disdain *Beliefs! As if you have any.*

Yet calmly Marus said, clasping his fingers across his sizable belly with an air of satisfaction: "You are very mistaken, Brother Byron. When Marus Mudrick walks out into the streets, when he stands at a pulpit, he is exposing himself to—whatever will happen, that is the will of God. This is the truth of my life, as I have explained many times."

Byron laughed, uneasily. He resented his brother taking on this vatic tone, that was so obviously hypocritical; yet, Byron never ceased to feel that, in some way, Marus believed what he was saying, while he was saying it.

"My identification is, *I am a Christian. I am a Christian minister who bears witness for Christ*—that is who I am."

In this, Marus Mudrick meant to establish his territory as a black Christian, like Martin Luther King Jr. and Jesse Jackson; unlike the visionary Malcolm X, and Marus's contemporary Louis Farrakhan, celebrants of an exclusionary black religion.

(Marus's only serious rival in black activist causes was the black Islamic leader known as "The Prince"—reputedly, an ex-convict who'd anointed himself Leopaldo Quarrquan. His headquarters were in Baltimore but Quarrquan often traveled to the New Jersey–New York City area, which Marus considered his territory. Byron had cautioned Marus not to provoke a feud with Quarrquan, for it would only go badly for Marus Mudrick, if he did: the Kingdom of Islam did not hold itself, even rhetorically, to the principles of Christianity. Quarrquan was reputed to have arranged for the assassinations of Kingdom of Islam rivals; he'd long been associated with the death of Malcolm X, whose murderers had never been identified. Yet in his reckless way Marus Mudrick charged his rival with "deceit" and "duplicity" within the black community, and "betraying Christianity"; in interviews, Marus dared to point out that at the time of Malcolm X's assassination in Harlem, on February 21, 1965, the head of the Kingdom of Islam Leopaldo Quarrquan had been living in Newark, only forty-five minutes away.)

Byron said irritably, "How can you call me a 'conservative'? I've been fighting for black rights in the courtroom all my adult life! As I am a lawyer, I'm bound by the law—to a degree. I do believe in revolution—legally. I don't believe in risking the lives of innocent, naïvely trusting people. Sending those people out to march on City Hall! What if the police had panicked and begun beating and shooting them? What if people had died?"

Marus frowned, and shrugged. He'd removed his glasses and their imprint was visible on the flat wide bridge of his nose. Thoughtfully he said, as if this were in confidence to his brother, "There must be sacrifice in revolution. At any time, any one of us might be chosen."

"You can choose for yourself, if you want to be a martyr. Martin Luther King chose for himself. But you have no right to choose for other people."

"You don't understand, Brother. I am the people's *leader*. They look to me for hope, and I give them hope. 'The Crusade for Justice for Sybilla Frye' is but one chapter in the epic of Marus Mudrick's life—it may be a prominent chapter, or a minor one. We don't—yet—know how far it will take us."

"What do you mean, 'us'? What about the girl?"

"The girl is blackness violated, scorned and debased. The girl is the perfect black victim."

"Well. Unless the girl comes forward soon with more information, and can describe her assailants more specifically, there isn't much farther we can go with this 'perfect black victim.' It was a terrible mistake for her mother to remove her from the hospital before the examination was complete and a rape kit was assembled."

Byron spoke contemptuously, as if to say *Rape kit! There was never any rape, and we know it.*

Byron spoke hotly, and waited for Marus to contradict him.

But Marus only said, stiffly, with a shifting of his lower body as if he were having digestive pains, "Nothing the Fryes did was a 'mistake'—they acted instinctively. It's unfair for you to judge them, Brother Byron, with your fancy law degree."

"You should have asked me to interview them, before you took on this case, Marus. Or at least to be present when you spoke with them initially."

"Why'd I do that? You'd of scared them off, Brother Byron. With your legal-ese and big words. Mao would have recognized Sybilla and Ednetta and honored them—peasants, the material for revolution."

"Mao? You're quoting Mao?"

"Mao spoke most clearly, Brother—'courage in battle, no fear of sacrifice, no fear of fatigue, continuous fighting' . . ."

"Quoting Chairman Mao! In your three-piece suit and elevated shoes. Fuck you, Brother."

Byron laughed incredulously. Had he moved out of his home, was he risking his marriage of two decades, for *this*? In an instant, not knowing why, he was furious with his brother and would have liked to strike Marus's smug, fat face.

Except, when they'd been boys, Marus had been the one to slap first, and hard.

Punch, pummel, pinch, kick. Hard.

Byron snatched up his worn leather briefcase, and headed for the door.

With brotherly mockery Marus called after him in his mellifluous preacher's voice: "Brother, bless *you*."

Safe House

He'd told them it wasn't safe.

In the (rented, run-down) row house on Third Street. In the two-floor duplex where she'd been living with Anis Schutt since before that trouble at the Polk Clinic when she'd had to quit and pay back money she hadn't even stole—and Sybilla had been a little girl. *That happy time. O Lord.*

Wasn't safe in Red Rock where she'd lived all her life. Where her friends and family lived, and Sybilla's friends and family. And Anis Schutt.

Gravely the Reverend explained: rumor was, Pascayne PD had a "hit" planned for her and her daughter.

Sometime before Christmas, possibly. If they remained in their house they were "living targets"—a SWAT sniper in plainclothes would be sent—so quick, they wouldn't know they'd been hit.

Ednetta was terrified. Sybilla said in a whiny voice, "Oh shit, Mama! Where we goin to live, then?"

For a few days they stayed with Ednetta's sister Cheryl and her kids which was a strain on the adults in such close quarters but wonderful for Sybilla and Martine who could share Martine's bed and watch TV together; but Martine went to school each weekday, and Sybilla had to stay home sulky and fretting. And Ednetta disobeyed Marus Mudrick's wishes by slipping back to the row house on Third Avenue, where Anis Schutt was living.

It was imperative, the Reverend said, that he could reach Ednetta at any time. If something happened, and he needed to contact her.

"He tellin us what to do all the time, seems like," Ednetta complained to her sister; and Cheryl said, in her snide-sister way, "You went to *him,* 'Netta."

"Sister Ednetta? Look at today's newspaper."

In Cheryl's kitchen, and the kids screeching. Ednetta cupped her hand over the receiver trying to explain to the Reverend that there wasn't any newspaper at her sister's and the Reverend said curtly, "Then get one. I'll call back in ten minutes."

Cheryl sent one of the boys out to fetch a paper.

At 939 Third Street the *Pascayne Journal* came every morning. Reverend Mudrick had paid for a subscription. Since what had happened to Sybilla, and the first of the articles in local papers, Ednetta had begun to read the local paper, or at least to quickly skim it, for the first time in her life on a regular basis.

Now, newspapers were accumulating on the front stoop of the row house, or moldering with wet on the ground. Anis rarely picked up a newspaper though when he was home he watched TV local news to check, as he'd say, who'd gotten arrested or killed that day he might know. (Seeing the face of someone newly deceased whom he'd known Anis would say with a pained smile *That do it for you, bro!*)

When the Reverend called back, precisely ten minutes later, Ednetta was skimming the front page of the *Pascayne Journal* anxiously.

Her eyes! Seemed like, these past few weeks, her eyesight was dimming.

And her left ear, where Anis had cuffed her—her hearing was fuzzy and diminished.

Cheryl had sent her kids out of the kitchen so Ednetta could hear the Reverend on the phone. Still, the place was noisy: damn TV on loud.

And where was Sybilla? (Ednetta dreaded the girl slipping out as she'd done a few nights ago, with Martine to pretend that Sybilla had "gone to bed, early.")

Reverend Mudrick told Ednetta to look on page seven of the first section.

Look for what? "Rookie Cop Death Ruled 'Gun Accident' Pending Investigation."

Grainy photograph of a boyish-faced young man with pale hair, a strong-jawed face, shy-friendly smile and dimples in both cheeks.

"Rev'end? What? I'm lookin . . ."

"There he is, Ednetta: '*Rookie Cop.*' "

Ednetta was confused. "Who—who's this?"

The caption beneath the photograph identified *Jerold M. Zahn, 27, Pascayne Police Dept.*

Was this someone Ednetta was supposed to know? She hated the Reverend talking to her like this, as often he did, and to Sybilla too, as if they were so stupid they had to be led by their hand.

Gravely Reverend Mudrick said: "Sister Ednetta, that is the 'yelow-hair' cop who raped your daughter."

Ednetta was so stunned, for a moment she couldn't speak.

"Oh—no . . . No, Rev'end, this ain't him."

"Call Sybilla. Let Sybilla make that decision."

"Rev'end, this ain't him. This some sad boy looks like he kilt himself with his gun . . ."

"This is no 'sad boy,' Sister Ednetta. This is the 'yelow-hair cop' who raped your daughter, she'd identified as best as she could under the circumstances. But now, here is his photo, and here is his name. 'Jerold Zahn.'"

Ednetta was rubbing her arm energetically. Aching joints, swollen knuckles. Her mother Pearline spoke of the "misery"—that was what Ednetta had now.

She'd been crying to Cheryl the night before *If only none of this had got started! All that damn girl's fault.*

"Call your daughter to the phone. Please."

Ednetta wanted to protest but dared not. Even on the telephone Reverend Mudrick exerted a powerful spell that left Ednetta feeling weak.

Ednetta went to fetch Sybilla back in Martine's bedroom. Though Sybilla had complained of school, having to study, do homework, take tests, now that she'd been temporarily excused from school attendance on the recommendation of Dr. Cleveland, she complained of missing school, and all her friends. She'd been sleeping in her clothes, it looked like. Her hair was like a bushman's springing out from her head and as she came slowly into the kitchen to take the phone, she was sucking her thumb.

Deftly Ednetta knocked Sybilla's hand away from her mouth. "Shhh, girl! It's the Reverend wantin to talk to you."

Sybilla made a face, shrinking away, but Ednetta pushed the receiver at her.

Sybilla took the receiver and pressed it against her ear. Her mouth was sullen. Cheryl had told Ednetta a rumor Ednetta didn't want to believe, that Jaycee Handler was back in Red Rock on parole, and had spoken of looking up Sybilla Frye.

Sybilla said little as Reverend Mudrick addressed her in his urgent voice, for Reverend Mudrick rarely allowed others to speak; he knew all the words beforehand, and so there was no need for anyone else to speak. Reverend Mudrick was like certain of her teachers except the teachers always came to an end, with the class period, while there could be no natural end to Reverend Mudrick's talk.

Sybilla did as Reverend Mudrick instructed, examining the photograph at the top of page seven of the *Pascayne Journal*.

Rookie Cop Death Ruled "Gun Accident" Pending Investigation.

Sybilla squinted at the young man's face. White guy, kind of boyish, good-looking. Was he some older kid at school, one of the few white guys? But couldn't be, if he was twenty-seven.

The Reverend was saying, "Sister Sybilla? He has committed suicide out of guilt for what he did to you. And now you can come forward."

Sybilla squinted at the photo. She'd jammed her thumb into her mouth and was sucking.

"Here is the 'yelow-hair cop' you saw, Sybilla. The one who was a little younger than the others. Take your time studying the photo."

Laughter began deep inside Sybilla, unless it was trembling. Her silly heart was beating quickly.

"Nah, Rev'end, that ain't him. I guess I didn't see who it was so clear. They had, like, this towel over my face so I couldn't see— 'blindfold.'" Sybilla began coughing. Close by Ednetta stood listening shaking her head *No, no!* but Sybilla ignored her.

Speaking gravely, yet forcefully, Marus Mudrick sounded as if he were in the kichen with Sybilla. Almost, she could feel his heavy warm hand on her shoulder where often he let it fall, seemingly by chance.

"Try again, Sybilla. Here is the 'yelow-hair cop'—you can see he's blond, and any kind of 'blond' hair would have looked to you like 'yellow' in your duress. He was a relatively young cop, you'd said—maybe thirty—one of the five or six or seven 'white cops' who raped you. See, 'Jerold Zahn' has killed himself over the shame and guilt of having raped *you*. He has killed himself because he knows that the Crusade for Justice for Sybilla Frye would soon have identi-fied him . . . Sybilla? Are you there?"

Sybilla mumbled an inaudible reply.

"We are going to identify 'Jerold Zahn'—we will come to Pas-cayne PD headquarters immediately."

Sybilla was staring at the photograph in the paper. A white boy, looked like a nice boy, even if he was some kind of cop—"rookie." There were white guys Sybilla knew, fair-skinned, part Anglo from the Islands so you couldn't tell if they were Puerto Rican or Jamaican or—whatever. This boy didn't look much like them with his white-looking hair. A certain kind of older fair-skinned boy like in high school or older, observing Sybilla Frye like he'd kind of like *her*. They weren't all nasty.

There were streets in Red Rock in an outlying district where some of them lived. She'd wanted to make that clear. In the inter-views, where Sybilla sat silent beside Reverend Mudrick while he answered questions, she'd wanted to interrupt sometimes and ex-plain that "white cops" had hurt her but she didn't hate all "white" people—she did not.

She'd had teachers . . .

And this boy, looked like he'd shot himself with his gun. That had to be sad.

"Nah, this ain't him, Rev'end. The one that did it was like older . . ."

"Sybilla, look again. Take your time."

"This ain't him, Rev'end."

Sybilla's voice was beginning to quaver. Ednetta was feeling so stressed, she was pacing at the doorway, hitting her fists light against her thighs. Her face was a net of wrinkles Sybilla hated to see—*No no no no no.*

Weakly Sybilla said she didn't think this was the man—"Like I say, he younger, Rev'end. The 'yelow-hair cop' I saw was not so young"—and Reverend Mudrick interrupted saying how fitting it was, at this time, that one of her rapists should kill himself out of fear of being exposed by the Crusade; being caught, arrested, and put to public shame. And Sybilla said that might be right but this wasn't the man. And Reverend Mudrick said this was the one who killed himself—"The guilt was just too much for him. Even a white Nazi-fascist cop."

Sybilla was shaking her head *no,* stubbornly.

Ednetta had come to stand square before her, staring at her face. But Sybilla's sly-drifting left eye avoided her mother's urgent gaze and her other, good eye was shimmering with tears.

The Reverend was saying, slowly, as one might speak to a retarded person, "This happens to be the Pascayne police officer who has killed himself, Sybilla. We are not going to have a choice of such officers, I think. Is your mother there? I can talk to her."

Quickly Sybilla murmured *No! Mama ain't here.*

"It's a crucial step, Sybilla. Here is our man—a gift and a blessing from Jesus. People are beginning to say, even in Pascayne, even among my brother's law students and Newark colleagues, that you might have lied, Sybilla—made the 'kidnapping' and the 'rape' up. Because you haven't identified a single 'white cop' so far. And now, when one of them is displayed before you, and you have plenty of time to deliberate and remember, you must seize it."

Sybilla sucked at her thumb, breathing quickly.

"D'you know what 'perjury' is, Sybilla? 'Filing a false charge' with the police? If you've lied, if there was never any rape and never any 'white cops,' the Pascayne PD will arrest *you*. The district attorney will get a waiver for your age, and try Sybilla Frye as an adult." Reverend Mudrick paused.

"Do you want to examine the photograph again? 'Jerold Zahn, twenty-seven.' It's natural that you mistook his light-blond hair for 'yelow hair'—the interior of the van would have been dim."

Sybilla said, with an angry little sob, "OK Rev'end. This him."

Quickly then before Reverend Mudrick could speak again she hung up the phone. Would have run blindly out of the apartment and into the drafty corridor and maybe tripped and flung herself down the stairs but her mother grabbed her and shook her, hard.

"Girl, what the hell you doin? That 'rookie cop' some mother's son feelin bad and kilt himself, and now—"

Sybilla jerked her arm away from her mother. With a sulky sort of triumph she said, "Go fuck y'self, Mama. This shit all comin from *you*."

Sybilla ran from the kitchen and into the interior of the apartment. Ednetta was too distressed to follow. Nor did Ednetta wish to answer her sister's prying questions. With the dazed helplessness of a creature staring at a cobra she stared at the telephone waiting for it to ring.

"Yelow Hair"

Y**es."**

And, "Yes. That him."

"You are certain, Miss Frye? This officer—'Jerold Zahn'?"

As instructed by Byron Mudrick she spoke quietly and without hesitation. She was not emotional: not sullen, not angry, not resentful, not vindictive, not anxious and not fearful. She did not betray uncertainty, or apprehension. Her eyes were partway closed.

"The young lady hardly knew the officer's name, Officer. No point in asking her that."

Byron Mudrick spoke curtly, with an edge of irony.

Third floor Pascayne City Hall, Family Services Division. On the morning of December 14, 1987, Sybilla Frye was seated at a table in an interview room making a formal statement to a woman officer from the Pascayne Police Department Juvenile Aid Bureau: identifying the "yellow-hair cop" who had raped her and participated in beating her on or about October 4, 1987.

Sybilla wasn't definite about the location of the assault. As Byron Mudrick had cautioned her, she should say that she believed she'd been kept captive in "some kind of van, like a police van" and that it had not been driven very far, but parked much of the time.

(Byron Mudrick had explained to Sybilla that this was to establish "jurisdiction"—"Otherwise they might try to say that the crimes were committed in a county other than Passaic, and pass the blame onto someone else.")

With Sybilla and Byron Mudrick were her mother Ednetta and Reverend Marus Mudrick, who were seated in chairs behind them, against a wall of the windowless room.

Byron Mudrick who was Sybilla's "legal counsel" was more comforting to her than Reverend Mudrick who seemed never really to look at *her*. Byron was softer-spoken, with a smile like her real daddy ought to've had, if she'd ever known him. (Anis Schutt who was her stepdaddy had a smile hard as steel. You never wanted to see that smile bare Anis's yellowy teeth.)

Sybilla was so grateful to Byron Mudrick! He'd insisted that his "juvenile client" meet with police officials and the Passaic County district attorney in the County Family Services Bureau office and not at police headquarters across the street, in order to avert a "nightmare scenario" of the rape victim accidentally encountering one or more of her yet-unidentified rapists.

"That would be a trauma we can avoid," Byron Mudrick said gravely. "The original trauma, the nightmare to my client, is irrevocable."

Family Services was a far friendlier setting than police headquarters, in any case. Ednetta Frye had come to this office a number of times in the past several years and believed she could remember having brought Sybilla with her at least once.

There would not be such hostility to the Fryes, in Family Services, as in police headquarters. They would be spared entering into what Reverend Mudrick called the "dominion of the Enemy."

Present also at the meeting were several Family Services officials, all women. And one of the social workers who'd come to speak with Ednetta Frye in her home several weeks before, whom Ednetta had ordered to leave.

The Pascayne Juvenile Aid officer, the Red Rock precinct captain, and the Passaic County district attorney sat at the table with Sybilla Frye and Byron Mudrick. Other officials, including several assistant district attorneys, sat behind the table in chairs against the wall.

This was a meeting highly charged with emotion! Sybilla sensed waves of repugnance for her, from the Enemy; though Byron had warned her and her mother what to expect, it was disconcerting. Sybilla wasn't used to being in places where people disliked *her*—like they had some special reason to dislike *her*?

Both Byron and Reverend Mudrick had cautioned her not to smile at the Enemy, and not to make eye-contact. Ednetta had been so nervous earlier that morning, she'd been in and out of the bathroom throwing up.

Sybilla was only vaguely aware of the hours of negotiation that had preceded the meeting. Numerous calls had passed between Byron Mudrick and the Red Rock captain and other police officials, and between Byron Mudrick and the district attorney and assistants. As soon as he'd announced to them that his client had "made an ID of one of her rapists" and wanted to meet with authorities to "confirm" it, the Enemy had reacted with alacrity.

The agreement was: Byron Mudrick would bring his client to City Hall to identify one of the "alleged rapists" and to make a brief, formal statement, but nothing more.

No "interview" with the Juvenile Aid officer. Not at this time.

Byron Mudrick insisted that Sybilla Frye hadn't fully recovered from the violent trauma she'd undergone. To subject the fifteen-year-old to further trauma would be an outrage.

Sybilla wore a long-sleeved white silk blouse with a little bow, a dark pleated skirt, dark woolen stockings and shoe-boots. In the shallow crevice of her throat, a small gold cross glittered.

Her hair had been hot-combed and plaited and fixed in place with plastic barrettes. She might have been a middle school student, and not a high school student; her almond-shaped eyes were both downcast and alert. The only visible scar on her face was a tiny white comma in her left eyebrow.

No ear-studs, no bracelets or rings. And her fingernails neatly filed, short and unpolished as a child's nails.

"Miss Frye? Will you look at these, and tell us if this is the same man . . ."

Several photographs of a young man with light blond hair were shown to Sybilla. In none of these was the young man smiling and there were no visible dimples in his cheeks.

Might've been Jerold Zahn, or someone else. Sybilla sensed a trick.

"My client says no, she doesn't recognize this man. If this is Jerold Zahn or someone else, she doesn't recognize the photo." Byron paused. In a voice heavy with sarcasm he said that his client had only "glimpsed" the rapist—"In not ideal circumstances and in a state of pain and terror."

Sybilla pointed to the original photograph, which had appeared in the newspaper. This was the one!

"My client is certain that the man in this photo is the man she remembers from the assault. 'Jerold Zahn'—a positive ID."

Buzzing in the room. Shock, outrage. Sybilla wasn't listening.

Sharp raised voices—male. And Byron Mudrick answering, quick and efficient.

But Sybilla wasn't listening. It was all a haze. It was all happening somewhere else. And Sybilla wasn't looking. Downcast eyes, shy and stricken. Deep inside, she wasn't even there.

Jaycee saying to her *S'b'la we gon see each other when I get out, that a promise.*

The look in Jaycee's face when his sister Shirley appeared with Sybilla in the visitors' room at Mountainview—and Jaycee expecting to see his little sister Colette.

Damn she was crazy for Jaycee Handler. Never minded he was at Mountainview where she could just think of him and not have to worry about the kind of things you'd worry about, if you were a girl, and a guy like Jaycee "liked" you.

But now God damn, she was so shamed!—Jaycee seemed to forgot her. A week at least he'd been out of Mountainview. Must be parole—probation? Martine was the one to tell her, knowing how it would hurt.

Except—it was maybe better if Jaycee didn't try to come around right now.

She'd have to explain some things to the Reverend—not sure what she'd tell him. Fuck it!

Fuck sometimes she wished he'd killed her, like he said he would do.

All the day before Marus Mudrick and Byron Mudrick had coached her and rehearsed her these few words to utter, how to breathe (through her nose), how to move her head, her eyes, where to look, where not to look, how to clasp her hands together in front of her when she wasn't required to point to a photograph—(for instance). How she must not "lock eyes" with anyone in the room—any of the Enemy.

The Family Services people, and the social worker—they'd be wanting to speak with her, get her attention, but—*no*.

And going into City Hall, and afterward leaving City Hall: walking between the Mudrick brothers, and Mama close behind, so the photographers, journalists, TV people (Reverend Mudrick had alerted) could observe her but not take advantage of her. Byron Mudrick and Marus Mudrick would speak to selected reporters and TV interviewers on the steps of City Hall only after Sybilla and her mother were safely enclosed in the waiting car with dark-tinted windows.

Rape Victim I.D.'s One of Six Alleged "White Cop" Rapists.

Between them they'd coached her until she'd wanted to lay her head down on the table and just cry. Until she'd screamed and wept and laughed the high wild laugh Mama said was a crazy-girl's laugh it scared her to hear. And Mama held her arms pinned to her sides to quiet her saying it would be all right, the Reverend had explained why it was necessary, and had to be done, and would be over soon.

They'd promised *Just this once, Sybilla. Just say what we have prepared for you to say. Not a word more. Then we will leave. You will never have to see them again we promise.*

Until now it had been mostly Reverend Mudrick who'd done all the talking. In this meeting-place in Pascayne City Hall it was Byron Mudrick who did most of the talking in his quick-snappy way reminding Sybilla of a whip, a whip you could snap, a whip to snap into the face of the Enemy.

Sybilla was rubbing her eyes. So sleepy! She never slept right any longer even with Martine cuddling beside her and snoring quiet like a cat.

His snores she'd hear through the house, in their old place. Hoped they would never go back to that damn stinky place.

"Sybilla?"—Byron Mudrick nudged her gently.

Oh here was a surprise: yellow Post-its on the table before her.

Not close in front of Sybilla so she might've grabbed and torn them if some wild impulse had come over her but about eighteen inches away. The Juvenile Aid policewoman had had these, in a folder. It was surprising and disorienting to Sybilla to see the Post-its she'd forgotten, or mostly forgotten, confused with a vague memory of the St. Anne's emergency room and Mama clutching at her like crazy trying to protect her from the medics and that female detective asking questions—looked like Puerto Rican—dark straight eyebrows, straight nose, beautiful eyes and beautiful smooth tanned-olive skin—real kind to Sybilla saying *Maybe it would be easier to write, Sybilla? Here.*

The Post-its had been hers. The detective. For a brief second flashing like a short thread through the eye of a needle Sybilla recalled the woman, then forgot her. They were confronting her with the Post-its hand-printed in pencil:

WHITE COP

WEAR A BAGDE

YELOW HAIR

AGE 30

Yes. Shook her head *yes*.

Yes she recognized these.

Sybilla's heart beat hard in protest. They'd promised her she would not have to answer questions only just say what she'd memorized. Yet, questions were being asked, and Byron Mudrick was answering them in his quick curt whip-snap way; and sometimes, Marus Mudrick would interject a cutting remark, and Byron might turn to Ednetta seated behind them blinking and staring like a drunk woman, and Sybilla would cringe hearing her mother stammer *What—what did you say? What?*

The hostility in the room! She'd been warned to expect it, she'd been warned to expect the hatred of the Enemy, for of course they would deny that one of their own, Police Officer Jerold Zahn, had committed a heinous crime, but there was something more than just hatred, Sybilla thought—the looks in the faces of the women from Family Services, and the social worker—like they were all but saying aloud *You poor girl! What has been done to you, Sybilla Frye!*

Hiding her face in shame. Hiding her eyes.

"No. My client will not answer any more questions today. And yes, we will consent to a polygraph. So long as I am involved in the choice of the polygrapher who will not be an employee of the Pascayne Police Department or, indeed, any law enforcement bureau in this state." When Byron paused, Marus Mudrick quietly interjected: "And not a 'white' polygrapher."

(Polygraph? Was this—"lie detector"?)

(Sybilla felt faint. Hunched over her tight-clasped hands. The buzzing in her ears, a quick beat-beat-beat of blood. Byron Mudrick had promised—*Don't even try to listen, what will be said. By them and by me. These are tactics of law. The Enemy has no defenses. The Enemy is flummoxed. And that means fucked.*)

Byron said: "Yes. We will insist upon choosing the polygrapher ourselves."

Byron was on his feet, signaling the end of the meeting. Affably he said, "We'll hope to schedule the polygraph before the end of the year, if you can meet our criteria. In the meantime, we've made some progress—my client has made the first identification of her rapists. She will soon give a full statement. By then her memory may have returned at least partially, so that she might identify others of her rapists among the Pascayne Police Department. We will want to examine photographs—we will want a 'lineup.' But this is enough for today—this is more than enough. You can investigate 'Jerold Zahn,' one of your own. Determine why this twenty-seven-year-old white man shot a bullet into his brain, and why at such an appropriate time as the Crusade for Justice for Sybilla Frye was coming into prominence. Officers, look a little harder for the suicide note. Interrogate the family. They've taken the note and hidden it, and it's up to your skilled detectives to find it and reveal its guilt-laden contents to the world. And now, we are leaving."

Byron spoke calmly and with much satisfaction. His lawyer's diction, clipped and precise, he'd cultivated since moot court in law school in emulation of certain of his revered elders. Sharp as an arrow, young Byron Mudrick! He was seeing lately that his very integrity had held him back, as a clubfoot holds back a runner. Around him he'd seen lesser individuals, like his twin brother, rise to prominence, make names and reputations for themselves, lavishly profiled in the white liberal press. And now, belatedly, it was Byron Mudrick's turn.

The Enemy's outrage he felt like waves of deafening sound, that can scarcely be registered yet is felt deep in the guts, and it made him happy as mere words could not make him happy. *We are doing this. The Mudrick brothers are playing this hand. Trump card! See what you can do, assholes.*

Not all of the Enemy was white. But those *of color* who worked for the Enemy were enemies by association.

One of the D.A.'s assistants was a dark-skinned Hispanic in his mid-thirties who looked with particular disdain upon Byron Mudrick. No doubt, his law degree was from Rutgers–New Brunswick and not Rutgers-Newark. Or Penn. He'd spoken only briefly at the meeting, not to Byron but to his boss the district attorney, but Byron had detected a New Jersey accent, nasal, possibly Camden-area, like his own. Arrogant bastard looking with contempt upon *him.*

There were two other dark-skinned individuals among the Enemy: a middle-aged supervisor from Family Services, and the social worker who'd had the Frye family in her caseload. Tight-curly hair trimmed close to her head like Klarinda's hair, and that professional-black-woman air of moral rectitude Byron found so exasperating in his wife—he couldn't bear it! She was staring at Byron Mudrick as if she were frankly, openly disgusted with him, and wasn't about to disguise it.

He felt a pang of hurt, and anger. Wanting to say *Sybilla Frye is our scourge to harrow Hell. See what the fuck you can do to stop us.*

The Prize

"See, Brother? What is meant by 'escalation.'"

Marus Mudrick laughed deep in his throat. As the elder of the Mudrick twins he'd taken a lifelong delight in surprising, impressing, intimidating and awing his younger brother.

It was so: following the identification of a young, recently deceased police officer in the Pascayne PD as one of several "alleged rapists" of Sybilla Frye, the Crusade for Justice for Sybilla Frye leapt prominently back into the media.

New York Times, New York Post, People, Associated Press, *Philadelphia Inquirer,* Newark *Star-Ledger, Pascayne Journal* . . . Photographs of Jerold Zahn on the front pages of newspapers, on TV news. On NPR, a forty-minute interview with Byron Mudrick.

Twenty-seven-year-old Pascayne police officer Jerold Zahn, who died in a "gun accident" on December 11, has been identified by the fifteen-year-old rape victim as one of "six or seven" local law enforcement officers who allegedly kidnapped, beat, and gang-raped her in Pascayne, in early October, in a case that has yielded few suspects.

Reverend Marus Mudrick of the Care Ministry of Central New Jersey and the victim's legal counsel Byron Mudrick are charging the Pascayne Police Department, Pascayne city officials, as well as the Passaic County district attorney's office with "criminal conspiracy" to cover up the crimes. The Mudrick brothers are demanding a specially convened New Jersey State Commission to investigate whether their client's civil rights were violated, in addition to the pressing of criminal charges. ———

"We will not rest until there has been justice for Sybilla Frye, as for the hundreds of thousands of other, similarly violated and debased black victims of our time," Byron Mudrick told reporters on the steps of City Hall last Monday after a meeting with police and prosecutors. "Sybilla Frye is but the first, and will not be the last."

Byron Mudrick, 44, professor of law Rutgers-Newark Law School, has been a civil rights activist since 1961, an officer and legal counsel of the NAACP, a member of the ACLU, the National African-American Legal Defense Fund, the Lawyers' Guild, the National Bar Association, and the National African-American Christian Fellowship.

Had to laugh how the (white, elitist) media leapt like circus animals through Reverend Marus Mudrick's flaming hoops. Byron had had his differences with Marus over the years—some betrayals, for which he'd never forgive his brother—(though it was pragmatic to pretend to forget)—but he had to admire Marus lifting the hoop ever higher, fanning the flames brighter, the fools leapt nonetheless. And the money came in.

Marus took care to provide a Newark, New Jersey, P.O. box for donations to "The Crusade for Justice for Sybilla Frye," or "Sybilla Fry"—a name variously misspelled, yet Marus's bank in Newark would honor it.

Donations came in checks, frequently in cash. No tax records were made of the cash donations, Byron supposed. Marus made it a point to oversee his assistants at the Care Ministry when they opened envelopes containing donations—"Not that I don't trust my girls, but it's cruel for them to be tempted and feel guilt if they succumb."

Mail donations varied from three thousand to seventeen thousand within the space of a week following the identification of Jerold Zahn, that had caused a small media sensation not only locally, in the New Jersey–New York area, but across the country, with the Associated Press and *USA Today* running detailed articles. Of course, these were figures reported to Byron, by his brother Marus.

When Byron mentioned to Marus that he hoped none of the donations were "disappearing"—(as substantial sums had "disappeared" during Marus Mudrick's directorship of another non-profit activist organization in the early 1980s)—Marus said coldly, "As the tide rises, all flotsum an jetsum gon rise with it. You workin *pro bono,* Brother Byron. All the world know *that.*"

In the insolent urban-black dialect this was a double slur: a suggestion that, for Byron, reaping publicity meant more than mere money.

Many of the donations were small-denominational bills, fives, tens, twenties. Many contained carefully handwritten notes addressed to Sybilla Frye, expressing concern for her, advice and prayers. *May God be with you Child, take care the Men do not expoit you allso.*

This penciled note, with a donation of a single much-folded ten-dollar bill, Byron read with a pained smile, guessing that the donor wasn't referring to white men.

In the wake of Marus's tireless campaigning, black celebrities were rallying to the Crusade. Not just donations but pledges of scholarships for Sybilla Frye—"One hundred thousand dollars to send Sybilla to an Ivy League university of her choice. The white man will not dare bar her!" (This was boxing promoter Don King, a longtime friend of Marus Mudrick.)

Bill Cosby, Muhammad Ali, Whitney Houston, Michael Jackson, Esmeralda Mason—through their assistants these celebrities called to pledge support and money for the Crusade.

Esmeralda Mason, a Pulitzer Prize–winning black poet and memoirist, offered her home in Montclair, New Jersey, as a "safe house" for the Fryes. Marus accepted with gratitude: he wanted to move the Fryes out of Red Rock, believing the mother and daughter too easily approachable by (black, ambitious) individuals wanting to make use of Sybilla for their own purposes.

One of these individuals, Byron had learned, was Leopaldo Quarrquan, the Black Prince. Unlike the soft-bodied Marus Mudrick, Quarrquan was an ascetic who prayed and fasted daily; he was rail-thin, with a blunt, shaved head and hollow-socketed eyes; his followers considered him a saint, and a "warrior" in the crusade of the Kingdom of Islam to convert Christian blacks to their true, native-African religion. Rumor was, Quarrquan wanted to meet Sybilla Frye, and had no interest in meeting her through Reverend Mudrick and the Care Ministry.

"He wants to convert this good Christian girl to black Islam. He wants to damn her soul."

Byron smiled, seeing his brother so incensed. In the matter of black activist-religious territory, Marus Mudrick considered himself the indisputable leader of east-central New Jersey.

"S'b'lla! My God guess what!"

Seemed like, every other day Ednetta shrieked for Sybilla to come downstairs to hear some good news.

In a Lincoln Town Car, the new young heavyweight boxing champion Mike Tyson came to visit Sybilla in the Mason residence in Montclair; and to leave with her his Rolex watch, impulsively slipped from his massive wrist and pressed into her hand—"This for you, S'b'lla. You gon be taken care of by good people." Sybilla had been deeply moved. Sybilla had come close to fainting. She had never seen Tyson box even on TV—she'd never seen a boxing match in her life— but she knew who Mike Tyson was and could not believe that the twenty-one-year-old world-class athlete had traveled some distance, from Catskill, New York, just to see *her.*

Mike Tyson was handsome!—what people might say *ugly-handsome.* He was not very tall—probably not more than six feet— with broad muscled shoulders and a very thick muscled neck. His eyes had an Asian, almond slant, not unlike her own. His face was strong-boned, though boyish, untouched by scars or bruising, for the new young heavyweight champion boasted of having *never been hit.* His voice was surprisingly high-pitched, and gentle; his gaze was kindly, though stern with rage against the terrible hurt Sybilla Frye had suffered.

Sybilla stammered something breathy and banal—she'd be embarrassed afterward, recalling!—that she'd never seen any boxing match in her life but when she did, she would see *him box.* And Mike Tyson thanked her and told her a secret he had not ever told anyone else: "Boxing is what 'Mike Tyson' is known for, but not what 'Mike Tyson' *is*."

Sybilla would regret afterward, she'd been too awe-stricken to ask about this. *What Mike Tyson is.*

And he'd confided in her, though he had a "white family"—trainer, managers—he hated to look out into the crowd at a boxing match like in Vegas, all those "rich white" people—yelling and screaming for him and his (black) opponent to kill each other.

"Boxing ain't no 'sport'—it's like ancient Rome, 'gladiators.' But I'm the best there is, right now."

Sybilla had no idea what Mike Tyson was saying except she felt the wonderful dark warmth of the young man's eyes, that were like no other eyes she'd ever seen.

The meeting with Mike Tyson was an emotional one for Sybilla, who would not soon recover from it.

"Oh Mama! Mike Tyson he come to see *me*. He left me this!"

But Marus Mudrick, who'd arranged for the meeting, and had been close by in an adjoining room listening, interrupted to inform Sybilla that the watch was a contribution to the Crusade; it wasn't a personal gift to Sybilla Frye.

"Rev'end, Mike Tyson give this to *me*. He did!"

Sybilla spoke in a childish whine.

"Sybilla, that is untrue. Mike Tyson's press agent and I conferred on this issue, and it was agreed, if Tyson saw you, he would leave a 'donation' to the fund. And I will take that, now."

Marus Mudrick held out his hand. Sybilla refused to respond.

Ednetta was summoned. Ednetta slipped the oversized watch off Sybilla's wrist and handed it to Marus Mudrick.

Sybilla ran off to cry.

Ednetta said, "Rev'end, it a shame, y'know—S'b'lla she so downhearted all the time, an this was makin her happy. Couldn't she have the watch? Is it some kind of expensive watch?"

"No. It is not a particularly expensive watch. But it's a man's watch, and would look ridiculous and pretentious on her wrist, even if we had it fitted to her size."

On the phone Sybilla complained to her cousin Martine she missed badly, in this "big old boring house" in Montclair, how unhappy she was. "I hate them all! Fuck them all I wish they would die, this means Mama, too."

"S'b'lla! You don't mean that."

"I do! I do mean that."

"You don't mean your mama, don't say that."

Martine sounded shocked. Sybilla felt a thrill of nastiness, you had such power over people you loved, or who loved you.

Sybilla lay sprawled on her stomach on "her" bed in this ladywriter's house, on a fancy silk comforter she didn't give a damn if she soiled with her shoes. Sucking her thumb and shutting her eyes to see Mike Tyson's ugly-handsome face drawn close to hers. Wait till Jaycee Handler found out, Mike Tyson had come to see *her*! Left her a present, even if the Reverend took it away again.

"He said I was pretty, M'rtine. It wasn't any bullshit about 'justice' or—anything . . . Just he said I was pretty, and he was lonely too, being so famous like he is, and always made to ride in a limousine with a driver, and not allowed to drive a car himself." Sybilla paused, stifling a sob. Even as she stared at his face, Mike Tyson was fading.

The Crusade

On NJN-TV the man was being interviewed. An older man, white-haired, ashy-skinned, with ravaged eyes and a halting but forceful voice.

Our beloved son has been defamed, desecrated. He was deeply, tragically unhappy and utterly blameless. He was—Jerold was—one of the kindest, most generous and most gentle people . . . It is a horror, it is not believable, that these people should insult our unhappy deceased son, for reasons of race-hatred . . . Jerold was a friend to so many people, who loved him—he had not hurt a single person in his entire life. He'd loved being a police officer, it had been his dream since he'd been a boy.

Quickly, Ednetta switched the channel. Then, she switched off the television set.

Then, she left the room.

"As long as you wish to stay, dear Ednetta and Sybilla! You are always welcome."

Esmeralda Mason had returned to the house in Montclair. She'd been in Key West, Florida, for a literary conference, she said, at which some of her own work had been discussed.

Ednetta wondered at the word—*work*. Was writing poetry, or any kind of writing, *work*? It did not seem like any *work* Ednetta herself had ever done and its rewards, in Esmeralda's situation at least, seemed grossly disproportionate to its effort.

Ednetta had been impressed by the many books on Esmeralda's shelves. Especially, she was impressed by the books with *Esmeralda Mason* printed on the bright covers. She'd never met anyone who was a *poet* and a *writer*, who had books with her name printed on them, and her picture on the back covers. Nor had Ednetta ever met any educated person so kindly, friendly and interested in *her*, in a way the social services people only just pretended to be interested, so they find out some damning fact about you and drop you from their caseloads cutting you off without a cent.

Esmeralda Mason's house was very special. Kind of house you'd see on TV or in a movie. More than one "living room" and in each room a "fire place" with gleaming brass fixtures—plus a "dining room" with a crystal chandelier—an "atrium" that was like a greenhouse with tangles of lush green jungle-plants, brilliant red flowers big as a man's head, several antique cages of birds—"finches"— "canaries"—"macaws"—"parrots"—"cockatoos." You needed a person to just clean up after these messy birds, spreading newspaper on the floor of the fancy cages and scrubbing at the bars to rid them of bird-droppings. The canaries sang so much, they made Ednetta nervous reminding her of females chattering at a distance and none of it adding up to anything. Sybilla complained that even the prettiest birds *smelled*.

Ednetta had tried to read Esmeralda Mason's poetry which squiggled down the page like trace marks made by some kind of wriggly insect—but she was too nervous and skittish to sit still. There was something scary about poetry—either it hit too hard, right into the brain and with no warning, or it made no sense at all like a voice you heard through a wall. And most of the time Ednetta was distracted: waiting for a phone to ring, or someone to knock on the door. Seems like, things were always happening in their lives now, like a train with unscheduled stops.

Reverend Mudrick had forbidden Ednetta to call home, to speak with Anis Schutt whom the Reverend didn't trust—(as Marus Mudrick did not ever trust, on principle, any man with whom the women under his protection were involved: there can be only one dominant male in a female's life, and Marus Mudrick was that dominant male)—and so when Ednetta tried to call Anis, at her old number on 939 Third Street, she was terrified that the Reverend would find out.

But Anis rarely answered the phone. Since the Crusade had entered their lives, Ednetta was in fear of losing her husband—for always, with a man like Anis, there were other, willing and reckless women.

Esmeralda Mason was warmly sympathetic with her house guests. She had a way of speaking to them while gazing into their faces as if memorizing them, that made them feel both flattered and uneasy. Also, she kept insisting upon making them tea—herbal tea, "camomile," that tasted to Ednetta like dirty socks soaked in water—which Ednetta was too polite to decline. Sybilla thought it was weird—their hostess had house-servants, at least three they'd sighted coming and going, yet, when they were together, Esmeralda tried to serve *them*. Sybilla wondered if it was some rich lady's way of behaving? Some black rich lady, wanting you to know she wasn't stuck-up but had her background like anybody else, doing housework for white folks. Or pretending that. Sybilla laughed saying, if she had Esmeralda Mason's money, she wouldn't ever cook or lift a hand to make anything for herself, just *order in.*

Ednetta agreed. "Some day, we gon be 'millionaires.' Rev'end Mudrick promised."

Ednetta spoke hopefully, stroking her arthritic arm. This cold wet New Jersey winter the *misery* was so awful, she wanted to just lay down and cry or drink up as much as she could out of Esmeralda Mason's store of fancy wines and whiskeys.

If Sybilla heard, Sybilla only shrugged a skinny shoulder and rolled her eyes as if this kind of Mama-talk was embarrassing to her.

"Rev'end Mudrick did promise that, S'b'lla. *You* didn't hear."

When Esmeralda Mason appeared, Sybilla went stiff and slipped away soon as she could, like a feral cat. It was some silly notion of Sybilla's, Esmeralda made her shiver wanting to put her into some *damn book.*

Esmeralda Mason was a stolid, stocky woman with a puckish elfin face. Her skin was leathery-dark. Her gray-white hair had been buzz-cut. She wore soft drapery-like clothes, elaborately brocaded tunics over trousers that flared like pajamas. Ednetta had calculated she was forty-nine years old—born in 1939. She laughed often, and loudly, at remarks of her own which Ednetta didn't comprehend. Gold flashed in her teeth. Each evening, Esmeralda came downstairs from her "up-stairs study" at 6:00 P.M. to have a drink and "unwind" from her writing, before dinner which was prepared by a Jamaican cook.

A cook! An inky-black *Jamaican cook*! Ednetta was astonished.

One evening over drinks—a dark, fruity wine Ednetta loved, that rushed straight to her brain to numb her thoughts—Esmeralda confided in Ednetta that she, too, had been assaulted, as a girl growing up in Baltimore. "I've written in my poetry and memoirs about this, which possibly you've read. My point is black or white attacker, it hurts the same. That nasty thing they do, it's made to hurt."

Ednetta had a chilling sensation—was Esmeralda the kind of female who likes other females? A *lesbian*?

It was suspicious to Ednetta: Esmeralda Mason had not once
ever complained of a man, an ex-husband, children. She hadn't even
thought to ask Ednetta about her other young children, staying with
her sister Cheryl, let alone Ednetta's grown children scattered in several cities.

Esmeralda said, after a second glass of wine, in a lowered, husky,
confidential voice, "Dear Ednetta—'Sister Ednetta,' as Marus calls
you—if your daughter is telling the truth, she is a tragic figure who
must be avenged. If she is not—exactly, in every syllable—telling
the truth, she represents other, tragic black figures who must be
avenged. Therefore, as I have told Reverend Mudrick, I am in support of the Crusade for Justice for Sybilla Frye—officially. I will
never abandon you."

Ednetta wanted to think that this was a friendly thing to say but
Ednetta didn't know how to reply. The way in which Esmeralda Mason smiled at her, a crinkly-sisterly smile, a smile of complicity, made
her want to slap the woman's elfin-leathery face, that she should dare,
so openly, to doubt Sybilla.

A sick sensation came over Ednetta—maybe all the "celebrities"
felt that way? Whether Sybilla Frye and her mother were telling the
truth, or were God-damn shameless liars, didn't matter? It was the
Crusade that mattered.

Ednetta didn't tell Sybilla what their hostess had told her, but next
day Ednetta insisted to Reverend Mudrick that they were leaving
Montclair as soon as they could—"This place just too fancy and boring, for us. Look out the window you see *trees*. S'b'lla miss her friends
like Mart'ne an those girls."

"You want to leave *there*? And return to—your life in Red Rock?"

Marus Mudrick was incredulous. Ednetta felt the insult, that their

Red Rock lives were so debased, the Reverend couldn't even hide his disdain.

"Yes, Rev'end. That is what I am sayin."

"And Sybilla, she feels the same?"

"S'b'lla *hate it here*. The only nice thing about this place was Mike Tyson comin to see her, and givin her his watch—she wasn't 'lowed to keep. That girl so heavy-hearted, it gon take two point five million to cheer her, at the least."

Reverend Mudrick stared at Ednetta. For a long moment he didn't speak. Then he said, in an even voice, "Sister Ednetta, I have no idea what in hell you are talking about. And I suggest that you have no idea, either. And I suggest you keep your quasi-thoughts to yourself, sister. Is that understood?"

Ednetta staggered back, shocked. For an instant the furious male glaring at her out of the Reverend's eyes was indistinguishable from Anis Schutt.

Rumor was, Byron Mudrick heard from several sources, the Black Prince was traveling to Pascayne sometime soon in January to meet Sybilla Frye.

The Black Prince was determined, it was said, to convert "the shamed black girl" to the Kingdom of Islam and lead a "Thousand-Man March" through the city.

When Byron spoke of this alarming news to his brother, Marus muttered a crude expletive and laughed. "The 'Black Prick' ain't comin within a mile of my girls. How's he gon get to them? Past *me*?"

"'Lie detector'? But how can they *tell*?"

Sybilla was terrified of the test, which Byron Mudrick had

scheduled for January 11, in the same "neutral" setting—the third-floor windowless room in Family Services.

Ednetta assured her, Reverend Mudrick would not let anything happen to her. He'd promised, neither Sybilla nor Ednetta ever had to be interviewed or questioned by the Enemy.

On the morning of January 11, Byron called authorities to postpone the polygraph to January 15. Eventually, January 15 would be postponed to January 31.

The reason, Byron Mudrick explained, was that his client was not yet prepared for a "recrudescence of her terrible trauma."

Or, the reason was, Byron Mudrick had discovered some "mitigating problem" in the selection of the polygraph tester. (Born in the Caribbean and now a citizen, he didn't quite qualify as an American black descended from African-American slaves.)

News of these postponements made their way into the media. In some reports, the Passaic County district attorney's office spoke of the Mudricks' *obfuscation* and *refusal to cooperate* in the investigation into Sybilla Frye's charges; in other reports, friendlier to the Mudricks, the brothers were quoted claiming that their client was being *systematically intimidated—harassed with threat of legal rape.* There continued to be disagreement over the qualifications of polygraphers.

Attorney Byron Mudrick declared in a local TV interview: "My client is eager to take a polygraph test, and to expose to the world the conspiracy forged against her. But only under circumstances that are fair and objective—not prevailing racist. And that is a high standard to meet in Pascayne, New Jersey."

Ednetta told Sybilla it would be all right. No one would make her take some nasty test hooked up with electric wires. Both the Fryes were coming to understand the lawyerly way of speech—though a lawyer said a thing publicly, he did not (necessarily) mean it; the fact that he'd said a thing publicly was a (probable) sign that he did not mean it.

Reverend Mudrick had forbidden the Fryes to watch TV interviews with him and Byron unless he'd expressly approved of the interview, but one afternoon in late January Sybilla happened to see the Mudrick brothers on an interview program on a New York City channel, discussing the Crusade. It made her feel dizzy—dazed—to hear her name evoked—so many times! And to see photographs of herself, and of Jerold Zahn . . . (By this time, Sybilla had come to believe adamantly that Jerold Zahn, twenty-seven, was the "yelow-hair" rapist.) She hadn't been prepared for a skeptical question—*Why should anyone believe your "client"—or you? Police have said there is no rape kit—there is no "evidence" of rape.*

Before the Mudricks could reply, Sybilla switched off the TV. Her heart was beating so hard she felt like fainting!

This was the Enemy, from whom she'd been protected until now.

But what was shocking to Sybilla, and confounding, was that the interviewer who'd asked this nasty question was a black man. Saying such a thing to the Reverend and to Byron Mudrick!

"This would not be an 'interview,' Sybilla—it would be a 'conversation.' "

Though the brothers had assured Sybilla repeatedly that she wouldn't have to endure interviews, even by friendly interviewers, yet it happened that they'd arranged for an "exclusive conversation" with a reporter from the *National Inquirer,* which would take place in the office of the Care Ministry, in Newark. When Sybilla rebelled,

Ednetta was charged with explaining to her that the "conversation" would be just "relaxed talking" with the Mudricks and with her, Ednetta; really, all Sybilla needed to do was sit quietly, nod *yes* or *no* from time to time. Bitterly Sybilla said, "Mama, they payin for this? How much?" Ednetta said, confused, "The newspapers don't 'pay'—the Rev'end told me. Like on TV, they don't pay you for 'news.'"

Sybilla said sulkily she bet the Reverend was being paid. Him, and the *damn lawyer*.

Ednetta slapped at Sybilla—"You got a fresh mouth, girl! You know you already got in trouble with that mouth."

"Bet they bein paid a whole lot, Mama. Like—a thousand dollars."

"Just don't you let them hear you sayin such things, S'b'lla. Let me promise you—if somebody has to talk, not just the Reverend and the lawyer, I will talk."

Eventually, Sybilla gave in.

A photographer accompanied the reporter to Care Ministry headquarters where the tape-recorded "conversation" lasted four hours at the end of which Sybilla was yawning and falling asleep. She hadn't had to say much, after all—the adults did all the talking.

Soon after the Fryes left Esmeralda Mason's beautiful house in Montclair to return to stay, temporarily it was hoped, with Ednetta's grandmother Pearline Tice in the overheated, airless, cluttered apartment on Eleventh Street, it was revealed by the Passaic County district attorney that an "unassailable alibi" had been established for the accused police officer Jerold Zahn for several days in succession in early October.

This was the occasion for a number of TV news bulletins: first, a photograph of the young police officer who'd been, it was hinted, falsely accused as an "alleged rapist," followed by interviews with Julio Ramos, the young, Hispanic assistant district attorney, standing on steps outside the county courthouse, glossy dark hair blowing in the wind.

Ramos was claiming that, contrary to the "positive identification" by the "alleged rape victim," Police Officer Jerold Zahn had been working full-time on October 5, 6, and 7, as well as earlier that week. There was no record of any absence of his from the PD, and his training officer and his fellow rookies had given sworn statements to this effect.

Off-duty, Zahn had spent time with others on at least two occasions. Ramos said: "It is the conclusion of this office that Jerold Zahn has been misidentified by the rape victim. The investigation into Jerold Zahn as the 'yellow-haired'—alleged—rapist of Sybilla Frye is now closed."

Pressed for further comment by the interviewer, Ramos said, with carefully enunciated disdain, "The involvement of civil rights activist attorney Byron Mudrick in these charges is shocking, and a disgrace. A once-respected attorney has turned to race-mongering. It is not a surprise that 'Reverend' Marus Mudrick would be a party to such reckless accusations, the defamation of an innocent man who is no longer living, under tragic circumstances, but—"

Byron switched off the TV. He was stunned, sick.

Shocking, disgrace. The ugly words echoed in his brain.

Still—his lawyer's mind continued to work, like any precision machine—it was possible to discredit the "alibi." Not likely that the young man's whereabouts could be totally accounted for, during those several days; quite possible to argue, convincingly, or in a way to undermine the Enemy's credibility, that Zahn would have had plenty of time, during the night, to have participated in the multiple rapes of the fifteen-year-old black victim.

When he learned the news, Marus was furious. Not that Jerold

Zahn had been provided posthumously with a convincing alibi, but that the Passaic County district attorney was disrespecting *him*.

"Brother, this is *war*."

"Sybilla."

Sybilla had been summoned to meet with the Reverend. Mama hovered nearby, anxiously.

Sybilla had trouble *seeing* the man. Had to half-shut her eyes.

"Here is another of your 'rapists,' Sybilla. We have located him and the surprise is—well, you can see the surprise."

Sybilla stared at the newspaper photograph of a youngish Hispanic-looking man. He looked familiar—but who was he?

"The obvious surprise is, this rapist isn't 'white.' He is a *light-skinned Hispanic*. Which suggests that we have no bias against 'whites'—that is now obvious. All you could have seen of this person's face in the van in which you were kept captive was a blurred but unmistakable image, at a time of great distress."

Sybilla continued to stare, uncomprehending.

"Who you sayin this is?"

"Julio Ramos. You wouldn't know the name."

Soon then, Marus Mudrick called a news conference not only to "adamantly re-confirm" the identification of Jerold Zahn as one of the Pascayne PD rapists, but to announce the identification of a second rapist by the rape victim—"Julio Ramos, assistant district attorney, Passaic County district attorney's office. One of the district attorney's cynical 'minority hires'—made without an adequate background check—a despicable political hire that has backfired—has exploded in the (white) face of the district attorney."

This grave accusation was made to a hastily assembled gathering of media people within eight hours of Julio Ramos's news conference. In mimicry of Ramos standing on the steps of the courthouse bareheaded and his hair blowing in the January wind, Reverend Marus Mudrick stood on the steps of that very courthouse in a camel's hair cashmere overcoat, bareheaded, his dense, oily dark hair stirred by the wind.

Fewer media people than usual had shown up at the news conference, since it had been so recently called. But more were arriving, and would arrive, including a Manhattan-based journalist from the BBC and a feature writer for *New York*.

For more than an hour, Marus Mudrick stood on the steps of the Passaic courthouse in the January wind, taking questions from the media and posing for cameras. He spoke eloquently, angrily, wildly—his voice lifted, and fell, and lifted again with the cadence of evangelical righteousness. It was not possible to believe that the Reverend did not, in his deepest heart, believe in the absolute truth of his words. At one point, Reverend Mudrick dramatically tore up a "dishonest, blackmailing document—a subpoena" issued by the district attorney's office, to intimidate him and his attorney-brother Byron. When reporters and TV people arrived too late for the ritual tearing-up of the subpoena, Reverend Mudrick obliged them by repeating it, with another sheet of paper, and allowing the pieces to blow in the wind. Black individuals in the gathering applauded him as he denounced the "lying, heinous, down-dirty-dishonest conspiracies of the Nazi-racist-white police of Pascayne, New Jersey, and the Passaic County D.A. office to hide from the public the identities of rapist Jerold Zahn and rapist Julio Ramos—to obfuscate, prevaricate, and eradicate the vicious kidnapping, beating and rape of a young black girl-victim left then to die in a filthy factory cellar on the other side of the river . . ." In the freezing air, Reverend Mudrick's breath steamed in vehement little puffs.

Among the gathering of disparate individuals, a number of whom were white, there were those who challenged the Reverend more sharply than usual; one was a tall white straggly-haired heckler in a soiled parka who tried to interrupt the Reverend several times, charging him with "race-baiting" and "race-mongering"—shouting, "Remember what happened to Reverend Martin Luther King Jr.! Got to pay a price for not knowing your place, Reverend Marus Mudrick! One day you might—I'm just saying *might*—have to pay that price . . ."

These shocking words, an obvious threat against Reverend Mudrick's life, roused much indignation among the crowd, who shouted down the heckler. Reverend Mudrick, however, only just smiled at his adversary, and said, "No, let the man speak! This is the white-racist speech that is too often silenced, allowing the assassins to do their work without warning." Bravely Reverend Mudrick opened his camel's hair coat, that had not been fully buttoned, and said, "Sir, I am not afraid of you. I am not afraid of the lynch mob that backs you and the white establishment that tacitly condones you. I am not wearing a bulletproof vest, and I am not myself armed . . ."

Quickly the heckler backed off, and walked away, as if the courage of the harassed Reverend had demoralized him. Infuriated individuals shouted after him. Sullen-faced police officers assigned to protect the Reverend and to forestall violence had been moving purposefully toward him but did not follow him as he broke stride and began to run away.

"If you stand up to a racist, he will always back down. At the heart of the racist is a sniveling coward." Reverend Mudrick spoke breathlessly as if, now that the threat had dissolved, he was able to reveal his vulnerability.

After a heated hour the news conference began to disband, and a TV journalist for WHNY-TV asked if he might interview Reverend Mudrick for another half hour, on the courthouse steps.

It was this interview that Byron Mudrick saw that afternoon, in his Newark law office.

Byron Mudrick had known nothing of the news conference called for the steps of the Passaic County courthouse. He had known nothing of his brother's abrupt decision to accuse a Passaic County assistant district attorney of rape, with the announcement that the rape victim had identified "Julio Ramos."

So quickly the accusation had come, following Ramos's statement about Jerold Zahn's alibi, it could not help but seem, to even the more sympathetic observers, that Marus Mudrick was retaliating against the young Hispanic prosecutor.

To endure this nightmare interview, Byron had to pour himself a small glass of whiskey. In recent weeks he'd been bringing a bottle—bottles—to his law office, to calm his nerves. *Self-medicate* it was called. Klarinda would understand, would pity him and (possibly) forgive him. Not immediately but—in time. Klarinda would say *Didn't I warn you, Byron! Your brother.*

Byron had received a phone call from an alarmed law school colleague, to turn on his television, quickly. The press conference in Pascayne had more or less ended, but the live WHNY interview was just beginning. Through a roaring in his ears Byron heard the interviewer ask if Marus Mudrick and his brother Byron were not afraid of "defamation lawsuits"—"charges of slander or libel"—"publicly charging two individuals of rape"—and there was Marus Mudrick's boastful answer, "Brother, I am not afraid of justice. Reverend Marus Mudrick has never been afraid of justice. And there is no libel of the dead, my attorney-brother Byron will explain to you."

"But of the living?—Julio Ramos?"

"When the Crusade finishes exposing that rapist-race-criminal, Ramos will think he *is dead.*"

Marus Mudrick spoke with zest, rubbing his hands together. On the wrist of his left hand, a handsome gold-banded wristwatch was visible, and at the cuffs of both shirtsleeves, gleaming gold mono-grammed cuff links.

Much of this interview Byron would not recall afterward. The shock was too great, like a blow on the head with a hammer. His hand shook as he lifted the whiskey to his mouth—so clumsy and uncoordinated, he couldn't locate his mouth with the glass.

Already the phone was ringing. Quickly Byron removed the receiver from the hook.

Imagining a phone ringing, ringing, ringing in some vast empty space—a morgue.

In the paralysis of that terrible hour foreseeing: professional shame, disbarment, public and sustained pillorying in the (responsible) press, the disintegration of his marriage and the embarrassment of his children. Worse, a defamation lawsuit brought by Julio Ramos against the Mudrick brothers that would leave them both penniless and their reputations shattered.

At least, Byron Mudrick penniless and his reputation shattered.

He swallowed a large mouthful of whiskey. With a shaking hand he poured another drink.

The Martyr

First glance, he was a young white man in tight dark clothes, with a shaved head. Out of nowhere veering purposefully in the Reverend's direction.

Second glance, as the Reverend was to see him, close-up from a distance of less than three inches, he was a very light-skinned black man, easy to mistake for Caucasian; not young, but so slender and lithe as to seem young, like a dancer, or a skater. He was just slightly taller than the Reverend. His eyes were tawny lynx-eyes. His nose was a Roman nose just slightly flat and broad at its tip. On his upper lip a thin mustache and beneath his lower lip a small triangle of a goatee of scarcely more substance than a shadow. He appeared to be smiling with unusually white, small teeth—*Rev'end Mudick?* This person, this stranger, whom Reverend Mudrick seemed to recognize, the kind of hip mixed-blood black boy, Caribbean most likely, and not an urban-American-born black like the Reverend himself, for whom the Reverend felt a confused but pleasurable swirl of emotion, and to whom he was (irresistibly, inexorably) drawn. *Rev'end Mudick? This for you* as out of the stranger's tight dark-suede coat there came a swift-flashing blade of twelve inches of which at least ten inches were sunk into the fatty flesh between the Reverend's ribs in less time than was required for the breathy message murmured kiss-close in the Reverend's ear *The Prince tell you, man—God is good.*

Abruptly on his knees on the cold unyielding pavement. In utter astonishment as pain came too quick and too vast for the stricken man to realize. Initially he'd thought that he had been hit—struck—by a boy's tight fist—which would have wounded him sufficiently in his pride, for he'd imagined that in the stranger's lynx eyes there had been a sly look of recognition, and of desire; fumbling his hands to clutch at the stranger wiping with rude expediency the bloodied knife blade on the Reverend's clothing (the camel's hair coat which the youngish-seeming man had managed to tug open just enough to thrust the blade inside). He tried to call for help but no words came—a hoarse croaking sound as of asphyxiation. Tried to heave himself to his feet, to assure staring observers that Reverend Marus Mudrick was unharmed, had not been stabbed to the heart by one for whom he'd felt an unwise instant's attraction.

Tried to heave himself to his feet, though now blood was flowing down his trouser-leg, and onto the pavement, that he might relive those last, incomprehensible several seconds, and comprehend them; and reverse his fate; his brain brightly flooding with ideas, alternatives—how descending the ten or so concrete steps at the conclusion of the rally he might have turned to the right, and not to the left; might have walked with aides from the Care Ministry, and not by himself as he often preferred at such public moments amid a battery of flash cameras that then, inexplicably it seemed, hardly a minute later, had abandoned him to the dark-clad smiling stranger who'd seemed at first glance to be *white* and to be extending his hand to be shaken—a *friendly white*. And his limousine at a curb at least thirty feet away. (Why wasn't the driver outside, and attentive to him? Didn't he pay Manuel to act as a kind of bodyguard, as well as a part-time chauffeur?) There were individuals awaiting him with whom in the triumphant adrenaline-surge following the applause of the rally Reverend Mudrick didn't much want to speak—the good, boring faithful, converts to the Reverend's cause, black faces shiny with tears, white faces hopeful that the revered Reverend would pause as he sometimes did to warmly shake their hands, embrace them and call them Brother, Sister!

But—he'd turned away. Away from safety. Away from those who were known to him, and whom in his complacency Reverend Mudrick might take for granted to continue to revere him, even if, fairly obviously, he *was* ignoring them, or at least pretending not to see them—their smiling faces, their tears of sympathy and hope.

Turned away, feeling vigorous, terrific—buoyed up by waves of applause, and a mostly adulatory (if somewhat small) audience (though fewer media people than he'd anticipated, and most of these black). Broad smile aimed at cameras, hand uplifted in victory. He'd worn a new suit tailor-made for his "unique" figure, at J. Press in Manhattan—svelte dark wool-flannel, double-breasted coat, waistcoat tight-fitting and "slimming." He'd been lavishly barbered earlier that day. In his rich strong baritone he'd led the chant at the conclusion of the rally—*Crusade for Justice for Sybilla Frye! Crusade for Justice for Sybilla Frye!* His sense was that the ad hoc collection had been a generous one—(he'd check later that night). Not a major rally—Thursday evening in the Newark-North Community Center—sponsored by local non-profit "Good Neighbors Mission" whose director Reverend Mudrick knew well, from previous crusades; neither Sybilla Frye nor her mother Ednetta had shared the stage with Reverend Mudrick tonight; nor was Reverend Mudrick's attorney-brother Byron with him. (Marus had to smile: his younger brother was furious with *him*. See how long that lasted! Byron Mudrick was of zero interest to the world without Marus Mudrick promoting him, and he knew it. And stuck-up Klarinda knew it. *They all did.*) Not a major rally but the following Sunday he'd be taking the Crusade to a new, other level in conjunction with the New York City–based activist organization CUAR—Citizens United Against Racism—at the New School where there was the possibility—(Marus would know in another forty-eight hours) that Norman Mailer might appear to introduce Reverend Mudrick . . . And then, turning to the dark-clad stranger, expecting his hand to be vigorously and warmly shaken, he felt—instead—

Such shock! On his knees, and clutching at the arm of the stranger, as if to forestall falling to the pavement; clutching at the man's legs, absurdly stretching his fingers, as the assassin leapt away.

Yet not thinking *assassin*. In the shock of the moment confusing the dark-clad stranger with the homeless alcoholic white man whom he'd paid twenty-five dollars to "heckle" him in Pascayne a few days ago—memorably, he'd thought—very convincingly; so convincingly, no one on his staff apart from the staffer who'd hired the man, and certainly no one in the audience, had known that the "heckler" was shouting prepared words.

Even Byron hadn't known. Though possibly, Byron had suspected, since Marus had occasionally hired white individuals to heckle him at public events, always with dramatic results, and if Byron learned, he'd disapproved.

Marus smiled bitterly, thinking of his brother. *Marus you are going too far. This is hubris, Marus. Do you know what* hubris *means?*

And Marus had replied with scarcely disguised contempt *Yes, Brother. I know what* hubris *means. Do you know what* cowardice *means? Do you know what* prig *means? Do you know what* race-traitor *means?*

But—this stranger was not in the Reverend's hire. This stranger was not a white man but one chosen perhaps because he resembled a white man. Insolently wiping his bloodied knife on the Reverend's coat and concealing it then inside his own coat as he walked with that air of almost gravity-less grace to a waiting minivan, and was driven away south on Ferry Street in the direction of the Passaic River visible only as a wide dark band emptying into further darkness.

He a white man, we all saw him!—happened too fast for anybody know what was happenin he just come up to the Rev'end an it look like the Rev'end knew him an was goin to shake his hand, then next thing the Rev'end on his knees and on the sidewalk an the man gone—he just gon like some ghost. And he white—we saw that.

The Broken Doll

*S**he say, You find some answer to this. Some way to explain this.
Whatever Anis do to you, he aint the one hurt you bad as you is, you
hear me? Some other ones came along and did this to you, hurt you
worsen he hurt you, 'cause he your daddy and he aint gon hurt you so bad,
that's a fact. So you find it.*

Find what, Ma?

She'd heard the screams upstairs. Just come into the house and the
younger children with her, she'd sent them back outside to run play
in the alley and not come back till she called them. Hearing the
man's shouts overhead. The girl's screams and pleas. Starting up the
stairs she'd felt the violent thuds and thumps and heard the sound of
something breaking. And she thought *He will kill me, too.* And in terror hanging back not knowing what to do until the screams came so
bad, she rushed blindly into the room and there came Anis head-on

charging *her*—struck her with just his body, blind drunk fury in his face as he propelled himself at her to exit the room and next thing she knew she was on the floor, blood drops like dark rain falling from—where, she wasn't sure—between her teeth? Head ringing and buzzing but she pulled herself to her feet, and was all right. Saying to herself *'Netta you all right.*

He'd slammed out of the house. He was gone, she knew he would not return for a night and a day at least and possibly a second night and a second day. And desperately she thought *He will get hisself killed. They will shoot him dead.*

The sobbing girl she found huddling in a corner of the room behind the torn-apart bed. Wedged between the bed and the wall. One of the girl's old dolls split-headed, broken and crushed on the floor like the man had set his heavy foot upon it, and his weight.

The soft blue-wool blanket splotched with blood, Anis had dragged over her, to hide her.

A sign that he loved her, Ednetta knew. Hide her shame, and keep her from cold. And from the sight of somebody staring inside the room, to see her how she would not want to be seen.

Ednetta gripped Sybilla's head in her hands. Turned her head, to see how bad it was.

Blood in the girl's hair like grease. And blood down her face like tears. Her eyes beginning to swell. Lips cracked and bleeding. In his rage she understood had been a despairing rage he'd torn the girl's clothes, battered her with his fists. He'd been cursing and sobbing, she knew. Hated the rage that came over him like liquid fire how the rage came into him and how it hurt *him,* he could not prevail against it.

This girl Sybilla was her most vexatious child. Sassy-mouth daughter she'd had to love but it was a hurtful love like a pebble in your shoe.

Ednetta screamed at the girl she'd provoked him! God damn you look now what he done, you know Anis have a hard life, now they will send him to prison the rest of his life. Anis die in that nasty place, girl it will be on your head.

Your stepdaddy he love you, girl. He try to love you. He help support you, like you his own daughter. And this how you thank him actin like some slut.

Girl, you open them eyes. You look at *me*.

She'd been with that boy, that was it. That Jaycee Handler the girls always talking about, nudging Sybilla in her ribs like it was a joke. And Anis not happy with Sybilla staying out of school and the kind of people she hangin with. Anis saying, if that girl gets pregnant, 'Netta, ain't no joke. If that girl shames us, that ain't no joke you know that.

People never knew, Anis took family serious. Anis took the responsibility for the kids serious. Looking at Ednetta like he'd be hurting *her,* she didn't control the daughter. She'd told Anis she thought that the boy was incarcerated, she'd heard it was Mountainview, talk was maybe Jaycee wouldn't survive, havin enemies there. But that never happened. What happened was, Sybilla went to see Jaycee with his sister Shirley, and Ednetta the last to know. And Sybilla fourteen years old!—just havin her birthday, so she was fifteen. This news that came (belatedly) to Ednetta, she had to know that Anis knew, too. Worse then, Sybilla had stayed away from the house overnight fearing Anis, and when she came back like a sniveling little dog with his tail between his legs there was Anis. She knew, Anis had to discipline her. He'd warned her enough times and all the kids knew, the girl disrespecting him would have to be punished. That big girl of Ednetta's always sassing Anis Schutt behind his back or without any actual words only just *thinking,* he could discern this. That cast in her left eye seemed always to be mocking him *Fuck you asshole-stepdaddy, you don't know shit what I'm doing.*

Wasn't Anis's fault, such provocations.

Ednetta believed that was the way it had been.

Sybilla lay shuddering in Ednetta's arms on the bed, where Ednetta dragged her up. Maybe a mistake, the blood would get in the bed worse than it was soaking down into the mattress already brown-blood-stained and urine-stained, but she had to comfort the girl—that beating was bad. Sybilla smelling of her body where she'd wet herself and maybe worse. Girl was sweaty and had vomited on herself. He'd had to discipline her, but he had not used a strap this time. There were no strap-welts on the girl's chest, buttocks, back Ednetta could see. If she had to take the girl to a doctor nobody would ask about the strap. Other questions they would ask, Ednetta had worked out ways to answer. If no bone was broke, only maybe a rib sprained, that would be OK. Ednetta thought it would be OK. But she would have to take her for some kind of medical treatment—like stitches in her eyebrow where it was all bloody and the skin kind of loose—anybody seeing Sybilla would know there'd been a bad beating, and cops might find out. And if the girl went back to school, damn teachers askin questions! They put away Anis for the rest of his life and he die in that nasty place and Ednetta in her bed alone mourning him. Or, Anis die on the street if the cops tried to take him.

The father of Sybilla, he die like that on the street like a dog. But not in Pascayne, in New York. Some street in the Bronx where he end up, only age thirty-six or -seven. But Ednetta had set her heart against *him,* the shit he'd done to her. And Sybilla never knew that father, or any of the younger children. And Anis never ask.

In Ednetta's arms Sybilla lay snuffling like something was broke in her nose. Like a guilty beat dog, that has given up. Swollen eyes, swollen mouth, Ednetta hoped no teeth were loose. Didn't want to think of how the girl was beneath her torn clothes that Anis complained of through the summer, his stepdaughter out on the street like some slut, and people knowing she was *his*. Then this last straw, Jaycee Handler he knew to be a punk selling crack to hooker crack-heads. Anis in such a fury he hadn't known what he would do, like bringing a match to a curtain, see how the fire flare up—nobody to stop it, once it start. She was shivering bad herself. She was tasting blood in her own mouth. She said, S'b'lla, we got to find some way. It up to us. When she was feeling strong enough she half-carried the girl out into the hall and to the bathroom, kicked aside the mess and ran hot water into the tub. Hoped to hell the younger children weren't sitting on the stoop. Or hanging at the back door like hungry pups. Last thing Ednetta wanted was some damn nosy neighbor coming over. Hard to get Sybilla into the tub without her slipping and falling. Like something broke in her head, she can't stand without teetering. Even her littlest right toe looked like it was crooked. Then in the tub Sybilla lay stiff with pain, moaning like some kicked dog. With a washcloth Ednetta washed between her legs. Gentle as she could but the girl started whimpering. A swirl of blood, fading into the water. Ednetta didn't ask how bad it was there, had to hope there wasn't something torn inside, she'd have to be taken to the clinic to have fixed.

Thinking *A girl is yourself. A daughter is yourself one more time. You got to love her no matter how vexatious she is, she ain't got nobody but her mama.*

After the bath that was steamy-hot and left them both dazed and sleepy Ednetta dried the girl in the biggest, best towel and whispered some baby talk in her ear and slipped her arm around the naked skinny waist where the bruises were starting, and walked her back to the bedroom, straightened the bed and another time the two lay together in each other's arms exhausted and drifting off to sleep.

Sybilla whispered *Mama, you gon forgive me?*

The Convert

Thereby are you baptized in the name of the Prophet—'Aasia Muhammad.'"

She was kneeling at the altar of the First Temple of the Kingdom of Islam of Newark, New Jersey, as the Black Prince baptized her into the faith. She was kneeling trembling and scarcely daring to breathe her eyes fixed upon the altar floor and the Black Prince's rather small, narrow feet in black leather boots visible beneath the hem of his white silk robe.

The ceremony in the Temple had been lengthy. The small gathering of the faithful murmured prayers and responses in a language she could not comprehend, that seemed wonderful to her. Several times she'd become light-headed from having fasted and slept only a few hours the previous night and from the excitement of the occasion.

"As you are 'Aasia,' so you are *hope*. And you are a vessel of *hope* for others."

With his fingertips the Black Prince touched her bowed head. She felt that touch through her being—like an electric current rendering her helpless. The Black Prince who was a "soldier" of Faith—a "warrior" of Allah—was praying over her in the strange, startling language that came to his tongue as readily as the more common, English language she'd been hearing all her life.

She'd been instructed how to reply. Faltering, determined to prevail, she murmured the responses she'd memorized that were incomprehensible to her except as words of magic. This, the very speech of Allah.

But it was beautiful speech! Uttering such words she felt that she might turn into a tropical bird with rich royal-blue feathers, cream-colored neck plumes, astonishing sea-green tail. Her speech was musical, mysterious. She could spread her wings, and *fly*.

That morning, early she'd been bathed by Sisters. Her hair had been stiff-plaited and affixed to her head with hairpins. Slowly then and with elaborate care she'd been clothed in white undergarments and in a white nylon skirt to her ankles and a long-sleeved white nylon tunic that fitted her slender body loosely. Over the plaited hair, a white nylon head covering like a nun's.

White is the color of *purity, virginity*. White was Aasia Muhammad's color.

" 'Great is the happiness of the daughter of the Prophet . . .' "

Among females of the Faith, there were "daughters"—"sisters"—"brides"—"wives." At fifteen, Sybilla Frye would be a "daughter."

Eagerly and anxiously she'd taken lessons in the Faith. Numerous times she'd practiced the ritual of conversion. With her Sister-instructress she had practiced the act of submission—first, on her knees, and her head bowed, and then sinking forward slowly in submission until she lay prostrate on her chest, belly, legs and her arms flung out above her head on the altar floor.

This is the posture of *utter acquiescence,* she'd been instructed. No one is so vulnerable to Allah as at this moment, prostrating herself on the Earth.

And Allah looks with love upon those who prostrate themselves in this way which is the way of the child.

Ednetta who'd accompanied Sybilla to her lessons had been astonished to see her sassy, rude, vexatious daughter so *obedient*. Sybilla had taken a mischievous pleasure in surprising Mama.

Too bad, there was (yet) no Temple of the Kingdom of Islam in Pascayne. This conversion ceremony, specially arranged by the Black Prince for Sybilla, took place in the Newark Temple, in a neighborhood not unlike Red Rock near the river.

It was mid-February: a low bleak sky like dirty pavement. The Passaic River turgid and lead-colored. In her beautiful white clothes with a coat flung over her shoulders Sybilla had been cold, shivering almost convulsively. She'd wiped at her eyes, and at her nose. Ednetta had pressed tissues upon her, that Sybilla wadded and pushed up inside her sleeves; how awful it would be, mortifying!—if as Sybilla advanced to the altar on the arm of an elder Sister, in her beautiful clothes, one of the wadded tissues would fall out of her sleeve.

Damn but Sybilla's eyes continued to water, uncontrollably. Since that bad beating, her left eye seemed particularly weak.

In another year or two, "Aasia Muhammad" could be betrothed. Her Sister-instructress in the Kingdom had told her that in the African countries of Morocco, Nigeria, Libya, Kenya, girls of fifteen, even fourteen, or thirteen, were frequently betrothed. To remain a girl, a child, was not desirable in the Kingdom, when one could become a "bride" of the Prophet, and a "wife" to a designated husband.

"'Aasia Muhammad.' Daughter of the Prophet you will rise . . ."

Aasia Muhammad! She had never heard so beautiful a name.

No longer was she "Sybilla Frye"—already the name sounded coarse and common to her ears.

Already that old, outgrown life had become repellent to her. A life of squalor, ignorance, shame, sin . . .

Things she'd done. Things she'd allowed to be done to her.

Years ago, in sixth grade. So young.

Older boys had given her beer in cans. She'd shared their beer. They'd given her joints to smoke, or to try to smoke. What they'd claimed to be crack she'd sniffed up into her nostrils so tender they'd bled. And the guys laughing at her.

Taking money from men hanging at the edge of Hicks Park. Taking money for Sybilla Frye to go with these men into the (nasty-smelly) men's lavatory or out behind the storage shed.

They'd give her small change to keep. Called her *Dog-face* which was cruel and unfair because everybody knew, Sybilla Frye was one of the sexy-attractive girls.

Except for the gap between her front teeth, and that damn eye so they'd call her *Cross-eye*. Which wasn't true, either.

Jaycee hadn't been the first. Jaycee'd been the one broke her heart.

He'd fired a gun at another boy. Jaycee always insisted, the boy he'd shot had been shooting at *him*.

It was something God must've decided, that Anis hadn't murdered her for disobeying him. Showing her ass like a slut in the hot summer, and her little titties in a T-strap shirt, had riled him worse than she'd known, but going out to Mountainview with Shirley, he hadn't even found out about it for certain, only just heard some damn rumor, he'd lost control. Sybilla tried to call him *Daddy* like he'd wanted but came out wrong, he'd thought she was sassing him, and maybe sometimes she was, it happened like that in school sometimes too, you rolled your eyes or made a smirk-face and a teacher saw you, and you hadn't even meant it. Anis Schutt had murdered his first wife but not every-body knew he'd (maybe) murdered another woman, too, whose body had never been found but was believed to be dumped in the river off the Pitcairn Bridge.

And maybe Mama knew? For sure, Aunt Cheryl knew. And Martine knew. You had to feel pity for Mama, not a bad-looking woman for her age but so sad and desperate to keep her man. And everybody knew, Anis Schutt used 'Netta Frye for his convenience like some old wife the husband doesn't glance at or give a damn for long as she cooks for him, cleans his clothes for him and crap like that. So trusting she'd given Anis some of the Reverend's money, with a promise of more. Sybilla had known, Anis had hated Ednetta for that money, *shame-money* he'd called it, but he'd taken it from her just the same.

Anis Schutt wasn't in this Temple this morning. Anis Schutt had nothing to do with Sybilla converting to the Kingdom of Islam and for all Sybilla knew, Ednetta was keeping it a secret from him.

All this issue with Reverend Mudrick and them, the "Crusade"— all the publicity, and people talking—Anis just kept away.

Now, Reverend Mudrick was in a hospital here in Newark. For some time it had not been known if he would live or die but—so far as Sybilla had been told—he had *survived the racist attack.*

Whoever had tried to kill him had aimed for the heart. Poor man had had surgeries to repair the heart damage, Sybilla felt queasy just to think of.

It was a fact, she hadn't *liked* the Reverend. Hadn't *liked* him to touch her, or breathe on her his breath that smelled like garlic or whiskey or meat. But she had *revered* him as so many did. And she had *feared him.*

Soon after the stabbing, the Black Prince had entered their lives through intermediaries in Pascayne.

It was very flattering to Ednetta, and to Sybilla—that Leopaldo Quarrquan of the Kingdom of Islam had wished to see *them.*

Unlike Marus Mudrick, Leopaldo Quarrquan was head of an entire religion. Marus Mudrick was a guest preacher in AME churches,
but was not the head of any church; it was explained to the Fryes, the
Black Prince was equivalent to the Pope who is head of the Roman
Catholic faith which is worldwide. As the Pope was head of a religion
for white people worldwide, the Black Prince was head of a religion
for black people worldwide.

The Black Prince described himself as a soldier of Allah— a "warrior." The Kingdom of Islam was both an ancient religion of "near-
prehistoric" time (A.D. 700, East Africa) and a "revolutionary" new
religion founded in 1979 by Leopaldo Quarrquan.

It was believed that the Black Prince was the reincarnation of
the Kingdom's earliest leader, whose name, roughly translated into
English, was Leopaldo Quarrquan (900 B.C.–846 B.C.). You were in the
Black Prince's presence only briefly before you realized that here was
an extraordinary individual, very like one who has been transported
from an ancient time to the present time and is bemused by what he
sees. As the Black Prince was a warrior, so he was surrounded by a
staff of (male, young) aides, with shaved heads; but they kept at a little
distance, so that, in public, the Black Prince appeared alone as if in sol-
itude. The Black Prince never raised his voice but spoke softly—you
had to listen to hear him. Not like the AME preachers who shouted,
cajoled, even wept from the pulpit, like actors on TV.

The rumor was, the Black Prince was armed at all times, as there
were "bounties" on his head issued by his enemies both white and
black.

First time they'd seen the Black Prince, the Fryes had been in awe
of the man. His way of moving was kingly—his face was like something sculpted out of stained wood—his eyes heavy-lidded, "African."
His head and his jaws were clean-shaven. His age was somewhere
between forty and fifty, though he appeared much younger. It was

said that in another lifetime, as a young man in his twenties, he'd
been convicted of murder. He'd served a sentence for manslaughter in
a Maryland maximum-security prison, seventeen years. In the prison
he'd converted to the Nation of Islam; shortly after being released
from prison, having served his maximum sentence, he quarreled with
the leaders of the Nation of Islam and founded his own, more "mili-
tant" and "revolutionary" Kingdom of Islam.

In prison, he had renamed himself. His old, "white" name had
been cast off and his new, "black African" name was Leopaldo Quarrquan. Each morning he rose at dawn, though earlier during the dark
months: never later than 6:00 A.M. His diet was rigorous. He ate spar-
ingly, fruits, vegetables, and grain. He abhorred the very thought
of pork or any unclean food like shellfish. He abhorred all drugs including most medications, for which the faithful had to apply for
permission to take. He never drank alcohol, nor even carbonated
soda, which were forbidden the faithful. He did not believe in ice
cubes to cool any drink. He lived an ascetic life, often at prayer. He
threw himself full length on the floor, on his prayer rug, utterly sup-
plicant in prayer. He prayed with such fervor, he threw himself into
a trance and none dared approach him at such a holy time. He was
an ordained warrior of Allah claiming that, in a vision, the Prophet
himself had put into his hand a sword blessed by Allah. The Black
Prince could never marry for he abhorred the "animal life." He was
not a private citizen, a civilian. He did not pay any state or federal
taxes for he had no income. It was a violation of the principles of the
Kingdom of Islam to cooperate in any way with any secular govern-
ment. And so, to avoid arrest and persecution by the IRS, it was arranged that an aide would fill out Leopaldo Quarrquan's income tax
forms and file them. Money received by the Kingdom of Islam was
almost entirely donations, tithed by the faithful; occasionally, there
were singular, large donations from black celebrities, athletes and

businessmen. Even secular blacks contributed to the Kingdom of Islam, in those urban areas in which the Kingdom exerted power and influence, where small businesses might depend upon the intervention of the Kingdom's staff.

There was an alternative, controversial vision of the Black Prince in which it was acknowledged that he had married as a young man, and had put aside his wife as a female unworthy of a warrior of Allah. Later, the Black Prince had married one of the "brides" of the Prophet, a pure young woman with whom he did not cohabit; she had borne him several children but only the sons were brought to him on a regular basis. The Black Prince wore a white silk robe with a sash, a white silk tunic, white trousers beneath. His heavy-lidded eyes were large, intelligent, grave, and bemused as with the folly of humankind through the centuries.

Meeting Sybilla, the Black Prince had said in his powerful subdued voice: "I have been sent to you, 'Sybilla Frye,' to save your soul from the white devil's Hell in which it has languished. Through the love of the Prophet I will bring you to your true home in the Kingdom of Islam from which you have been exiled these many centuries."

Ednetta would say afterward *It was as if the Prince had touched S'b'lla's heart. Just reached inside her rib cage and touched her beating heart, the change that came over her.*

This had been at a time when rumors circulated in Red Rock that Reverend Mudrick had been murdered.

In all the news media it was being declared that Marus Mudrick had been executed by a racist white, possibly a member of the New Jersey Ku Klux Klan, after one of his rallies in support of the Crusade for Justice for Sybilla Frye. Then, the news was modified to state that the Reverend had not died but was in critical condition, in Newark Presbyterian Hospital. Bulletins were issued from the Reverend's bedside in Intensive Care by his distraught brother Byron.

There were prayer vigils at the Camden Avenue AME Church, and at other churches in Red Rock and Newark. The Fryes did not attend these vigils, as they did not visit the Reverend in the hospital, for their presence would have caused too much of a distraction.

In his pulpit Reverend Denis wept angrily: *Brother Marus is a martyr to the cause of justice for black people everywhere. He is our Martin Luther King Jr. But he will not die in vain. He will not die.*

Yet, days and weeks passed, and Reverend Mudrick remained in the hospital, having endured several cardiac surgeries. And there were said to be other, ancillary medical problems, complicating the Reverend's recovery.

"Aasia Muhammad, Blessed of Allah, daughter of the Prophet and vessel of hope you will rise, and speak after me . . ."

The Black Prince spoke in an incantatory voice, in English; then, in a deeper and more guttural voice, in the mysterious "speech of Allah"—Ednetta had no idea if this was a true language, like Arabic, or an invented language known only to Leopaldo Quarrquan.

Amid the rows of seats reserved for women and girls on the left side of the Temple Ednetta sat alert and uneasy; like these daughters, sisters, brides, and wives of the Prophet she wore a head scarf to cover her hair. Their clothing was long, loose, and light-colored, while Ednetta wore dark, somber clothing in recognition of the perilous condition of Reverend Mudrick, so abruptly wrenched from their lives.

Ednetta had tried to discourage Sybilla from so quickly converting to the Kingdom of Islam, after the violence to Reverend Mudrick.

She'd appealed to the girl, to have faith in the Reverend, that he would return to health, and again lead the Crusade; but Sybilla had been frightened, and flattered by the attentions of the Black Prince, who reminded her (she said) of Mike Tyson, not in his appearance but in his manner which was kingly, gentle and kind. Calling her *Sybilla,* and speaking of the *languishing of her soul.*

Byron Mudrick could not lead the Crusade as his brother had done, that was certain. Since the stabbing, the attorney had scarcely contacted Ednetta; he'd been terrified by the attack on Marus, and feared for his own life. Worse, he'd told Ednetta it was "inevitable" that they would all receive subpoenas to appear before a Passaic County grand jury, soon to be convened by the district attorney, to investigate the charges filed by Sybilla Frye.

So long as Sybilla had refused to speak with authorities, the Crusade had operated, so to speak, beyond the law; as soon as Sybilla had "positively" identified both Jerold Zahn and Julio Ramos, under the direction of Marus Mudrick, the district attorney's office had initiated its investigation. Byron had lamented to Ednetta that it had been a "dangerous, reckless and vindictive act" of Marus's to specifically name Julio Ramos as one of Sybilla's rapists; they would all be sued for hundreds of thousands of dollars, if not millions, and he, Byron Mudrick, would lose his license to practice law. If only Marus had consulted with him, before calling news conferences! Ednetta had wanted to press her hands over her ears. She'd wanted to cry to Byron Mudrick that his brother Marus was a martyr to the Crusade who'd risked his life for justice for Sybilla while he, Byron, was a coward who didn't have any faith in any of them. *My daughter name those men 'cause they the rapists, that why, Mr. Mudrick! She a black Joan of Arc. Marus know that.*

Still, Ednetta was anxious now she'd be served a subpoena, and made to testify in a courtroom. You had to swear on a Bible to tell the truth and if you lied it was perjury, which was a crime in itself apart from any other crime. And if you lied on the Bible, Jesus would be betrayed. She'd heard of people struck down dead who'd swore on a Bible and lied and God had punished them as they deserved. There was just no way out except as Byron Mudrick said refusing to answer the subpoena, fleeing the State of New Jersey before they could be arrested which was no option for him, as an attorney. *Stuck like Tar Baby* was Byron's sad joke on himself.

But the new development in the Fryes' life was the Kingdom of Islam. No one had anticipated *that*.

Now Sybilla was a convert to the Kingdom, and re-baptized "Aasia Muhammad"—maybe the law wouldn't pursue her? Maybe they would see she'd been just an ignorant young girl, failing in school and in trouble with her family, but now a good Muslim girl, and not prosecute her? The Black Prince had been confident that the "notoriety" of the Crusade would not follow Sybilla into her new life, and Ednetta wanted to believe this.

But Ednetta Frye was the girl's mother, and her legal guardian, even if Sybilla had converted to Islam. (This had been explained to her.) So long as she remained living in Pascayne, New Jersey, or anywhere in New Jersey, she could be served a summons at any time.

The Black Prince was intending to continue the Crusade for Sybilla Frye, but in his own way. He had access to "dimensions of wealth and power" far beyond the reach of Marus Mudrick, of whom he spoke with a sneering sort of pity.

He'd informed Ednetta of his plans for "Aasia Muhammad" without asking permission from her. He wasn't polite and deferential to her as Reverend Mudrick had been, at the start at least.

Ednetta thought it was because the Kingdom of Islam was a warrior religion and not a religion of peace like Christianity. Kingdom of Islam faithful did not believe in "turning the other cheek" as Jesus had taught—this was "weakness." Kingdom of Islam, surrounded by enemies both white and black, believed in striking the first blow; that was the history of the Kingdom, from its earliest, "pre-historic" era.

If you were declared an enemy of the faith by the Black Prince, it was a directive from the Prophet that you should be executed, and no one except the Black Prince could intercede.

No one had been arrested in the attempted murder of Marus Mudrick though there'd been dozens of witnesses to the attack, and the Newark Police Department claimed the Mudrick investigation was "high-priority."

Ednetta was determined to remain a member of the AME Church, for the time being at least. The Black Prince would sway her to conversion perhaps, in time; but in the meantime Ednetta could not abandon her many relatives who belonged to the church; she could not break the heart of her grandmother Pearline Tice. It was true, she felt the powerful attraction of the Black Prince who taught that Christianity was a "slave religion" that had "emasculated" black Africans; yet, she could not abandon the hope of Jesus in her heart, and the hymns she'd sung in the church on Camden Avenue since she'd been a girl.

Ednetta didn't like it that her daughter was a Muslim convert—but maybe it would be good for Sybilla, to dress modestly, and associate with girls nothing like the girls who were her friends in Red Rock. It would be good for Sybilla to be kept away from boys—the wrong kind of boys—and men. Good for Sybilla not to live with Anis Schutt any longer.

All that was over. That part of the girl's life, that was Ednetta's life as well. When the girl had come swaying on her feet to her, swollen-faced and bruised, but smiling like a drunk little girl proud of herself for doing something right for once—*Mama, look.*

Upside-down she'd scrawled words in Magic Marker on her naked body. The hard little bruised and bitten breasts with red-berry nipples, the skin taut against her ribs, the flat belly she'd written in black ink you could just manage to read—NIGRA BITCH KU KUX KLANN.

Mama, see? They don this to me. This what they done, an the other, an they left me like this, and you found me . . .

Quickly Ednetta said *Not me. Better somebody else, not your mama.*

So it was happening, without Ednetta ever agreeing, that Sybilla wouldn't be returning to Red Rock after this day. She wouldn't return to that nasty high school where there were drugs, stabbings and shootings and all kinds of ugly sex acts right in the school building, and the teachers and administrators helpless to stop it, or indifferent, and that was a good thing, Ednetta thought—but it was a surprise, and something of a shock, to learn that Quarrquan had arranged for Sybilla to live in Newark, in a Muslim household only a block from the Temple; Ednetta had just learned that she could only see her daughter with the permission of this "foster" family, and with the permission of the Black Prince. There was no doubt, Sybilla would be better off enrolled in a special girls' school taught by instructresses in the Faith. The girl's Christian religion hadn't gone very deep in her, Ednetta supposed.

Or maybe, it had been beat out of her by her stepdaddy's fists.

"From this hour forward, in the name of the Prophet and in the name of Allah, you will live in *hope,* Aasia Muhammad! And you will bring *hope* to others dwelling in darkness and yearning for the light . . .

"Your heart must be open to Allah. For all is Allah, and there is not anything that is not Allah."

The Sisters

D ry-swallowing the white pill, that left a bitter taste on her tongue.

If the Black Prince knew! But the Black Prince would not know.

It was the Sisters' task, to prepare Aasia Muhammad for the rally.

Bright blinding lights, restless noise of the crowd like those big green insects eating—one of the plagues of Egypt.

The mother wasn't allowed near Aasia, by decree of the Black Prince. Ednetta Frye shamed and humiliated and nothing Aasia could do, she'd turned away from *all that.*

The Black Prince was addressing the crowd. The Black Prince in his radiant white robe, arms lifted in a blessing.

The Black Prince spoke the language of the Prophet. No more beautiful and sacred language had ever been uttered, than the language of the Prophet.

The audience did not know this language. Yet, the audience was

eager, like children, to echo the Black Prince's words in an incantatory call-and-response.

She was one of those seated on the platform beside and behind the
Black Prince. Eyes lingered on her hungrily. She was cloaked in white,
and her long white sleeves to her wrists. And her long white skirt covering her ankles. And her white head scarf covering her tight-plaited
hair stiff as a Brillo pad, that was itching her scalp without Mama to
intervene.

Eyes lowered. Always, eyes lowered. The eyes of strangers moving over her hungrily, she must not acknowledge.

*The black girl shamed and debased by "white cops." Hurt so bad, only
the Kingdom of Islam has saved her and will demand justice for her and for
her sisters shamed and debased by "white cops."*

High up inside her, there was a sharp pain. It was not a steady
pain but a quick-darting pain you could forget, until it recurred. This
pain was too strong for the white pill to numb so it was always a
surprise when it came sharp as it did—but then, it was not a constant
pain. At first she'd thought *I will start to bleed. In these white robes!*

But there was no blood. None of *that blood.*

For weeks now, there'd been none of *that blood.* After the beating she'd been having a period every fifteen days, twelve days, and
bad cramps, but now the periods seemed to have stopped. She'd overheard the Black Prince saying she'd become too skinny, and a black
girl does not look good if she is skinny. A daughter of the Prophet
should exude health.

On the platform she sat as still as she could. This pose, the white
pill did help.

Sat with her shoulders raised, her ankles crossed. Hidden beneath
the long white skirt. And her head bowed, and her eyes near-shut.

It was easier, to keep her eyes shut. It was not a good idea to be
glancing out into the audience, looking for faces.

Among strangers you look for a familiar face. How many times she'd seen Mama in an audience!—also Aunt Cheryl, Grandma Tice, Martine, Anis Schutt . . . Seeing Anis Schutt in some tall thick-bodied man at the rear of rows of seats or standing in the aisle not sure if he's staying, and that was a shock to her, she'd regret. But also she'd seen teachers out in the audience, a woman like that neighbor who'd found her in the fish-factory cellar, faces not attached to names and in any case these were not the actual people, it was stupid for her to imagine they were, that they'd come some distance to see *her*.

(Oh!—she'd heard, Jaycee Handler had been interviewed in the *National Inquirer*. Claiming Sybilla Frye had come to visit him in a youth facility at the time she'd said she was being held captive by "white cops" in Pascayne.)

(She'd heard this nasty lie. And other neighbors were telling of her and Mama, on Third Street. There was talk of a "grand jury" in Passaic County to investigate Sybilla Frye, Ednetta Frye, and the Mudrick brothers. The Black Prince had comforted her, now she was a daughter of the Prophet of the Kingdom of Islam the secular state had no authority over her. He would protect her, he promised. Any summons or subpoena served to her, the Black Prince would tear up on the steps of the Pascayne courthouse, for Allah had ordained him as the protector of Aasia Muhammad and the secular law would not dare confront him.)

Tonight was Trenton. A nighttime rally in the Trenton Armory, estimated three thousand people in the chilly, high-ceilinged place though she could not see them clearly even if she'd dared to lift her eyes, for there were bright lights shining onto the stage.

Against the night sky of Trenton was an illuminated sphere like a fallen moon, she'd marveled at it as they'd driven south into the city and was told that was the state capitol building for this city was the *capital city* of New Jersey.

Several cities she'd been taken to, in just these few weeks she'd become Aasia Muhammad, a daughter of the Prophet. Sweetened goat's milk she was given each night by her Sister-Mother to help her sleep, for her new family did not like her screaming in the night, in fear of bad dreams. And the sweet milk, like the white pill, helped numb the sharp-needle pains high inside her and if she was lonely for Mama, her Sister-Mother would hold her, and rock her to sleep.

On cue, "Aasia Muhammad" would rise from her chair, and move to center stage, where the Black Prince looming above her in his radiant garments would take her hand. The Black Prince would lead her to the pulpit where a blinding light awaited her like a burst sun. The Black Prince would introduce her to the reverent audience and she would speak her careful, memorized words.

"Hello! I am 'Aasia Muhammad'—I am your sister in the Faith. My name was once 'Sybilla Frye.' You know of me—a 'shamed black girl.' But now, I am one of you. The Prince is seeking justice for me bringing war against the white Enemy. Please help him in this righteous war, and Allah will bless you."

Inanely she was smiling, as the audience erupted into cries and sobs. Gently the Black Prince tugged at her arm, not at all impatiently for it was not the way of the Black Prince, to betray impatience with any of the faithful in a public setting.

A glance of disgust was enough, to wound. Aasia Muhammad understood.

She'd stumbled, returning to her seat. For a terrible moment it seemed that she might faint—fall clumsily onto the platform. Such a fainting spell had not been practiced, and would be an outrage to the Black Prince.

But she did not faint. A ripple of apprehension, then relief ran through the audience, that understood how she'd been kidnapped, beaten, raped, tortured, left for dead . . . Any weakness of the daughter, the faithful would forgive.

Following the deafening applause she was led offstage. She would not see the Black Prince again that night. Perhaps, she would not see him for many nights.

In the sharp cold air that smelled of a river she was being walked to a waiting car. She was homesick suddenly for that other river—nobody ever gave a glance to, in Red Rock. But you could see it walking to school, and you could smell it. And by Grandma Tice's building you could see it. Her legs were feeling weak as a child's legs. The pavement here was covered in something white and gritty like metallic filings—she was trying to recall the word for *snow*. Out of nowhere a figure approached her, a woman with a face that seemed wrong—a white face, like a joke-mask.

" 'Sybilla Frye'? Excuse me—please—you don't know me, Sybilla, but I—I am—I'm the sister of Jerold Zahn . . ."

It was forbidden to Aasia Muhammad to speak with strangers unless directed by the Black Prince. For all strangers are the Enemy.

She did not speak, but she paused to stare openmouthed at the white-face woman.

Not a woman but a girl. A girl her age? Older? With anxious eyes, a wounded mouth.

There'd been white girls at school who'd been friendly to Sybilla and Martine. She'd been friendly to them.

Well, not really—just seeing them in the girls' restroom where nobody was supposed to smoke, or out back of school, or at the Wawa. White girls hanging out with black guys, sharing joints, cans of beer, street-jive-talking.

"Sybilla Frye? I'm the sister of—Jerold Zahn . . ."

The name was one of those knives thrown at her. The Black Prince had cautioned her never to reply, she would be protected from the Enemy, yet she heard her voice startled and faltering:

"Who you sayin? Don't know no 'Jer'd Zehn.' "

The Sisters were moving her along. The Sisters hissed at the white girl to get away, before she was hurt.

"Please, Sybilla! You accused my brother of a terrible thing—you know it wasn't true, please will you admit it? We are begging you, please . . ."

Aasia was shaking her head *No no.*

Aasia did not remember that name. Or, Aasia could not speak with the white-face Enemy.

Left behind in the parking lot the girl called after them. Forlorn as a child, calling after them. Aasia heard *Please please please we loved my brother so much* like an echo in one of those bad dreams.

"Still Alive"

She knows me—of course. She knows what she has done to me and to Jerold and my family. She knows.

I think she is sorry for what she'd done. She will not recant, but she is sorry. I think I saw that in her eyes.

In one of her eyes, that locked with mine. The other eye appeared to be damaged.

We can forgive her, I think. The others, we can't forgive.

But the girl, we need to forgive the girl.

Daddy? I spoke to her in Trenton last night, the girl.

In her eyes I could see how sorry and shamed she was.

We couldn't speak. They were taking her away.

Yes—she knew me. She recognized Jerold's name.

She said, I am sorry.

With her eyes, she said this.

We have to forgive. There is no other way.

Exhausted she slept at his bedside. On all sides, machines were monitoring the father's life. When she wakened with a start she saw that her father was very still, scarcely breathing. In another ten minutes, her brother Lyle would be bringing their mother. How cruel it would be if Daddy died before Mom arrived to say good-bye to him, she prayed that God would not be so cruel.

But her father was still alive, steadily breathing. The machines were monitoring his life. If there was a sudden crisis, another stroke, the machines would signal an alarm. She leaned over her father, with a pang of joy she felt the faint breath.

Still alive.

Ten-Thousand-Man March

*K*ill *you one of them. The time come now.*

That black-feather thing tormenting him. Ain't gon die a righteous death if you fail in this, Anis.

It was like the thing had him by the throat. Way it say *Anis* you could hear the disrespect.

He'd found the gun on a shelf in the closet and was carrying it now in his left-leg-trouser pocket. Seemed like the right time at last.

Been meaning to take time to clean and oil it. Had not fired the damn thing in—how long?—had to be years.

Then, he'd missed who the fuck it was he'd been aiming at. Anis in that old rattletrap Plymouth, and the motherfucker in some big-ass SUV cuttin him off on Crater by the bridge, and Anis aimed out the window and fired and the look on the motherfucker's face!—had to laugh, remembering.

Bullet just went wild, he guessed.

Driving on Crater now, why he was thinking of this.

Camden Avenue was blocked by cop vehicles. All day he'd been hearing about the "rally"—"march"—"Black Prince"—"Sybilla Frye."

Nobody would say to Anis Schutt *Ain't that girl your stepdaughter? 'Netta Frye's girl?*

Nobody would dare say to Anis Schutt *You gettin any of that money they're making on that girl? She your daughter ain't she?—or was?*

Anis wasn't living in the row house on Third Street any longer. Collection agency tryin to get him to pay eight hundred dollars back rent and "damage" but fuck that, he'd just laughed. Last he'd heard, Ednetta was taking away the younger children to live with relatives in South Carolina. Told him she wasn't afraid of any "grand jury"— she would swear to tell the truth the whole truth so help me God and she would *tell the truth* in the white man's face about them cops raping and beating her girl—but must've changed her mind, he'd have told her it was a God damn good idea to change her mind, news came to him the woman was gone.

Did he care, fuck he *did not care.*

Fourteen years they'd been together. Except for Anis staying away sometimes but the place with 'Netta was *home.*

He'd never have another *home,* he guessed. All right with him.

Last three days he'd been drinking to numb the pain in his back and legs. Each day starting earlier and the alcohol made him feel heavy like lead in his veins. Used to be, drinking made Anis feel happy but no longer.

'Netta sayin the same with her. Plus God damn di'betes made her crazy-hungry why she put on weight.

Last year or so, the pain in Anis's back and legs was worsening. Had to sit down where he could, outdoors there's not many places to sit shake out his damn right leg the pain came so bad. Misery in wet cold weather. He'd been young not giving a damn for how he took care of hisself, like the guys on the truck with him. Calling him *old man* like they felt sorry for him but didn't respect him.

Driving to Twelfth Street he was blocked again. God damn!

Pascayne PD cruisers, uniformed cops and cops in riot gear along the street like the U.S. Army. And he'd been seeing people running in the street, that age the TV called *youths*.

Cursed turning the car around in the street not giving a damn if he blocked other vehicles or scraped against some motherfucker parked at the curb. The more you were boxed-in, the more you felt needing to get out. Close behind him a driver sounded his horn and Anis leaned the palm of his hand on his own horn, hard. Thinking *Somebody gon die tonight asshole, you keep that up.*

Camden blocked at Washburn, too. More people on the street, and more cops.

It was the Ten-Thousand-Man March, he'd been hearing about. Everybody talkin about. Two men he worked with were planning to march, they'd said. Anis thought they had to be crazy, he'd just laughed. Assholes! Like they was Reverend Martin Luther King Jr. and anybody'd give a shit about what happened in Pascayne that was one of the shit-holes of New Jersey.

A march along Camden Avenue to the Pitcairn Bridge and across the bridge to City Hall and the courthouse. Had to be two miles, maybe three. *He* couldn't march a mile or half-mile or a block, Christ!

Some Black Muslim march. They'd taken up Sybilla Frye, the Reverend had had to quit his Crusade.

It wasn't the Nation of Islam, Anis had some respect for. It was the other black Islam-religion, started by some punk incarcerated in a prison and tellin himself Allah gives a shit for *him*.

(Had Mudrick died? Killed by some racist white man the cops didn't stop from stabbing him? Asshole boastin he didn't carry a gun and didn't wear a bulletproof vest what'd he think would happen to him? Couldn't remember if Mudrick had died but it served the motherfucker right, interfering in Anis Schutt's family life.)

The girl had a new name now—not a name he could pronounce. Some Arab-name. African-name. Ednetta telling him like she was embarrassed, she couldn't pronounce the name either. And S'b'lla wearing a head scarf now, she'd have screamed with laughter seeing any friend of hers wearing on the street.

The one thing the Black Muslims did was protect their women. Keep the women covered up, and stayin indoors all they can. Hard to see how that sassy-mouth Sybilla gon keep indoors.

Missed her. The girl, and the younger children. And 'Netta.

Shit, they gone from him now. Had to happen sometime. His own kids growed up, and gone. He'd never see this lifetime and they'd been on bad terms.

He'd been seeing posters for the march. Close-up of a face that was meant to be "Sybilla Frye" but was some other black girl, Anis could tell. The picture was blurred on purpose so you mostly saw ugly swollen-shut eyes, mouth, a bloodied nose and the caption was WHITE COPS DID THIS and information about the TEN-THOUSAND-MAN MARCH scheduled for March 7 which was this day.

The posters had appeared everywhere in Red Rock the previous week, all along Camden, on the sides of buildings and on fences, on storefronts, on doors—hurriedly torn down by Pascayne cops as well as neighborhood residents who didn't want trouble with the Pascayne cops.

Since there'd started to be stories in the papers and on TV about the *black girl kidnapped by white cops* it was a sensitive time in Red Rock. More dark-skin cops on the street, you could see that was deliberate. But any-skin-color cop is a white cop, people in Red Rock figured.

Lookin like Washburn was blocked—why in hell? People marchin on Camden ain't gon come down here.

Police-cruiser blockade at Eighth Street? Also, Barnegat. Had to be, the cops had orders from the mayor to shut down Red Rock. Traffic backed up and everybody honking his damn horn and the God damn city buses detouring from Camden onto side streets too narrow for them to pass oncoming traffic. Plus kids runnin in the streets. There were looks in the cops' faces—Anis perceived, even in the faces of dark-skin cops—like in boxers' faces before a fight. You work yourself up, your blood is up, you ready yourself to break some motherfucker's face, and you are *ready*.

All the cops armed, and *ready*.

Anis tried another block, and was stopped. God *damn* he wasn't ever gon get home except to abandon his car and *walk*.

And his knees hurtin so bad, fuck he could *walk*.

You could see the cops was sectioning off Red Rock so people were boxed in. Except for the marchers on Camden who could walk in the street, in wide, wavering rows holding posters and pictures of "Sybilla Frye" (in fact, it was the picture on the poster, which was not "Sybilla Frye") as well as pictures of other black faces (gunned down or incarcerated) and some of them pictures (it looked like) of black men in full-dress uniform like in the Army or Marines. Nobody could walk mostly anywhere. Driving a vehicle was impossible unless it was one of the police vehicles everywhere you looked.

Cops boxing in Red Rock like the inhabitants was cockroaches. At the time of the 1967 riot it was reported the police chief had said that, about cockroaches, meaning black people without any doubt. He'd sworn he was misquoted but there was no doubt. White folks in Pascayne hopin there's a "riot" tonight so the mayor can call in the National Guard, and tanks.

Anis was seeing cops in riot gear. Cops with riot shields lining Camden Avenue so if marchers wanted to quit the march they couldn't—had to keep moving forward.

Along side streets Anis could see cops erecting barricades.

If you wanted to cross a street on foot you had to make your way the length of a block to get around the barricade—except the cops were yelling at people trying to walk in the street. And if families had gotten separated from one another, cops were refusing to allow even small children to slip through the barricade. (Anis saw some small children crying, their mother on the wrong side of the barricade. Felt a flash of disgust, a woman got to be a damn fool, or drunk or high on crack bringing children out onto the street at such a time.)

It was the old story of Red Rock and Pascayne. If you don't tear up your place of residence, trash and burn it, nobody gon give a shit about you. But if you do that, you got to live in the rubble.

No way to win. Anis knew that. Ten-Thousand-Man March for justice but also to "celebrate" being black. Anis had to laugh, some people believin anything.

He was sorry he'd missed the start of the march. Had to suppose the Black Prince and his shave-head guards were at the head and (maybe) Sybilla was walking with them?—in white female robes, and one of them Muslim scarves on her head?—if she was, there'd be white-clad Sisters walking with her. Not Ednetta, they'd sent the mother away.

If Anis had been standing at the curb watching for her, unless she'd pass within a few feet he wouldn't have seen was the girl really *her*. This the way of the Kingdom of Islam, they made their women and girls dress "modest." He guessed she'd never lift her eyes to look at him, as she would not look at any man standing at the curb.

Never meant to hurt you so bad, S'b'lla. You know that.

All you accomplished now, you and your damn-drunk mama, is broke up our home. Thank your little slut-ass for that.

Her and her mother, he'd never forgive. Taken what he'd done to the girl like it was something actual he'd meant to do, and not Anis losing his temper like he did sometimes. Damn bitches *knew better.*

Ednetta saying the doctors would tell the cops and the cops would come and arrest *him.* And Anis sayin, shit how'd anybody prove any fuckin thing. You don't know nothin about the law, 'Netta you head up you fat ass.

That fat-ass female! Jesus he was glad to be rid of *her.*

This woman he was staying with now on Twelfth Street, never tried to get the last word. Anything Anis said, she'd agree real quick. Younger than 'Netta and a cashier at Walmart. That sick-eager look in her face, she'd be grateful for any kindness and Anis Schutt the man for such a woman.

Everybody boxed-in here, blowing his horn. Sounding like cattle braying. Anis pressing the palm of his hand down hard against his horn though shit, he knew better, seeing cops up ahead in the street making people open their trunks. That shit Anis didn't want nothing of, carrying his gun like he was.

(The heavy gun he kept in the left-trouser-leg pocket of his coveralls. Anis left-handed all his life so the schoolteachers tried to teach him right but never succeeded only just made him stutter till he got out of grade school. Anytime Anis feel a stutter come on he think of them teachers an wishin he could strangle them and nothin to do with race. The coveralls loose-fitting like Anis has lost weight which maybe he has, or lost height, which definitely he has like a doctor say on TV, a man can lose one inch of his spine a year he don't take in enough calcium.)

It was a cop-tactic, *boxing-in.* They'd *boxed-in* pedestrians on the street in 1967 with barricades, then squeezed tighter. Like an animal pen and the animals pissin theyselves knowin they was to be slaughtered. On the highway they came up behind you in a squad car not running its siren, and another squad passing you, and goes ahead then slows down; and a third car comes up alongside you and you are *boxed*.

This they did to the Hispanic boy they'd shot back in the fall on the Turnpike claiming he was going for his weapon when his hands were in full view on his steering wheel. And that boy, turned out, was a first-year National Guardsman—but the white cops not knowing *that*. One squad car came up behind him making no sound or signal, and the others closed in forcing him to brake onto the shoulder of the highway with a claim he'd been speeding and "reckless endangerment"—some shit like that. Meaning they wanted to shoot a dark-skin boy, like a hunter gets it into his head he wants to kill some animal.

Since Lyander shot down like a dog, Anis has known he will kill a white cop only not *when*. Shit, since Anis twelve years old, he has known. The black-feather Angel of Wrath chiding him, how long he's going to wait? And what if he dies first? If the white cops *kill him first*?

This was a sobering thought: if Anis waited too long to kill a white cop, one day it would be too late. *Sorry-ass nigger ain't you gon be embarrassed!*

It was like 'Netta's girl. How long you gon wait before the girl havin sex right in that house, and the two of them laughin at you like you was some asshole old helpless blind man. He'd had to discipline them all, 'Netta couldn't control even the younger children saying *shit* and *fuck* to their mama and her not able to stop them. 'Netta always bawlin sayin she loves the children too much to discipline them, feels sick if she has to whip them, and Anis say, you want me to do it, then I will. And you keep your fat face out of it then.

This fish-net-top the girl was wearing, last summer. You could see right through it, Jesus! And skinny little straps falling off her shoulder like she didn't notice, or didn't give a damn. And the short-shorts all

the girls wore, you could see half their asses like little half-moons, and
that soft pale goose-pimple flesh there, Anis stood dead-still staring
and blinking; and he's seeing Tana just turning away from him, slim
girl, the side of her face, the way she touched her hair with her hand
like to stroke it, and her slim legs, and feeling weak seeing Tana and
him so old now, could be his young wife's daddy at least. A hot flush
came into his face, the girl was seein him, and giggling. But it was
Sybilla giggling like that, not—not the other.

Most of the time Sybilla shrewd enough to wear a shirt over
herself, and when Anis was home most of the time she'd wear her
jeans that was stiff with dirt, and keep out of his way like all of the
woman's children had learned to do, like you'd keep out of the way
of a bull to respect it. What he brooded on wasn't whether the young
girl was having sex—(he had to know she was, wouldn't be normal if
she wasn't)—but whether she'd get pregnant and have a baby and the
upkeep of the baby would fall on *his head*. Like some ugly mongrel
sneaking into a yard where there's a special-breed dog, mating with
the female and you had to bring up the pups, take care of them like
they were your own. Family Services checks didn't add up to shit,
everybody knew. You had to be punished for any new baby in the
household, Family Services made sure of that.

These things, and many other things triggered his rage. It was
like a rim of small blue flame on a stove, turn the burner-dial fast to
the left and a hot yellow flame burst out. He'd be talking with somebody could be 'Netta, or a stranger, or somebody at work, or one of
the kids, and the way the person shifted his face, or wiped at his nose,
Anis understood there was a judgment against him. Sybilla always
trying to slide away from him, sideways on the stairs, and that scared
cross-eye look to her, that freaky left-eye of her, made him mad; and
worse mad, when she giggled to show she wasn't scared, and she *was
scared;* and it fucked him up bad, that his stepdaughter and the other

kids were *scared as hell* of him when he tried to be nice to them, God damn they had to know, he'd heard 'Netta telling them, Anis was the main financial support of the household, but they scared as hell of him as much when he was nice to them as when he was blind drunk and wanting to slam them against the wall.

Every time he went out, driving slow under the speed limit so the cops would not stop him, he could see them—their cop-eyes following *him*.

Nigger motherfucker don't have the balls to murder us, think we don't know it?

Laughing openly at Anis and other black men on the street. The cops were high on being hated, it made them excited to know how the residents of Red Rock yearned to murder them but had not the courage.

One of the old men saying to Anis *You think you'd be ashamed livin here. That shit you take from them.*

The old man scratching his crotch, laughing. Most of his teeth were missing. His jaws appeared misaligned. Anis felt the sick horror, the old man was Death. Liver spots on his skin you could see darker than his skin like paint-spots. Old man lived on the street or in vacant houses with his mattress, shopping cart and crap. A veteran of some war—"world" war—he'd had medals, a long time ago—Anis vaguely remembered unless it was another old bastard like a vulture fixing nasty eyes on him laughing at him. Then he'd start coughing, wheezing and scraping up clots of phlegm, Anis turned aside in disgust and walked away.

That evening, he'd come home early. And there was Sybilla in the kitchen rinsing dishes in the sink sulky and careless like she's tryin to break them to spite her mama in the next room watching TV. And seeing Anis (she ain't expected to come home so early) she shut off the faucets and hurried upstairs to her room like a scared cat and

Anis came after quiet-like not raising his voice. *Why're you hiding in here?* he'd asked and the girl mumbled she *was not hiding. Why are you acting like you got some secret from your daddy?* and the girl mumbled she wasn't acting like anything, she was just minding her business. And Anis said *Why'd you run upstairs, didn't say hello to your daddy?* and when the girl not answer backing off and hiding her face he'd asked *Why're you acting like some guilty bitch? Won't meet your daddy's eyes like you're afraid of—what?* And the girl saying in her soft-scared voice she wasn't guilty of anything, tried to lift her eyes to Anis's face he saw this was true, and felt sorry for her, she was just a little girl begging him so. Saying *If I go to school and they see I am beat-up they will ask me about it like last time and send a social worker here and Mama will get in trouble and blame me and I ain't done nothing wrong Daddy, I swear.*

There was 'Netta calling up the stairs anxious and neither of them was hearing her.

So Anis had mercy on the girl seeing she called him *Daddy,* that time.

Nothing was so clear to him, he must kill the enemy.

Yet, if he began to kill the enemy but not enough of the enemy, they would kill *him.*

The Angel of Wrath chided him for his cowardice. Muttering to himself cursing as he dumped stinking garbage into the rear of the truck. The fury in his face was such, the other men kept their distance from Anis Schutt.

He'd see a cop cruiser on the street, and freeze where he stood. His hands like claws inside the smelly gloves twitching, so badly he wanted to strangle those throats.

His mind was clouded. He'd stop at the Blue Star tavern and wake in some other place.

Then back on the sanitation truck. The smell of it, even in cold weather when the garbage was frozen, nothing could lessen the stink of the truck, in his hair, his clothes, his lungs. Seeing then a police cruiser pass and the faintness would come over him, once he'd fallen from the truck onto the street, the men shouted for the driver to stop and they hauled him to his feet, and his vision was blotched like strobe lighting but he summoned back his strength, and insisted he was all right.

Jesus help me, I have got to kill some of them. They comin to kill me an my children.

Jesus give me a sign? How I can do this one thing, to put my heart at rest.

At the Blue Star seeing on TV how Pascayne cops are the highest paid in New Jersey, on account of the police union contract negotiated eighteen years ago. Cops making extra money working overtime. Cops with seniority retiring with such high pensions, the city ain't got enough money for schools, road repair, sewers, clinics, finishing buildings started ten years ago.

He's waiting for a sign. Gripping the steering wheel, and his arthritic hands like claws. On Camden Avenue the marchers were still passing. Anis squinting and staring through the badly cracked side-window of the car, amazed there were so many. Feeling the reproach *You a man, you be walking, too. Ten-Thousand-Man March and Anis Schutt sittin on his ass, too weak to be a man.*

Traffic was edging forward, but again stopped. He saw a street sign—EAST VENTOR. Dead-end by the river. That nasty smell of the river. Boarded-up warehouses and factories. Shouts on the street, cops surrounding a vehicle ahead. Anis steeled himself waiting for gunfire thinking *If the first shot is fired, that will be a sign.*

He hadn't practiced with the gun. Didn't know if the damn thing would fire.

His heart pained him, thinking of Lyander. Him and Lyander

hadn't seen each other in almost two years, news came to Anis the boy had been shot dead. For a long time he didn't think about it, and he didn't let the woman talk to him about it. (A woman has a way of slipping inside a man's grief like a hand inside his trousers, once it's there, you aint goin to push it away even if you don't want it. But it's disgusting to you, and the woman goin to pay.) But now, since Sybilla an all that, he'd been thinking about Lyander and how the boy had died in the street, and the last voices he'd heard had had to be white cops shouting to one another *Nigger down! Finish him.*

And later they would say *Refused to throw down his weapon. Firing shots. Ordered him to stop but he would not comply.*

Later they would add *Evidence of drug psychosis.*

Shameful to Anis, he'd lived so long in this city, and such a coward.

Even now he's thinking with a part of his brain if he can turn the damn Plymouth around, drive back where he came from, take that backstreet by the river by the railroad yard then uphill to, what is it, Depp Street, maybe the Ten-Thousand-Man marchers are past that block of Camden, and the cops have opened it . . . Trying to turn the car around and both rear wheels jolting up over a curb, there's a fierce-looking white cop pounding the hood with a billy club and another cop shouting at him from a few feet away. God damn he hadn't seen them.

The cop with the club is rapping hard on the windshield like he'd like to break it. Telling Anis to put his hands where they can see them, on the steering wheel. But the other cop shouting for him to lower his window.

Anis frozen-still behind the wheel. Cops shouting at him the way cops do, repeating their words louder, angrier-sounding and Anis's brain like something stunned with a sledgehammer—not sure what to do except he knows it's better to stay still than to move.

Sweating, and his heart pounding with the strain. They were

shouting at him through the window asking him for his driver's license and vehicle registration. How many times Anis has been stopped by cops in Red Rock and across the river! Each time like it will be the last time, you make a wrong move.

Not sure how to react. Shut-mouthed, silent like he didn't know the language. Or, quick to obey.

Silent might be mistaken for resistance. Quick-to-obey might be mistaken for mockery.

You didn't want to move too much, or too quickly. White cops anxious they gon be shot-at tonight and primed to shoot first.

The (older, thick-face) cop yelling at him to lower his window was louder than the other (younger, pimply-face) cop and standing closer to him so Anis lowered the window moving slowly and deliberately. The kind of old-style window you crank by hand, and that takes time. Black man, thick-neck black man in smelly work clothes, scarred-looking face, heavy-lidded eyes, mouth not smiling—the cops were excited having cornered their prey, but like their prey they could not know precisely what would come next.

Slow-moving like a crippled old animal. Yet in the predators' eyes, a dangerous old animal.

Anis considered asking the angry cops what the "parade" was all about?—shaking his head to indicate he wasn't one of *those blacks*.

Considered asking them if there was some way he could get back to Depp Street, or was all the streets blocked by that damn "parade" . . .

The Smith & Wesson .45-caliber revolver heavy in the left-leg deep pocket of his work-pants. He'd had the revolver in the glove compartment, now in his pocket. Moving the gun from the closet to the car, from the car to his pocket had to mean something. Seeing the posters—WHITE COPS DID THIS. He'd come to believe—almost—that *white cops had raped his daughter like everybody say* and that fact was unbearable. A man just could not live with it, and be a man.

The button on that pocket had pulled off long ago. Say he reached into the pocket, seized the gun, could he raise it and fire, before the cops shot him? Brain calculating the odds even as he was smiling now, trying to smile at the cops, friendly-seeming lifting his hands so the cops could see yes, OK, he did not have a weapon and did not appear to be the kind of black man who carried a weapon, except of course there is no black man who does not carry a (hidden, deadly) weapon, and the cops knew this, they'd been trained to know this, sharp-eyed, excited and eager.

Yet, they'd allowed Anis Schutt to reach into his rear pocket—slowly—and to remove his wallet. In the midst of jammed traffic, a dozen cops in view in just this section of the street, red lights flashing. Allowed Anis to open the wallet with his splayed fingers, and fumble for the laminated New Jersey license, miniature photo of a glaring black man likin to rip out your throat with his teeth. And—slowly, his lower back seizing with pain—reaching over to the glove compartment, to fumble for the registration. Closely they watched Anis through the lowered car window and through the smudged windshield as one might watch an animal not only deadly-dangerous but unpredictable and Anis continued smiling at them, feeling muscles in his lower mouth twitching and straining against the assault of pain.

The cop's voice, now he wasn't shouting, sounded high-pitched, querulous. "'Anis Schutt'? Seems like that's a name I know."

Anis sat quietly. Arms on the steering wheel now, big-knuckled hands visible.

The cops talked together loudly, like Anis was deaf.

"Y'heard of him? 'Schutt'? We know him, do we?"

"Yah. 'Schutt.' He's—ya know who he is?—the father of 'Syb'la Frye.'"

"Fuck he is! Jesus."

Still, Anis sat quietly. The pain in his back was suspended as if in anticipation of a greater pain, from another source, to which the afflicted man must give one hundred percent of his attention.

"Mr. Schutt, you the father of that girl? 'Syb'la Frye'?"

Shook his head *no*.

Shrewdly the younger cop said, "You livin with her, though? Says here '939 Third Street'—right?"

Shook his head *no*.

"No? You ain't? Changed residence, and this driver's license ain't up-to-date?"

Anis mumbled an inaudible reply. The cops asked him to repeat what he'd said so he repeated what sounded like *Just moved out Officers. Meanin to change that.*

The younger cop took the auto registration to a nearby cruiser to run a check. Anis was feeling light-headed the way you'd feel if small strokes of lightning were striking your brain. Reasoning *So many people here, they ain't gon just shoot me. Too public.*

The narrow street was jammed. Behind Anis, a city bus was stalled. Vehicles were being abandoned. Drivers were shouting at one another. Cops were yelling, brandishing billy clubs. There were no pistols in sight. Not yet.

The old police tactic, from union marches of long-ago, Anis had been hearing all his life, is the cops fire at a "sniper"—the sniper "returns fire"—cops discharge as much ammunition as they can, hundreds of rounds of bullets, as long as ten minutes solid firing, in the direction of the rooftop, the building, the hiding place where the "sniper" is crouched. You're in the "cross fire" you hit the pavement and lay right there, don't even try to crawl away.

Or even if you lay still not breathing sometimes they shoot you anyway. Cop bullets flying wild.

Cops blocked his view. Anis couldn't see the marchers on Camden Avenue. But he believed they were still marching—hundreds, thousands of marchers—ten thousand? And all for justice, for Sybilla Frye?

Again he thought *They ain't gon shoot me this time. Feels like, they gon let me go.* A sensation of disappointment came over him though also relief. Though also dismay. Fuck!—he'd have to return to his old, debased life. Have to crawl into his skin like crawling into a befouled bed.

Now came again the God damn spine-pain, like a vise gripping his lower back, obliterating all thought.

The second cop returned. Anis had been thinking the cop would just hand back the registration and the driver's license and tell Anis Schutt to sit his ass still in the vehicle until the street was opened up, but turned out, both cops had more questions to ask and there was an excitement in their voices a signal for trouble.

Where was Anis headed. Where did he come from. Where did he work. Where did he live if it wasn't Third Street.

And where'd he been at the time his "daughter" had been kidnapped in October.

To these answers, Anis mumbled replies. In the midst of his mumbled words stuttering, stammering like a terrible quake beginning deep inside his body and moving out. Last time they'd stopped him, Anis had not stuttered, he was sure.

Looking at their prey with contempt but also pity. If he'd been a true black man like a Kingdom of Islam warrior he'd have shown it by now, the white cops is thinking.

Now ordering Anis Schutt to release the lock of his trunk, which Anis did with careful, deliberate motions. In his rear-view mirror he saw the younger of the cops staring into the trunk, moving a few items, sour-faced seeing nothing suspicious. The cop then peering into the rear of the car, saw nothing suspicious yet in loud voices both cops ordered Anis to step out of his vehicle.

Was this happening? He'd thought that it was not going to happen. In the jammed traffic, some vehicles were being closely inspected but most were not. Vehicles driven by black youths were the ones being searched. Lone drivers and middle-age or older drivers, not. But they were asking him if he was carrying a concealed weapon or anything that was "sharp" and he tried to answer them saying *No sir* but the spine-pain came so sudden, he nearly fainted. "Oh Jesus God"—whisper like a prayer escaped his lips.

His right leg lost strength, a nerve tingling and aching from his buttock to the sole of his foot.

"Watch it!"—the elder of the cops regarded him with a kind of involuntary sympathy, ravaged-looking black man, wincing pain in his face. There is no disguising such pain. "Lean against the car, Mr. Schutt."

They hadn't drawn their pistols. They had captured their prey but not a dangerous prey after all. The pain came so bad, even leaning onto the car, grabbing at the roof wasn't enough to keep him standing. Apologizing to the cops *Sorry, oh Jesus I am sorry, my leg . . .*

He was on his knees on the pavement. White cops standing over him uncertain what to do with him. He'd tried to stand, you could see he had tried. But he had not the strength, he'd sunk to his knees on the pavement. And it was a confused time. Not far away, there were pounding feet. Black boys running. Cops shouting at them. Sounds of sirens. Like a wounded animal Anis groaned aloud in misery, indignation, fury scrambling to haul himself back to his feet, to stand upright and confront the cops pitying him. And the older cop gripping his arm as if to help him, and the younger cop hovering close, and both of them talking to him and the words had no meaning, he'd ceased listening for there went Anis's hand into the left-leg pocket, fumbled to grip the gun, nickel-plated handle, and his finger on the trigger that was always larger than you expect, and in a movement graceless but expedient as all of Anis's movements had been since the cops had first approached him in his vehicle he managed to remove the heavy revolver from the pocket, aimed it upward, and fired—a quick shot—and another shot, and another—the first bullet struck the older cop on the underside of his jaw blowing much of the jaw away, second bullet seemed to have struck the cop's forehead above his right eye tearing away bone and gristle, and the third bullet, and the fourth and fifth bullets, striking the younger cop in his face and neck where the bulletproof vest couldn't save him so taken by surprise his face was an utter blank like a moon, in an instant shattered and bloody, broken.

The white cops were down. Within seconds it had happened. Anis gripped the gun lifting it in both hands, in an ecstasy of triumph aiming the long barrel at whoever was approaching, and another time fired, the final bullet, though his finger continued to jerk the trigger on the emptied chambers even as he was being shot, he hadn't seen where the final bullet had gone, eyes shut as he dragged himself along the pavement, beyond the front grille of his vehicle; in his confused memory this was a dead end on Ventor, by the river, he would crawl into someplace on the dock, a hiding place of the kind boys knew about, one of those big pipes into which he'd crawled as a boy; a pipe not so long you couldn't see the dim halo of daylight at the farther end, and you could hide there. Still, they were firing at him. Yelling at him and at one another and their shouts sheer sound, animal-sounds of rage. The long-barrel gun had slipped from his fingers. Dragging his useless legs, his broken spine. Muscled shoulders, thick-muscle neck, they were firing in a half-circle around him crouched and each of them aiming to kill. And his face pressed now against the part-collapsed chain-link fence, and his torso, outstretched arms . . .

This was the dead end of Ventor he could not crawl past to get to the dock and the river and the big open pipes, Anis Schutt would die here straining against the badly rusted fence like an animal that has crawled away to die amid mummified remnants of newspaper, styrofoam litter caught in the chain-link fence where even now he could anticipate the weight of a booted foot on the back of his neck. *Shooter down! Finish him.*

Afterword

Though it is set decades later, *The Sacrifice* is strongly linked to my novel *them* (1969). The Detroit "riot" of July 1967—(more accurately called, by individuals who'd lived through it, the Twelfth Street Riot)—as well as the Newark "riot" of July 1967—resulted in a number of carefully researched studies into "black urban civil disorder" in subsequent years, but these were not available to me at the time of the composition of *them*.

Among the many books, articles, and online materials consulted for *The Sacrifice* are three which have been of particular interest:

The Algiers Motel Incident by John Hersey (1968)
The Report of the National Advisory Committee on Civil Disorders (1968)
The Special New York State Grand Jury Report in the Tawana Brawley Case (October 7, 1988)

053115367